DRAGON AND LIBERATOR

★Denotes a Tom Doherty Associates Book

A TOM DOHERTY ASSOCIATES BOOK | NEW YORK

DRAGON AND
LIBERATOR

THE SIXTH DRAGONBACK ADVENTURE

TIMOTHY ZAHN

DRAGON AND LIBERATOR

Copyright © 2008 by Timothy Zahn

Edited by James Frenkel

A Starscape Book
Published by Tom Doherty Associates, LLC
175 Fifth Avenue
New York, NY 10010

www.tor-forge.com

Library of Congress Cataloging-in-Publication Data

Zahn, Timothy.
Dragon and liberator : the sixth Dragonback adventure / Timothy Zahn.—1st ed.
    p.   cm.
"A Starscape book."
ISBN-13: 978-0-7653-1419-2
ISBN-10: 0-7653-1419-3
1. Adventure and adventurers—Fiction.   2. Genocide—Fiction.   3. Dragons—Fiction.
4. Orphans—Fiction.   5. Science Fiction.   I. Title.

PZ7.Z2515 Dm 2008
[Fic]—dc22

                                                                                    2008003000

First Edition: June 2008

Printed in the United States of America

0 9 8 7 6 5 4 3 2 1

To Anna—

For all you do, and for all you are

DRAGON AND LIBERATOR

One month.

The words echoed through Draycos's mind as he lay in his two-dimensional form against Jack Morgan's back, arms, and legs. *One month.*

One month left until the refugee fleet carrying the remainder of his K'da people and their Shontine symbionts arrived here in the Orion Arm of the Milky Way galaxy. One month until their long, wearying journey would be over.

One month until they flew into the ambush that Arthur Neverlin and the Valahgua were preparing for them.

Or perhaps even less than that. After two years in hyperspace, they could easily be a week or two early for their rendezvous.

Draycos raised his head a little from Jack's shoulder, his eyebrow ridges and spiny crest pressing up against the boy's shirt. Through the windshield of the car Jack had borrowed from a used-vehicle lot, he could see the Brummgan town of Ponocce City laid out in front of them. Its ugly color scheme, thankfully, was shrouded by the darkness of night and the city's mediocre streetlight system. Three miles straight ahead, its lights reflected against the low clouds, was the spaceport where some of the enemy forces were even now being gathered together.

Draycos swiveled his head around, lifting his eyes over the

back of Jack's shirt. Directly behind the car, rising over the low houses around it like a breaking ocean wave, was the tall ceramic wall that surrounded the Chookoock family estate.

There were some very unpleasant memories tied up with that wall and the evil people who hid behind it. Draycos could imagine how Jack must be feeling right now as the memories of his brief time as a Chookoock slave were forced back upon him.

Draycos? Jack's thought flowed into the K'da's mind along the strange telepathic link the two of them had somehow developed. *You okay?*

Yes, Draycos replied. *Why do you ask?*

You're twitching your tail against the back of my knee, Jack told him. *I thought maybe you were nervous.*

Draycos hadn't even realized he'd been doing that. *My apologies,* he said, bringing his tail to a halt.

No problem, Jack assured him. *It tickled, that's all.*

In the distance behind them, Draycos caught a flicker of reflected streetlight from the gate set into the white wall. "The gate's opening again," he said aloud.

"Got it," Jack said, picking up the portable sensor he'd brought from the *Essenay* and pressing it against the side window. "Geez, how many soldiers have they got in there, anyway?"

"Well, we've had around three hundred come through here, if that helps any," Alison Kayna's voice came from the comm clip attached to Jack's left shirt collar.

"Yes, thank you, I *can* do basic math," Jack growled. "You want to keep it down?"

"Relax—they can't possibly hear me," Alison said. Her tone managed somehow to be reassuring and sarcastic at the same time. "We're all the way up at the top of the hangar on one of the loading-crane supports."

"Good," Jack said tartly. "Keep it down anyway."

They'll be all right, Draycos assured him.

I know, Jack said.

But the boy's words couldn't hide his tension. Especially since it was the same tension Draycos himself was feeling.

Because it should be him and Jack skulking around the Chookoock family's main shuttle hangar. It should be him and Jack watching the Brummgan mercenaries gathering for transport to the ambush point. It shouldn't be Alison and Taneem.

Especially not Taneem. The young female K'da was intelligent and likable, and she'd certainly shown herself willing to put herself at risk for Draycos and his people.

But she'd spent most of her life as little more than an animal. Her transformation to full, sentient being was less than two months old. She still needed more learning and experience before she would be ready for even a normal K'da life.

And the circumstances she and Alison were in right now were anything but normal.

Restlessly, Draycos lashed his tail. He should have put all four feet down right from the start and insisted that he and Jack take this part of the plan.

The problem was that Alison was just as stubborn as Draycos was. And, unfortunately, she'd also had logic on her side. She and Taneem had already successfully opened one of the K'da/Shontine safes, and that experience was worth more than any coaching that Alison could give Jack. Even Jack had admitted that. And to be fair, she *had* proved she was capable of handling herself.

But all the logic in the universe didn't help. Draycos's emotional core was still tied up in knots of frustration and concern.

"Here they come," Jack said. "Looks like just three vans in this convoy. Uncle Virge?"

"Ready, Jack lad," the voice of the *Essenay*'s computerized personality came from the comm clip.

The first van reached their position. Jack held the sensor steady against the window as it rolled past, followed closely by its two companions. "Okay," he reported as the vehicles' taillights continued down the dimly lit street. "Uncle Virge?"

"First one seems to be all personnel," Uncle Virge said slowly as the computer sifted through the data Jack's sensor had sent it. "Looks like our standard fifteen armed Brummgas."

Draycos grimaced. Alison's theory was that the Patri Chookoock's role in this conspiracy was to supply Brummgan soldiers to crew the ships that would be attacking the K'da and Shontine refugees. Apparently, she'd been correct.

The Patri Chookoock was donating the soldiers and crews. Arthur Neverlin, once chairman of the board of the megacorporation Braxton Universis, was supplying the planning. Later, when the K'da and Shontine were all dead, he would probably also provide the marketing system they would use to sell the technology from the looted refugee ships. The Valahgua, deadly enemies from the K'da and Shontine's own far distant part of the galaxy, were providing their horrible and unstoppable Death weapon.

That left only the attack ships themselves. Presumably, Colonel Maximus Frost of the Malison Ring mercenaries would be supplying those.

And all that the unsuspecting refugees had standing between them and genocide were Jack, Draycos, Alison, and Taneem. Two young humans, and two K'da.

And a single month of time.

"Bingo," Uncle Virge's voice cut into Draycos's thoughts. "Second van has five armed Brummgas, plus one very big chunk of metal."

Draycos felt Jack's muscles tighten beneath him. "How big?" the boy asked.

"A little shorter than you and quite a bit wider," Uncle Virge said. "And I'm getting an unknown on the particular alloy."

"That's it," Alison said positively. "That's the safe."

Draycos lifted his head again to look at the vans' retreating taillights. Each of his advance team's four ships had had one of those safes aboard, a safe that had contained the location of their planned rendezvous with the incoming refugee fleet.

But Neverlin's ambush of the team had killed all the K'da and Shontine except Draycos, leaving all four safes in his hands. Two had been wrecked when Neverlin's men attempted to open them. Alison, under threat to her life, had opened the third for them.

Three safes down. One still left.

And the final safe had at last been brought out from behind the protection of the white wall and was heading toward the hangar where Alison and Taneem were waiting.

"Don't sound too eager," Uncle Virge warned. "The third van has another fifteen Brummgas."

"Not a problem," Alison said. "I've got enough sopor mist canisters planted to blanket the whole hangar. I just need to make sure all three vans are inside before I trigger them."

"Just make sure they don't have gas masks on before you do it," Jack warned.

"You want to walk me through it, just to make sure I do it right?" Alison asked tartly. "Relax, will you? I know what I'm doing."

"I hope so," Jack muttered as he set the sensor on the seat beside him and started the car.

They'll be all right, Draycos reassured him as the boy pulled out into the Ponocce City traffic. *We'll be only a few minutes behind this last group. If there's trouble, we'll be in position to help.*

Sure, Jack said. *Help me watch for cops, will you? I'm going to see if I can get a little more speed out of this crate.*

There was a distant, muted thunk. Across the hangar from where Taneem and Alison crouched on the wide crane supports, the large doors on the north wall began to roll up. "This should be them," Alison murmured.

Taneem didn't answer. Her heart was beating rapidly, a cold sense of dread twisting like morning chill through her. Very soon now, the waiting would be over.

And she was terrified.

She'd been in dangerous situations before, certainly. Several of them, in fact. But never had she found herself facing the sheer numbers of Brummgas wandering restlessly around the hangar floor below them. There were twenty-three of the aliens— Taneem had counted them five times—all of them carrying guns and wearing thick body armor. If Uncle Virge was right, the vans outside those opening doors carried another thirty-five of the aliens.

"You all right?" Alison's soft voice asked into her thoughts.

With an effort, Taneem lifted her silver eyes from all those guns and focused on Alison's calm face. An odd thought ran through Taneem's mind: a girl of Alison's mere fourteen years had no business being so calm in the middle of this much danger. "Yes, I'm fine," she said, trying to keep her voice from shaking.

"The waiting's always the hardest part," Alison told her. "But try to relax. If this goes down like it's supposed to, neither of us will have to do any fighting."

And if it doesn't go down like it's supposed to? Taneem wondered. But there was no point in bringing that up.

The doors below finished opening, and three vans pulled inside. They rolled past the milling Brummgas and pulled up behind the two shuttles waiting by the much larger doors at the south end of the hangar. There had been ten such shuttles when Taneem and Alison had first arrived, which had left the hangar in pairs as each group of new passengers arrived and was loaded aboard.

At first Taneem had hoped the shuttles might provide the answer to their problem. Alison had brought along the transmitting device that Colonel Frost had used to track the *Essenay* to Rho Scorvi, and Taneem had hoped she and Alison could plant it aboard one of the shuttles and find the refugee rendezvous point that way.

But Alison had explained that the shuttles would simply be taking the Brummgas to another ship or group of ships waiting out in deep space. Those ships would then continue on, while the shuttles returned to Brum-a-dum.

Across the hangar, the doors closed again with another thunk. On the floor below, the van doors opened and the Brummgan soldiers began filing out. "Okay," Alison said, getting a grip on her remote trigger. "Here we go." Flipping up the protective cover, she pressed the button.

Nothing happened.

"Alison?" Taneem asked anxiously, looking down at the Brummgas still filing out of their vans.

"It's okay," Alison assured her. "This is a Type Four sopor. Takes longer to start working, but also keeps them asleep longer after the mist dissipates."

Taneem flicked her tail. Certainly Alison ought to know how her own weapons worked.

And then, all across the hangar, the Brummgas went limp and collapsed onto the floor.

"See?" Alison said as she pulled on her full-helmet gas mask and tossed a coil of rope over the edge of the track. "Here we go. Stay here until I call you." Getting a grip on the rope, she rolled off the support and started sliding down.

Taneem watched her go, scratching her claws nervously against the metal of the track support. If the Brummgas down there were faking . . .

But no one moved or opened fire, and a few seconds later Alison was safely down. Drawing her small Corvine pistol from its holster, the girl dropped the backpack off her shoulder and pulled it open. "Clear," her muffled voice came from the comm clip fastened to Taneem's ear. "I'll get the MixStar started."

Alison headed toward the middle van. Taneem watched her go, thinking about her MixStar safecracking computer. She'd seen the device in action, and it still amazed her that such a powerful device could be concealed inside a belt and a pair of shoes. Alison reached the van, peered into the open door, and disappeared inside.

"Taneem?" Draycos's voice came softly. "Are you all right?"

"I'm fine," Taneem assured him. "The sopor mist seems to have worked properly."

"Keep an eye on the Brummgas anyway," Draycos said. "Watch for twitching or movements like someone might make in their sleep. If you see anything like that, let us know immediately."

"They'll be fine," Alison said before Taneem could answer. "Okay, the MixStar's running. I'll go find a spot for the tracer." She reappeared from the van and jogged over to the rear of the nearest shuttle, ducking beneath its engine section.

This was the part that Taneem still didn't quite understand.

The tracer would do them no good attached to the shuttle. Jack, Alison, and Draycos all knew that. So, presumably, would Colonel Frost.

Yet Alison seemed to think Frost might not think Jack and Alison knew that. She had tried to explain that Frost might therefore believe that was the reason why she and Taneem had invaded the hangar this way.

It would be simpler if they never knew Alison and Taneem had been here at all. But Taneem had to admit that was probably impossible. Not with the Brummgas having been put to sleep this way.

There was so much she still had to learn.

"Alison!" Jack's voice snapped with sudden urgency in Taneem's ear. "More traffic heading your way."

"I thought Uncle Virge said there were only twenty-five vans on the Chookoock grounds," Alison said.

"These aren't vans, they're cars," Jack gritted out. "Four of them, loaded to the gills with humans."

"And," Draycos put in tautly, "Frost and Neverlin are among them."

CHAPTER 2

Alison felt her stomach tighten. Frost and Neverlin were *here*? She'd assumed both had slipped out during the Malison Ring raid on the Chookoock estate twelve days ago and escaped off-planet.

If she'd only known. But it was too late to worry about that now. "ETA?" she asked.

"Maybe two minutes before they pop the door and see your handiwork," Jack said.

"Taneem, get down to the hangar floor," Draycos ordered. "And hold your breath—the sopor mist may not yet have completely dissipated. Alison, the west door won't be visible to them as they enter. Go out that way and head south—we'll circle around and pick you up."

Alison looked back under the shuttle's drive nozzles toward the three vans and the north door beyond them. Draycos was right—two minutes would be enough for her and Taneem to make their escape out the west door.

But if they left now, they'd never get another crack at that safe.

"Alison?" Jack asked. "You copy that?"

Alison came to a sudden decision. "We're trying the safe first," she said, getting out from underneath the shuttle and sprinting for the van. The rope hanging from the ceiling twitched violently as Taneem finished her slide onto the hangar floor. "Come on, Taneem."

"Alison—"

"We've got a minute and a half," Alison cut him off as she reached the van and climbed inside. "Maybe more if Frost sees the carnage and decides to take it slow."

"Are you *crazy?*"

"Probably," Alison conceded, crouching in front of the safe as Taneem crowded into the van beside her. "Now shut up and let me work."

The MixStar was nearly finished. "Let's check out the fail-safes," Alison said, holding out her hand.

Taneem touched the hand with her paw and went two-dimensional, vanishing up Alison's sleeve. As she did so, the comm clip popped off her ear. Alison caught it in midair, stuffing it into a pocket as she turned around and pressed her back against the door of the safe. The K'da had a special trick in their 2-D form for looking "over" walls that would let her see into the safe.

She felt the subtle wriggling as Taneem adjusted herself. A moment of stillness, then a second wriggle, and her head slid around over Alison's right shoulder. "The third and fourth indentations," Taneem whispered.

"Got it," Alison said, glancing at the display strip on the inside of her mask. "Don't worry about breathing—the mist has dissipated."

The MixStar had finished its work. "Combination is three-seven-twelve-nine-twenty," Alison said. "We're opening it now. Taneem?"

Lifting a paw from Alison's forearm, the K'da stuck two of her toes into the third and fourth indentations in the safe's sidewall. "Hurry it up," Jack said. "They've reached the door and stopped. Probably wondering why no one's opening it for them."

"Fifteen seconds," Alison promised. She keyed in the combination and pulled the break bar.

To her relief and satisfaction, the door swung quietly open. "Got it," she announced. Reaching in, she scooped up the handful of data diamonds lying on the safe's floor and shoved them into her side pocket along with Taneem's comm clip. "And we're out of here," she added, getting a grip on the break bar and starting to close the heavy door.

And without warning, the hangar was rocked by a thunderous explosion.

Alison gasped, grabbing the edge of the safe as the blast lifted the van an inch off the floor and then slammed it back down again. Someone was shouting into her ear, but for those first few seconds she couldn't hear anything but a loud ringing.

But at least she was still conscious. If she hadn't been inside the van when the concussion blast went off, she'd be flat on her back right now.

Abruptly, the ringing cleared. "—blew the door and are coming in," Jack was saying urgently. "All of them, and they're spreading out to cover the whole hangar."

"I'm coming in," Draycos added, his voice dark and grim. "Find somewhere to hide until I get there."

"You'll never make it," Alison said quickly. She could hear the widely separated sounds of squealing brakes as the cars came to a halt in four different parts of the hangar. "They're too spread out, and there's no cover. They'll kill you."

She heard a sudden whistling sound from the comm clip as Draycos left the car and sprinted through the night air. "My life isn't important," he said over the whistling. "The data diamonds you've obtained are all that matter."

"No, they're not," Alison snapped, looking frantically around her for inspiration. "How do we convince StarForce this is on the level without a genuine K'da to show them?"

"You have Taneem."

"Who was born and raised on Rho Scorvi," Alison countered, knowing that she was running out of time. The first thing Frost would check once his men declared the area secure would be his precious safe.

The safe.

And with that, she knew what she had to do. "We're getting into the safe," she said, grabbing the MixStar. Crouching down, she stepped into the big metal box.

"You're *what*?" Jack demanded. "Alison—"

"My mask can give us air for six hours," Alison cut him off, sitting down facing the safe door with her knees tucked to her chest. It would be a tight fit, but not too bad. The door's inner plate, she noted, had several small access holes to the lock mechanism that were big enough for her to get a couple of fingers into. "We'll be safe until then, so take your time and pick your moment. Don't try to rescue me—either of you. Understand?"

"Yes," Draycos said reluctantly.

"Good," Alison said. Taneem, she noted uneasily, had gone rigid against her skin. Was the K'da claustrophobic? She hoped not. "Also, don't worry if you can't catch up with us before the six hours run out. Taneem and I will just play it by ear. I can get to the lock from in here, so we won't be stuck."

"Understood," Draycos said, his voice tight but steady. "Good luck."

Alison could hear heavy footsteps now, and the echo of terse commands. Bracing herself, she got a grip on the door and pulled it closed. There was a soft click as the lock reengaged.

And she and Taneem were alone in utter darkness.

"Taneem?" she murmured softly toward her shoulder. "You all right?"

There was no answer. "Taneem?" Alison tried again. "Come on, girl; we've been in worse scrapes than this one."

"Have we?" Taneem whispered back, her voice shaking. "Have we really?"

Alison grimaced. Actually, they probably hadn't. "We're going to be fine," she assured the K'da. A sudden thought occurred to her, and she dug her mascara tube from her kit. "Let's see if we can hear what they're talking about out there."

Unscrewing the end from the tube, she placed it into her ear. The burglar's pickup was designed to let her listen into safes from the outside. There was no reason it shouldn't let her listen the other direction, too. Switching on the microphone half of the tube, she pressed it against the safe wall beside her.

"—Morgan, I tell you," Colonel Frost's voice growled faintly in her ear. "It's exactly the sort of crazy stunt he and that frunging K'da of his would pull."

"Very likely," a second voice answered.

Alison felt a shiver run through her. *That* voice was *very* familiar: Arthur Neverlin, once the number-two man at Braxton Universis. The man who, five months ago, had framed Jack for theft and murder and then blackmailed him into helping with his plan to kill Cornelius Braxton and take complete control of the huge corporation.

Only Jack and Draycos had turned the tables on him. They'd saved Braxton's life and sent Neverlin scurrying for the shadows where he'd been lurking ever since.

Which probably meant Neverlin hated Jack as much as Colonel Frost hated Alison.

Alison's father had once told her it was good to have all your enemies grouped together in the same place. At the time, she'd thought it sounded like a reasonable idea. Now, she wasn't so sure.

"Which brings up the question of what he was trying to accomplish," Neverlin continued. "Morgan wouldn't waste his time just trying to tweak us."

"I think it's pretty obvious this is what he was after." There was a sharp rap on the side of the safe. "Question is, did he get in or not?"

"There's one way to find out," Neverlin said. "Unfortunately, since we don't know how Kayna opened the other one, we'll probably destroy it if we try."

A sudden cold chill ran down Alison's back. In her hurry to get out of sight, she'd completely forgotten the fact that the K'da and Shontine had booby-trapped these safes to protect the precious information inside them.

Booby-trapped with a small but powerful bomb, in fact. A bomb that was currently pressed up against the side of Alison's head.

"Yeah." Frost bit out a curse under his breath. "She did something—she *must* have done something—that the other safecrackers we hired didn't do. But I've been over that recording a hundred times, and for the life of me I can't figure out what it was."

"Yes, she was a very clever little girl, our Alison," Neverlin murmured, his voice even more snakelike than usual. "I do hope we run into her again someday."

"In the meantime, we have to decide what to do about this

safe," Frost said. "Do we open it and see if the data diamonds are still there, or not?"

"Not, I think," Neverlin said. "I generally dislike destroying something I might someday find a use for. Besides, even if Morgan has the rendezvous location, there's nothing he can do to stop us. Certainly not without warning."

"*If* the flaggers you bribed in StarForce stay bribed," Frost countered sourly. "If you ask me, people who are willing to take money to watch your backtrail are just as willing to change sides for a better offer."

Alison grimaced. So Jack's guess had been right. Neverlin had people in high places watching and waiting for Jack and Draycos to surface. If the two of them had gone to StarForce or the Internos government when all this started, as Uncle Virge had urged, they would probably be dead right now.

And Alison herself would be off somewhere about her own business instead of sitting here locked in a coffin-sized alien safe. Sometimes, she reflected, it didn't pay to play the what-if game too deeply.

"Don't worry about the flaggers," Neverlin said. "Money isn't the only thing that can ensure a man's loyalty."

Another voice called something, the words too faint for Alison to make out. "What?" Frost called back.

The other voice grew louder as its owner moved closer, until it was loud enough for Alison to understand. "—under the edge vent," the other said.

"Well, well," Frost said, a sudden malicious amusement in his voice. "So Morgan thinks he's clever."

"Get away from us with that thing," Neverlin snapped.

"Relax; it's not a bomb," Frost soothed. "It's the hyperspace tracer I planted on his ship a couple of months back."

There was a slight pause. "Really," Neverlin said, all calm and icy again. "Interesting."

"More stupid than interesting," Frost countered. "He must think we're amateurs. Dumbarton, check it for booby traps and bugs and then put it in my car."

"Yes, sir." A few soft footsteps and the other was gone.

"So you think Morgan was being stupid?" Neverlin asked.

"Don't you?" Frost countered.

"Oh, I wasn't referring to his foolishness in thinking these shuttles would take their occupants someplace worth tracing," Neverlin said. "I was referring to the fact that he accurately guessed our need for the Patri Chookoock's soldiers. *And* that he guessed it early enough to plant himself in here before our own security perimeter went up. I wonder what else he may have guessed."

"What he *guessed*?" Frost asked, his voice going cool. "Or what he might have been *told*?"

"An interesting conclusion for you to jump to," Neverlin said, matching his tone.

Alison smiled tightly to herself. Maybe some of the seeds of distrust she'd tried to plant between Neverlin and Frost were starting to grow.

"I didn't mean you, naturally," Frost said. "And my own troops are completely trustworthy. But the Patri didn't seem too thrilled about you taking away both his soldiers *and* this thing." He tapped the safe again.

"Though not nearly as unhappy as he was about that Malison Ring raid on his estate two weeks ago," Neverlin countered.

Frost grunted. "And whoever the frunging idiot was who put that particular centipede in their shirts is going to pay for it," he promised darkly. "I don't believe for a minute it was really General Davi who ordered it."

"Regardless, it's one more reason for the Patri to perhaps be reevaluating his part in this."

"Let him reevaluate," Frost said. "We've got all the Brumm-gas that we need, and once we're off Brum-a-dum there won't be any way for him to call them back if he changes his mind. Anyway, he'll come around again once it's done and there's loot to be passed out."

"Indeed." Neverlin paused. "There is, of course, one other possibility. I understand we have a new fighter pilot on the payroll."

"Former StarForce Wing Sergeant Jonathan Langston," Frost said, his voice suddenly as thoughtful as Neverlin's. "He claims Morgan betrayed him."

"*Claims* being the key word," Neverlin said. "What exactly do we know about him?"

"He and his Djinn-90 disappeared somewhere in the vicinity of that canyon on Semaline," Frost said. "He claims he was held captive by the inhabitants—"

"There's that word *claims* again," Neverlin put in. "I don't want claims, Colonel. I want facts."

"Don't worry, I'm watching him," Frost promised. "Meanwhile, what do we do about this?" There was another thunk as he tapped the side of the safe.

"We'll take it with us as planned," Neverlin said. "But not on either of these shuttles, in case Morgan had more surprises up his sleeve. The first group of transports should be back soon from the transfer point. We'll deploy for siege and wait for them."

"Do you want to call the Patri for reinforcements?"

"I hardly think that necessary," Neverlin said, and Alison could imagine the other's detestably oily smile. "We can handle this ourselves."

"Yes, sir," Frost said. "I'll deploy the troops."

There were a few faint footsteps, and then all was silence again. Alison held the microphone against the wall another few seconds, just to be sure, then turned it off and replaced the earphone end. "You heard all that?" she asked quietly.

"Yes," Taneem murmured from her shoulder. "What do we do?"

Alison started to take a deep breath. She remembered in time that they needed to conserve air and made it a shallow breath instead. "We settle in, try to relax, and wait."

The Malison Ring mercenaries were piling out of the cars in the distant hangar, their weapons held ready as they spread out across the floor. "Come on; come on," Jack muttered under his breath, squeezing the steering wheel of his borrowed car as if he were trying to break it. He should *never* have agreed to this stupid plan. "Come *on*."

And then Draycos was there, a black shadow sprinting toward him through the other shadows of the building site between Jack and the hangar. Jack stretched out his arm toward the open window, and as the K'da dived through the opening he caught the boy's hand with his front paws and slithered up his sleeve. "Go," Draycos ordered tautly. "Not too fast."

Jack clenched his teeth. But Draycos was right. Even with the horrible urgency pressing in on them he couldn't simply peel away as if the entire Internos police force were on his tail.

And so, with an air of casual unconcern, he pulled the car away from the curb. An honest citizen driving away from an honest errand, not a guilty would-be thief running from the scene of the crime.

He played the role for three blocks, until he was out of sight and hearing of the men back at the hangar. Then, stomping hard on the accelerator, he kicked the car to high speed.

"Careful," Draycos warned, his head rising from Jack's shoulder to look out the boy's shirt. "Frost might have backup watchers even this far out."

"Doesn't matter," Jack gritted out, the red-tinged image of Alison and Taneem buried alive inside that safe hazing over his eyes like a vision of the ground floor of hell. "Even if he did, it's too late for them to stop us."

"What's your plan?"

"We go in full bore," Jack told him. "Uncle Virge, get prepped to fly, and activate all weapons systems."

"Are you sure that's wise?" Uncle Virge asked cautiously. "They'll surely have heavy weaponry in there with them."

"They'll never get a chance to use it," Jack said. "No warning—we're just going to blast away at the hangar with everything we've got."

"But Alison and Taneem—"

"Are inside three inches of hardened metal with their own air supply," Jack cut him off. "Draycos?"

"Yes, you're right," Draycos agreed, a cautious hope in his voice. "They should be well protected against any of the *Essenay*'s weapons."

"That's the nice thing about some traps—you can get them to work in either direction," Jack said, a grim and not entirely pleasant thrill rippling through him. After months of running and ducking and hiding, he and Draycos were finally going to take the battle to the enemy.

He was still psyching himself up for combat when a delivery truck pulled out of a blind driveway directly in front of him.

He jammed on the brakes. But he was going way too fast, and it was already way too late. With a horrible crunching of metal and plastic, he slammed full tilt into the truck's front left side.

For a short eternity the car spun and twisted terrifyingly around him. Then, abruptly, it came to a halt. Breathing heavily, Jack peered between the milky white balloons of the car's emergency protection system as they slowly receded back into their compartments.

He'd ended up half turned around, facing back toward the truck. The front left side of the other vehicle was a shambles, though not nearly as bad as the mess Jack had made of his own car. "Draycos?" he panted.

"I'm unharmed," the K'da said from his shoulder. "You?"

"I'm okay," Jack assured him. With a grating creak, the truck door opened and the Brummgan driver climbed rather shakily to the ground. "Looks like the other guy is, too."

"We'd best get out of here," Draycos warned. "The accident will hardly have gone unnoticed."

Jack looked through his broken windows. All around them Brummgas had stopped their cars or had appeared in open doorways or were peering out of windows. "No kidding," he said, pulling the door release and leaning against the panel.

For a wonder, it wasn't jammed, and with an ear-piercing shriek he got it open. With his hands shaking with reaction, it took another half minute to get his seat belts off. He had just gotten them clear when a large hand reached in, grabbed his left upper arm, and hauled him bodily out of the car.

And he found himself staring up at the dark Brummgan eyes and gleaming golden collar ring of a police officer. "Your vehicle license?" the Brummga demanded.

Jack felt his heart sink. *Oh no.* "Sure," he managed, pointing back into the car. "It's in the storage compartment." If he could get into the car and out the other side . . . "I'll get it."

But he'd barely started his turn when the grip on his arm tightened and pulled him back again. "This vehicle plate shows it stolen," the Brummga growled. "You come now to jail."

Jack? Draycos's urgent thought came.

From overhead came a faint whine. Jack looked up to see a formation of three long-range shuttles appear, losing altitude as they flew toward the Chookoock family's private hangar.

Frost's shuttles had returned.

And if the mercenaries were monitoring the police comm system, the sudden frantic flurry of reports claiming a dragon had attacked a cop would bring them down on him and Draycos in double-quick time.

Jack?

Don't bother, Jack told him wearily, his earlier thrill of anticipation burned into ash.

He was being put into the rear seat of the police car when he saw the Chookoock shuttles lift again into the sky. He watched them head for the stars, his stomach knotted tight enough to hurt.

Alison and Taneem were on their own now.

CHAPTER 3

The returning shuttles arrived sooner than Alison had expected. Far too soon, unfortunately, for Jack and Draycos to have had time to put together a rescue plan.

Neverlin and Frost were probably thinking along the same lines. They wasted no time getting their troops and the safe aboard and lifting off again.

Alison tried her burglar's pickup a couple of times during the flight. But the safe had apparently been secured someplace away from the passengers, and the background rumble of the engines masked whatever anyone might be saying.

There wasn't much conversation going on inside the safe, either. Taneem would answer any questions that Alison asked her, mostly questions about how the K'da was doing. But aside from that she lay quietly against Alison's skin, neither speaking nor moving.

Maybe she was conserving oxygen. More likely she was just terrified.

The flight didn't last long. An hour and a half after lifting from Brum-a-dum, Alison felt the subtle jolt as the shuttle docked with another vessel. A few minutes later the safe was rocked onto a lift cart and rolled through the shuttle's hatchway. Ten minutes and several turns later, they reached their destination. Another short flurry of rockings and bumps to get them off the cart, and the safe came to rest.

And once again silence descended.

For the next two hours Alison kept her microphone pressed against the safe wall, splitting her attention between the occasional and very distant background noises and the indicator on her gas mask canister.

The gas mask was a marvel of engineering. Along with a small oxygen tank, it included a catalytic reactor that could take their exhaled carbon dioxide and split it back into carbon and oxygen. Without such a converter, a mask that size wouldn't have kept her and Taneem alive for even a single hour, and several times during their quiet vigil Alison gave silent thanks that her father had provided her with such exotic and expensive equipment.

But even so marvelous a gadget had its limits. The carbon storage tube slowly but steadily filled with a black, sootlike powder as the oxygen tank just as slowly but steadily drained.

Finally, just under four hours into their ill-fated mission, Alison decided it was time. "It's been quiet out there for two hours," she told Taneem as she put away the microphone and got out her light. "It should be safe for you to take a look."

"All right," Taneem said softly.

Alison pressed her back hard against the safe's rear wall. She felt the familiar movement across her skin as Taneem leaned in her strange fourth-dimensional way over the metal. There was a pause, and somehow Alison had a sense that the K'da was surprised.

There was another wiggle, and Alison looked down through her open collar as Taneem's gray-scaled head and silver eyes slid back around onto her shoulder. "Is it clear?" she asked.

"Very clear," Taneem said. "And very familiar."

"How familiar?"

"Very," Taneem said again, a hint of wry humor finally peeking through her tension. "We're in the room containing the second safe you opened for Colonel Frost on our journey from Semaline to Brum-a-dum."

Alison felt her mouth drop open. "We're aboard the *Advocatus Diaboli*?"

"Unless there are two such rooms," Taneem said. "You're surprised by this?"

"Well, no, I suppose it makes sense," Alison had to admit. "Neverlin will certainly want to be on hand for the big attack. I guess I'm just surprised he'd risk his own ship instead of bunking in with Frost and the rest of his people on their warships."

"Perhaps he wishes to travel in comfort," Taneem suggested.

"There's that," Alison agreed dryly. "Malison Ring ships aren't known for the kind of luxury Neverlin's accustomed to."

"Malison Ring," Taneem said, her voice suddenly thoughtful. "What about them?"

"I was just noticing the curious similarity between your names," the K'da said. "Alison, Malison. Odd that I never noticed that before."

"Pure coincidence," Alison assured her. "*Malison* is an old Earth word meaning a curse. I presume General Davi was thinking he would be a curse to his enemies when he set up the group twelve years ago."

"They began so recently?" Taneem asked. "I assumed they were older than that."

"Not this group, no," Alison said. "But they certainly aren't Davi's first experience with mercenaries. He worked for two other groups, and was one of the commanding officers of a third before he started his own."

The K'da cocked her head, an odd-looking gesture as she lay flattened against Alison's skin. "You seem to know a great deal about them."

"Not really," Alison said. This was starting to drift toward dangerous territory. "Everything I just told you is public record."

"Is General Davi's voiceprint also public record?"

Alison grimaced. She'd hoped Taneem had forgotten that part of the trick she and Uncle Virge had pulled on Frost and the Chookoock family. "Like I told Uncle Virge, my dad got that for me. The voiceprints and tonal patterns of important people can come in handy."

"As we saw," Taneem agreed.

"But that's neither here nor there," Alison said, training her light on the inside of the safe door. "Let's get out of here, shall we?"

There were, as she'd noted earlier, several small holes in the inner sheet metal. In the single hurried glance she'd had before shutting them inside the safe, it had looked like the holes would give her access to the lock mechanism.

It took her less than a minute to discover that they didn't.

Don't panic, she ordered herself firmly as she probed around inside with her fingers. The holes had to be there for *some* reason, after all. If she couldn't manipulate the lock itself, perhaps there was an emergency release back there somewhere. All human-designed safes this big had such releases, in case someone accidentally got locked inside.

But she couldn't find any such switch.

"Is there trouble?" Taneem asked softly.

"I can't find a way to spring the lock mechanism," Alison

told her. "We're going to have to try something else. Something a bit risky."

The K'da shifted position on her skin. "I'm ready."

Alison grimaced. It was more than just a little risky, she knew. But with their air running out, it was all she could think of. "You remember that trick Draycos has where he can lean over a wall, like you did just now, only then fall all the way over and come out the other side?"

"Yes, of course," Taneem said cautiously. "He also said no other K'da in history has ever had such an ability."

"I know," Alison said. "But I think you can do it."

"I can't," Taneem said, an edge of fear starting to creep into her voice. "I'll fall off and—I'll *die,* Alison."

"You won't die," Alison said firmly. "You can do this as well as he can."

"I can't," Taneem insisted. "Draycos is a powerful poet-warrior. I'm not."

"It has nothing to do with Draycos's warrior training," Alison said. "It has to do with you and me. You as K'da, and me as human."

"I don't understand."

Alison wrinkled her nose. This was hardly the time and place she'd planned on springing this on either of the two K'da. But under the circumstances, Alison didn't have much choice. "I know Draycos has been walking you through the encyclopedia section of the *Essenay*'s computer," she said. "Has he shown you the drawings and paintings of dragons from Earth legends?"

"I've seen some of them, yes."

"Didn't it strike you as odd that we would have so many legends of that sort?" Alison asked. "Especially from so many different cultures and peoples?"

Taneem had gone very still. "What exactly are you trying to say?"

Alison took a deep breath. "I'm saying that I think the K'da originally came from Earth."

"That can't be," Taneem said. "Draycos told me his people are coming here from a far distant world in a very different part of the galaxy."

"And so they are," Alison agreed. "But he also says the whole group of them were kidnapped from their home world by passing slavers thousands of years ago. I think they just don't realize how far they traveled before they were able to fight their way free."

"And what of my own people?" Taneem asked. "The Phookas living on Rho Scorvi?"

Alison grimaced. Those Phookas weren't living on Rho Scorvi anymore, she knew. She and her associates had made sure of that. "You were probably survivors of one of the battles the slavers used you for," she said. "You found the Erassvas—or they found you—before your time limit was up and discovered they could serve as hosts."

There was a rhythmic tapping against Alison's leg as Taneem twitched her tail restlessly. "No," she said. "This can't be. You're just guessing."

"There is some guesswork involved, yes," Alison agreed. "But I've got at least one bit of evidence on my side. Do you happen to remember the name Draycos said their original hosts were called?"

"The Dhghem."

"That's right," Alison said, vaguely surprised that Taneem would remember such a jaw-cracker of a word. "A while back, just for fun, I looked it up. Turns out it's the old Indo-European root word for *human*."

Taneem didn't say anything but just kept tapping her tail against Alison's leg. "I'm not the only one thinking along these lines, either," Alison went on. "A couple of nights ago, while we were waiting for Frost to start moving the Brummgan mercenaries, I caught Jack in the dayroom looking through some of the old Earth dragon legends."

"But how can this be?" Taneem asked at last. "We aren't like any other Earth creatures."

"You aren't like any other creatures, period," Alison said. "I'm just saying it looks more and more like you were originally designed to be companions and friends to human beings. *Specifically* to human beings, in fact. That's why Draycos can do things with Jack that he couldn't do with the Shontine. Certainly things you and the other Phookas couldn't do with the Erassvas. With a human host, you're finally becoming the way K'da were truly meant to be."

"You say we were designed," Taneem said. "Designed by whom?"

"No idea," Alison said. "Passing aliens, some ancient human civilization's genetic engineers, God Himself. Take your pick. The point is that you and I are the same human/K'da team that Jack and Draycos are. If Draycos can drop safely off Jack's back over a wall, so can you."

"Perhaps," Taneem said. "But whether you're right or wrong, we have no choice, do we?"

"Not that I can see," Alison admitted. "I'm sorry."

The tapping tail slowed and then stopped. "Then I will do it."

"Thank you," Alison said. "All right. You remember that it was the third and fourth indentations. The combination is three-seven-twelve-nine-twenty. You line up the little diamond on the rotator with the right place around the rim, push the center of the rotator until it clicks, then go on to the next one."

"I understand," Taneem said. "*Twelve* is the one and two, correct?"

"Right, but the dial isn't marked with human numbers," Alison said, feeling a fresh layer of sweat ooze out onto her forehead. She'd worked with safes for so long that she didn't even think anymore about the fact that most of them used entirely different number systems. "When I say *twelve* I mean the twelfth symbol around from the top. I think it's a squiggle with a short line angled through it. The very top symbol is what I call twenty, the symbol just to its right is one, the next is two, and so on."

"I see," Taneem said. "I should have realized that. I'm sorry."

"No problem," Alison said. "You ready?"

"Third and fourth indentations; three, seven, twelve, nine, twenty," Taneem said. "Yes, I'm ready."

"Then let's go for it," Alison said, pressing her back firmly against the metal again. "Good luck."

She felt Taneem move into position, peering over the wall. There was a moment of anticipation that reminded Alison somehow of her first experience gazing down from the end of the swimming pool's high-dive board.

And then, suddenly, Taneem was gone.

Alison twitched violently in reaction. The movement bumped her head against the self-destruct bomb set into the safe's ceiling.

She rubbed gingerly at the spot. As if she'd needed that reminder that her fate was now directly tied to Taneem's. If the K'da had fallen wrong and disappeared into that strange fourth-dimensional space, then Alison was also dead. Either her air would run out or someone else would open the safe and the bomb would blow her head off. . . .

She was almost startled when, with no fuss at all, the safe door swung open at her feet.

She blinked sudden tears of relief from her eyes as Taneem's gray-scaled face peered in at her. "You were right," the K'da said, her jaws cracking open in a wry smile. "Number twelve *was* a squiggle with a line through it."

"Ah," Alison said, filling her lungs with fresh air as she worked her way out of the safe. Stretching stiff muscles, she looked around.

The room was dark except for the handful of small red night-lights marking the door and the tastefully concealed emergency kit. Another door led off one of the side walls, its lack of red night-lights showing that it wasn't an exit.

"What now?" Taneem asked quietly.

"Shh," Alison warned, touching her finger to her lips. She pulled out her mascara tube again as she moved carefully to the door. If Neverlin had any brains, he would have left guards outside in the corridor.

He had. Two of them, she guessed, from the sounds of their breathing.

Just as carefully she backed away again to the farthest corner of the office. Taneem, her silver eyes glittering in the darkness, padded silently over to join her.

"There are bad people out there?" the K'da murmured.

Alison nodded. "Two, I think," she said. "But don't worry. It doesn't sound like they're planning to come in and snoop around."

"Unless we give them reason to do so."

"So we make sure we don't," Alison said, trying to think.

Originally, a quiet look around had been first on her list of things to do. Once she had some idea of how many men and Brumm-gas were aboard, she would have a better idea of where the two of them might be able to hide for a few days.

Unfortunately, both parts of the plan required her to leave the office. With a pair of Malison Ring mercenaries standing guard a foot outside the door, that was going to be a little tricky.

"I see no place where we may hide for long," Taneem said into her thoughts. "Unless your breath mask can be restored?"

"It can be recharged somewhat, yes," Alison said. "But not entirely. Certainly not enough to get us through a whole day or more in the safe."

"Then we must find a new place," the K'da concluded. "Shall I begin a search?"

Alison frowned. Then, suddenly, she understood. The last time they were aboard, Taneem had taken herself on a brief tour of the ship's ventilation system. "It could be dangerous," she warned. "And not just from the ducts themselves. If anyone spots you, we're both dead."

The K'da twitched her tail. "So will we be if we stay here."

"I can't argue with that," Alison conceded. She looked around, spotted the vent in the wall just below the ceiling. "Let's get the grille off."

Three minutes later, Taneem climbed up on Alison's shoulders and eased her head and forepaws into the open vent. "It looks clear," she said, pulling her head briefly back out again to look at Alison. "I'll be back as soon as I can."

Alison nodded. "Good luck."

Taneem put her head back into the opening. Pulling with her forepaws, she slid the rest of the way in, and with a flick of her tail she was gone.

Pulling out her flashlight, Alison turned it to its lowest setting and put it into the duct to give Taneem something to look for when she headed back. She then put the grille back into position, fastening the bolts just tightly enough to keep it in place.

And once she'd done that, there was nothing for her to do but wait.

CHAPTER 4

She waited for a grand total of maybe two minutes. Then, being careful not to make any noise, she set out to explore the office.

The last time she'd been in here, when Frost had had her break into Neverlin's desk safe, he'd kept her in the main room. Her first task, therefore, was to see what was beyond the side door.

There were, as it turned out, two other rooms in the suite. One was a private washroom, the other a secure communications nook with a direct link to the ship's radio and InterWorld transmitters.

There were, unfortunately, no exits from either room.

She got a drink of water from the washroom and then returned to the main office, a fresh idea occurring to her. It was right after she'd opened this particular safe that Frost had fulfilled his part of their bargain and given her the satchel she'd gotten from Virgil Morgan's Semaline lockbox.

More important, that was the point where Frost's interest in the *Advocatus Diaboli*'s various safes had suddenly stopped.

Something in that safe had apparently been very interesting to Neverlin's ally. It might be worthwhile to see what that something was.

She'd already opened the safe once, which theoretically

meant she already had the combination. But there was always the chance that Neverlin had changed it since then.

Anyway, it wasn't as if she didn't have a few minutes to spare. Pulling out her burglar's tools, she got to work.

It was just as well she'd checked. Neverlin had indeed changed the combination. Using her MixStar computer to track down the new sequence, she got the safe open.

Inside was a two-inch-thick stack of papers, plus half a dozen data tubes. Setting the data tubes aside, knowing they were probably encrypted, Alison pulled out the papers and set them on her lap. With her light clipped to her shirt collar, she started going through them, wondering which one had caught Frost's attention.

Five pages from the top, she found it.

She had finished looking at the papers, and was going through the desk's drawers, when Taneem returned.

"The ship is very quiet," the K'da said after Alison had helped her back through the opening. "I saw only two humans seated in the main control rooms."

"The bridge," Alison identified it. "Probably Neverlin's night-shift crew. Any passengers out and about?"

"The ducts carry the smell of many Brummgas," Taneem said, a brief shiver running through her. "I think there are also a few other humans."

"Frost and some of his men," Alison said. "At least now we know where we stand. Which is more than Frost can say right now."

"What do you mean?"

"I mean I found out why he was almost on my side for a while during our little vacation on Brum-a-dum." Alison held up the interesting paper she'd found. "I helped him find out that Neverlin's trying to do an end run around him."

"What's an end run?"

"Actually, in this case it's more of a double cross," Alison said. "Remember that we figured out earlier how Neverlin was going to get the ships he needed for his attack? That Frost was going to steal them from one of the planets where the Malison Ring is fighting one of their wars?"

"Yes," Taneem said. "Only it was *you* who figured that out, not *us*."

"Oh," Alison said, momentarily thrown off-track. "Yes, I suppose it was. But it doesn't really matter who came up with the idea."

"Yes, it does," Taneem said, a bit primly. "Draycos says a person must always give proper credit for cleverness and resourceful thinking. Especially if that same person is equally quick to assign blame."

Alison grimaced. "Let me guess. Jack was grousing again about me opening the other safe for Neverlin?"

"Actually, at the time I believe they were discussing your plan for getting through Frost's security cordon into the Chookoock hangar back at the Ponocce Spaceport," Taneem said. "Jack thought your Trojan Horse idea was very clever."

Alison felt her eyebrows crawling up her forehead. "*Jack* actually paid me a *compliment*?"

"And Draycos agreed." Taneem twitched her tail. "Is that so hard to believe?"

"From Draycos, no," Alison said. "From Jack, yes. But never mind that." She tapped the paper. "The point is that Neverlin has contracted with a Compfrin company to buy a dozen surplus KK-29 system patrol ships."

"Those are fighting craft?"

"Very much so," Alison said. "Probably not as powerful as

the ships Frost could get from a Malison Ring base. But they'll be plenty good enough."

"Draycos has told me that the refugee ships are well armed."

"Which won't matter a twig against the Valahgua's Death weapon, will it?" Alison countered. "Which is why Neverlin can get away with a relatively small attack force. All he needs is to keep the defenders busy while the ships carrying the Death slip inside the perimeter and start killing everyone."

Taneem's eyes flicked around the room. "Do you think any of the Death weapons might be aboard this ship?"

"I'd sure keep one close to hand if *I* was Neverlin," Alison said. "You didn't happen to smell anything besides humans and Brummgas, did you?"

"I don't think so," Taneem said. "But there were cooking aromas that might have disguised other scents."

"And of course, you don't know what a Valahgua smells like," Alison pointed out. "Well, we can look into that later. In the meantime, we've got work to do."

"Finding a way out of here?"

"Actually, that shouldn't be a problem," Alison assured her. "I was referring to the need to share this little news flash with Jack and Draycos."

"How do we do that?"

"You'll see." Putting the papers and data tubes back in the safe, Alison resealed the door. "Come on—the link's in the other room."

The *Advocatus Diaboli*'s InterWorld transmitter, she found as she settled into the nook's comfortable armchair, was already set on standby. Either someone had been sending or receiving messages earlier or else someone was planning to do so in the near future.

Either could mean there was someone paying attention to the bridge's InterWorld control station. If so, that someone might notice a transmission coming from a supposedly empty office, and wonder about it.

But they would just have to risk that. The longer she and Taneem sat here in Neverlin's office, the greater the chance someone would accidentally stumble over them.

It was the work of only a minute to key in the *Essenay*'s own InterWorld frequency and pattern information. Mentally crossing her fingers, she tapped the microphone switch. "Jack?" she called softly. "Come on, kiddo; look alive."

"Alison?" Uncle Virge's voice came back. "This is a relief, lass. Where are you?"

"Aboard the *Advocatus Diaboli*," Alison said. "And we don't really have time for chitchat."

"Understood," Uncle Virge said. "First things first. Did you get the rendezvous location?"

"I have the data diamonds," Alison said. "Unfortunately, the K'da reader Jack brought back from the *Havenseeker* is still on your side of the universe."

"Neverlin must have one of his own."

"Which isn't anywhere in his office," Alison said. "Either it's in one of the other shipboard safes or else he's carrying it with him. I'll try to get my hands on it, but I'm not too hopeful."

Uncle Virge muttered something under his breath. "In other words, we've got to find a way to get you out of there."

"You don't have to sound so unhappy about it," Alison said archly. "But that's not why I called. Tell Jack to haul his carcass out of bed—I need to talk to him."

"Jack's not here," Uncle Virge said grimly. "He wrecked his car getting back to my part of the spaceport."

Taneem gave a little gasp, her breath briefly warming the back of Alison's neck. "Are they all right?" Alison asked.

"They're fine," Uncle Virge said. "But before they could get away from the scene, Jack was arrested for car theft."

Alison wrinkled her nose in disgust. She'd begged Jack to simply buy the stupid vehicle in the first place and be done with it. But he'd said that would be too expensive, and that the paperwork would take too long anyway.

She should have argued harder. Too late now. "Can you get him out?"

"I can't exactly show up at the jail with bail money," Uncle Virge said huffily. "And he hasn't tried to contact me."

"Probably doesn't have enough privacy to get to his spare comm clip," Alison said. "I guess he and Draycos will have to figure it out on their own. In the meantime, take a message for him."

She relayed the information about Neverlin's private collection of patrol ships. "I don't know when he's planning to send crews to pick them up," she finished. "But if Jack can get to the depot on Bentre before that, maybe he can do something."

"Such as?"

"Such as making sure Neverlin doesn't get them," Alison said patiently. "Now that the Malison Ring has been alerted to the fact that something fishy is going on with Frost, he shouldn't be able to just waltz into one of their bases and commandeer a large number of their ships. If we can also deep-six these KK-29s, Neverlin should find himself in a bind."

"He'll still have the Valahgua and their weapons."

"Sure, but the fewer ships he has to throw at the refugee fleet, the better the chances the K'da and Shontine will be able to paste all of them before they get close enough to use the Death."

"I don't know," Uncle Virge said doubtfully. "I'm thinking about the three hundred Brummgas Neverlin's already shipped off Brum-a-dum. Even fully crewed, a dozen KK-29s won't carry more than seventy-two of them. Either he's *very* confident that Frost can grab more ships or else he has those extra ships already stashed away somewhere."

"We *do* know he's got several Djinn-90s," Alison pointed out.

"Which are single-seat fighters," Uncle Virge countered. "Three-seaters if you throw in the optional gunner and observer. He *can't* have enough of those to need three hundred Brummgas."

Alison scratched her cheek. Unfortunately, he had a point. "I'll see what I can find out about that," she said. "In the meantime, you and Jack see what you can do about those KK-29s, all right?"

"I'll give him the message," Uncle Virge said heavily. "Provided he gets out of jail before they fly."

"If he doesn't, Taneem and I will just have to deal with them," Alison said. "I've got to go. *Don't* try to call me here."

"Thanks, I *had* figured that part out," Uncle Virge said sardonically. "Take care of yourself, lass. You *and* Taneem."

"I will. Good luck."

She keyed off the microphone. "Do you truly believe you and I can handle all this by ourselves?" Taneem asked.

"What, you mean that thing at the end?" Alison asked. "No, of course not. That was just for Jack's benefit. Sometimes the best way to get someone on the job is to hint that he can't do it."

"That seems rather . . . I don't know the word."

Alison sighed. "The word is *cynical*," she said. "Or maybe *manipulative*."

"You *can* change," Taneem reminded her quietly. "All people have that capability."

"I know." Reaching down, Alison scratched Taneem briefly behind her ears. "But to tell you the truth, I kind of like myself just the way I am. Go back out to the main office and listen at the door, will you, while I close down here?"

Taneem nodded and trotted back out of the nook. Alison leaned over to close the door between them, then quickly reset the transmitter's frequency.

The man waiting at the other end of the connection picked up instantly. With the word *manipulative* running through her mind, Alison launched into the report she hadn't wanted Taneem to hear.

Fortunately, this one was much shorter than the conversation with Uncle Virge had been. Within a minute she was finished and had signed off. Resetting the controls to their original positions, she rejoined Taneem in the main office.

The K'da was by the door, her ear leaned against it. "Any change?" Alison called softly as she sat down at Neverlin's desk.

Taneem shook her head as she moved away from the door. "Both guards are still there," she said, coming to Alison's side. "You have a plan?"

"I do," Alison said as she keyed on the desk computer terminal. The system was code-locked, of course, but Alison had her own version of Jack's sewer-rat technique for getting into uncooperative computers. "The trick with military organizations like this is to know how things get done," she continued. "The key is that every order goes through at least two levels of command before it gets where it's supposed to go."

"Even in a group this small?"

"Even here," Alison assured her. The mole program did its

work, and the menu came up. Scrolling down the assignment roster, she found that the two guards currently standing outside the office door were a human named Rennie and a Brummga named Grisfel.

"What I'm doing now is issuing a new set of orders to the night duty officer," she explained as she typed. "I'm telling him to send our guards out there to the main conference room for a brief consultation with Colonel Frost."

Taneem was silent a moment. "But surely they'll quickly discover the orders are false."

"Of course they will," Alison said. "But they won't be able to trace which of the ship's computers sent the message." She smiled grimly as she added a second order to the list. "And you might be surprised how easily suspicious minds like Neverlin's and Frost's can be nudged in the wrong direction."

She logged both orders and shut down the computer. "Come on aboard," she said, holding out her hand. "One last job and we'll be ready to go."

Selecting the largest and longest-range needle transmitter from her sewing kit, she slid it into the carpet beside one of the desk legs, out of the normal traffic pattern, the way her father had taught her. The carpet wasn't thick enough to hide the needle completely, but no one was likely to see it unless he was specifically looking for it.

Then, making sure she hadn't left behind any other trace of her presence, she stepped to the door and set her burglar's pickup microphone against the panel.

Frost's mercenaries were nothing if not efficient. Barely two minutes later she heard a faint comm clip voice from outside the office. There was a short, half-heard conversation, followed by a quiet order to the guard's companion.

Followed by the sound of two sets of footsteps moving away down the corridor.

"Is that it?" Taneem murmured from Alison's shoulder when the footsteps had faded into silence.

"That's it," Alison said. Steeling herself, she opened the door.

She'd half-expected to discover that the trick had failed, that she would find herself facing men and Brummgas with drawn weapons and evil grins. But the corridor was deserted. Getting her bearings, she headed forward. "Where are we going?" Taneem whispered.

"You'll see," Alison whispered back. Another corridor cut across theirs directly ahead. She paused to check around the corner, then turned into the cross-corridor and headed outward toward the ship's hull.

A minute later, they had reached their destination.

"What is this?" Taneem asked, lifting her head from Alison's shoulder to study the red-rimmed door in front of them.

"One of the ship's lifepods," Alison said, running a finger across the thin, multicolored seal pasted across the edge of the door. "Two weeks' worth of food and water and air for four people. Perfect place to hide until we reach the rendezvous."

Taneem seemed to digest that. "And the catch?"

Alison lifted her eyebrows at her symbiont as she pulled a small coil of nearly invisible but incredibly strong monofilament thread from her shirt cuff. "The *catch*?"

Taneem shrugged, a sideways flip of her crest. "Jack says that when something looks too good or too easy there's always a catch."

"Talk about *cynical*," Alison commented, taking the cap off her pen and carefully setting the loops at the ends of the monofilament into small grooves in both cap and pen.

"Is he wrong?"

"In this case, no," Alison said. Setting the pen and cap on the deck, she pulled out a pair of thumb caps and worked them onto the tips of her thumbs. "See this seal? It's designed to break easily so that people can get into the lifepod in an emergency. But once it's broken, it's broken."

"Showing that someone has been inside?"

"Exactly," Alison said. "It's supposed to discourage people from sneaking inside and pilfering any of the goodies."

"But you have a way to repair it?"

"Not exactly." Picking up the monofilament again, Alison gripped the pen and cap in opposite hands and set the thread against the door by the end of the seal. Pressing the thread firmly against the metal with her protected thumbs, she eased the thread beneath the seal. "The plan is to get the seal off but keep it intact."

It was a technique she'd practiced many times under her father's watchful eye. But she'd never had to do it in the field, and rather to her surprise she discovered it actually worked. The monofilament slid smoothly beneath the seal, cutting through its adhesive and releasing it from the metal.

Her biggest fear was that the seal would simply fold itself back onto the door as the thread passed beneath it. Fortunately, that didn't happen. Instead, the seal curled slightly away from the metal as she worked, eliminating that danger.

A minute later, she was finished. Praying that Neverlin hadn't added any entry alarms, she touched the release.

He hadn't. The door slid open, the pod's lights came on, and she slipped inside.

"Are we going to close the door?" Taneem prompted, peering out Alison's shirt back into the ship.

"Patience," Alison said, pulling out her multitool and getting to work on the control panel plate beside the door. "Closing the door normally starts a ten-second eject countdown."

"Oh."

"Oh, indeed," Alison said. "We'd really like to keep that from happening. Especially since I'm not sure what happens to a lifepod ejected while the ship's still running on the ECHO stardrive."

"But you *can* keep that from happening?"

Alison grimaced. "We'll find out in a minute."

The plate came off. Nudging the bundle of wires out of the way with her screwdriver, she located the right one and popped the end out of its socket. "That should do it," she said, tapping the door control.

She watched the status display carefully as the door slid shut, counting down the seconds to herself. Fifteen of them later, she finally started breathing again. "Yes," she said, closing the multi-tool. "That did it."

"Not quite," Taneem said. "Would you press your back against the door a moment?"

Frowning, Alison complied. Taneem shifted around on her back, probably checking the corridor one last time.

But no. Something else was happening, something that felt subtly different from anything else Alison had experienced with her companion.

She squeezed her hand into a fist, a fresh wave of tension flowing into her. If Taneem fell off into the corridor, this whole thing would have been for nothing.

And then, to her relief, she felt the K'da's weight shift again as she came fully back onto Alison's skin. "There," Taneem said with satisfaction. "I've smoothed the seal back into place on the door."

Alison blinked. "How in the world did you do *that*?"

"I leaned over the wall as if preparing to fall to the other side," Taneem said. "Only instead I merely leaned one paw over and pressed it against the seal."

"I'll be sniggled," Alison said, eyeing the K'da with new respect. "That's a new one on me. As a matter of fact, I don't think even Draycos has tried that one. Nicely done."

"Thank you," Taneem said. "I was afraid it would be seen."

"It might have, at that," Alison agreed. In actual fact, she knew, the flowing air currents out there would eventually have reattached the seal more or less where it was supposed to be.

But Taneem was so proud of her accomplishment that Alison had no intention of popping her bubble. Besides, this way the seal was back in place that much sooner.

"I'm glad I could help," Taneem said. "What now?"

"Now the evening is finally over." Alison yawned widely. "I don't know about you, but I'm beat. Let's check out the food supplies and then see about getting some sleep."

CHAPTER 5

As far as Jack could tell, the Ponocce City Police Station was as badly organized as the rest of Brummgan society.

His first stop after being hauled from the patrol car was an office for the usual round of fingerprinting, retinal scans, and other biometric readings. Then he was put into a small holding cell, then sent back to the first office to redo the fingerprints, then over to a second office for no particular reason he could figure out, and once more back to the first office.

Eventually, he ended up in a block of group cells two levels underground that seemed to be stocked mostly with drunks.

Disorganization, Uncle Virgil had often said, was a con man's best friend. In this case, though, none of the chaos did Jack any good. His forced wanderings never took him into a room or corridor with a window, and there were always too many armed Brummgas between him and the doors for him to make a break for it. Draycos, with his warrior's training and eye, agreed with that assessment.

Which wasn't to say either of them liked it.

Four hours, the words whispered through Jack's mind. The thought felt as restless against Jack's mind as Draycos's two-dimensional form felt against his skin. *We've been here four hours.*

Thanks, I can count, Jack thought back sourly. *I'm still open to suggestions.*

Draycos didn't answer. Not really surprising, since well before the first hour was up the two of them had discussed and eliminated pretty much every possible plan.

Jack still had the backup comm clip hidden in his shoe. Unfortunately, there was no one to call with it. The *Essenay* could hardly tackle a police station all by itself, certainly not with Brummgan military aircraft stationed within a couple of miles.

And even if Uncle Virge caught the Brummgas napping and was able to blow a hole in the side of the building, Jack and Draycos were currently sitting right where the pile of rubble from that blast would land. No future in that at all.

Alternatively, Draycos could roll off Jack's back through the plastic doors of their cell and take out the two guards playing cards across the room. But there were a half-dozen surveillance cameras in the cell block, and all the Brummgan inefficiency in the galaxy wouldn't save them once the building was aroused.

They have to eventually take us out of here, he reminded Draycos. *They'll take us to trial, or a more permanent prison. Sooner or later, we'll get our chance.*

Again, the K'da didn't answer. Again, Jack didn't need a telepathic connection to know what his symbiont was thinking.

Eventually, certainly, they'd be out. But whether they would be out in time to save Draycos's people was an entirely different question.

Let alone whether they'd be out in time to save Alison and Taneem.

"Human!" a deep voice called. "Human Macavity!"

"Yes, I'm here," Jack called back. He worked his way through the milling drunks to the door, sternly warning his hopes not to get too high. Chances were they'd simply messed up his fingerprints again and were hauling him back up to the second floor to retake them.

"You are summoned," the guard rumbled, sliding the door open for Jack.

A second guard joined them as they walked to the elevator. They got in, and the first Brummga punched one of the buttons.

Only it wasn't the second-floor button. This time, they were taking Jack to the tenth floor, only two floors down from the top of the building.

And that high up, where the senior officers and administrators probably had their offices, there were bound to be windows.

Though we will *be ten floors up,* Draycos reminded him.

I know, Jack agreed. *But at least it's something.*

The elevator let them out into a far nicer hallway than anything Jack had seen in the building so far. The guards led him to a thick door, opened it, and nudged him none too gently inside.

The room was reasonably large, clearly someone's office, with a cluttered desk in the middle and a low table and a pair of guest chairs in front of it. The lights were on low, probably a nighttime setting. A man sat behind the desk, his face in shadow. Three large Brummgas stood behind him, their handguns out and pointed at Jack.

And on the side wall to Jack's left was the most beautiful sight he'd seen since crashing his car: a large window looking out onto the lights of the city below.

They had their way out.

"Thank you," the man at the desk said to Jack's escort. "You may leave."

The guards backed out, closing the door behind them. "Welcome, Mr.—*Macavity,* was it?" the man said, gesturing to the farther of the two guest chairs. "Please; sit down."

Jack crossed toward the chair, trying to get a better look at the man's face. The voice seemed familiar, but he couldn't place it. "I expect you're wondering what you're doing here," the man continued as Jack sat down.

"I think the charges were vehicle theft and reckless driving," Jack said, shifting in the seat as if arranging himself. As he did so, he brought one foot up slightly, lifting his heel an inch off the floor. *Draycos, can you get to my comm clip?*

He felt movement across his skin, then a touch of weight as the K'da's forepaw lifted slightly from the back of his leg just above the ankle. *I think so.*

Get it, Jack told him. *See if you can slide it under my clothes up to my neck.*

"I meant what you were doing *here,* in this office," the man said, gesturing around the room. "I gather you don't recognize me." Leaning forward, he flicked on the desk light, bathing his face in a soft glow.

Jack felt his muscles tighten. He did indeed know the man. His name was Harper, and he worked as a bodyguard for Cornelius Braxton.

The head of Braxton Universis . . . and a man who might have been involved in the murders of Jack's parents eleven years ago.

"I see now that you do," Harper said. "Good. That should save some time."

"Time is usually worth saving," Jack agreed. Draycos had the comm clip out of his shoe now and was working it up along the back of the boy's leg. So far neither Harper nor the Brumm-gas seemed to have noticed anything. "Do you suppose your friends back there could point those guns somewhere else?" he added.

"Sorry," Harper said, smiling faintly. "After what happened to Slavemaster Gazen a couple of weeks ago, they feel it would be wise to keep you under guard at all times."

Jack looked sharply at the glowering aliens. Those were *Chookoock* family Brummgas?

"Yes, we're from the Patri Chookoock, Mr. Macavity," Harper said, correctly interpreting Jack's sudden change of expression. He raised his eyebrows slightly. "Correction: Mr. *Morgan*."

A shiver ran up Jack's skin. *Uh-oh.*

Steady, Draycos calmed him.

"You've caused us a great deal of trouble, Mr. Morgan," Harper went on. "Luckily for you, the Patri Chookoock is prepared to be lenient."

"In exchange for what?" Jack asked, the words coming out with difficulty. If Harper was working with the Chookoock family, it meant he must actually be one of Neverlin's men.

Or it could be even worse. It could be that Neverlin and Braxton had patched up their differences and Braxton was now a full partner in the plot to kill Draycos's people.

Either way, everyone in the room right now knew about Draycos.

Calm yourself, Jack, Draycos's cool thought whispered through his sudden surge of panic. *They want something, or they would have killed us already.*

Jack's heart was thudding hard enough for him to hear. *We can't take that chance,* he thought back.

We have no choice, Draycos said firmly. *They're too widely separated for an attack. Stay calm and watch for an opportunity.*

Jack had been trying to keep his swirl of emotion out of his face. But Harper wasn't fooled. "Relax," he said, smiling faintly. "There's still a chance you can walk away from this with your life. I understand you know a young lady named Alison Kayna."

For a split second Jack thought about denying it. But there didn't seem to be much point to that. "We've chatted once or twice," he admitted.

"That's good," Harper said. "Because the Patri Chookoock is even more annoyed with her than he is with you."

"Yeah, I'm not surprised," Jack said. The comm clip pressed against the waistband of his jeans, and he pulled in his stomach a little to let Draycos keep it moving.

"Ah, so you know about her little rampage through his estate," Harper said. "Excellent. That means you've been in contact with her since then. Tell us where she is and you can go free."

Briefly, Jack wondered what Harper's reaction would be if he told him Alison was settled in somewhere aboard the *Advocatus Diaboli*. "Hard to say," Jack told him instead. "The girl's always on the move."

Harper's smile hardened a little. "But you *would* be willing to help us find her?"

"Well, she's not in *here*," Jack said, half-turning both directions as if checking the room's corners behind him. The movement, he hoped, would hide the slight rippling of his shirt as Draycos slid the comm clip the rest of the way to his neck and attached it to the inside of his collar. "Afraid I can't help you look anywhere else just now."

"I think we can fix that," Harper assured him. "In about fifteen minutes a private shuttle will land on the roof of this building. You, I, and our three friends will take the elevator up there, get in, and take a ride to the Chookoock estate."

His face hardened. "Where you'll tell us everything the Patri Chookoock wants to know. One way or another. Guaranteed."

Stay calm, Jack, Draycos said again.

Jack took a deep breath. He'd had all he could take from the Chookoock family during the month he'd been their slave. And most of *that* had been just their casual day-to-day cruelty, the sort they would inflict on any of the helpless beings under their control. The thought of the kind of focused torture Harper was hinting at chilled him straight to the bone.

But Draycos was right. Panic would gain him nothing but a frozen brain.

Besides, even if Harper knew about Draycos, he'd never seen just what a poet-warrior of the K'da could do. That might give them the edge they would need.

In the meantime, Jack had fifteen minutes before the shuttle arrived. Maybe he could put the time to some use. "I'm sure we can come to some arrangement," he told Harper. "So tell me. How long have you been working for Mr. Neverlin?"

"Let's talk about you instead," Harper said. "How long have you—?"

"Because I'd have thought that after the *Star of Wonder* fiasco Braxton would go over his whole staff with a laser slicer," Jack interrupted. "How did you get missed? Or are we talking a brand-new alliance?"

"We know you were on Iota Klestis during the attack on the K'da/Shontine advance force," Harper said, ignoring the question. "What we *don't* know is how you learned about it far enough in advance—"

"What new alliance?" one of the Brummgas rumbled.

Harper frowned up at him. "What?"

"It said there was new alliance," the Brummga said, gesturing toward Jack with his gun. "What did it mean?"

"He was talking nonsense," Harper said. "The only alliance is the one we're already part of."

"It also spoke of Braxton," one of the other Brummgas said.

And suddenly two of the three guns that had been pointed at Jack were pointed at Harper instead.

"Are you *insane*?" Harper demanded, his voice low and ominous as he looked up at them. "Do you have any idea who I am?"

"We know who you claim," the first Brummga said. From Jack's comm clip came a soft murmur, too soft for Jack to understand. "Maybe you should be more closely asked at."

Jack, get ready to roll off the chair to your right, Draycos's thought came urgently. *Steady . . . now!*

Jack fell to his right, dropping sideways to land flat on the floor. He caught a glimpse of Harper and the Brummgas turning sharply to look at him.

And with a thunderous explosion, the window disintegrated. *Go!*

Jack climbed unsteadily back to his feet, blinking back the swirling dust now filling the room. Through the ringing in his ears, he could hear Uncle Virge's voice shouting faintly from inside his shirt. "Come on, lad! Hurry!"

Jack looked toward the side wall. Where the window had been was now a gaping hole. Beyond the hole, hovering on its lifters with its ramp gesturing invitingly, was the *Essenay*.

"Hurry, lad," Uncle Virge said again. "They'll be on us anytime."

"Right," Jack muttered, and he headed toward the ruined wall.

He was halfway there when he heard the flat crack of a gunshot.

He spun half-around, dropping reflexively into a crouch. Harper was still seated at the desk, with two of the Brummgas still standing over him. The aliens were waving their guns wildly, their pea-sized brains probably still trying to sort out whether they should be pointing the weapons at Jack, Harper, or the new threat that had suddenly appeared outside.

And then, as Jack watched, there was another pair of gunshots. The two remaining Brummgas jerked and toppled backward out of sight behind the desk.

It was only then that Jack saw the small gun in Harper's hand.

There was a sudden surge of weight on Jack's shoulders, and Draycos leaped out of his collar.

But Harper was faster. Instantly, he lifted both hands, pointing his gun at the ceiling. "Truce," he called.

The word was barely out of his mouth before Draycos reached him. Jack caught his breath, but the K'da hadn't missed the signs of surrender. He leaped up onto the desk but instead of delivering a killing or stunning blow merely slapped the gun out of Harper's hand with his paw.

"Jack, lad, come *on!*" Uncle Virge snapped. "They're scrambling pursuit fighters."

"On our way," Jack called back, starting again toward the ramp. "Come on, Draycos."

Draycos flicked his tail and hopped backward off the desk, his eyes still on Harper. "Take me with you," Harper called, his hands still in the air. "We may be on the same side."

"You've got your own shuttle coming," Jack reminded him. "You can take that one."

"With three dead Brummgas behind me?" Harper countered. "Don't be ridiculous."

Jack hesitated. Harper was probably right about that.

Question was, could Jack and Draycos trust the man? Jack looked at Draycos, but the K'da was looking back at him. Waiting for *him* to make the decision.

And as he gazed at those glowing green eyes, a memory popped back into Jack's mind: he and Draycos on Sunright, with Jack unwilling to go charging back into danger to rescue Alison and some of their fellow Whinyard's Edge soldiers. *A warrior does that which is right,* Draycos had told him. *Not because he may profit from it. Because it is right.*

If they left Harper here, the man was dead. Pure and simple. Either by the hand of the Brummgan legal system or by the far more personal hand of the Patri Chookoock.

And there was always a chance he and Harper *were* on the same side. "Come on, then," Jack told him.

Turning back to the ruined wall, he steeled himself and leaped the two feet across to the end of the ramp. Draycos was right behind him, with Harper a close third. "We're in," Jack called toward the airlock's camera/speaker/microphone module. "Close up and head to the roof."

"Right," Uncle Virge said.

"Wait a second," Harper protested as the ramp slid back into place and the outer hatch closed. He started toward Jack, stopping abruptly as Draycos stepped warningly into his path. "The *roof*?"

"They'll be looking for someone running," Jack called back over his shoulder as he headed for the cockpit. "So instead we go to ground."

The *Essenay* was already settling onto the roof beside the police station's set of big relay dishes when Jack reached the cockpit. "Hull-wrap on, everything else power crash-down," Jack ordered the computer as he slid into the pilot's seat.

"Got it," Uncle Virge said, the cockpit's lights and power indicators already winking out. "Jack, lad, bringing on another passenger—"

"Save it," Jack said. He turned as Harper came up behind him, Draycos close on his heels. "Just relax, Mr. Harper. It's under control."

He saw Harper's eyes flick to the single part of the board still showing indicators. "Chameleon hull-wrap?" he asked.

"That's right," Jack confirmed. "A very good one, too."

"It still won't fool them forever," Harper warned. "We may look like a section of roof from above, but there's no way to hide the ship's actual bulge from anyone looking straight across the rooftops at us."

"We aren't going to stay here forever," Jack assured him. "As soon as those fighters and police aircars get far enough away, we'll be making a break for it."

"And at night a sideways look isn't going to do anyone much good anyway," Uncle Virge added. "Trust me, we've done this before."

"I'll take your word for it," Harper said, glancing around. "I give up. Where are you?"

"Uncle Virgil's not actually here right now," Jack said, tensing a little as he always did whenever someone asked about his dead uncle. "He just added a personality simulation to the computer so I wouldn't get lonely when he was away."

"Interesting." Harper leaned over Jack's shoulder toward the P/S/8 designation plate on the computer-interface board. "That kind of personality simulation usually requires at least a P/S/11. You must have upgraded your system somewhere along the line."

"Actually, I think the ship came already equipped with a

P/S/11," Jack said. "I think what Uncle Virgil did was *down*grade the designation plate."

"We've got a shuttle incoming from the northeast," Uncle Virge reported. "The police are moving to intercept."

"That'll be mine," Harper said. "Or, rather, the one the Patri was sending for me."

Jack sent him a sideways look. "Awfully nice of him."

"Relax; I'm not with them," Harper said. "Really. I just spun them that yarn to get myself into the police station."

"Ah," Jack said, wondering whether to actually believe that. "He's going to be furious when he finds out you killed three of his soldiers, you know."

"No more furious than he'll be when he finds out I lied to him about being one of Neverlin's associates." Harper consulted his watch. "Which should be any time now, depending on when the answer to his query gets back from the *Advocatus Diaboli*."

Jack frowned at him. "You *knew* he would check up on you?"

"Of course," Harper said. "But I also know how long it typically takes messages to transfer back and forth between underlings and superiors. I figured I had enough time, especially given how eager the Patri was to let me sneak you out of jail and into his hands."

A shiver ran up Jack's back. "You play dangerous games."

"*You* should talk," Harper countered. "From where I sit, it looks like you're involved with Neverlin up to your lower lip."

"Jack's involvement is purely accidental," Draycos put in.

"And then we have you," Harper went on, looking over his shoulder at Draycos. "I can't wait to hear *your* story."

"Jack, I believe it's time," Uncle Virge spoke up. "They're all far enough away."

Jack nodded. "Rev us up."

The board lit up again as the computer reactivated the *Essenay*'s systems. Jack gave everything a quick look, then got a grip on the control yoke. "You might want to hang on to something," he advised Harper. "This could get a little bumpy."

"Keep it slow and casual as long as you can," Harper cautioned. "The more you look like someone out on an innocent late-night errand, the longer it'll take them to notice you."

"Thanks, I know the drill," Jack told him. "Here goes."

He eased the *Essenay* away from the roof, turning off the chameleon hull-wrap as he did so, and headed at a leisurely pace at right angles to the current focus of the searchers' attention.

For the first thirty seconds he thought they were actually going to pull it off. Then, three of the fighters turned away from their confrontation with the Chookoock shuttle and swung onto an intercept course. "That's it," Jack said, grabbing the thruster control. "Hang on, everyone." Mentally crossing his fingers, he jammed it to full power.

He needn't have worried. The fighters' pilots had apparently been motivated by little more than curiosity about the unidentified craft's presence over the city. By the time Jack's burst of speed turned their idle questions to sharp-edged certainty, the *Essenay* had too much of a lead.

Six minutes later, with the fighters still trying to play catch-up, Jack keyed in the ECHO. The starry sky in front of them flashed with the usual brief rainbow, and became the blue of hyperspace.

And they were safe. For now.

"Nicely done," Harper said. "Now what?"

"We find someplace to drop you off and get on with our lives," Jack said, frowning at the navigation display. With the data diamonds holding the refugee rendezvous information still aboard the *Advocatus Diaboli,* the new plan had been for him and Draycos to go to Driftline, where Alison had deduced Frost had been heading when he'd been ordered to Semaline to pick her up.

Of course, that had been a month ago. Frost and Neverlin could easily have changed their plans since then. But Driftline was the only lead they had.

But Uncle Virge had already laid in an ECHO course. Not for Driftline, but some obscure planet named Bentre at the edge of Compfrin space. "Uncle Virge?" Jack asked.

"We'll talk later, Jack lad," the computerized personality said firmly.

"Whatever," Jack said, catching the cue. Apparently, whatever was going on, it wasn't something Uncle Virge wanted to discuss in front of company.

"Meanwhile, we'd be more comfortable in the dayroom," Draycos put in.

"Good idea," Harper said, turning and working his way out of the cockpit. "I'm looking forward to hearing your story."

"I'm sure you are," Jack said, following him out. "Almost as much as we're looking forward to hearing yours."

CHAPTER 6

Alison had just unwrapped a pair of ration bars when the receiver she'd set in her ear picked up the sound of a door opening and an indistinct murmur of human voices. "Hold it," she said softly, gesturing to Taneem. "We've got company."

The K'da stepped to her side, pressing her ear to Alison's just as the muttering voices began to resolve into words. "—*hell* were they thinking?" Neverlin was snarling.

"What do you want me to say?" Frost bit back, sounding every bit as angry as Neverlin. "This isn't a field operation with enemies just across the mortar zone, where you double- and triple-check everything. This is supposed to be a secure operations base. You get an order, you assume it's legit."

"An order to abandon your post?" Neverlin countered acidly. "An order to leave a guard station unmanned? Maybe your troops need to hear a lecture on basic security technique."

"Trust me," Frost said darkly. "They'll *definitely* be hearing a lecture."

There was a soft thump, the sound of flesh slapping against metal. "Well, at least he didn't get it open," Neverlin muttered.

"How do you know?" Frost countered. "Kayna got *hers* open without blowing off the door. How do you know Mrishpaw didn't use the same trick she did?"

"I *don't* know," Neverlin said. "But I intend to find out."

The voices fell silent. "Mrishpaw?" Taneem asked quietly.

"That was the other order I logged from Neverlin's office," Alison told her. "I sent a message to Mrishpaw to report to Frost at the aft sensor room. Naturally, Frost wasn't there."

"But why do they suspect him of trying to get into the safe?" Taneem asked. "They must realize both orders were false."

"And they also realize both were for the same purpose," Alison agreed. "But their assumption will be that someone wanted to sneak *into* the office, not out of it."

"But Mrishpaw went to the aft sensor room, not the office," Taneem said, clearly still confused.

"Yes, he did," Alison agreed. "But since most of the rest of the ship was asleep, probably no one saw him. That makes it his word against Neverlin's suspicions."

"Suspicions of one who is an ally."

"True, but remember these people are allies purely from common interest," Alison reminded her. "They don't especially even like each other. They certainly don't trust each other."

"Ah—Mrishpaw," Neverlin said. "Come in. No, no—over here, by the safe."

The hidden needle picked up the thud of Brummgan footsteps crossing the room. "I must congratulate you," Neverlin went on. "You and the Patri Chookoock both. You must have seen something Kayna did when she opened that other safe. Something the rest of us missed."

"Sir?" Mrishpaw asked. Brummgan voices were hard to read, but Alison had no trouble hearing the bewilderment in this one.

"The safe, Mrishpaw," Neverlin said. Another slapping of flesh on metal. "Tell me, how exactly did you get it open?"

"Sir?" Mrishpaw asked again. With his molasses mind in a

swirl of confusion, he was clearly having trouble coming up with anything new to say.

"You can drop the innocent act, Private," Frost said tartly. "You know, Mr. Neverlin, it's just occurred to me that the only really solid report we have of Morgan's K'da being on the Chookoock estate also came from Private Mrishpaw. Yet we know now that both Morgan *and* his K'da were actually on Semaline at the time."

"No," Mrishpaw protested, finally finding his tongue or his brain or both. "It was on the estate. It attacked Sergeant Dumbarton and me."

"So you reported," Frost said. "However, Sergeant Dumbarton himself doesn't remember seeing anything but a blur."

"It attacked other guards, too," Mrishpaw said, sounding puzzled. "The ones who fought the slave riot. They saw it, too."

"Oh yes—the big impressive K'da warrior attack," Neverlin said contemptuously. "Leaving—let me see—three Brummgas knocked unconscious, none dead, and the rest escaped without so much as a scratch. Must have been his day off."

"*Panjan* Gazen was also killed," Mrishpaw said. His confusion was starting to edge into alarm now as he finally saw where the conversation was going.

"By slaves armed with sticks," Neverlin said contemptuously. "The fact is that every report of a K'da being on Brum-a-dum came from you or one of the Patri Chookoock's other people."

"You're here, Private," Frost said. "The Patri Chookoock is a long ways away, where he can't hear. If you have anything to say, this is the time to say it."

"*Panjan* Gazen was also killed," Mrishpaw repeated, sounding thoroughly miserable. He was being railroaded, and he knew it. But he was all muscle and stamina, and he couldn't think of anything to say in his defense.

Alison could almost feel sorry for him. But then she thought back to the Chookoock estate, and how Mrishpaw had accepted without protest Frost's order to kill her in cold blood, and her sympathy faded away.

"Very well," Frost said. "Pending further investigation, you're confined to quarters. Dismissed."

Again there was the thud of Brummgan footsteps across the office floor, followed by the sound of a closing door. "Unless you'd prefer I have him executed?" Frost asked.

"I don't know," Neverlin said. During the confrontation there had been no hint of hesitation in his voice. Now, though, Alison could detect both doubt and suspicion. "In point of fact, we don't actually *know* the K'da was on Semaline with Morgan. We only have Langston's statement on that."

"I was thinking the same thing," Frost agreed slowly. "On the other hand, those false orders definitely came from somewhere inside the *Advocatus Diaboli*. Langston isn't here. Mrishpaw is."

"Mrishpaw and eleven other Chookoock family Brummgas," Neverlin rumbled. "By the way, speaking of Morgan, it seems he's slipped through our fingers again."

"What?" Frost demanded. "You said the police had picked him up."

"They did, and were holding him as ordered," Neverlin said grimly. "Unfortunately, someone calling himself Springer showed up at the Chookoock estate claiming to be one of my men. He convinced the Patri that Morgan and the K'da were already working on escape and volunteered to take a couple of Brummgas to the station and get them out."

Frost swore under his breath. "Idiot. Why didn't he check with you first?"

"Springer apparently had him convinced that Morgan was

already halfway to the jail block door and there wasn't time," Neverlin said. "The Patri decided instead he could check with me while the others went off to fetch the prisoners."

"And?"

"Suffice it to say the police station now has a brand-new hole in the tenth-floor wall, three dead Chookoock soldiers, and one prisoner and one visitor unaccounted for."

"How convenient for Morgan," Frost said. "You think the Patri might have deliberately helped him to escape?"

"One would hope the Patri is smart enough to know what it would mean to try changing sides at this late date," Neverlin said contemptuously. "No, I think he simply got conned by this Springer character. I'm leaning toward him being someone sent by your friend General Davi to retest the waters."

"One would hope General Davi is smart enough to leave well enough alone," Frost growled. But Alison could hear the half-hidden discomfort in his voice. "More likely he's one of Braxton's people, still trying to track you down. That, or else the Internos government has finally started to take notice of all this."

"Fortunately, whoever he is, he's hitting the curve too late to stop us," Neverlin said. "And whatever he wants with Morgan, getting three of the Patri's soldiers dead in the process will now have bought him a great deal of additional trouble."

"Unless it was the K'da who killed them, not Springer," Frost pointed out.

"I doubt the Patri will really care about such details," Neverlin pointed out. "Besides, as I said, he's far too late to stop us."

"Maybe Springer can't," Frost warned. "I'm not so sure about the Patri. If he gets it into his slow-motion brain that Springer *was* one of us, there to pull some kind of bizarre double cross, he might decide to retaliate."

"With his men already here and out of communication with him?" Neverlin countered scornfully. "That would be a neat trick."

"On the other hand, double crosses can come in all sorts of odd flavors," Frost said, a subtle change in his voice. "They might even involve, oh, say, a set of twelve Compfrin KK-29 patrol ships."

There was a short, dark silence. "Very good, Colonel," Neverlin said at last. The words were calm enough, but there was something in his tone that sent a shiver up Alison's back. "But let's not overstep the dramatics. Ever since the raid on the Chookoock estate you're no longer flying beneath the Malison Ring's radar. I felt it might be unacceptably dangerous for your men to go to Driftline as originally planned for those Rhino-10s. I therefore went ahead and set up a backup plan, just in case."

"Nice speech," Frost complimented him. "Very believable. Unfortunately for you, I happen to know that this particular backup plan was made long before the Malison Ring had ever even *heard* of the Chookoock family."

There was another short silence. "I see," Neverlin said, his voice still calm. "So you gave Kayna a little safecracking practice on the way to Brum-a-dum."

"I thought it would be a good idea to give her skills a real test before I brought her in front of you and the Patri," Frost said. "Imagine my surprise when I discovered that bill of sale among your private papers."

"Imagine," Neverlin agreed politely. "But as I said, it was a backup plan."

"Was it?" Frost countered. "Or was the plan to abandon me and my men on Driftline and do the job on the refugee fleet without us? Leaving us to face General Davi's tender mercies?"

"You're here for your tactical abilities, Colonel," Neverlin said coldly. "I suggest you start proving you have some. Do you really think I'm foolish enough to tackle an armed fleet with nothing but a handful of KK-29s and a ship full of Brummgas?"

"*And* your tame Valahgua and their Death weapons."

"Even with them we need everything we have, and everything more that we can get," Neverlin assured him. "I trust you'll remember that."

"*I* remember it just fine," Frost said. "I just wanted to make sure you did, too. What was your plan for retrieving the 29s?"

Neverlin snorted gently. "The original plan was to swing by Bentre after I'd dropped you and your men off at Driftline and have the Brummgas collect the ships and fly them to Point Two. Now, with this Mrishpaw thing, I may not want all of your men leaving my ship just now."

Alison pricked up her ears. Point Two. The ambush location?

"Don't worry, we won't need to use anyone from the *Advocatus Diaboli*," Frost said. "I've already sent a group of my fighter pilots to Bentre in one of the other shuttles."

"Have you, now," Neverlin said, and there was a sudden edge of caution in his voice. "And they're already on their way?"

"If not, they will be soon," Frost said. "They were to leave as soon as the troop carrier signaled that it was safely on its way to Point One. They should reach Bentre in four days, at which point they'll pick up the 29s and fly them directly to Point Two."

"Yes," Neverlin murmured. "That should make everything so much more convenient."

"Meanwhile, Sergeant Chapman and a team are on their way to Driftline to see about those Rhino-10s," Frost continued. "By the time we're ready to move to Point Three, we should have all the ships we need."

Alison grimaced. So much for Point Two being the end of the line.

"Excellent," Neverlin murmured. "You do still mean *we,* correct?"

Frost chuckled. "Relax, Mr. Neverlin," he said. "As you said, we need all of us to make this work."

"I'm relieved to hear it," Neverlin said, back on balance again. "Langston isn't with either raiding party, is he?"

"Don't worry," Frost assured him grimly. "He's at Point One getting drilled in proper Malison Ring combat technique." He paused, and Alison could imagine his thin smile. "And he's under the impression that Point Two is the actual rendezvous point. If he *does* have a knife up his sleeve, whoever he tries to call will show up in the wrong place."

"Let's just make sure he doesn't have a chance to make any such calls," Neverlin said.

"No problem," Frost said. "I've got him aboard the *Foxwolf.* No InterWorld transmitter *there.*"

Neverlin grunted. "As far as we know."

"The Valahgua supposedly know what their enemies' long-range transmitters look like," Frost reminded him.

"Supposedly," Neverlin said. "How many of your men are on the *Foxwolf* at the moment?"

"Seventeen," Frost said. "Three shifts each at command, helm, engineering, hyperdrive, and monitor room, plus two swing crewers. Plus Langston."

"Do we have Brummgas who can handle those jobs?"

"Yes," Frost said, and Alison could hear a frown in his tone. "Do we *want* Brummgas handling those jobs?"

"The question is whether I want any Brummgas aboard the *Advocatus Diaboli,*" Neverlin said tartly. "And right now, I'm thinking I don't. As soon as we reach Point Two you'll swap them off to the *Foxwolf* for twelve of your men."

"I'd strongly recommend against that, sir," Frost said, his voice suddenly formal. "The *Foxwolf* is the key to this whole operation."

"Don't worry; your men will still be in command," Neverlin said. "And we can certainly swap them back before we reach the rendezvous. But for the moment I want the Brummgas as far away from me as possible. *And* from my InterWorld transmitter."

"As you wish," Frost said. "I still think it's a mistake. Brummgas make good soldiers, but they're not built for thinking."

"There won't be any serious thinking to be done until the attack," Neverlin said. "By then, we'll have your men back aboard." He paused, and Alison heard the sound of footsteps as he headed for the door. "I'm going back to bed. Let me know if anything else happens."

A second set of footsteps joined the first. There was the sound of a door opening and closing, and then silence. Alison waited a minute, just to make sure, then pulled the receiver from her ear.

"Four days," Taneem murmured.

"What?" Alison asked.

"He said four days until his soldiers reach Bentre," the K'da said. "He also said Jack was no longer in jail."

And Alison had left a message with Uncle Virge urging Jack to also head directly to Bentre. "Yes, I know."

"Do you think Jack might be able to get there before they arrive?" Taneem asked hopefully.

Alison tried to visualize the map of the Orion Arm. "Theoretically, yes," she said. "But knowing Jack, he'll want to skulk around a bit first. Make sure everything looks okay before he goes in."

"So he and the mercenaries will arrive at the same time."

Alison grimaced. "Probably."

For a minute neither of them spoke. Alison ran the scenario over and over in her mind, trying to think of a way to warn him.

But she couldn't come up with one. The only way out of the lifepod now would break the seal, which would alert everyone aboard that they had a stowaway.

She couldn't afford for them to know that. Not yet.

"And Langston is here," Taneem murmured into the silence.

"So it would seem," Alison said, wincing. The StarForce wing sergeant Jack had sprung from unjust imprisonment on Semaline.

Jack had thought Langston died when the Malison Ring mercenaries raided the canyon where Jack had been imprisoned. Clearly, the other man had lived through the experience. And not only had he survived, but he'd apparently made a deal with Frost.

The question was, was it a genuine deal? Or was Langston playing some game of his own?

"It'll be all right," Taneem said. "Jack has Draycos with him. They'll be all right."

"I know," Alison said. She looked down at her hands, only now remembering the ration bars she was holding. "Here," she said, giving one to Taneem. "Eat up, and then we'd better get some sleep."

CHAPTER 7

"Interesting," Harper said when Jack had finished his story. "And you say there's a whole fleet of these K'da things on its way?" He looked over at Draycos, who was lying on the dayroom floor to his right. "No offense," he added. "I didn't mean *things*."

"No offense taken," Draycos assured him, stretching his forelegs leisurely.

Or at least, it looked leisurely. But Jack knew better. Draycos's posture was calculated to make him look perfectly harmless while he and Jack tried to figure out who Harper really was.

To Jack's private annoyance, he wasn't much closer to that goal than when they'd started.

Harper had listened closely to the story of the K'da/Shontine refugee fleet, the betrayal of Draycos's advance team, and their various run-ins with Neverlin and his fellow conspirators. Through it all he'd nodded at the right spots, been intensely interested at the right spots, and expressed amazement or outrage at the right spots.

But there was something about the man that still bothered Jack. Something he couldn't quite put his finger on.

"And Kayna has been your partner in all this?" Harper asked.

"Yes, at least starting with Rho Scorvi," Jack told him.

Maybe that was what it was. Maybe it was Harper's preoccupation with Alison that didn't quite feel right. It was almost as if, to him, the survival of Draycos's people was only a footnote to the main story. "Though mostly she's been a pretty unwilling ally," he added, deciding on the spur of the moment that it might be better for Alison if he downplayed her role.

"I don't doubt it," Harper said dryly. "I wonder what her reasons are for sticking around."

Draycos stirred. "Alison has been a good and faithful friend," he said. His tone was mild, but there was a familiar edge beneath it. Apparently it hadn't occurred to him to distance Alison from them.

"I'm sure she's behaved admirably," Harper said. "I'm simply wondering what she's looking to get out of this."

"You think she's the profiteering type?" Jack asked, probing delicately. So far, Harper had been conspicuously silent about what he knew about Alison.

"That's certainly been her history with Braxton Universis," Harper said. "About ten weeks ago she broke into one of our computer systems and made off with a highly valuable trade secret."

"You're certain it was her?" Draycos asked.

"Positive," Harper said grimly. "Because a week after that, she walked right into one of our research labs and walked out again with some actual hardware. *That* time we got her on camera."

"And I suppose you want the stuff back," Jack said. "Is that why you were at the Avrans City spaceport on Bigelow a couple of months ago?"

Harper's forehead creased slightly. "How did you know about that?"

"Because I saw you," Jack said. "Alison had just sprung me from the Malison Ring recruiting station and we were heading back to her ship. She spotted you hanging around and talked me into taking her for a ride to Rho Scorvi instead."

"Really," Harper said, eyeing Jack closely. "You hadn't mentioned that part of your story."

Jack shrugged. "It didn't seem important."

"Everything Kayna does is important," Harper said. "Including whatever she's up to right now. You *do* know where she is, don't you?"

"Not really," Jack said truthfully. He had no idea where exactly the *Advocatus Diaboli* was, after all. "But enough about Draycos and me. What's *your* story?"

"You've basically just had it," Harper said. "Kayna stole something from Braxton Universis. I was sent to find her and retrieve it. Along the way I discovered she'd linked up with you, who Mr. Braxton was already interested in."

"Why?"

"Because you'd saved his life," Harper said, looking puzzled. "Mr. Braxton notices things like that. Anyway, I was told to watch you and see if and when Kayna showed up. When you got arrested, I decided to get you out, so I went to the Patri Chookoock and spun him a soap bubble. He bought it, and we're here. End of story. So where do you think Kayna *might* be?"

"She *might* be almost anywhere." Jack looked over at the dayroom's computer module. "Uncle Virge? What do you think?"

"I don't know, Jack lad," the computerized personality said thoughtfully. "He's certainly taking the whole story very calmly."

"You mean like he's heard it all already?" Jack suggested, watching Harper's face closely.

The other's expression didn't even twitch. "That's ridiculous," he said.

"Is it?" Jack countered. "You may not have noticed—actually, I suppose there's no way you *could* have noticed—but I kept the story to only the stuff Neverlin and his buddies already know."

"As a matter of fact, I *did* notice some fuzziness in places," Harper told him. "But someone in your line of work must know that lack of reaction alone isn't a solid indicator. Of guilt, or anything else."

Jack raised his eyebrows. "*My* line of work? Excuse me, Mr. Harper. *My* line of work at the moment is trying to stop genocide."

Harper inclined his head. "My apologies. As I said, Mr. Braxton is interested in you. His backcheck of you and your uncle was most thorough." His face softened. "You've obviously been through a lot. I understand that."

"And *I* understand when someone's trying to change a subject," Jack countered. "That's point number two against you. Point number three is that even though you seem to know all this, you still made an effort to look as if you didn't."

Harper shook his head irritably. "This is ridiculous," he bit out. "Fine. If I'm not who I say, then who *am* I?" He folded his arms across his chest. "Because if I'm with Neverlin—"

In a single smooth motion Draycos sprang to his feet and leaped in front of Harper, landing practically in the man's lap. His front paws caught on the other's forearms, his claws digging lightly but with clear warning into Harper's sleeves. His bared teeth were inches from Harper's face.

"I'd advise you not to try anything stupid," Jack warned, standing up. "I've seen those claws cut through solid metal."

"So have I," Harper said, keeping perfectly still.

"Really?" Jack asked, crossing over to him and patting him down. His hand touched a small flattened cylinder in Harper's coat pocket near the other's right hand. "When?"

"Don't you remember?" Harper asked. "He scratched something in the base of Mr. Braxton's rejuvenation cylinder."

"Ah. Right." Nudging Harper's hand aside, Jack dug into the pocket and pulled out the object.

It was exactly what he'd expected from the shape: a palmgrip, two-shot tangler. "What have we here?" he asked the room in general as he held it up.

"It's a tangler," Harper said. "A completely non-lethal weapon, you'll note."

"Which just means whoever hired you wants me alive," Jack said. He pressed the weapon against his palm, noting how neatly and invisibly it nestled there, then dropped it into his own pocket. "At this point, that's not all that encouraging."

"Jack, use your head," Harper said patiently. "If I was working for Neverlin's crowd, why in Orion's armpit would I have brought you out of that holding cell and into the upper part of the police station where we would have a better chance at escape? Why not just leave you behind plastic until the paperwork was done, then take you out in a car where your ship's rather illegal collection of firepower couldn't have done anything without killing you?"

There was a short silence. "He has a point," Draycos said.

"I agree," Jack said. "I also notice you haven't let him up from that chair."

The K'da's tail lashed the air. "At this point, I'm not inclined to take chances."

"I agree with that, too," Jack said. "I guess our options are to handcuff him here in the dayroom or handcuff him to the cot in Alison's cabin." He raised his eyebrows at Harper. "Feel free to jump in with a vote."

"You're making a mistake, Jack," Harper said, his voice low and earnest. "I can be of great help to you. I'll prove myself any way you want—just tell me how."

For a long moment Jack was tempted. With Neverlin, Frost, a bunch of Malison Ring mercenaries, and at least three hundred Brummgas against them, he and Draycos were sorely in need of fresh allies.

But Draycos was right. It was way too late to start taking chances. "Sorry," Jack said. "Even if I knew what side you're on, I have the feeling that side could shift without much warning."

"I understand," Harper said. "Actually, in all honesty, I'd probably do the same in your place. I won't make trouble."

"Not that you could," Jack said. "Draycos, watch him."

Jack left the dayroom and went to the rear of the ship's living space, where all his theft and safecracking equipment was stored. Digging out two sets of handcuffs, he returned to the dayroom and cuffed Harper's left wrist and right ankle to the chair. "That should do for now," he said as he stepped back again. "We'll try to come up with something more permanent later that'll let you eat and sleep more or less comfortably."

"I'll look forward to it," Harper said dryly. "Can you at least tell me why we're going to Bentre?"

"I don't even know myself," Jack said candidly. "Uncle Virge?"

"I don't know if I should," Uncle Virge said hesitantly.

"It's fine," Jack said. "Just tell us."

"Alison called while you were in jail. She found out that Neverlin has twelve newly purchased KK-29 system patrol ships waiting to be picked up from the Progline Skyport on Bentre. She also gave me the name they're registered under."

Jack frowned at Draycos. "Does that mean Frost has given up on the idea of hijacking ships from Driftline?"

"She didn't say," Uncle Virge said. "All she said was that you should try to get to Bentre ahead of Neverlin and sabotage the ships."

"What are these spacecraft like?" Draycos asked.

"Six-man fighters, though one can fly it in a pinch," Harper said. "Pilot, copilot, and four blister gun stations, two on either side."

"Sounds like some serious firepower," Jack said.

Harper shrugged. "Serious enough," he said. "Just how well armed is this fleet of yours, Draycos?"

"Extremely well," Draycos said grimly. "But if the Valahgua are able to get close enough to use the Death, all their weaponry will be useless."

"I still don't get this Death thing," Harper said. "How can this beam thing go straight through armor plating like it's not there? Wouldn't something that penetrates hull metal more easily than even gamma rays also tend to go straight through the crewers without causing much damage?"

"The Death is not a form of radiation," Draycos said. "It's possibly a vibration of space itself, which seeks out the core of a living being and destroys that core and its connection to the rest of the universe."

Harper snorted. "Can we steer clear of the philosophy aspects?" he asked. "I'm looking for the physics of the thing."

"I don't know the physics." Draycos paused, his tail arched in thought. "Perhaps an analogy would help. Suppose you wished to destroy the center of a planet. A normal weapon would first have to blast away layer after layer of crust and mantle until the core was exposed. Agreed?"

"Agreed," Harper said. "So?"

"The Death does things differently," Draycos said. "In this analogy, it would be like a weapon that could ignore the outer planetary layers and seek out and destroy the core directly."

"That would be some weapon," Harper acknowledged. "But living beings aren't planets."

"No, but we all have a core of life within us," Draycos said. "Somehow, the Death is able to focus on that core."

"Still sounds like magic," Harper declared. "But never mind that. If you're right about its range being only a couple of hundred miles, the K'da and Shontine ought to be able to take out Neverlin's force long before they can get close enough to use it."

"Especially if we can get to Bentre and eliminate the ships he's planning to pick up there," Uncle Virge added.

Jack scratched his cheek. A rather outrageous plan was starting to form in the back of his mind. "Who said anything about taking them out?" he asked.

Draycos and Harper both looked sharply at him. "Alison did," Uncle Virge said, his voice as wary as Draycos's expression. "She was *very* specific."

"I'm sure she was," Jack said. "But why destroy them when they can be more useful in one piece?"

"If you're thinking you can get the refugee rendezvous from their course settings, forget it," Harper warned. "Neverlin's bound to have at least two midway points along the way."

"I know," Jack said. "That just means we'll have to hitch a ride."

"Hitch a *ride*?" Uncle Virge all but gasped. "Jack lad, there's nowhere in one of those things where you can possibly hide."

"And even if you could find a spot, what then?" Harper added. "It's going to take days to reach wherever they're going. You going to sit there quietly that whole time?"

"Something like that," Jack said. "Draycos? You game?"

"I don't know what exactly you have in mind," Draycos said. "But I have no better suggestions to make. At any rate, we have three and a half days to work out a proper plan."

"Make it four," Jack said. "We'll want to skulk around a bit first and check out the area."

"Four days, then," Draycos said. "Regardless, I'm with you."

Uncle Virge gave a snort. "And these were the two," he muttered, "who were so keen on not taking chances."

CHAPTER 8

Bentre was exactly the way Jack had expected: quiet and sparsely settled. Best of all, it was inhabited by the mostly easygoing Compfrins, who usually didn't ask awkward questions.

It was the perfect place, in other words, for someone planning genocide to pick up a few attack ships.

"Ah, yes—the spacecraft for *Sidj* Kimtra Varn," the manager of the Progline Skyport said, peering at his computer display. "Twelve KK-29s, surplused from the Grimnau Customs Office." He peered intently at Jack's face. "You are not *Sidj* Varn, are you?"

"No, I just work for him," Jack said. Human faces were hard for Compfrins to distinguish between, but he wasn't quite ready to try to pass himself off as either Neverlin or Frost.

"Allow me then to greet you and welcome you to Bentre," the manager said. He pulled out a handful of papers and a stylus and pushed them across his counter toward Jack. "Here are the release-and-possession forms that must be completed. I trust you brought a pilot for each vessel? These craft cannot be slaved together as some ships can."

"Yes, I know," Jack said, gently pushing the papers back toward him. "Actually, *Sidj* Varn just asked me to stop by and make sure the ships were here and ready to go. Another group will be coming by later to actually take possession."

"You will save them valuable time if you complete the forms now," the Compfrin suggested, pushing the forms back again.

Compfrins weren't nosy, Jack reflected, but they could definitely be pushy. "The other group will do that," Jack said firmly, trying to imagine Neverlin's reaction to the news that someone had stopped by his secret-weapons stash and done his paperwork for him. "And I really must go."

He left the office before the manager could protest further. *So we know now that Frost's men haven't already retrieved them,* Draycos's thought whispered into Jack's mind.

Getting in ahead of the opposition is always a good start, Jack agreed, looking around. The spaceport had a dozen somewhat dilapidated hangars of various sizes scattered across the grounds, including the one where he'd parked the *Essenay*. Filling the space between the hangars were a variety of other vehicles. Most of them were light personal aircraft, anchored to the ground by thin wires to protect them against gusts of wind.

Should be that one over there, Jack said, nodding toward the westernmost of the hangars as he got into one of the rental carts lined up outside the office. He dropped some coins into the slot and got a grip on the steering lever. *Let's go see what kind of bargain Neverlin got.*

They had passed the last line of tethered aircraft between them and the hangar when the comm clip on Jack's collar suddenly came to life. "Jack lad, I'm picking up a shuttle with Brumm-gan markings, coming in from the west," Uncle Virge said tightly. "Could be Frost's pilots."

Jack shot a look over his shoulder at the sky. "How close?"

"Close enough," Uncle Virge said grimly. "You need to get under cover, right now."

Jack looked around. Problem was, there *was* no cover, at least nothing he could get to quickly.

But there *was* something he could use as camouflage. "Right," he said, shifting direction toward a group of airplanes about fifty yards from the east side of Neverlin's hangar. "Any idea how many Brummgas are aboard the shuttle?"

"My infrareds can't pick out individual bodies through that kind of hull," Uncle Virge said. "But if we assume twelve pilots plus the shuttle's own crew, the overall IR sum would say they're all human, not Brummgan."

Jack felt his throat tighten. He'd assumed Frost's buddies would be busy stealing Malison Ring ships, and that Neverlin would assign this particular duty to his tame Brummgas. None of that bunch was particularly clever, and most of them had probably never actually seen Jack.

But many of Frost's mercenaries had. Way too many of them.

So much for his chances of running some sort of scam on them.

What's our plan? Draycos asked.

Jack looked over his shoulder again. The fiery glow of the incoming shuttle's drive could now be seen against the cloud-speckled blue of the sky. *There's no time to get to real cover,* he told the K'da. *So we're going to go with the classic technique of hiding in plain sight.*

The shuttle was on its final approach as Jack pulled up to the group of aircraft and stopped. "Uncle Virge, I've got a Lightsparrow-66 here," he said, glancing at the nearest airplane's markings as he got out. "I need the location of any outside equipment bays."

"Right. Give me a minute."

Making sure to keep his face away from the incoming shuttle,

Jack stepped around to the back of his cart and opened the storage compartment. It was mostly empty, but in one corner he spotted a forgotten screwdriver and a socket wrench. "Uncle Virge?" he prompted, scooping them up.

"Both wing engine pods have access ports on their inboard sides," Uncle Virge reported. "Three bolts along the top, then swing down the panel."

Jack looked at the nearest engine pod, spotted the three bolts. "Got it," he said, turning to it and setting to work with his borrowed screwdriver. He was facing the hangar now, which would be a little risky when Frost's men started piling out. On the other hand, once Jack got the panel open, it should block his face from anyone who looked in this direction.

Sure enough, as the last bolt came loose the panel swung down just low enough to hide everything above his chin. *Draycos?* he called silently. *Can you see anything?*

The K'da moved across his skin, sliding down to where he could look through the neck of Jack's shirt. *They're landing near the hangar,* he reported. *The shuttle's stern is turned toward the door.*

With its weapons turned outward, ready to shoot at possible trouble. Frost's men weren't taking any chances. *Are they all staying at that end of the building?*

No—two of them are heading this way.

Jack winced, moving his elbows briskly and visibly as he pretended to work on the plane's engine. If the mercenaries were suspicious enough to come over here and check him out . . .

Wait, Draycos said, and Jack could sense the relief in his voice. *They're turning to go around the side of the building. They're just checking the hangar's exterior.*

Jack breathed a quiet sigh of relief. At least he and Draycos weren't going to have to fight.

But that brought up a whole different problem. If the mercenaries were suspicious enough to check out even the solid parts of the hangar's exterior, they weren't likely to leave either of the two doors unguarded. *Have they finished their sweep yet?*

Almost, Draycos answered. *They're moving around the corner—one last look on this side . . . there. They're gone.*

Did they seem interested in me?

One of them looked in this direction, but there was no indication he was suspicious, Draycos answered. *All is clear. We can get moving.*

Moving to where? Jack countered. *They're bound to be watching the doors at both ends.*

Across the distance came a soft, low rumble. "Uncle Virge?" Jack asked. "Is that what I think it is?"

"It's multiple engine prep," Uncle Virge confirmed. "Looks like they're in something of a hurry."

"The manager's going to be furious if they don't fill out his paperwork," Jack said, trying hard to come up with something. So much for his original idea of hitching a ride. That left only Alison's plan of wrecking the ships and keeping Neverlin from getting them. If Jack got the *Essenay* moving right away—and if they were extraordinarily lucky—they might be able to take out all twelve ships before the mercenaries got their own weapons on line.

At which point, there would be only one other chance for him and Draycos to find Neverlin's attack force. They would have to get to Driftline before Frost finished stealing those Malison Ring ships, and figure out how to hitch a ride from there.

And if they failed there as well, Alison and Taneem would be on their own. Completely and utterly on their own.

Go to the side wall directly across from us, Draycos instructed, an edge of determination in his tone. Perhaps he was thinking about

Alison and Taneem, too. *They won't be watching for an intrusion there.*

Of course they won't, Jack said, suddenly understanding what Draycos had in mind. Ducking under the engine pod panel, confirming for himself that the mercenaries were out of sight, he headed toward the hangar at a brisk jog.

He reached the wall and pressed his back against it. *How's it look?* he asked.

Very possible, Draycos said. *Move to your left about ten feet. There's a wide tool cabinet near the wall which I can enter behind.*

I hope you're keeping the odds in mind, Jack warned as he moved along the wall and settled into his new position. *There are at least fourteen of them, and only one of you.*

Don't worry, Draycos assured him. *I'm not planning to fight even one of them, let alone all fourteen.*

Jack frowned. *Then what's the plan?*

To arrange transport, of course, Draycos said. *Return to the airplane you were pretending to fix, and have Uncle Virge locate and monitor their transmission frequencies. I'll join you soon.*

Jack felt a surge, and Draycos was gone.

Draycos pushed against Jack's skin with his rear paws, and with a slightly dizzying rush he fell over the wall into the hangar.

He dropped into a low crouch behind the tool cabinet, flicking his tongue a few times to taste the air. There were indeed only humans in this group, he concluded. Twelve of them, he estimated, which implied the entire transport crew was still in their shuttle. Easing to the edge of the cabinet, he cautiously looked around it.

The twelve KK-29 patrol ships were set out in neat rows, four rows of three each, all of them facing south toward the hangar's main doors. Two of the mercenaries were walking slowly through the rear two rows, doing a visual check of drive nozzles and missile tubes. Occasionally one of them leaned over to peer at the underside between the landing skids.

Four more men, including the two who'd walked along Jack's side of the hangar, were standing at the open north-end door, facing outward with weapons at the ready. The shuttle itself, Draycos noted, with its own weapons turned outward, would do an adequate job of guarding the southern end.

Under most circumstances, the arrangement would have created a proper and logical defensive perimeter. In this case, unfortunately for them, they were all facing the wrong way.

All six ships in the first two rows were giving off the low rumble of spacecraft being readied to fly. Waiting until the two roving men were out of sight, Draycos crossed the empty space to the nearest of the third-row patrol ships. With a final look around to make sure he hadn't been spotted, he dropped to his belly and crawled beneath it.

The Flying Turtle 505 transports Jack had flown in during his brief time with the Whinyard's Edge mercenaries had been designed to carry troops over battlefields. Those ships had thus been equipped with heavy armor plating on their undersides.

The KK-29s, in contrast, were designed to chase smugglers and marauders. Since they were expected to face their enemies during battle, their armor was concentrated instead in the nose sections.

And since weight considerations meant a fast-attack ship couldn't be invulnerable everywhere, Draycos found himself lying beneath a full collection of conduits, tubes, access ports, and vents. Protecting the whole thing was a single three-inch armor plate bolted over the maze, set off with long spacers to allow access to the equipment.

Perfect.

He didn't know what sort of fluids, hazardous or otherwise, the various conduits might be carrying. Fortunately, he didn't need to try his luck with any of them. Extending a single claw, he slipped it between a pair of tubes and pressed it against the inner hull of the ship itself. Quickly but quietly, he started cutting through it.

The metal was thicker than he'd expected, and he had to widen the cut twice before he finally felt his claw pierce the hull into the ship's crew compartment. He enlarged the hole a bit more, then rolled back onto his stomach and made his way to the front of the landing skids.

The first row of ships had already disappeared, and the second row had risen on their lifters and were preparing to follow. The guards at the rear door, he noted, had also disappeared, presumably preparing their own ships for lift.

The pilots of the three hovering ships started forward, their low-power drives kicking up a swirling cloud of dust. Taking advantage of the cover, Draycos ducked out from between the landing skids and sprinted back to the protection of his tool cabinet.

There he watched as the rest of the patrol ships flew away into the afternoon sky. The shuttle followed, and Draycos headed for the main hangar door.

He was nearly there when Jack appeared in the opening. "You all right?" the boy asked anxiously.

"I'm fine," Draycos assured him. "Is Uncle Virge monitoring their conversation?"

"Yes, he's on it," Jack said, holding out a hand. Draycos leaped toward him, catching the hand in midair and sliding up the boy's sleeve. *Everything's encrypted, but it's a simple cross-stitch and he says he can break it,* Jack added, switching back to telepathic communication now that Draycos was in contact with his skin. *What exactly did you do in there?*

You'll see in a few minutes, Draycos said. *We need to return to the ship right away.*

They reached the *Essenay* to find that Uncle Virge had started their own engine prep. "Where are they?" Jack asked as he headed for the cockpit.

"About a hundred miles up," Uncle Virge said tartly. "If we're going to catch them, we need to get going right now. In fact, we might already be too late."

Out of the corner of his eye Draycos saw Jack look down at the opening in his shirt collar. "We're okay," the boy said. "What are they talking about?"

"Nothing much," Uncle Virge said, the urgency in his tone starting to blend into the annoyance Draycos knew so well. "They're doing their final running checks and systems tweaking. If our noble poet-warrior has anything to offer in the way of— hold it."

There was a click from the board as Jack dropped into the pilot's seat. "—bit of trouble," a new voice came from the cockpit speaker. "Looks like I've got a slow air leak."

"You told me the pre-lift diagnostic came back negative," a second voice said accusingly.

"It did," the first voice retorted. "The leak's not in the air system. Must be in the cabin itself."

The second voice swore. "Blast it all, Chiggers."

"Lighten up, Sarge," Chiggers scolded. "Like I said, it's real slow. I can probably patch it with sealant and the torch from the onboard tool kit."

"*If* you can find it," Sarge warned.

"He can probably do that just with his breath," a third voice put in.

"Stow it, Driscol," Sarge snapped. "You think Colonel Frost is going to make jokes about us having to put down again?"

"Who said anything about *us* having to put down?" Chiggers asked. "There's an outpost town right on my glide path. You go ahead and I'll drop down and get this fixed. Shouldn't be more than an hour or two behind you." He snorted. "Fact is, the way Driscol flies, I might even beat you there."

"I don't like this," Sarge growled.

"Would you rather go back to Frost and tell him we left one of the 29s behind because you were afraid I might get lost?"

Sarge hissed an irritated sigh. "All right, fine. Just make it quick. Driscol, you stay with him."

"I don't need him," Chiggers put in before Driscol could respond. "Besides, he might run into my *breath* and hurt himself."

"Chiggers—"

"See you, Sarge," Chiggers said. "When I get to Point Two I'll tell Frost you're on your way."

There was a soft click as Chiggers shut off his transmission, and another as Uncle Virge closed down the speaker. "One of the ships is breaking formation," he reported. "He's heading back down."

Draycos lifted his head from Jack's shoulder for a better look at the display. The patrol ship was definitely curving back toward the surface. More important, none of the others seemed to be following. "Can you locate his landing point?" Draycos asked.

"He said there was a town on his flight path, and there are only two settlements of any real size along that vector," Uncle Virge said.

"Make for the first one," Jack told him. He looked down at Draycos again. "We *are* planning to meet him, aren't we?"

"Absolutely," Draycos confirmed, feeling a sense of relief. So far, this was working exactly the way he'd planned.

"And once we do that?" Uncle Virge prompted.

"He should have this Point Two already programmed into his ship's computer," Draycos said. "If we can retrieve that information, we can find them."

"And then what?" Uncle Virge countered. "Harper seemed to think Neverlin would put a couple of midway points into his schedule."

"And I'm sure he was right," Jack said. "Neverlin and Frost probably won't give anyone else the actual rendezvous point until the last minute."

"So I repeat: then what?"

"We'll figure out something," Jack assured him. "Let's just first make sure we get to Chiggers before he fixes Draycos's leak."

CHAPTER 9

The patrol ship was nowhere to be seen when the *Essenay* reached the settlement Uncle Virge had mentioned. "Wonderful," Uncle Virge growled. "Now what?"

"Calm yourself," Draycos said. "He must have found someplace out of sight to make his repairs."

"I only see two buildings big enough," Jack said, pointing out the canopy at the town stretching out in front of them. "Looks like both of them have doors big enough for the 29, too."

"Odd," Uncle Virge muttered. "I wonder what they want with hangars that big out here in the middle of nowhere."

"Don't know," Jack said. "Don't really care, either. Either of you have any preference as to which one we look at first?"

Jack felt some weight come onto his shoulder as Draycos lifted up his head for a better look. "He's in the farther of the two," the K'da said.

Jack frowned down at him. "How do you know?"

"There are swirl marks in the dust on the near side of that building," Draycos said. "The other has no such marks."

"Meaning something has just flown in there," Jack said, nodding agreement. Turning the control yoke a few degrees, he angled the *Essenay* toward the building Draycos had indicated.

"I don't know," Uncle Virge said doubtfully. "If it was me, I'd have come in strictly on lifters with no drive at all."

"That takes more time, and Chiggers is in a hurry," Jack reminded him. "Besides, he doesn't know anyone else even knows about this little patrol ship deal."

"It's still sloppy," Uncle Virge declared. "So what's the plan?"

Jack looked down at Draycos again. "Over to you, symby," he invited.

"The leak is near the rear of the cabin," Draycos said. "If he's found it and is in the process of sealing it, we should be able to slip in through the forward hatchway without being seen."

"And then we clobber him?"

"Basically," Draycos said. "Once we have the coordinates, it may be time for another talk with Harper."

Jack grimaced. Harper, handcuffed to the bunk in the *Essenay*'s second cabin, had so far been behaving himself. But that didn't mean Jack was ready to trust him. Far from it. "Let's first get the coordinates," he said. "Draycos, go grab me a tangler and holster from the storage room while I put us down."

He landed the *Essenay* four blocks away, shielded from view by the second of the town's two large buildings. With Draycos riding his skin, he headed out.

A few of the townspeople, all of them Compfrins, were out and about. Two or three of them gave Jack curious glances as he passed.

But no one asked him any questions or complained about his choice of parking spaces. Probably, Jack thought, they figured he was with the other human who had unexpectedly dropped in on them.

Hopefully, none of them would try to be helpful and tell Chiggers his friend had arrived.

There was a small, person-sized entrance on the wall around the corner from the building's main hangar-style doors. It was locked, but Jack had his burglar tools with him and it took him less than a minute to get it open. Holding his tangler ready, he slipped inside.

The building's walls were lined with fine-mesh panels that reached three-quarters of the way up the sides. The floor was heavy concrete, with a crosshatch of grooves that looked like wheel tracks of some kind. Several stacks of small boxes were lined up against the far wall.

The patrol ship filled most of the remaining space. It was sitting nose-in, its entry hatch open and the ramp lowered.

Aha, Draycos's thought came.

Aha what? Jack asked, looking around. There was no sign of Chiggers anywhere that he could see.

Uncle Virge wondered earlier why a distant settlement like this would have a full-sized hangar, Draycos explained. *You can see now that this is in fact a crop storage facility.*

Jack looked around. He could see no such thing. *I can?*

Of course, Draycos said. *Those mesh bins folded against the walls can be opened outward to create compartments for grain or vegetables.*

With their vertical supports on wheels rolling out along the tracks in the floor, Jack said, nodding as he finally saw it. *Well, that's one mystery solved. Good. Can we get back to the main subject at hand?*

He felt a bit of weight on his shoulder as Draycos lifted his jaws and flicked out his tongue. *He's definitely here,* the K'da said. *I can taste his scent.*

Jack took a deep breath and readjusted his grip on his tangler. *Okay,* he said. *Let's go get him.*

He crossed to the boarding ramp. As he reached the bottom, he heard a faint sound of clinking metal coming from somewhere deep inside the ship. *Not only home, but hard at work,* he commented, starting up the ramp. *You want to hop off now, or wait a little longer?*

I think I should wait until we're inside.

Jack stopped just outside the hatch. There'd been something odd in the K'da's tone just then. *What's wrong?*

I don't know, Draycos replied. *That metallic sound seems strange.*

Strange how?

I don't know. Too rhythmic, perhaps.

Jack peered into the hatchway. Directly ahead of him was the open inner airlock door, which opened into a narrow corridor leading to the cockpit at the bow and the gun bays and the rest of the ship farther aft. *So what do we do?*

We go in, the K'da said. *Just be careful.*

Grimacing, Jack stepped into the airlock. Nothing happened. He took two more steps to the inner airlock door, pausing there to look in both directions down the corridor. No one was visible. *You're sure that's Chiggers you're smelling?*

I'm positive, Draycos said. *The metallic sound seems to be coming from the left.*

Carefully, Jack took a step into the corridor and started to turn that direction—

"Move and you're dead," Chiggers said quietly from somewhere behind him.

Jack froze. *Draycos?*

He's too far back, the K'da said, his tone grim.

Just chill it, then. "I'm not moving," Jack assured the other. "Take it easy, okay?"

"Oh, I'll take it easy," Chiggers said. "I'll take it plenty easy. Drop the weapon and kick it down the corridor to your right."

Jack obeyed. "Now put your hands on top of your head," Chiggers ordered. "Fingers laced together."

"Yeah, yeah, I know the drill," Jack said, again doing as he was told. "I don't suppose we might be able to come to some agreement?"

"The only agreement I'm interested in is you dead and me rich," Chiggers said. "Where's that frunging dragon? Dragon? Show yourself—right now—or I kill him."

"I'm here," Draycos said, lifting the top of his head over the back of Jack's collar. "Don't shoot."

"I would if I had any sense," Chiggers muttered. "All right. Keep going—straight ahead—face to the wall. Back on his skin, dragon. *All* the way on. I so much as see your nose and he's dead."

Move all the way to the wall, Draycos's thought whispered into Jack's mind.

Way ahead of you, buddy, Jack assured him. He took two long steps forward to the far side of the corridor and leaned against the wall, pressing his chest firmly to the cold metal.

And with a flicker of sensation, Draycos leaned off his skin and fell over the wall.

"This ought to look really good on your service record," Jack commented, speaking loudly enough to cover any sound the K'da might make as he landed on the concrete floor below. "Neverlin and Frost have both tried to nail me and neither of them even came close."

"Yeah, and I'll bet you tried to talk *them* to death, too," Chiggers growled. The patrol ship vibrated slightly with the other's footsteps as he strode the rest of the way up the ramp and stepped through the hatchway. "What we're going to do—"

Abruptly, there was a hollow-sounding thud, followed by a sort of crumpling sound. "All right, Jack," Draycos said.

Jack turned around. Chiggers was sprawled half inside the airlock, unconscious. He was wearing a Malison Ring flight suit, though with the helmet still off. A large and unpleasant-looking gun lay on the deck near his right hand. "Nice job, symby," Jack said, stepping over and retrieving the weapon. "Too bad, though. I was looking forward to hearing how he thought he could put a K'da poet-warrior out of action without killing him."

"Perhaps keeping me alive was never part of his plan," Draycos said.

"Probably not," Jack conceded. Stuffing Chiggers's gun into his belt, he retrieved his tangler and peered aft down the corridor. "So if that noise isn't him working on the leak, what *is* it?"

"Obviously, some sort of bait," Draycos said. "Hence the unusual rhythm I noticed earlier. He must have become suspicious of my sabotage and decided to lie in wait to see if anyone came calling."

"And we walked right into it," Jack said, feeling his cheeks warming. Uncle Virgil had warned him over and over about both sloppiness *and* overconfidence. "If it hadn't been for your jump-the-wall trick, we'd have been up the creek for sure."

"We wouldn't have been there for long," Draycos said, his voice dark. "Still, without the trick I *would* probably have been forced to kill him."

"Lucky Chiggers," Jack murmured. Draycos was so civilized and pleasant most of the time that the boy sometimes forgot the sheer raw power that lay beneath those red-edged golden scales. "Let's get to the cockpit and see if all this was worth the effort."

It was.

"Here we go," Jack said, peering at the navigational display. "It's even called Point Two, in fact. It's out past Trintonias, about a two-day trip from your new home on Iota Klestis."

"If that *will,* in fact, be our new home," Draycos said.

Jack grimaced. Iota Klestis was probably still owned by the Triost Mining Group, which was itself owned by Braxton Universis. If Harper's appearance on Brum-a-dum meant that Braxton had now become a part of Neverlin's conspiracy, the K'da and Shontine would probably have to hunt up a new place to move into.

Assuming the refugees even survived that long. "We'll make it work," Jack told Draycos firmly. "Anyway, it's about a four-day trip from here. We'd better grab some supplies and get moving."

"Supplies?" Draycos asked, his tail curving in a frown.

"Didn't I tell you?" Jack asked. "We're taking the ship and heading to Point Two."

Draycos's neck arched. "We're *what?*"

"Well, we're sure not taking the *Essenay* into Neverlin's hornet's nest," Jack pointed out. "How did you think we were going to get there?"

"I assumed we would now try to make a deal with Harper and Braxton."

"I don't trust Harper," Jack said flatly. "*Or* Braxton."

"I believe Braxton to be trustworthy," Draycos said, a bit hesitantly. "From comments Alison has made, I gather she also has no reason to distrust him."

"Well, cheers for Alison," Jack said. "If it comes to *that,* I don't necessarily trust *her,* either. She and I might be on the same side at the moment, but she's not leveling with us. Not completely."

"Probably not," Draycos conceded. "On the other hand, the only people we'll find at Point Two will *definitely* not be on our side."

"Leave that to me, symby," Jack told him. Reaching to his collar, he turned on his comm clip. "Uncle Virge?"

"Right here, Jack lad," the computerized voice came back instantly. "You all right?"

"We're fine," Jack said. "You want to bring the *Essenay* over? We've got another passenger for you, and I don't feel like lugging him through the streets."

There was a short silence. "Another passenger?"

"Don't worry; I'm sure he and Harper will get along like a house on fire," Jack said. "Now, move it. We're on a schedule here."

Harper, as it turned out, was not at all pleased with his new roommate. "This is ridiculous," he fumed as Jack secured Chiggers to a thick metal cable fastened to one of the pipes on the far side of the cabin.

"I know," Jack said. "But what can I say? The *Essenay* hasn't got a proper brig."

Chiggers muttered something nasty sounding, his breath a puff of warmth against Jack's cheek as the boy double-checked the mercenary's handcuffs. The man was seething, but there wasn't a thing he could do about his situation. Not with Draycos standing watchful guard at his side.

"I've already told you I'm on your side," Harper said. "I can help you."

"And all who believe that raise their hands," Jack said, backing away from Chiggers. "Okay. You can both get to the food and water supply and the bathroom. But there's nothing either of you can use to cut your tethers or unlock your cuffs."

"You got something to keep me from killing him while he sleeps?" Chiggers demanded, glaring across at Harper. Without his fancy Malison Ring flight suit, Jack reflected, Chiggers looked and sounded more like a street punk than a big bad mercenary soldier.

Harper apparently thought so, too. "I'd be real careful about trying something like that, sonny boy," he said, his voice sending a shiver up Jack's back. "Half-asleep, I could still take you."

"I guess maybe we'll find out about that," Chiggers retorted.

"I guess maybe we won't," Jack put in. "Because Uncle Virge is going to be keeping an eye on you. Say hello to the nice men, Uncle Virge."

"I don't think you've really thought this through, Jack lad," Uncle Virge said darkly. "What if they *do* make trouble? For me *or* each other?"

"Then you crack open one of the sopor mist canisters from Alison's collection that I've hooked into the air system," Jack said. "There are three of them, wired separately, in case you feel like giving them more than one chance."

"And what happens when I've used up all the canisters?" Uncle Virge persisted.

"Then they'll *really* be sorry they made trouble," Jack said, watching both men carefully. "Because if and when you have to crack the third one, you're to fly them to Roarke's Mill on Cavendish while they're sleeping."

Harper frowned. Clearly, the name meant nothing to him.

Chiggers's reaction was far more interesting. There was a catch in his breath, and his eyes narrowed. "You wouldn't dare," he said.

"Oh yes, I would," Jack assured him.

"What's Roarke's Mill?" Harper asked.

"It's a hangout for killers and thugs," Chiggers growled.

"The Internos has tried a dozen times to clear it out, including hiring the Malison Ring and a couple of other merc groups to handle the grunt work. But the scum just keep coming back."

"It's also a hangout for less violent people, like con artists and safecrackers," Jack said. "Uncle Virgil and I visited the place a couple of times, and he still has acquaintances there. I'm sure that once Uncle Virge explains the situation they'll take good care of you until I come back."

"You send us there and we're dead," Chiggers said flatly.

"Very possibly," Jack agreed. "Reason enough for you to behave yourselves."

Harper shifted his shoulders. "Jack—"

"Have a nice time," Jack said, backing out of the room.

Draycos didn't speak again until they were loading their supplies aboard the patrol ship. "I still don't know what you're planning, Jack," he said. "But I have to agree with Uncle Virge. You may not have thought this through."

"I'm not all that crazy about it myself," Jack admitted. "But I actually *have* thought it through. Remember, I was brought up to be a con man. I know how people think."

"I appreciate your talents in that area," Draycos said. "But none of that will matter once they see you're not Chiggers."

"There are ways around that," Jack assured him. "Or at least ways to delay the magic moment. The bottom line is that Neverlin's group is on the move and this may be our only chance to hook up with them. If you've got a better idea, I'm all ears."

"You've already heard my idea: to make a deal with Harper and Braxton," Draycos said. "You've already rejected it."

"Though not without some regret," Jack said. "I'd love to

show up at the rendezvous with a wedge of Braxton Universis Security ships behind me. But I don't trust Harper *or* Braxton."

"So you've said." Draycos gave a quiet sigh. "Very well. If we're going to do this, we'd best be on our way."

Jack took a deep breath. "Yeah."

CHAPTER 10

The next four days went by quickly. Far too quickly for Draycos's taste.

Heading into battle was nothing new for him. Heading into battle without knowing everything his commander was planning also wasn't new.

But this was different. This was heading into a battle where he didn't even know the basic strategy Jack had in mind.

And never had he fought a battle with so much at risk. So terribly much at risk.

But worse than the concerns—and, yes, the fears—were the doubts that began to creep into his thoughts. The question of whether, ultimately, the risk he and Jack were taking was even worthwhile.

After all, the refugee fleet was hardly an easy target. There were fifty-eight escort warships, manned by experienced K'da and Shontine warriors who would be alert for every possible danger. Surely they could defeat Neverlin's force, no matter how many Death weapons the Valahgua had given them.

But what if they didn't? Neverlin and Frost would hardly be going forward with their plan if they didn't think they had a reasonable chance of success. What if they'd put together such a powerful force that even the refugees' escort was overwhelmed?

What if they *were,* in fact, able to destroy the fleet?

And if that was the case, what would he and Jack be able to do in the face of such a force? Could they get close enough to do anything, let alone to do enough to make a difference?

Probably not. Almost certainly they would be detected, identified, and killed long before they even got close enough to the attackers to use their new patrol ship's weapons.

But there was an alternative . . . because Draycos knew now that the K'da on those refugee ships were *not,* in fact, the last of their kind.

The Phookas of Rho Scorvi were also of K'da blood. Taneem's experience had shown they could also be K'da in heart and mind.

But they could never become true K'da without someone to teach them their people's history and heritage. Draycos could be that teacher. And wouldn't that be a better use of his life—*and* Jack's—than walking uselessly to their deaths?

It was a persuasive argument. A horribly persuasive argument, and over those four long days Draycos spent many hours struggling with it.

But in the end there was really no question as to what he had to do. Alison and Taneem were trapped aboard the *Advocatus Diaboli,* with no one but Jack and Draycos standing between them and their own deaths. Whether Draycos gained or lost—whether he lived or died—K'da warrior ethic demanded that he make every possible effort to save them.

Besides, how could he presume to teach the Phookas what it meant to be a K'da if he himself had failed this final test?

By the time the ECHO timer trilled its ten-minute warning Draycos was again at peace. Fifteen minutes from now he might very well be dead, and his host along with him. But he would die with honor, doing what he could to protect those who had put their trust in him.

He would die a poet-warrior of the K'da.

"Draycos?" Jack's voice drifted down the corridor from the cockpit. "Come on, buddy. Time to get aboard."

"Coming," Draycos called back, giving the controls in his chosen weapons blister one final check. Jack wanted them together when the ship came off ECHO, but at the first sign of trouble Draycos would hurry back here where he could man the patrol ship's weapons.

If he and Jack were going to die, Draycos intended to at least take as many of the enemy with them as possible.

He reached the cockpit as the ECHO timer was counting out its last twenty seconds. "Come on; come on," Jack said, holding his hand back over his shoulder.

Draycos set a paw on Jack's palm and slid up the arm of the Malison Ring flight suit the boy had taken from Chiggers. *Do you have an attack plan?* he thought as he settled into his usual position.

No, but I have a non-*attack plan,* Jack thought back. *Watch and learn, symby.*

The countdown reached zero. Jack pushed the ECHO lever forward, and the shimmering blue hyperspace sky faded back to star-sprinkled black.

There, stretched out in front of them, was Neverlin's attack force.

Draycos lifted his head from Jack's shoulder, studying the ships scattered across his field of vision. There was the *Advocatus Diaboli,* of course, the luxurious Braxton Universis corporate yacht that Neverlin had run off with. There were the Malison Ring Djinn-90 pursuit fighters, at least twenty of them, formed up in a defensive circle at the fleet's outer edge.

A large troop carrier was off to one side, probably the ship Neverlin had used to bring those three hundred Brummgas here from Brum-a-dum. Near it was a fueler ship, and Draycos could see the other eleven KK-29 patrol ships from Bentre clustered around it like hatchlings gathered alongside their mother at lunchtime.

And there was one more ship present, floating a few hundred feet from the *Advocatus Diaboli*. A large and agonizingly familiar ship.

It was the *Gatekeeper.* One of the four ships of Draycos's advance team.

Jack apparently spotted it at the same time Draycos did. *Geez,* the boy's startled thought echoed through Draycos's mind. *Is that one of your advance team ships?*

It is indeed, Draycos thought back grimly. Suddenly, Neverlin's strategy was as clear as the cold vacuum of space.

Hey, hey, slow down, buddy, Jack protested into Draycos's sudden flurry of thoughts and speculations. *Did you say something about a trap?*

Sorry, Draycos apologized, forcing his mind to slow down. Their telepathic link only worked if he and Jack were thinking directly at each other. Other thoughts could be sensed, but only as a wordless and rather distracting buzz. *Yes, it's a trap. But not for us. Do you see all the hull damage, especially in the forward part?*

Yes, Jack thought back, sounding puzzled. *I didn't realize Neverlin's team had hit you that hard.*

They didn't, Draycos replied. *That damage has been added since the Iota Klestis attack.*

He sensed Jack's sudden flash of understanding. *Got it,* the boy said. *They're going to pretend they're being attacked by the rest of the ships and go running to the refugee fleet for protection.*

Exactly, Draycos confirmed. *Many of the Valahgua can speak our language well enough to be mistaken for Shontine. They'll call for help, and the screening warships will almost certainly let them past the defense ring.*

There's no password?

There are several, Draycos told him. *But the Valahgua can feign transmission trouble, or claim that all senior members of the advance team were killed or incapacitated.*

And come to think of it, why shouldn't *the warriors believe them?* Jack agreed grimly. *As far as they know, there isn't a Valahgua for thousands of light-years.*

There was a ping from the control board. "Hey, Chiggers," Driscol's voice came from the speaker. "So you didn't get lost, huh? Too bad. Guess I lose the pool."

Jack took a deep breath. "Showtime," he muttered, and flipped the transmission switch. "Yeah, and my heart bleeds for you," he replied sarcastically.

Only somehow, it was no longer Jack.

Draycos twisted his head around to look up at the boy's face, a wave of disbelief running through him. Jack's face had subtly changed, his eyes gone dark and smoldering with resentment, a cynical twist to his mouth.

And his voice was Chiggers's voice, matching the mercenary's tone, phrasing, and attitude. It was as if Jack had flipped a switch and somehow become the mercenary.

"That's not the only thing that'll be bleeding if you don't get your tail over here and fuel up," Driscol warned. "Colonel wants us taking a turn at sentry duty."

"Colonel's going to have to wait," Jack growled. "I need to dock and get some repair sealant."

"You still leaking air?"

"No, now I'm leaking calozyne," Jack told him.

"Calozyne?" Driscol echoed, a sudden catch in his voice.

"Yeah, calozyne," Jack said impatiently. "You want me to spell it for you?"

"You sure it's not just your breath?"

"Smells more like your butt," Jack countered.

There was another click from the speaker. "Chiggers, this is Borkrin," Sarge's voice came on the line. "What's this about a calozyne leak?"

"It's a calozyne leak," Jack said. "What do you want me to say about it?"

"How about starting with how bad it is?" Sarge growled. "You need us to set you up an isolation bay?"

"Oh, frunge, no," Jack scoffed. "It's not going to kill anyone. But it's eating the lining off my nose, and I used all my sealant on the air leak. Can you set me a port with the *Advocatus Diaboli*?"

"Oh yeah, right," Sarge said with a snort. "Like the colonel and Mr. Neverlin want to smell it. Get yourself over to the *Foxwolf*. I'll have Reinking set you up a docking port there."

"Copy," Jack said, and tapped his transmission key, cutting off the radio. He took another deep breath; and as he did so, the resentful expression smoothed away. "I think we're in," he said. His voice, too, was back to normal.

It took Draycos another second to find his own voice. "Impressive," he said. "I had no idea you could do something like that."

"You like it?" Jack asked, getting a grip on the control yoke and turning them a few degrees to the left. "A little trick Uncle Virgil taught me."

"More than just a single trick," Draycos said. "It was as if you'd actually become the man."

"That's the best way to imitate someone," Jack said. "Body, mind, attitude, voice. Everything." He shrugged. "*If* you can do it. Most people can't. At least, not very well."

"Obviously, you're one of the few who can," Draycos said. "And all that after having heard only a few sentences from the man."

"Yet another useless talent for a reformed con man and thief." Jack shook his head sharply. *Okay, I think my brain's ready to go with the telepathy thing again,* the thought whispered across Draycos's mind. *Next job is to actually make it aboard the ship.*

Draycos turned his head to look out the canopy through Jack's collar. While they'd been talking, Jack had shifted their course toward the *Gatekeeper*. *Isn't the next trick to figure out which ship is the* Foxwolf? Draycos asked. *Going to the wrong one would be a dead giveaway that you aren't Chiggers.*

Not a problem, Jack said. *If you scratch the* Advocatus Diaboli, *the only ships big enough to dock this thing are your* Gatekeeper, *the fueler, and the troop carrier. Troop carriers and fuelers, if you'll recall from all that reading we had to do when I was in the Whinyard's Edge, are usually numbered, not named.*

Neverlin might have made an exception.

He didn't, Jack assured him. *Now that we know Frost's plan,* Foxwolf *is a perfect name for the* Gatekeeper. *It'll start out looking like it's running for its life, like the fox in a foxhunt. Once it's past the main defenses, it'll suddenly turn into a wolf and start ravaging its way through the fleet.*

Draycos felt his tail twitch. With his mind occupied with Jack's performance, he hadn't yet spotted the most important implication of the *Gatekeeper*'s presence here. *Which also means that's where the Valahgua will have mounted their Death weapons.*

Or at least most of them, Jack agreed. *I'm guessing Neverlin has at least one aboard the* Advocatus Diaboli, *just to make sure his own skin is safe.*

And if they could get aboard the *Gatekeeper* and disable those weapons . . . *Tell me about this calozyne you mentioned,* Draycos said. *What exactly is it? And there* isn't *any actual leak, is there?*

Believe me, buddy, if there was you'd know it, Jack said dryly. *It's a heat-exchange fluid for the laser chargers, and it stinks to high heaven.*

Odd, Draycos said. *Our heat-exchange fluids are odorless.*

Actually, calozyne smells the way it does on purpose, Jack said. *It's a safety feature, so that you know right away if you've got a leak. Firing lasers without being able to dump the heat is generally considered a very bad idea.*

Agreed, Draycos said. *But won't those aboard the* Gatekeeper *then know immediately that we have no leak?*

The minute they get close enough to get a good whiff, Jack confirmed. *That's why we'll have to hit first and fast and then go to ground. I hope you know somewhere aboard where we can do that.*

There are several such hiding places, Draycos assured him, gazing out at the *Gatekeeper* and forcing his brain to work. So far Jack had been carrying the burden of planning here. It was about time Draycos picked up his share of the load. *If we haven't got a leak, can we make one?*

Sure, but what's the point? Jack asked. *The minute the mercenaries in there see me, the game will be up.*

Unless those who meet us are Brummgas, Draycos said. *I doubt they'll be nearly so good at distinguishing one of Frost's mercenaries from another.*

Out of the corner of his eye he saw Jack frown down at him. *Probably not,* the boy agreed cautiously. *But we don't even know if there* are *any Brummgas aboard. Let alone that Frost will let them play reception committee.*

Actually, aside from the Valahgua manning the Death weapons, I expect nearly all aboard will be Brummgas, Draycos told him. *Very likely all those we watched being brought from the Chookoock estate, in fact.*

Okay, buddy, you've now officially lost me, Jack said. *I thought we'd just decided the* Gatekeeper *was their primary attack ship. Neverlin's certainly not going to leave that part of the scheme in Brummgan hands.*

They aren't here to handle the attack, Draycos said. *They're here to create the proper illusion. As I said earlier, the Valahgua can imitate Shontine voices well enough to fool the fleet's warriors. What they can't imitate is the heat signature of five hundred K'da and Shontine crew members aboard ship.*

He caught Jack's flicker of understanding. *So Frost has loaded the ship with warm Brummgan bodies?*

Exactly, Draycos said. *The refugee fleet's sensors can't read individual heat emissions through the hull but only the sum total. Three hundred Brummgas should be just about right.*

And the spectrum from a living being probably looks different from ordinary heaters or anything else Neverlin might have used, Jack said.

Exactly, Draycos said. *I'm sure Neverlin would have preferred to use humans, but I'm guessing neither he nor Frost had access to the necessary numbers.*

Hence the whole deal with the Patri Chookoock, Jack said slowly. *So if we can avoid the handful of Malison Ring mercenaries Frost has watching over the Valahgua and Brummgas, we may be able to push our own game a little longer.*

As long as we can, Draycos said. *The more quiet time we have to seek out and sabotage the Death weapons, the better.*

Ahead, the marker lights came on beside one of the *Gatekeeper*'s hatches. *There—that's our target hatch,* he told Jack, flicking out his tongue toward the lights.

I see it, Jack said. *Hop off, will you? I've got a job for you.*

What job? Draycos asked as he leaped out of Jack's collar to land on the deck behind him.

"Go to the nearest weapons blister and get under the control board," Jack said. "Right up against the inside wall there should be one or more blue-striped tubes labeled *coolant.*"

"Understood," Draycos said. Turning, he headed aft.

"And hold your nose," Jack's voice wafted down the corridor after him. "I wasn't kidding about the smell."

Five minutes later, with the stench of calozyne curling his nostrils, Jack brought the patrol ship to a smooth docking alongside the *Gatekeeper.*

Draycos was waiting for him at the hatch. "You were right about the smell," the K'da said as he laid his paw on Jack's hand and slithered up onto his skin. *What's our plan?*

We stay with the Chiggers story as long as possible, Jack told him. He started to take a deep breath, instantly changed his mind. He straightened the collar of his flight suit, checked that his tangler was riding loose in Chiggers's holster, and touched the hatch release.

The hatch slid open. Beyond the docking collar was a medium-sized bay with the same light tan walls and deck Jack had seen in the wreckage of the *Havenseeker,* back on that fateful day when he and Draycos had first met. Squaring his shoulders, trying to act as if he owned the place, he stepped through the hatchway into enemy territory.

But for the moment, anyway, the enemy seemed to be unaware they'd been invaded. The only other occupants of the bay were a pair of Brummgas working at an open access panel, and their only reaction was a curling of their own nostrils against the smell leaking out into their world.

Like I own the place, Jack reminded himself. "Hey—you," he called toward them. "Get me a sealant tube, will you?"

One of the Brummgas half-turned, his cheeks wrinkling in disgust. "Get it yourself," he said, pointing a thick finger at a tool chest along the wall. Turning his back on the insolent human, he returned to his work.

Smiling to himself, Jack headed for the toolbox. *Do we need to take the time to fix the leak?* Draycos asked.

Unfortunately, yes, Jack said. *The idea is that Chiggers came aboard, did his repairs, and then made himself scarce before anyone could find him and give him some other job to do. Vanishing without fixing the leak would look suspicious.*

Understood, Draycos replied. The K'da's tongue flicked briefly through the air beneath Jack's chin. *But be careful. I can taste a hint of human scent beneath the smell of the Brummgas.*

Plus a few Valahgua?

He sensed a darkening of Draycos's mood. *Yes.*

No problem, Jack said, trying to hide his sudden twinge of fear. A people who had defeated K'da warriors weren't a group he really wanted to run into. Even if their Death weapon *was* sort of cheating. *We'll just have to be a little extra careful, that's all.*

The toolbox contained two different tubes of sealant. Jack wasn't sure which would work better for a calozyne pipe, but for the length of time the repair needed to hold it probably didn't matter. Selecting the more expensive-looking tube, he headed back to the patrol ship.

The hole Draycos had sliced in the pipe was small and easy to get to. Jack squeezed a generous portion of sealant across it and watched a minute to make sure it was solidifying properly. Then, capping the tube, he went back into the docking bay and returned it to the toolbox. *Which way?* he asked Draycos as he straightened up again.

Take the door to your left, Draycos told him. *The Death weapons will most likely be mounted in the bow. Probably in the weapons bays, where they'll have an ample source of power.*

Sounds reasonable. Just point the way.

He was halfway across the bay when a figure stepped through the door ahead of him. It was a human figure, dressed in a Malison Ring uniform, peering down at a notepad in his hand.

Only it wasn't just one of Frost's men, a man who would know Chiggers at a glance. It was far worse . . . and it was the last person Jack had expected to see here.

It was StarForce Wing Sergeant Jonathan Langston. The man who'd helped him escape from Semaline.

A man Jack had thought was dead.

CHAPTER 11

In that single frozen heartbeat, Jack felt his mental camouflage being stripped away like the wrapper off a ration bar. Not only would Langston know Chiggers by sight; he was possibly one of the few aboard who would also instantly recognize Jack himself.

And with that, the quiet game Draycos had hoped for had come to an abrupt end. The minute Langston spotted Jack and squawked his name, the two Brummgas poking at their access panel would be on to him.

Jack and Draycos had to take all three of them out before that happened.

Jack dropped his hand casually to his holstered tangler. *I may not be able to get them all before someone yells,* he warned Draycos. *As soon as I start shooting, you'd better head forward by yourself to deal with the Death weapons.*

What about you?

I'll be all right, Jack told him, knowing full well it was a lie. A single squawk out of any of the three would draw the whole ship down on him. If they didn't kill him outright, they would haul him back to the *Advocatus Diaboli* and give him to Neverlin, which would pretty much amount to the same thing.

But that didn't matter. All that mattered was that he give

Draycos as much time as possible to find and destroy the Death weapons. *On three,* he said. *One, two—*

Wait, Draycos cut him off, an odd tone to the texture of his thoughts.

Jack flicked his eyes around the room, wondering what had caught the K'da's attention. There was nothing Jack could see that could possibly help them. He looked back at Langston, bracing himself.

Only Langston wasn't staring at him, his eyes wide, his mouth open, a shout of warning boiling out of his throat.

In fact, he wasn't looking at Jack at all. He was still gazing intently down at his notepad.

And he wasn't walking straight toward Jack anymore, either. Instead, he was angling across the bay toward the patrol ship. "Hey, Chiggers," he called casually, still not looking up. "Good trip?"

Answer him, Draycos prompted.

It took Jack another half second to put his Chiggers face and voice back in place. "I lived through it," he growled. "What's been happening here?"

"Not a thing," Langston said. He raised his eyes from his notepad, but now they were focused on the hatchway leading into Jack's patrol ship. "Looking forward to the big battle, though."

"*I'm* looking forward to the loot at the end of it," Jack countered.

"That'll be nice, too," Langston agreed. "See you later."

With that, he stepped through the hatchway and disappeared into the ship. *Move,* Draycos urged.

Abruptly, Jack realized he was standing still, staring at the hatchway where Langston had disappeared. *Now, that was just plain unreal,* he told Draycos as he got his feet moving again.

Not unreal, Draycos said grimly. *Deliberate.*

What are you talking about? Jack asked. *You saw the uniform. He's gone over to Neverlin's side.*

He most certainly has not, Draycos said, his tone leaving no room for argument. *There's no possible way he could have failed to see and recognize you. He deliberately gave you a pass. Gave us a pass.*

Jack grimaced. The K'da was right. He had to be.

Which meant that, somehow, Langston had talked his way into Frost's crew in order to help save the incoming refugees.

It also meant he was going to be in serious trouble when the balloon went up. Very serious trouble indeed.

I know that, Draycos said, answering Jack's unvoiced thought. *So does he.*

A shiver ran up Jack's back as he stepped through the door into a long corridor. Once before, he'd thought Langston had gone to his death to protect Jack and Draycos. Now Jack knew the man had lived through that particular ordeal.

Only to now be facing death for a second time. And again for Jack and Draycos.

He is a true warrior, Draycos said. *He has made his decision, and his sacrifice. It's up to us to make sure that sacrifice is not in vain.*

You got it, buddy, Jack said grimly. It was, he decided, about time he showed some of that determination and ruthlessness Uncle Virgil had hammered into him over their long years together. *Let's go find us some Death weapons.*

For the first few days of their time together in the lifepod, Alison and Taneem had done little but talk.

Most of the talking at the beginning was on Alison's side as she turned their forced idleness into an impromptu school. She taught Taneem everything she knew about the *Advocatus Diaboli,* about Neverlin and Frost and the Malison Ring, and more about Brummgas than anyone in the Orion Arm probably wanted to know. The lifepod they were in had some limited flight capability, and she spent one entire afternoon drilling Taneem on the theory and practice of space flight.

After that had come lectures on skulking, information gathering, and combat. Most of what Alison knew about the latter didn't directly apply to K'da, but she'd seen Draycos in action enough times to have some idea how he would deal with various combat situations.

Taneem didn't especially like that set of lessons. She didn't say anything, but Alison could tell. Taneem didn't like fighting, and the thought of possibly having to kill again made her sick.

But she also knew what was at stake. Whatever it took to save the K'da and Shontine refugees, she would do it.

Around the sixth day the lessons had mostly ended. Alison couldn't think of anything else to teach, and both of them were getting pretty tired of the seminars anyway.

After that, their conversations shifted to more personal matters. Alison told Taneem about her life growing up, while Taneem gave what little she could remember about her life as a Phooka.

By the ninth day, they'd run out of even minor things to talk about. Fortunately, the lifepod's equipment included a deck of cards, and Alison spent several relaxing hours teaching Taneem some of the games she and her parents and grandparents had enjoyed when she was a girl.

It was on the tenth day, and she was trying to come up with a way to modify the cards for some of the more specialized games she knew, when she heard the faint warbling of the ship's emergency alarm.

"What's that?" Taneem asked, bounding to her feet.

"Emergency alarm," Alison said grimly, stepping to the door and pressing her ear against the cold metal. She could hear the alarm itself more clearly, but there was no sign of the automated instructions that usually accompanied such an alert. "I don't hear any abandon-ship announcements," she told Taneem, digging out her receiver and turning it on. "Maybe Neverlin's got something to say on the subject."

She stuck the receiver into her ear as Taneem slithered up her sleeve onto her skin. "—want to get up here right away," Frost's voice came, soft and distant. Probably coming from the intercom on Neverlin's desk. "The *Essenay* has just come off ECHO outside our sentry ring."

"*Morgan?*" Neverlin demanded. "How in blazes did he find us?"

"I don't know," Frost said grimly. "And it's not *Jack* Morgan. It's Virgil."

Alison frowned down at Taneem's head lying across her shoulder. Jack had told them that his uncle Virgil was dead.

"Really," Neverlin said. "After all these months of looking for him, he finally surfaces. *And* at the most awkward time and place possible. Interesting. What does he want?"

"He wants to talk to you," Frost said. "Shall I blow him out of the sky and be done with it?"

"By no means," Neverlin said, and Alison heard the soft creak of a chair. "Certainly not until we know how he found us. I'll be right there." There was the sound of a door opening and closing, and then silence.

"Blast," Alison muttered, pulling the receiver out of her ear.

With the conversation shifting to the *Advocatus Diaboli*'s bridge, she and Taneem were now out of it.

"It can't really be Virgil Morgan, can it?" Taneem asked hesitantly.

"Not unless Jack lied to us," Alison said, gazing at the door. "Which I'm sure he'd do in a heartbeat if he thought it was necessary."

Taneem lifted her head from Alison's shoulder. "We need to listen in on that conversation."

"I dearly wish we could," Alison said. "Problem is, if we leave the lifepod now we're not getting back in without everyone knowing about it. Remember the seal on the door?"

"What if I simply go over the door?" Taneem suggested. "Or what if I went into an air duct? I think I remember seeing one running along the upper part of the corridor."

Alison looked at the top of the door. The K'da was right, come to think of it. There was a large duct running along both sides of the ship, designed to flood the lifepod boarding areas with air in a hull-breach emergency. "Problem with *that* is that once you're out there's no way to get in again," she pointed out.

"We have time to think of something," Taneem said firmly. "Right now, we need to find out who this man is and what he wants."

Alison chewed at her lip. It was risky, and they both knew it. Still, even if worst came to worst, it should merely mean moving her private timetable up by a few days. "All right," she said. "If you're game, let's try it."

"I am," Taneem said. "You'll need to get higher up against the wall."

"First things first." Alison pulled out the comm clip that Taneem had been wearing during their hangar raid on Brum-a-dum and clipped it to the K'da's ear. "Just so I don't feel left out," she said. "No, wait a minute," she went on, frowning. "That won't work, will it? You have to go two-dimensional to get over the wall."

"Why not try putting it in my mouth?" Taneem suggested.

"Oka-a-y," Alison said slowly, pulling the comm clip off Taneem's ear. The K'da opened her jaws, and Alison set the device inside between the rows of sharp teeth. "Be careful you don't swallow it."

Taneem nodded and flattened herself again across Alison's skin.

The comm clip didn't reappear. Apparently, it was indeed going along for the ride.

Something even Jack probably doesn't know, she thought as she pulled over one of the lifepod's chairs. Climbing up on it, she pressed her back against the wall above the door, twisting at the waist to give as much connection as she could to the area of the air duct.

She felt a flicker of sensation, and Taneem was gone.

Alison hopped off the chair, praying silently as she turned on her own comm clip. Even Draycos had never tried falling off into such an enclosed space before. If Taneem had miscalculated even a little . . .

"I'm in," Taneem's voice came softly from the comm clip. "Heading forward."

Alison exhaled silently. "Be careful," she murmured.

"Don't worry," Taneem said. "I will."

It was the third time Taneem had been inside the *Advocatus Diaboli*'s ventilation system. The first time, she remembered, she'd been nervous and confused and more than a little frightened. The second time, just a few days ago, she'd been only a little nervous, but very quiet and cautious.

This time, she found the ductwork felt almost like a second home.

Which wasn't to say she could abandon caution. Far from it. The ship had suddenly come alive, with crew members and Malison Ring mercenaries moving quickly through the corridors or settling themselves into various rooms. Whoever this person was who was pretending to be Jack's uncle Virgil, he'd stirred up a stingbug's nest.

By now the alarm had been silenced. Fortunately, there was enough commotion and conversation around her that she didn't have to worry too much about being heard. Still, she made sure to peek through each grille before she passed.

The bridge on a seagoing vessel, she remembered from the *Essenay*'s encyclopedia, was typically on the upper part of the deck. The *Advocatus Diaboli*'s bridge, in contrast, was buried away in almost the very center of the ship. It was on the middle deck, a little ways forward of the computer and ECHO room.

She reached the room to find that Neverlin had already arrived. "So far, he hasn't tried anything fancy," Frost was telling the other as Taneem eased her way to the edge of the nearest grille. From her position she could just see Neverlin and Frost, standing behind a pair of men in white uniforms seated at a control board. "He definitely hasn't activated any of his weapons."

"And you're sure it's really Virgil Morgan?" Neverlin asked.

Frost snorted. "I'm not sure about anything," he said. "It could be the Tooth Fairy for all I know. But he *is* alone out there."

"Are we sure about *that*?" Neverlin countered. "We don't

know what K'da look like on an IR scan when they're plastered across a human body."

"*We* know," a whispery voice replied. A very alien voice, of a type Taneem had never heard before. "I have studied the readings. The human is alone."

Neverlin turned around. "I see," he said, his voice subtly changed.

Carefully, Taneem moved forward a few more inches, trying to see the being who had spoken.

There, standing behind Neverlin and Frost, was a Valahgua.

There was no doubt in Taneem's mind that that was what this creature was. His head was wide and flat and bony, like a sphere that had been squashed down from above into a flattened disk. Dark eyes peered from beneath a brow ridge, and short tentacles writhed at both corners of his wide mouth. His body was wide and long but oddly slender from front to back.

The upper arm she could see was thick, splitting at the elbow into a much thinner forearm plus a muscular tentacle about the same length as the forearm. The hand at the end of the forearm was clenched into a fist, preventing her from seeing how many fingers he had. His legs were short and considerably thicker than even his upper arms.

The overall effect was as if someone had taken a legless crab and attached it to a wide door, then added limbs salvaged from an elephant, a human, and an octopus. It was a strange and rather ridiculous combination, and under other circumstances Taneem might have been tempted to laugh at it.

But these were the people who had made war against the K'da and Shontine. The people who, not content with driving them from their homes, were plotting with Neverlin and Frost to utterly destroy them.

There was no reason to laugh. No reason whatsoever.

"Fine; so he's alone," Frost said impatiently. Apparently, he wasn't as impressed or intimidated by the Valahgua as Neverlin was. "Can we get on with this before the entire StarForce comes roaring down on us?"

"Calm yourself, Colonel," Neverlin said. He gestured to one of the men at the control board. "Go ahead, Captain."

The other man nodded and tapped a switch. "This is Arthur Neverlin," Neverlin called. "Who is this?"

"Hello, Mr. Neverlin," a voice came over the bridge speaker. "This is Virgil Morgan. I understand you need me."

Taneem felt her crest stiffen. It was Uncle Virge's voice, all right. Which meant that the person they'd detected aboard had to be Jack.

But what in the whole rainbow did he think he was doing, marching up to Neverlin's front door this way? And if the Valahgua was right about Draycos not being in there with him, where was he?

The last time she and Alison had heard from Uncle Virge, Jack had been in jail on Brum-a-dum. Had something happened during their prison break?

Was Draycos dead?

The thought sent an icy flood of fear and horror through her. If Draycos was gone—if it was just her and Alison and Jack now—

She took a careful breath. *Panic freezes the will,* Draycos's words whispered through her mind.

She would not panic. Whatever happened, whatever *had* happened, she would not panic. Draycos would want it that way.

"Your information is a bit out-of-date, Mr. Morgan," Neverlin said. "Your safecracking skills are no longer required."

"I didn't say you needed my safecracking skills," Uncle Virge said. "I said you needed *me*. Tell me, how secure is this transmission?"

Neverlin glanced at Frost. "Secure enough. Why?"

"Obviously, because what I have to say is highly private," Uncle Virge said. "Let me lay it out for you. You've come into possession of one or more safes previously owned by a pair of symbiotic species. For convenience, let's call them, oh, the K'da and Shontine. Inside that safe or safes are supposed to be coordinates showing where a fleet of these beings will be coming into the Orion Arm. You with me so far?"

"Very much so," Neverlin assured him, his voice gone cool. "And not *supposed to be*. The coordinates *are* inside."

"What's inside are a set of numbers," Uncle Virge corrected. "No one said they were the actual coordinates."

The Valahgua made a strange gurgling sound. The tentacles around his mouth were writhing like startled stumpgrubs suddenly brought into the sunlight. "In fact, our friends here *do* say that," Neverlin countered. "Are you suggesting they're wrong?"

"I'm *saying*, not suggesting, that the K'da and Shontine were smarter than you realized," Uncle Virge said. "Turns out there's a modifier that has to be factored into the coordinates you found."

"An interesting story," Neverlin said. "Where exactly did it come from?"

"A little bird told me," Uncle Virge said. "A gold-plated, sharp-toothed bird named Draycos."

"And you came all this way just to give us this information?"

"I came all this way to *sell* you the information," Uncle Virge corrected. "More precisely, I came to sell you the location of the modifier data."

"Which is where?"

"Don't worry, it's close at hand," Uncle Virge said. "It's hidden in that impressive-looking ship you've got lying off your port-side bow."

"Of course it is," Neverlin said. "And you'd like us to all go aboard so you can show us?"

"*You* don't have to go if you don't want to," Uncle Virge said. "Give me an escort and I'll find it myself."

"Very generous of you," Neverlin said. "Tell me something, Mr. Morgan. After six months of dodging us, why are you suddenly being so cooperative?"

"Because I've come to the conclusion that you're going to win," Uncle Virge said. "I like being on the winning side."

"It pays better?"

"Absolutely," Uncle Virge agreed. "On the other hand, you're only going to win if you actually locate the fleet."

"Of course," Neverlin said. "Would you care to tell us how you found us?"

"*And* where exactly your nephew and his K'da friend are?" Frost put in.

"Who's that, Colonel Frost?" Uncle Virge asked. "Hello, Colonel. Don't worry about Jack and Draycos. I've sent them off on a wild-goose chase that should keep them out of the way until it's all over. As for telling you how I knew about Point Two, I'd be happy to. But only face-to-face."

"You can speak freely," Neverlin assured him. "I trust my associates completely."

"That's nice," Uncle Virge said. "Unfortunately, *I* don't. So do I get an audience with the new soon-to-be Master of the Universe? Or do I turn around and fly home?"

"Leaving us to wait for the refugees at the wrong spot?"

"Something like that."

Neverlin's lip twisted. "One moment."

He gestured, and the uniformed man touched the comm switch. "Colonel?" Neverlin invited.

"It's a trick," Frost said flatly. "He's up to something."

"I agree," Neverlin said. "The question is, what?"

"He wishes access to the K'da/Shontine vessel," the Valahgua said in his whispery voice. "That is obviously the motive behind this so-called modifier he claims knowledge of. You will *not* permit that to happen."

"Don't worry, Lordhighest; he's not getting anywhere near it," Neverlin assured him. "But I will admit to being intrigued. Colonel, instruct the fleet to prepare for immediate departure. We'll leave as soon as Mr. Morgan is aboard."

"We're taking him with us?" Frost asked, frowning.

"Him and the *Essenay* both," Neverlin said. "You have a problem with that?"

"Transporting a suspicious ship to Point Three?" Frost retorted. "*Yes,* I have a problem with it."

"Would you rather we negotiate with him here at Point Two?" Neverlin countered. "Giving anyone he may have talked to time to catch up with him?"

"I'd rather blow him out of the sky and be done with it," Frost said.

"That would be the wisest move," the Valahgua said.

"Perhaps," Neverlin said. "But as I say, I'm intrigued. Captain, signal all ships to prepare evasive patterns to Point Three. Each commander is to lay out his own course, with arrival six days from now."

The Valahgua alien rumbled somewhere inside his wide head. "I protest this plan most strongly," he declared. "We now take six days to reach Point Three? You had said it would take only four."

"It would," Neverlin confirmed. "But I think a couple of extra days of being undetectable by anyone else in the universe wouldn't be a bad thing right now."

"It could be a very foolish thing," the Valahgua retorted. "The K'da and Shontine could reach the rendezvous in as few as nine days."

"Which will still give us plenty of time," Neverlin assured him. "It's only a couple of hours from Point Three to the rendezvous."

"Is it truly?" the Valahgua asked. "What if this human has heard truly from the K'da?"

"He has a point," Frost said. "Once we're on ECHO we'll be out of communication with the rest of the fleet. If Morgan isn't lying, and if the rendezvous point actually turns out to be more than three days away from Point Three, we won't make it in time."

"Then they'll just have to wait for us, won't they?" Neverlin said tartly. "But they won't, because Morgan is blowing smoke. I'm sure of it."

"Then destroy him as the officer suggested," the Valahgua said.

"Not until I find out what flavor smoke he's blowing," Neverlin said. "Colonel—"

"You risk this mission for mere curiosity?" the Valahgua interrupted.

"I risk nothing, and this is far more than mere curiosity," Neverlin said coldly. "This man knew where Point Two was. I need to find out what else he knows. Before he dies. Colonel, have two of your Djinn-90s escort the *Essenay* here. While they do that, contact the team on Driftline and tell them to skip Point Two and head directly to Point Three once they've collected the Rhino-10s."

"Yes, sir," Frost said. "What about the *Foxwolf*?"

"What about it?"

"We still have only the single shift of my men aboard," Frost reminded him. "Do you want to swap the other two shifts back in?"

"What's your recommendation?" Neverlin asked.

For a few seconds Frost stared at the displays. "I'd say no," he said. "If Morgan has some trick planned, I don't want to be in the middle of a personnel change when he springs it."

"Agreed," Neverlin said. "Besides, I'd rather have your men instead of the Brummgas on hand here to watch him. Get the *Essenay* docked and then bring Morgan to my office." He raised his eyebrows. "Make sure you check him *very* carefully."

"Don't worry," Frost said softly. "We will."

Inclining his head to the Valahgua, Neverlin headed for the bridge door. Carefully, Taneem eased her way backward down the duct. "Did you hear all that?" she whispered when she was far enough away from the grille.

"Yes," Alison whispered back. "Can you find your way to Neverlin's office?"

"I think so," Taneem said. She reached a cross-duct and backed around the corner into it. "But can't you listen through the needle?"

"Yes, but it probably won't be loud enough for you to hear via comm clip," Alison said. "Besides, I'm curious to find out what this fake Virgil Morgan looks like."

"I understand," Taneem said, turning back into the main duct. "I'm on my way."

CHAPTER 12

The *Foxwolf*, as expected, was loaded to the gills with Brummgas.

They were everywhere. Some were lounging at consoles in various rooms, their wide bulks squeezed into chairs a couple of sizes too small for them. Others were running power cables along the corridor ceilings, apparently setting up special equipment. Others were simply milling around, or watching everyone else work.

Sure not working very hard, are they? Jack commented as he passed yet another group of idling aliens.

There's probably no need, Draycos said. *In an emergency, the ship could be handled by a mere thirty crew members. Even in full combat mode, it would require only another hundred and fifty.*

So why were there so many in your advance team?

Partly for companionship on the long journey, Draycos said. *Also, part of our job was to begin preparing areas of Iota Klestis for colonization.*

Which means Neverlin probably could have *gotten away with fewer people aboard,* Jack pointed out. *Brummgas or men. All the Valahgua would have to say was that everyone else was back on Iota Klestis, digging wells or whatever.*

A good point, Draycos agreed. *I wonder if the fleet will wonder about that, as well.*

Anything that looks odd to them works in our favor, Jack said. *But whether they wonder about it or not, it definitely works in our favor right now. The more big, dumb Brummgas there are wandering the halls, the harder it'll be for any of Frost's men to spot me in the crowd. A little luck and we may just get away with this.*

They had reached the center of the ship, and were passing a long room that Draycos said contained the K'da/Shontine version of the ECHO hyperdrive, when their luck ran out.

"Hey!" a human voice boomed just as Jack cleared the door-way. "You—is that Chiggers? Get in here."

"I'm busy," Jack called back in his Chiggers voice.

"You're gonna be busy mopping the deck with your face," the other retorted. "Come on; help me configure this frunging thing. We're heading out."

Jack felt his stomach tighten. They were going on ECHO *now?* Before Frost's raiding party even returned with their stolen Malison Ring ships? *Something's wrong,* he told Draycos.

I agree, the K'da replied. *But we have no choice but to play it through. Open your flight suit a bit more.*

"Yeah, yeah, I'm coming," Jack called, reversing direction and heading back to the room. As he did so, he slid a finger under the sealing seam at his flight suit's neck and slid it open to just above his stomach.

The mercenary was sitting at a console halfway across the room, his right side toward the door. He was scowling down at the displays as he worked at his control board. "What's the problem?" Jack asked, glancing around as he walked toward the other. There were four Brummgas in the room, too, making little snuffling noises of concentration as they worked at their own controls.

"Whole frunging alien frunging thing is the problem," the

man growled back. "We were supposed to have had a real ECHO system put in before we had to go anywhere else."

"Yeah," Jack said, forcing himself to maintain a steady stride. So far the other man hadn't actually focused on him, but the second he did it would all be over. Jack had to be within striking distance when that happened. "What do you want me to do?"

"Help me sort out this chicken scratching," the man said, flicking a finger toward a set of papers taped to the front of the console.

Almost there. "Sure," Jack said, picking up his pace a little. Almost there.

He was two steps away when the man finally looked up.

Keep going, Draycos urged.

For that first fraction of a second the man's expression went blank, his brain apparently slip-skidding like an amusement park bump car. Then, abruptly, his wheels seemed to catch traction again. His eyes widened; and as Jack closed the final step, he opened his mouth.

The warning shout never came. Through the opening in Jack's flight suit, looking for all the world like some shock-movie alien larva emerging from its reluctant host, Draycos's foreleg lanced out . . .

. . . the paw catching the man solidly around his throat.

The mercenary jerked backward, his wide eyes going even wider. Or, rather, he tried to jerk backward. But Draycos had him in a solid grip, and there was no escape.

He grabbed at the K'da's paw, trying to pry it loose. But Draycos had cut off the man's air supply, and as Jack watched tensely the clutching hands went weak and limp. Belatedly, he seemed to remember he was armed, and dropped his right hand to the gun holstered at his belt.

But it was too late. The hand scrabbled for a second at the gun, then went still. The man's eyelids sagged, the eyes behind them rolled upward, and he was out of the fight.

The controls, Draycos's thought whispered through Jack's mind.

Jack glanced around. The attack had been so quick and quiet that none of the Brummgas seemed to have noticed that anything had happened. Even now, with Jack standing close to the unconscious man and Draycos's half-hidden foreleg keeping the other from collapsing to the floor, there was little for them to notice. *What do I do?* Jack asked.

Move around behind him, the K'da instructed. *I first need to see if he finished programming in the target system.*

It was quickly apparent that the man had only gotten halfway through that part of the task. Fortunately, he'd written the coordinates on a small mark board taped beside the cheat sheets Jack had already noticed. With Draycos giving him step-by-step instructions, he got the rest of the destination programmed in.

The center section runs the countdown sequence, Draycos continued when Jack had finished. *Activate it with the two keys beneath the leftmost display.*

Got it. Jack touched the keys.

"Williams, what's the holdup?" a voice called from a speaker across the room. "Come on; get your butt off standby."

"Off standby and shaking," Jack called back. "Sequence is going."

"Who's that, Chiggers?" the voice demanded. "What are you doing in there?"

"Williams needed help; I'm helping," Jack told him. "What's going on, anyway?"

"Who the frunge knows?" the voice growled. "We're suddenly

doing a six-day evasive to Point Three instead of going straight there. Something to do with that Pergnoir-7 that blew in a few minutes ago, I think."

Jack felt his throat tighten. Wasn't that the class of ship Alison had said the *Essenay* was? "I suppose someone'll tell us when they figure we need to know," he managed.

"Sure they will," the voice said. "You said the timer's going?"

Jack looked helplessly around for the proper display. He had no idea which one it was.

Three minutes to full charge, Draycos told him.

"Three minutes," Jack said.

There was a grunt, and the other voice fell silent.

Do you think the ship he mentioned could be the Essenay? Draycos asked.

You know any other Pergnoir-7s that might be wandering around the area? Jack retorted, looking around. There didn't seem to be any external displays in the room. *We've got to find out what's going on out there.*

There's a monitor station out the door to the left, Draycos said. *They may have it activated.*

Good. Let me have his head.

The K'da foreleg stretching out through Jack's flight suit released its grip on Williams's neck. Jack eased the man's head against the chair's headrest, balancing it to stay as upright as he could.

The result wasn't very convincing, he knew. Especially since Williams's eyes were closed and his mouth hung slightly open.

But the Brummgas in the room didn't seem particularly attentive. Hopefully, the deception would last long enough. Stepping away from the slumped figure, Jack headed for the door.

Three Brummgas were in the monitor station, standing beside the too-small chairs and gazing at the wall of displays. Most of the screens showed views of the *Foxwolf*'s interior, but Jack spotted three that were linked to exterior cameras. One of them showed a telescopic view of the *Advocatus Diaboli*.

And docked beside it, looking like a baby whale nuzzling up to its mother, was the *Essenay*.

Before Jack could get more than that one quick look, there was a single warning hoot from somewhere, and the view dissolved into the blue of hyperspace.

Was it the Essenay? Draycos asked. *I couldn't tell.*

It was, Jack said grimly. *What in space is Uncle Virge up to?*

Draycos was silent a moment. *If it* is *Uncle Virge,* he said at last.

No, Jack said firmly. *Harper and Chiggers couldn't have gotten loose.*

We will hope not, Draycos said. *In the meantime, we have a job to do.*

Abruptly, Jack realized he was still standing in the monitor room doorway. *Right,* he said, trying to shake away the image of Harper or Chiggers running loose on his ship. *Where do we go?*

Look at the two monitors at the left end of the second row, Draycos said.

Jack did so. The two displays seemed to be showing different angles of the same room. Aside from a single large machine in the center, the room was mostly empty, though he could see the places where other equipment or chairs had once been bolted to the floor.

He focused on the machine. It was roughly cylindrical in shape, about six feet long, with rounded ends and a slight bend in the center. The surface was dark brown and covered with tiny black spots. At one end were a set of handgrips and a small square pattern of muted blue lights. The whole thing was mounted on a pedestal swivel arrangement. *Looks like a giant Polish sausage,* Jack commented. *What is it?*

Draycos's tone seemed to darken. *It is the Death.*

Jack swallowed hard. The device looked so innocent. Comical, even, for something that had caused so much destruction and misery.

He glanced across the other monitors. Now that he knew what to look for, and adjusting for the multiple views, it looked as if there were three more of the weapons elsewhere aboard. *Got it,* he said, backing out of the room. *How do I get there?*

Out the door and to your left, Draycos said.

Okay, Jack said grimly. *Let's go have us an old-fashioned wienie roast.*

He'd made it past one more doorway when there was a sudden hoot like the one he'd heard just before the *Foxwolf* went into hyperspace. "Medical unit to ECHO room," a Brummgan voice bellowed over hidden loudspeakers.

Looks like someone finally noticed Williams, Jack said.

There's a door up here on the left, Draycos said urgently. *Hurry— we need to get out of sight.*

Easy, Jack soothed him. Ahead, Brummgas were starting to stream into sight as they left their bored lounging and headed aft to see what was happening. *Hurrying people make other people wonder why they're hurrying.*

But you're going the wrong direction, Draycos objected. *You should be heading back to the ECHO room.*

Why? Jack countered. *I'm a fighter pilot, not a medic.*

But—

Trust me, Jack said. *First of all, there shouldn't be any bruises on*

Williams's neck yet, so they'll just think he's fainted or something. Nothing to get excited about. Second, there was no mention that it was a human who needed help. With the number of Brummgas aboard, Chiggers would naturally assume it was one of them.

Even so, wouldn't Chiggers at least want to know what the problem was?

Not Chiggers, Jack said. *I get the feeling he doesn't much care about anyone. And vice versa.*

Sure enough, none of the Brummgas gave Jack so much as a second glance as they lumbered past. Jack continued forward, keeping an ear cocked for the sound of any of Chiggers's fellow humans.

But to his surprise, he saw no one. It was as if Neverlin had simply turned the *Foxwolf* over to the Brummgas and Valahgua. *This doesn't make any sense at all,* Jack commented as Draycos directed him into another corridor. *The way Alison was talking, it didn't sound like Neverlin trusted the Patri Chookoock any farther than he could push him uphill.*

Perhaps he's relying on the Valahgua to keep the Brummgas in line, Draycos suggested. *Certainly they have the most to lose if something happens to the ship or the Death weapons.*

Good point, Jack agreed, trying to think. Back on Brum-a-dum, he knew, Alison had tried to sow a little dissention between Neverlin, Frost, and the Patri Chookoock. Maybe he and Draycos could stir up a little distrust of their own between the Valahgua and Brummgas.

The Number Two weapons bay is around the next corner to the left, Draycos warned. *The Death weapon is mounted in the bay's auxiliary control room.*

Any idea how many Valahgua might be aboard?

There will be at least nine, Draycos said. *A Death weapon requires* one operator and one controller. There will also be a Lordover in command aboard this ship, plus a Lordhighest in overall command, probably on the Advocatus Diaboli *with Neverlin and Frost.*

How good are they at hand-to-hand fighting?

Adequate, Draycos said. *But the K'da and Shontine are far better. It is only the Death that gives the Valahgua their advantage.*

Ah. Though at nine-to-one odds, Jack noted privately, the Valahgua didn't have to be particularly good to still win out in a straight-up, toe-to-claw fight. He and Draycos would have to make sure that didn't happen.

He rounded the final corner and found himself facing an orange-rimmed door fifteen feet away, flanked by a pair of armed Brummgas. *That it?* Jack asked.

That's it, Draycos confirmed. *You'll need to bring me as close as you can.*

Easy, Jack cautioned as he strode toward the guards. To his eye, the Brummgas didn't look particularly alert. Certainly not as alert as someone guarding the ultimate weapon ought to look.

In fact, come to think of it, they looked bored and even a bit resentful.

Small wonder. Here in the middle of a ship populated entirely by their friends and allies, guard duty would seem pretty unnecessary.

They would have a rude awakening on that point soon enough. In the meantime, a pair of bored guards opened up some intriguing possibilities. *What did you call the Valahgua head honcho again?* he asked Draycos.

The Lordover, Draycos said. *You have a plan?*

I'm thinking we might try the subtle approach first, Jack told him, glancing casually around. Besides the two guards, there didn't seem to be anyone else around. *We can always kick butt later if we have to.*

"What do you wish?" one of the guards demanded.

"What do you *think* I wish?" Jack retorted. "The last diagnostic on the big gun came back a little iffy, and the Lordover wanted me to run a quick check."

The Brummgas looked at each other, and Jack held his breath. If they decided to call the Valahgua to check on the order, Draycos was going to get some exercise after all. "Come on; come on," Jack growled, waving toward the door behind them. "I haven't got all day."

"No one is permitted to be inside with the weapon," one of the Brummgas rumbled.

"No one is permitted to be *alone* inside with the weapon," Jack countered. The trick with Brummgas was to stay one step ahead of their mental processes. "Read your standing orders sometime, will you? So open up and we'll all go in together."

The aliens exchanged a second uncertain glance. "All of us, together?" the same one asked.

"I'm not supposed to be in there alone, remember?" Jack reminded him, putting some strained patience into his voice. "Besides, I'm going to need an extra hand or two."

"Yet the orders also state that we cannot leave the door unguarded."

"Then you wait out here, and your buddy can come in with me, and everyone'll be happy," Jack said.

The Brummga drew himself up. "No," he stated firmly. "He will stay. *I* will go." He gestured, and his companion stepped back to the door control. "But I will watch you closely," he added warningly.

"Fine by me," Jack said. "Can we please just get to it?"

The Brummga gestured again. His companion keyed the control, and the door slid open. Squaring his shoulders, Jack stepped between the aliens and into the doorway.

And found himself face-to-face with the Death.

Viewing it on the monitor, Jack had been able to appreciate both its comical appearance as well as its more deadly aspects. But no more. Here, standing in its presence, he could see nothing amusing about it at all. The device reeked of destruction and anger, of hatred and pride and a lust for power.

All tools and weapons, Uncle Virgil had once said, could be used for both good and bad. They could be a help in Jack's work, or could throw a snarl-up in his path.

But the Death was different. There was no useful task to which it could be put, no role of defense or creation that its technology could provide. All it could do was kill, without discrimination or restraint or mercy.

It was pure evil.

Jack felt a cold shiver run up his back. Uncle Virgil, he knew, would have immediately looked for ways the Death could be of use to him, as either a prize to ransom or a commodity to sell to the highest bidder. Jack himself, a year or two ago, would probably not have approved, but he would probably not have voiced any serious objections, either.

Not so the Jack Morgan of the present. This Jack Morgan could recognize the need to destroy this device. And he was ready and willing to do so.

Six months of living with a poet-warrior of the K'da had turned Jack into a person he'd never thought he could be. A person he'd never even dreamed he could be.

He was going to do what was right. Not because he stood to gain a thing from it, but just because it was *right*.

And despite the danger all around him, it felt good. It felt *really* good.

Jack?

With an effort, Jack shook away the sudden rush of feelings. The self-evaluation and warm fuzzies could wait until later. Right now, he had a job to do.

He eyed the Death, doing a quick mental calculation. Assuming the device hadn't been moved since his visit to the monitor room, one of the two cameras in the room had to be directly above the door, while the other was across in the far left-hand corner. A simple, straightforward arrangement, and one that covered the room quite adequately.

Unfortunately for Frost, the people who'd installed them had made the classic mistake of mounting both cameras out of the way near the ceiling. As long as Jack kept his head down, he should be able to keep his face off the monitors.

He stepped inside, looking down at his waist as he pulled out his multitool. *Have you gotten close enough to Valahguan equipment over the years to know what kind of fasteners they use?* he asked Draycos.

I have, Draycos said. *They're like human-style screws, but with a triangular hole in the end.*

Jack winced. His multitool had screwdriver blades with both cross-headed and square-headed tips. But a triangular tip was something new. *I suppose it's too late to tell them I need to go get a tool kit?*

Definitely, Draycos said. *But I think one jaw from your needle-nose pliers will work.*

I hope you're right. Jack reached the Death and leaned over the blue-light panel as if examining it. *Control circuitry?*

Beneath a cover plate on the underside, directly under the status light display.

Jack finished his examination and crouched down beside the weapon, using its bulk to block the relevant camera's view of his face. He found the access cover plate right where Draycos had said it would be, held in place at its four corners by the odd-looking triangle-holed screws. Mentally crossing his fingers, he opened his needle-nose pliers and inserted the tip of one jaw into the nearest screw.

The fit wasn't perfect, but it was close enough. *Be careful—the thread is left-handed,* Draycos warned. *It works the opposite way from human designs.*

Thanks. Jack turned the proper direction, and the screw began to loosen.

"You don't have right tools," the Brummga said, sounding more confused than suspicious. "Why don't you have right tools?"

"You've got to be kidding," Jack said with a snort. "Those Valahgua tools are for sissies." He got the panel off and laid it aside, then flicked on his flashlight and pointed it up into the opening.

Inside was a maze of wires, four rectangular circuit boards with neat rows of small components, and a few larger, thumb-sized modules wired separately into the system. Jack had dealt with his share of electronic designs over the years, but this one was completely unlike anything he'd ever seen.

But there were certain constants in every electronic design, constants forced by the laws of physics. Control circuits, which always ran on low voltage, were connected together by thin wires. Power supplies, which ran much higher voltage, required thicker wires and heavier insulation.

And if the high-voltage current from the power circuits ever wandered over into the control circuits, trouble was pretty much guaranteed.

Reaching a hand to the top of the weapon, Jack tapped one of the handles. "Hold it right here," he told the Brummga. "Keep it real steady. And *don't* bump any of the controls."

The Brummga did as instructed. Pulling out one of his multitool's special blades, Jack touched it to one of the thicker wires. The indicator light remained dark, confirming that there was no current flowing there at the moment. He checked two other wires, then replaced the sensor and pulled out a slender knife.

The operation took less than a minute. "Okay, I think I got it," he announced as he began screwing the cover plate back into place. "But don't let go until I tell you."

He finished with the plate and stood up, vigorously rubbing his forehead to again block any view of his face. "Thanks," he told the Brummga as he turned and strode back to the door, bowing his head as if he were checking on his multitool as he put it back into his pocket. "I'll let you get back to your exciting guard duty."

Jack left the room and headed back down the corridor. *That went well,* he thought toward Draycos, his skin itching as it always did when he had his back to people he'd just conned. *What now?*

Now we get under cover, Draycos said. *Take the second door to the right.*

Right. Jack chewed at his lower lip. *On the other hand, what's the hurry? They're going to be on to us soon enough. It seems to me we should squeeze everything we can out of this time of blissful ignorance.*

If we do, we run the risk of being caught in the open when the alarm is given, Draycos warned.

It's still worth a shot, Jack said. *Where's the next nearest weapon?*

A few rooms forward in the Number One weapons bay, Draycos said. *From the camera image, I believe this one's mounted in the bay's main control room, instead of in auxiliary control. That room is right up against the hull, and we'll need to use a different door to reach it.*

Then let's do it, Jack decided. *Just show me where to go.*

Very well, Draycos said. *Take the next turn to the left.*

CHAPTER 13

Neverlin had told Frost to search the man calling himself Virgil Morgan before allowing him aboard the *Advocatus Diaboli*. Frost had apparently taken that order very seriously, because Taneem ended up crouching by the grille overlooking Neverlin's office for nearly half an hour before the man finally arrived.

When he did, he wasn't at all what Taneem had expected. For one thing, he didn't look or smell anything like Jack, as she would assume a relative should. He was a large man, slightly bigger even than Frost, who was walking closely and watchfully behind him. He had broad shoulders and a way of moving that somehow brought the best Phooka dancers to Taneem's mind.

His clothing was another surprise. Instead of Jack's casual jeans, shirt, and jacket, he was wearing a distinguished-looking white uniform.

A moment later, she realized it was the same uniform she'd seen earlier on the *Advocatus Diaboli*'s bridge crew. Apparently, Frost had decided not to let the man even keep his own clothes but had pulled a spare uniform from the ship's stores for him to wear.

But all of this Taneem noticed only secondarily. Her main attention was focused on Neverlin.

And on Neverlin's sudden and violent reaction to the man's

entrance. "What the *hell?*" he all but gasped, twitching back from his desk. "Frost!"

"Hold it," Frost snapped, grabbing the man's right wrist.

Or rather, he tried to grab the man's wrist. Before he could get a solid grip, the other twisted his arm smoothly out of the mercenary's grip.

Neverlin twitched again, shoving himself even farther back from his desk as if expecting an attack. But the newcomer simply stood where he was, making no attempt to do anything at all. "Hello, Mr. Neverlin," he said calmly. "Nice to see you again."

Snarling a curse, Frost got another grip on the man's wrist. "You know him?" he demanded.

"Oh yes, I know him," Neverlin bit out. "His name's Harper. He's one of Cornelius Braxton's bodyguards."

Frost's shoulder twitched, and suddenly his other hand was pressing a gun against Harper's side. "Big mistake, friend," Frost said softly.

"Actually, the mistakes are all on your side," Harper said, his voice still calm. "What Mr. Neverlin failed to mention—because Mr. Neverlin doesn't know—is that I'm not actually working *for* Braxton anymore."

"Meaning?" Frost asked.

"Meaning that in all your grand and detailed planning for this operation, you never once thought about putting a spy on Braxton himself," Harper said, his voice suddenly hard. "Did you actually think he was just going to go about his business and forget about you?"

"Let me guess," Neverlin said. "You're volunteering for the job?"

"Don't be absurd," Harper said contemptuously. "The time for that is long over. Fortunately for you, someone else had the foresight to approach me months ago with an offer I decided was worth the risk."

"Does this person have a name?" Frost demanded.

"Yes, a name you know quite well," Harper assured him. "The Patri Chookoock."

Frost snorted. "And you expect us to just believe that?"

"Of course not," Harper said. "By all means, call him and ask." He eyed Frost over his shoulder. "Only be sure none of his Brummgas are within eavesdropping distance of the InterWorld transmitter when you do."

"Meaning?" Frost asked.

"Meaning you've been infiltrated," Harper said bluntly. "One of the Brummgas, possibly more than one, has been suborned."

"By whom?" Neverlin asked. "Braxton?"

"Worse—the Malison Ring." Harper looked at Frost again. "Possibly General Davi himself."

A shadow seemed to cross Frost's face. "That's ridiculous," he insisted. "Davi has no idea what's going on here."

"Like he had no idea you were holed up on the Chookoock estate?" Harper asked pointedly.

"That had nothing to do with Davi," Frost growled. "It was some con Morgan stirred up. Morgan, or the Kayna girl."

"Speaking of Morgan," Neverlin said, "if you're really working for the Patri, why this Virgil Morgan masquerade?"

"With all due respect, Mr. Neverlin, kindly start using your brain," Harper said. "Our conversation out there could have been picked up by anyone in your fleet. Would you really have wanted me to simply announce my true identity and mission to the Malison Ring's spies?"

"A good point," Neverlin said. "Again, why Virgil Morgan?"

"Because everyone here knows you've been trying to find Morgan to get him to open the K'da/Shontine safes for you," Harper said patiently. "He's the one person who could show up without raising anyone's suspicions."

"So how exactly do *you* know about any of this?" Frost asked. "If your job was to keep tabs on Braxton, how do you know what General Davi and the Malison Ring are up to?"

"Because Davi and Braxton have had several long conversations together over the past couple of weeks," Harper said. "Sharing their various pieces of the puzzle, as it were." He raised his eyebrows. "And Davi in particular sounded like he's been getting a steady stream of new pieces."

There was a short silence. Taneem wondered if Neverlin and Frost were thinking about Mrishpaw and his supposed attempt to open the K'da safe.

Probably. If Taneem could put those pieces together, surely Neverlin and Frost could.

"All right, you're off the hook," Neverlin said at last. "For the moment. But we *are* going to call the Patri."

"Fine," Harper said. "As I said, just make sure the Brummgas are out of earshot."

"Easily done, since there aren't any aboard the *Advocatus Diaboli* anymore," Neverlin said. "They're all on the troop carrier and the *Foxwolf.*"

"Good," Harper said. "Well, that's all I have. The Patri just wanted me to get out here and alert you to the infiltration." He cocked his head. "You have any other questions? It's been a long day, and I want to go back to the *Essenay* and rest a bit before dinner."

"I'm afraid you won't be going back to the *Essenay* any time soon," Neverlin told him. "At least, not until we've cleared your story with the Patri. But I'm sure you'll find our accommodations adequate."

"Just one more question," Frost said. His gun, Taneem noted, was still pressed against Harper's side. "If you're working for the Patri, why did you blast out of the Ponocce City Police Station with Jack Morgan instead of just taking him back to the Chookoock estate?"

"Because I needed to find out if Morgan had also been in contact with Braxton or the Malison Ring," Harper said. "To do that, I needed to gain his trust. I also needed his ship if I was going to pull off this Virgil Morgan charade. Too many of the Brummgas had seen the *Essenay* and might be suspicious if I showed up flying an entirely different ship."

"And part of the trust building was to kill three of the Patri's Brummgas?" Frost demanded, digging the muzzle of his gun a little harder into Harper's side.

Harper didn't even flinch. "I told you the Chookoock family had been infiltrated," he said mildly. "I never said all the traitors were here in your fleet."

There was another short silence. "We'll be sure to ask the Patri about that when we talk to him," Neverlin said, his voice neutral. "Where's Jack now?"

"*And* his dragon," Frost added.

"Yes; his K'da," Harper said, shaking his head. "Damnedest thing I ever saw. Actually, I didn't do anything with either of them. I didn't have to. They went off somewhere, brought me back a roommate, then disappeared again."

"You didn't ask where they were going?"

"I didn't care where they were going," Harper said. "All I needed was his ship, and he was handing that to me on a platinum platter. I waited until he was gone, popped my cuffs, and plugged in the Point Two coordinates the Patri Chookoock had given me."

"This roommate you mentioned," Frost said. "What was his name?"

"No idea," Harper said. "We were never introduced, and the only times he opened his mouth were to be loud or insulting. Or both. I dumped him with the local cops just to get rid of him."

"What did he look like?" Frost asked, his voice gone suddenly dark. "And where exactly did Morgan pick him up?"

Harper shrugged. "Medium height, slender build, rusty brown hair, thin face, and we were in the middle of nowhere on Bentre. Why?"

Frost snarled a curse. "Chiggers."

"Who?" Harper asked, frowning.

"That's impossible," Neverlin said, ignoring the question. "He was seen boarding the—" He broke off. "*Wasn't* he seen boarding the *Foxwolf*?"

"You tell me," Frost said, stepping around Harper and heading for Neverlin's desk. He got two steps before he abruptly stopped. "*Frunge* it all. We can't even call over and check."

"Who's Chiggers?" Harper asked again.

"One of our pilots," Neverlin said grimly. "He got separated from the group picking up those KK-29 patrol ships you probably saw on your way in." He looked at Frost. "We *thought* he'd made it back safely."

"Blasted kid," Frost bit out. "Sir, we have *got* to get word to the *Foxwolf* right away."

"How?" Neverlin countered. "Besides, it's probably way too late to sound an alarm now. Morgan and the K'da have undoubtedly already made their presence known."

Frost swore viciously. "And six days before we can even get help to them."

"Six *days*?" Harper demanded. "Where are we going, Ghossta's End?"

"We're doing an evasive to our next rendezvous point," Neverlin told him. "We thought it would be a useful distraction for anyone who might be monitoring you."

"Terrific," Harper said heavily. "How big a force is the *Fox-wolf* carrying?"

"Three hundred eighteen Brummgas, plus five of my men and a new recruit we're not entirely sure of," Frost said. "Plus nine Valahgua."

"Against a fourteen-year-old boy and a K'da." Harper pursed his lips. "Not too bad."

"You haven't seen the K'da in action," Frost said grimly. "I have. They'll have their work cut out for them."

"Still, they do have those nine Valahgua," Neverlin added. "One would think that after all these years they'd have *some* idea of how to deal with K'da."

"I guess we'll find out," Harper said.

"I guess we will," Neverlin said. "And we can always make do with a few less Brummgas if we have to."

He waved a hand. "But I'm forgetting my manners, and you *did* say something about wanting to rest before dinner. Colonel, would you escort Mr. Harper to his stateroom? There's an empty one forward that he can use."

"Certainly." Frost gestured back toward the office door. "Mr. Harper?"

Carefully, Taneem eased back from the grille and backed her way along the duct. This time, she waited until she was two turns away from the office before speaking. "Alison?" she whispered. "Did you hear all that?"

"Yes," the girl's voice whispered back. "Interesting."

"Did you know all of this when you made it look like Mrishpaw had broken into Neverlin's office?"

"I'd never heard a word of it," Alison told her. "It's beautifully convenient, though."

"I suppose." Taneem hesitated. "Do you think Jack and Draycos are really over in that other ship?"

"I don't know," Alison said, her voice tight. "But it sounds like the sort of crazy stunt they'd pull."

"Is there anything we can do to help them?"

"You heard Neverlin," Alison said. "As long as we're in hyperspace, we're cut off from the rest of the ships."

"Then what do we do?"

"The only thing we can," Alison said. "We keep an eye on things here and try to plan what we'll do when we reach Point Three. *And* we keep stirring the fire beneath Neverlin and Frost and see if we can get this alliance to implode."

"To what?"

"To fall apart," Alison explained. "To self-destruct."

"Oh," Taneem said. "What do you want me to do now?"

There was a soft, thoughtful hiss from the comm clip. "See if you can find out where Neverlin and Frost have put Harper," she said. "If he's really working for the Patri Chookoock, we'll want to see about pointing some of Neverlin's suspicions in his direction."

"You think he might not be?"

"Might not be what?"

"Working for the Patri Chookoock."

"Who knows?" Alison said. "If he's not, coming aboard like this would be a pretty crazy thing to do. On the other hand, Cornelius Braxton is famous for pulling crazy stunts."

"It sounds like he and Jack would get along very well," Taneem suggested.

"Probably," Alison agreed. "Off you go now. But be careful."

"I will." Getting her bearings, Taneem turned toward the bow and headed for the forward group of staterooms.

CHAPTER 14

As always, Taneem took her time, checking each grille as she passed. As always, her excessive caution proved largely unnecessary. Now that the *Essenay* had been docked and the immediate crisis was over, both crew and passengers were relaxing again. Certainly none of them seemed to have the slightest interest in the air ducts running along above their heads.

During her most recent investigation of the ship, just after she and Alison had escaped from the safe, Taneem had noted that most of the forward cabins were occupied by Brummgas, usually four to a room. Now, with all the aliens having been sent to the *Foxwolf,* their places had been taken by human Malison Ring soldiers.

Still, even through the confusing mix of other human scents wafting through the ducts, it didn't take her long to find Harper's new home.

Back in the office, both Harper and Neverlin had mentioned Harper's desire to rest. But as Taneem eased an eye around the edge of the grille, she discovered he wasn't resting at all. Instead, he was walking slowly around the room, his hands running gently over the walls and furnishings, his head moving back and forth as he looked closely at everything.

His movements seemed strangely familiar. Taneem frowned, trying to figure out why.

And then it hit her. Just as Alison had done on their very first visit to this ship a month ago, Harper was searching for hidden microphones and other spy devices.

Carefully, Taneem settled down into a comfortable position inside the tight fit of the duct. This would, she knew, take some time.

It didn't take as long as she'd expected. Within fifteen minutes Harper had finished his sweep. Still looking around as if making sure he hadn't missed anything, he took off the white uniform jacket he'd been given and sat down on the edge of the bed.

But he didn't lie down. Instead, he rolled up his shirtsleeves past his elbows, exposing his forearms. Holding his left arm close to his eyes, he placed the fingernails of his right hand against the inside of his left wrist.

For a moment nothing happened. Harper held the pose, his fingertips making small movements against the skin as if he were scratching some delicate itch.

And then, to Taneem's horrified astonishment, he peeled the skin straight back off his arm.

Taneem gasped, her tail twitching violently in reaction. The tip hit the inside of the duct, giving off a muffled metallic clang.

Harper's head jerked up, his right hand still gripping the flap of skin. His eyes darted around the room, his face suddenly grim and deadly.

Taneem froze, afraid to breathe. For a long minute Harper continued his visual sweep. Then, to her relief, he lowered his eyes again to his forearm. Resettling his grip on the flap of skin, he continued pulling it away from his arm.

And now Taneem saw what she should have spotted in the first place. He wasn't pulling off his own real skin but merely a flap of something that *looked* like skin.

And as the flap came free, she could see several small, flat objects embedded in the flap's underside.

Neverlin had warned Frost to search Harper carefully. It looked like Frost hadn't been careful enough.

The strip of false skin extended nearly the entire way from Harper's wrist to his elbow. He finished pulling it off and laid it beside him on the bed, then spent a minute vigorously rubbing the real skin that had been covered by the patch. Switching arms, he removed another strip of skin from his right forearm and laid it beside the first.

Again, he took a moment to rub at the arm where the strip had been. Then, removing a slender item about as long as one of Taneem's claws from the first strip, he stood up.

And headed directly toward the room's air grille.

Taneem was back up into a crouch in an instant, easing her way backward down the duct as quickly as she dared. Before she had made it to the next corner she could hear the faint sounds as Harper began unfastening the screws holding the grille in place.

She made it to the corner and backed around it, not stopping until she was completely out of sight of Harper's room. "Alison!" she whispered urgently.

"What is it?"

"I think he heard me," Taneem said, feeling scared and thoroughly miserable. It was like her first time in the air ducts all over again. "I'm sorry—I made some noise when he started peeling off his skin, and now he's opening the grille—"

"Slow down; slow down," Alison cut her off. "What do you mean, he peeled off his skin?"

"On his arms," Taneem said. "Only it wasn't real skin. Only I didn't know that, and I gasped, and now I think he's coming in after me."

"Okay, just relax," Alison soothed her. "First of all, he's way too big to get anything but his head into the duct. Can he see you where you are right now?"

"No," Taneem said, feeling her heart slowing down a little. Looking down at her paws, she saw that the extra blood from her panicked reaction had turned her gray scales black. "No, I'm around a corner."

"Good," Alison said. "Now tell me: did he jump up and head for the grille as soon as you made your noise?"

From the direction of Harper's room came the faint sound of the grille being pulled free of the duct. "No, he finished pulling off the skin first," Taneem said, lowering her voice a little more. "Then he took out something from the inside of one of the pieces and came over to the grille."

"Then I think you're okay," Alison said. "Just hang there a minute and listen."

Taneem nodded, feeling herself calming down. If Alison wasn't worried, she probably shouldn't be, either. The scales on her paws, she noticed, were starting to go back to their usual gray.

For a moment there was silence. In her mind's eye Taneem saw Harper with his head sticking into the opening, looking both ways down the duct.

She flicked her tongue out a few times, tasting the mixture of human and unidentified scents flowing through the ducts. Some Earth animals, she'd read in the *Essenay*'s encyclopedia, could smell or otherwise sense fear and anger. Distantly, she wondered if a properly experienced K'da could do the same.

And then, she heard the sound of the grille being put back in place. Another minute of scratching as the bolts were replaced, and then all was silent again.

She waited another minute, just to make sure. "Alison?" she whispered. "I think he's done."

"He didn't spot you?"

"No."

"Good," Alison said. "Okay. I want you to look back around the corner—carefully—and tell me what you see."

Taneem frowned. What could there possibly be to see besides an empty duct?

But Alison knew about these things. She must have her reasons. Moving forward, Taneem eased her head back around the corner.

The grille, as she'd guessed, was indeed back in place.

But the duct was no longer empty.

"There's something there," she said, frowning even harder. Was that what she thought it was? "I think—Alison, he's put the two strips of skin into the duct."

"That's what I thought he was up to," Alison said, sounding grimly pleased with herself. "He got the stuff in past Frost okay, but didn't want to risk getting caught with it on him. *Literally* on him, in this case."

"What *is* it?" Taneem asked, eyeing the strips with a mixture of fascination and distaste.

"Let's find out," Alison said. "Why don't you scoot over there and grab them?"

Taneem felt her whole body go rigid. *"What?"*

"Keep your voice down," Alison admonished. "What's the big deal? You sneak over, you pick up the goodies, and you get out. Couldn't be simpler."

"But what if he *sees* me?"

"He won't if you're careful," Alison said. "Come on, Taneem. If this is something he doesn't want Frost and Neverlin knowing about, we definitely want to take a look."

Taneem curled her tail into a grimace. "All right," she said with a sigh. "I'll try."

She edged around the corner and down the duct. There was no reaction that she could sense. Her heart pounding again, she eased up to the grille and peered through it.

Harper was lying on his back on the bed, one arm across his chest, the other resting across his eyes. Without taking her own eyes off him, she scooped up the two flaps of skin and retreated hastily back down the duct. "I've got them," she whispered to Alison.

"Great," Alison said. "Find a safe place to talk, and let's check them out."

Having already had one narrow escape, Taneem was in no mood to try for another. She therefore made her way to the very back of the ship, to the very end of the air duct system, where she could taste no humans or Brummgas nearby.

Finding a spot midway between the air-pumping room and a darkened machine shop, she laid her new prizes out in front of her. "All right, I'm ready," she said.

"Good," Alison said. "Describe the items for me."

Taneem leaned close, studying the flaps of skin with the light from her own glowing silver eyes. "First are two small, flat pieces of plastic. The end of one of them has a funny sort of shape, like a sort of squished X."

"Does it look like it would snap open into a square shape if you opened it up?"

Taneem frowned. Then she saw what Alison meant. "Yes, it does," she said. "The other piece of plastic is just flat."

"Screwdrivers," Alison identified them. "Probably started out as a set of three, only Harper used the crosshead one on the grille. What else?"

"Two small half cylinders that look like they fit together to make a complete tube," Taneem said. "There's another tube, a solid one, that looks like it would fit inside the other one."

"Anything there that looks like needles?"

"I don't see—oh yes, there they are," Taneem corrected herself. "They're on the other flap. There are five of them."

"Knockout needles, with either a hypo or a spring-load launcher to deliver the goods," Alison said. "Harper certainly came ready for trouble. What else?"

"Two wide, flat, round containers," Taneem said. "Also a flat tube sort of like the one you have for your toothpaste."

"Any writing on either of them?"

Taneem looked closer. "The tube says 'akid well putty.'"

"*Acid* well putty? *A-c-i-d?*"

"Yes," Taneem said. "Acid well putty. The round containers say . . . they just say 'keyhole.'"

"Beautiful," Alison murmured. "Thank you, Mr. Harper. Grab everything and bring it back here. We're in."

"I don't understand," Taneem said as she tucked the strips of skin under her forelegs and headed down the duct toward Alison's lifepod. "How can you put a keyhole inside a container?"

"This isn't a normal keyhole," Alison explained. "It's an acid-based paste that's supposed to be able to eat through any normal door material. You're supposed to set it over the lock where it'll either expose the mechanism so you can get at it or else eat away the bolt itself. Hence, keyhole."

Taneem winced. "It sounds dangerous."

"It is," Alison confirmed. "It can eat human flesh even faster than it eats doors. But if you know what you're doing it can get you out of a tight jam."

"I thought you could get out of the lifepod any time you wanted," Taneem said, frowning. "Or did we take it because we don't want Harper getting out of his stateroom?"

"Actually, right now we don't really care what Harper does or doesn't do," Alison said. "What *we* want is a way to get you back in here with me."

Abruptly, Taneem understood. "We can use the acid against the duct wall!"

"You got it," Alison said. "You saw how relatively thin the metal was where you popped into the duct. That's because the lifepod acts as that part of the ship's outer hull. We shouldn't have any problem making a hole big enough for me to stick a couple of fingers through."

She was right. Following Alison's directions, Taneem first squeezed out a semicircle of the putty beneath the spot where the acid was to go. Then she half-turned the acid container's seal and nestled it against the wall with the putty holding it in place.

The smell, once the acid started working, was incredibly strong. Midway through the operation Taneem had to retreat down the duct and wait near one of the grilles.

By the time Alison called her back, five minutes later, it was finished. The acid had eaten away the metal of the duct, leaving a small hole between it and the lifepod. Again at Alison's instruction, Taneem folded the flaps of skin and their remaining contents and put them gingerly into her mouth. Alison stretched two fingers through the freshly made hole, and Taneem slithered up her arm and back onto her body.

Taneem had barely made it onto Alison's skin when she leaped out of the girl's shirt collar. In the same motion, she spat the two folds of flesh onto the deck. "Ackleh!" she gasped, trying to drive the taste from her mouth.

"That good, huh?" Alison said, stepping around her and retrieving the flaps.

"No, that bad," Taneem said, wiping her tongue back and forth across the inside of her teeth. "It tastes like real flesh."

"It is," Alison said. Her voice was calm enough, but Taneem noticed she was taking care to touch the flaps only with her fingertips. "You take a sample of someone's skin, grow the right-sized strip in a lab, then paste it back over his own arm or leg or whatever."

Taneem shuddered. "Why would anyone do that?"

"For exactly the reason Harper did it: so you can sneak in your goodies without anyone spotting them." She began prying out the remaining items, again touching the skin as little as she could. "A good scanner will pick up any synthetic you try to use. This way, they can even pull a DNA sample from the fake skin and it'll match up with any other samples they take."

"It's still disgusting," Taneem said. "Is this a common practice?"

"It's a very *un*common practice," Alison said. She removed the last item and began folding the empty skin strips together. "Harper obviously has access to some very sophisticated and expensive equipment."

Taneem thought about that as Alison took the roll of skin to the lifepod's disposal container and pushed it through the opening. "But why would the Patri Chookoock go to so much trouble?" she asked.

"I don't know," Alison said, stepping to the sink and washing her hands. "But your question assumes Harper is genuinely working for him."

"You don't think he is?"

Alison shrugged. "I find it hard to believe one of Braxton's top bodyguards would turn traitor as easily as Harper makes it sound," she said. "And this"—she gestured to the collection of items she'd taken from the fake skin—"looks a lot more like Braxton's budget than the Patri's."

"Do you think Braxton sent Harper to find Neverlin?"

"That's certainly the logical assumption," Alison agreed.

Taneem pricked up her ears. There had been something odd about the way Alison had said that. "Are there other possibilities?" she asked.

Alison smiled. But it was a slightly brittle smile. "There are always other possibilities," she said. "But there's no point in trying to dig too deeply into this. Don't forget, we don't even know for sure that Harper's not exactly who he claims to be. His little bag of tricks could be some game the Patri's pulling on his allies."

"Because they're only allies of convenience," Taneem murmured.

"Exactly," Alison said.

"What about us?"

Alison frowned. "What do you mean?"

"Are *we* only allies of convenience?" Taneem asked, her eyes steady on the girl.

Alison seemed to brace herself. "We're genuine allies, Taneem," she said, her voice low and earnest. "More than that, I hope that we're friends."

"I hope that, too, Alison," Taneem said. "Because I trust you."

Alison laid her hand on the K'da's head. "I trust you, too, Taneem," she said. "We have to, you know. Because we're all we've got."

"I know," Taneem said softly.

"And we're going to get through this," Alison continued. "Come on; let's get something to eat."

She turned toward the supply cabinet. "And after that," she added over her shoulder, "you can tell me your impressions of Harper, Neverlin, and Frost."

"And the Valahgua?"

"Yes," Alison said grimly. "Especially the Valahgua."

CHAPTER 15

They were on their way to the *Foxwolf*'s Number One weapons bay when Jack felt the sudden change in the air around them.

It wasn't anything obvious or big. Rather, it was a combination of small things. The ship seemed to go oddly quiet, as if dozens of casual conversations had been broken off or reduced to whispers. The background rumble of thudding Brummgan feet likewise softened, as if the big aliens had suddenly found reasons to stand still.

And as the background noises faded, they were replaced by a sense of watchful foreboding.

The enemy was on to them.

I think we've worn out our welcome, buddy, Jack warned as he continued down the corridor.

I know, Draycos agreed. *We'd better get to cover.*

Jack chewed at the inside of his cheek as he kept walking. According to Draycos's directions, the weapons bay should be right around the next corner. *How far is your bolt-hole from the weapons bay?*

Not far, Draycos said. *In fact, there should be an access point from the bay's interior.*

So if we can get in, we can wreck the Death weapon and go straight down the rabbit hole?

Theoretically, yes. But that would require us to get past whatever defenses they've now organized around the Death. I don't think we can take the risk.

I don't know, Jack said thoughtfully. *Unless Langston changed his mind and turned us in, they have to still be thinking it's Chiggers going around doing God only knows what. We ought to be able to keep them thinking that way at least long enough to get through the next set of guards.*

If that is their assumption, Draycos warned. *If not, even now they'll be setting a trap for us.*

I'm sure they are, Jack agreed. *But even laying a trap implies they don't realize who we are. If they knew they had a K'da poet-warrior aboard, there should be alarms going off all over the place right now. Followed by massive quantities of gunfire.*

Assume for the moment that you're right, Draycos said. *What would be our plan?*

Assuming I'm right, we should still have one surprise attack's worth of slack left, Jack said. Reaching into his side pocket, he slipped Harper's two-shot tangler into his palm. *I'm thinking we march straight up to the guards like we own the place, hit them with Harper's tangler, then go in and wreck the Death weapon. Then we do a quick fade into the woodwork and work on our new strategy.*

Very well, we'll try it, Draycos said thoughtfully. *But save the tangler for future use. When we reach the Brummgas, just get me as close to them as you can.*

Okay, Jack said doubtfully. *You sure we want to reveal you this soon?*

Trust me, Draycos said. *Just get me close. And let your arms hang as limp as you can.*

Jack frowned. As *limp* as he could?

But there was no time to ask about it. He turned the corner and found himself once again facing a door and a pair of armed

Brummgas. He didn't break stride but continued confidently toward them.

The aliens were trying hard to look casual, and they were doing a rotten job of it. Their postures were stiff, their studiously unconcerned faces included masses of tense muscles in throat and jaws, and their hands hovered way too close to their holsters.

But at least they hadn't drawn the second Jack appeared around the corner. It was looking like his take on the situation had been right. *As close to them as I can get, right?*

Yes. If possible, get between them.

"What do you wish?" one of the Brummgas asked, his voice as pretend casual as his face.

"I need to take a look at the big gun," Jack said. Staying with his last script ought to make everyone think he didn't suspect they were on to him. That should persuade them to give him a little more rope to play with. "The Lordover wanted me to run a quick check on it."

"Very well," the Brummga said. Unlike the last time, Jack noted, neither of the aliens made any move toward the door release. "Come," the Brummga added, gesturing Jack forward.

Obediently, Jack stepped toward them. As he did so, one of the Brummgas unglued himself from the deck and started forward. *Careful,* Draycos warned. *He's going to try to intercept you, with the other staying out of reach as backup.*

I'm on it. Waiting until the Brummga was nearly to him, Jack half-turned as if he'd heard something behind him. As he did so, he gave a little sidestep, just enough to sidle him smoothly past the approaching Brummga. Jack turned back, doing the same step in reverse, and landed squarely between the two aliens. *There you go, buddy.*

Arms limp, Draycos reminded him. The Brummga already in

motion braked to a halt and reversed direction. Both aliens were now moving in on him. Jack felt a surge of weight on his chest and inner arms as the K'da came partially off his skin, pressing out against his flight suit.

And to Jack's astonishment, his arms abruptly swung upward of their own accord, his hands jabbing straight toward the Brummgas' throats.

There was no time for him to even begin curling his hands into fists. But there was no need. As it had been Draycos's forelegs that had swung Jack's arms upward in the first place, it was also his paws that lifted just far enough off of Jack's palms to slam with devastating force against the Brummgas' throats.

The two aliens dropped like stunned moose, slamming to the deck with a double thud the whole ship must have felt. *Quick— inside,* Draycos urged as he melted back onto Jack's skin.

Jack jumped over the prone Brummga blocking his way and hit the door release. The door slid open, and he sprinted inside.

To find himself facing three more Brummgas.

They were standing between him and the Death weapon, their mouths widening with surprise even as their eyes began to narrow with anger.

Uh-oh, Jack thought toward Draycos, the momentum of his forward rush faltering. The Brummgas reached for the guns belted at their sides—

With a flash of black-tinged golden scales, Draycos shot out of Jack's collar, his rear paws shoving hard against the boy's chest as he arrowed straight for the Brummgas. There was a blur of paws and tail, and all three Brummgas went down.

"I'm guessing we're finished with the subtle approach?" Jack suggested, rubbing his chest where the K'da's paws had shoved against the skin.

"There was no other way," Draycos said, turning to the Death weapon. "You eliminate the cameras. I'll deal with this."

"Right." Jack leaned down to one of the unconscious Brummgas and pulled out his gun. A single three-shot burst from the weapon shredded the camera over the door. He turned to the one in the corner of the room, waved cheerily at it, and shot it out, too. "Now what?" he asked, tossing the weapon aside and looking back at Draycos.

The subtle approach was definitely over. Half of the Death weapon was already scattered across the deck in mangled pieces. Draycos was still working on the other half, quickly but methodically shredding it with his claws. "There," the K'da said, flicking his tail toward the hull-side bulkhead.

Jack frowned. Then he spotted it: a narrow, rectangular section of wall that was a slightly different color from the plates around it. It was small, extending vertically only from his eyes to his knees, its width slightly less than that of his shoulders. "What do I do?" he asked as he stepped over to it.

"Push at the top and bottom and slide it to your left."

Jack gave it a try. The panel resisted his first attempt. He tried again, pressing harder. This time it gave way and obediently slid away to the left, revealing a narrow passageway. "Got it," he called, easing his head into the opening. It was hard to tell in the faint light leaking in from their room, but the passageway seemed to go a considerable distance in both directions, bending visibly to the right as it followed the curve of the hull.

The floor wasn't solid but was made of a thin, fragile-looking meshwork, with a lot more of the narrow passageway directly below it. If the passageway had a ceiling, he couldn't see it in the dim light.

"Inside," Draycos said, loping over from what was left of

the Death. He reached Jack's side and turned to face the door, crouched ready to leap. "Hurry—I can feel footsteps approaching."

Ducking his head, Jack turned sideways and got one leg through the opening, easing his weight onto the meshwork. To his relief, it was stronger than it looked. He got his other leg in and held out his arm. "Ready," he said.

Still watching the door, Draycos flipped his tail onto Jack's hand and slithered backward onto his arm. *That was different,* Jack commented. The panel, he saw, had a pair of handles on the inside. Gripping them, he gave the panel another sideways shove. It slid back into position and closed, cutting off the light from the room and leaving Jack in pitch-darkness.

Just in time. Pressing his ear to the panel, he heard the faint sound of the room door opening, followed by the much louder noise of thudding Brummgan feet.

Hold still, Draycos ordered. His head and part of his upper body rose from Jack's shoulder, the passageway picking up a faint green glow as the K'da's eyes rose from the concealment of Jack's flight suit. Draycos reached up with a paw and with two quick slashes cut off a section of bar running along the inner side of the passageway. *Brace it against the entrance,* he instructed, passing it down to Jack's hand. He sank back onto the boy's skin, leaving only his eyes and the top of his head still three-dimensional.

Silently, Jack moved the bar into place, wedging it between the movable panel and the rear of the passageway. Draycos had cut the bar perfectly, he noted, even to the point of angling the ends slightly so that it would lie flat against both sides. *Got it,* he said. *Where now?*

To your left, toward the bow, Draycos instructed. *The hull curves inward more strongly in that direction.*

Do we care how strongly the hull curves? Jack asked as he set off. The corridor was just a little wider than his shoulders, allowing him to walk straight instead of having to sidle.

The Brummgas and Valahgua are too big to fit in here, Draycos said. *But they can still reach in and shoot.*

Jack swallowed. *Oh.*

Ahead, the light from Draycos's eyes showed their path blocked by a fat metallic cylinder decorated with a pattern of angled stripes and spots. It was nearly three feet high and filled the corridor's entire width. Between the sections of stripes and spots Jack could see multiple holes dotting its surface. *What is this place, anyway?* he asked as he got one leg up over the top of the cylinder.

It's called the tween gap, a space between the inner and outer hulls, Draycos explained. *In an emergency—either serious combat or an imminent crash situation—the gap can be flooded with a material called* ghikada. *It comes out as a vaporized fluid, solidifying quickly and filling the gap.*

We have something like that, Jack said, nodding as he shifted his weight onto the cylinder. It was like riding a short but very fat horse. *It's called crash foam. It's designed to absorb some of the impact in an accident.*

This is somewhat different, Draycos said. *Solid* ghikada *is stronger even than hull metal. Its function is not to absorb damage but to provide an extra shell of protection around most areas of the ship. It was the reason the* Havenseeker *survived its crash landing on Iota Klestis as well as it did.*

Handy stuff, Jack said as he dismounted off the far side of the cylinder. *How come you wait to the last minute before using it? Why not keep the tween gap filled all the time?*

Because ghikada *is strong but unstable,* Draycos said. *It holds its full strength for only about two hours. After that it begins to soften, and after a few more hours it has melted completely into a liquid form.*

From somewhere behind them came the metallic sound of something hammering against the inner hull wall. *Sounds like they've figured out where we've gone,* Jack said. *You say this tween gap goes everywhere in the ship?*

Everywhere except the weapons bays themselves and the three navigational bubbles, Draycos said. *Those areas need to be open to the outer hull in order to function.*

In other words, those sections of the tween gap would be dead ends. *We should probably avoid those places,* Jack said. *Getting trapped with your back to a wall is generally considered bad form.*

Don't worry; I have an entirely different refuge in mind, Draycos assured him. *We'll need to go up a level to reach it.*

Jack looked at the sheer walls beside him. *How do we do that?*

Just past the next ghikada *cylinder will be a vertical section of mesh I'll be able to climb.*

They reached the mesh a few minutes later. Draycos came off Jack's back, and with Jack gripping his tail he began to climb.

By now the hammering behind them had stopped, but Jack thought he could hear the hiss of a cutting torch. Apparently, the Brummgas and Valahgua had given up trying to get the door open and had decided on the more direct approach.

They reached the next level up, and with Draycos again on Jack's back they continued heading forward. A few minutes later, they reached another of the tween gap access doors.

Draycos spent a few minutes with his ear pressed against the wall, listening for signs of activity. Then, at his direction, Jack pulled on the handles and slid the panel open.

The room beyond was unlit, but in the glow from Draycos's eyes Jack could see that it was long and narrow and low ceilinged.

Nearly the entire floor space was filled with cylinders, longer but thinner than the *ghikada* containers and sporting a different stripe/spot pattern. They were connected to each other and the deck by a confusing array of pipes, all of which seemed to have unique stripe/spot patterns of their own.

Wait here, Draycos said. Again bounding out of the boy's collar, he made his way nimbly across the cylinders and piping to another small door at the far end of the room. There he again pressed his ear against the panel and listened.

A minute later, he straightened and crossed back to Jack. "The area outside appears to be deserted," he murmured. "We should be safe here for a while."

"Good," Jack said. Gingerly, he stepped into the room, trying not to slip on the cylinders. "What is this? More *ghikada*?"

"Fire suppressant," Draycos identified it. "This room handles fire control for most of the upper/forward sections of the ship."

"And the Brummgas and Valahgua don't know about it?"

"They may," Draycos said. "But only if they bothered to examine the rest of the data diamonds Alison retrieved from the safe at the Chookoock family estate."

Jack frowned. "You kept your ships' schematics in a *safe*?"

"The complete schematics, yes," Draycos said with a sort of grim amusement. "The set freely available on the ship's computers has certain gaps and omissions."

"Such as this room?"

"Such as several of these rooms, the tween gap areas, and most of the equipment crawl spaces," Draycos said. "They also indicate the ventilation ducts are narrower than they actually are."

"Too narrow for K'da to get through, I suppose," Jack said. "Man, you guys really planned ahead."

"We were traveling to unknown space, to meet peoples we knew little about," Draycos reminded him quietly. "We had to be prepared for attack and betrayal."

Jack felt a shiver run up his back. "I'm glad we're on the same side," he said. "Still, even if they found the actual schematics, I doubt the Brummgas and Valahgua could squeeze in here anyway. I just wish I knew how many humans Frost has aboard."

Draycos was silent a moment. "Actually, no one *has* to come in here after us," he said reluctantly. "The Death, as you'll recall, can penetrate any thickness of material."

Jack felt his stomach tighten. "That *does* kind of put a damper on things, doesn't it?"

"Though it's not necessarily as bad as it sounds," Draycos assured him. "For one thing, the weapons below us are long-range models, hardly suitable for lugging around the ship."

"True, but they hardly need to move them, do they?" Jack countered. "All they have to do is get everyone out of the way and sweep the whole hull area right from where they are."

"That *is* a possibility," Draycos conceded. "However, recall the situation at Iota Klestis. There, according to Alison's theory, each Death weapon was programmed with a limited amount of operational time. If that's still the case, they may hesitate to waste any of that time and energy on us. Certainly not with major combat still lying before them."

"Sure, but who says they've got that same setup here?" Jack asked. "Our theory was that the weapons at Iota Klestis were gimmicked because the Valahgua didn't want Neverlin and Frost double-crossing them and getting hold of functioning Death weapons. Going into full-blown combat is an entirely different scenario."

"Not necessarily," Draycos said. "The Death is their sole

advantage over the peoples they've destroyed or conquered. Without it, they would have been victorious over few, if any, of their victims."

He lashed his tail contemptuously. "They certainly would never have driven us from our homes without it. No, they can't afford for its secret to escape their control."

"That's good to hear," Jack said. "Paranoia can be useful, as long as it's in the other guy."

"True," Draycos said. "Though that doesn't mean that they might not feel it worthwhile to spend a few seconds of power if they should locate us. We must continue to be quiet and vigilant."

"I'm with you on that," Jack said.

"The other reason not to worry overly much," Draycos continued, "is that I'll be doing everything in my power to destroy the remaining Death weapons as quickly as I can."

"I'm with you there, too," Jack said. "Do bear in mind, though, that they're on to us now. It's not going to be nearly so easy to get access to the blasted things."

"We'll find a way," Draycos promised. "Meanwhile, we need supplies. You stay here while I go find food and water."

"You want some company?"

"Thank you, no," Draycos said. "There are ways about this ship that only a K'da can travel. You just rest. I'll be back soon."

"Fine," Jack said. "But don't get greedy and go after any of the Death weapons alone. I want a piece of them."

"Don't worry," Draycos promised grimly. "You'll have your full share."

He crossed to the door and again listened for a minute. Carefully opening it, he peered outside and then slipped out into the corridor beyond.

Jack took a deep breath, let it out in a long sigh. He was tired, he realized suddenly. Tired, and tense, and worried.

But not worried about himself. He had Draycos at his side, after all, a trained poet-warrior of the K'da.

Instead, to Jack's mild surprise, he discovered he was worried about Alison.

And Taneem, too, of course. But mostly he was worried about Alison.

It was a rather annoying discovery, actually. Alison herself, he knew, was probably not worried about *him*. And she certainly gave the impression that she knew how to take care of herself, as well as knowing everything else.

Still, he couldn't help feeling some concern.

With an effort, he pushed the thoughts away. They were probably Draycos's fault, he decided, these unwanted feelings about Alison. He'd probably picked them up while the K'da was riding his skin. Draycos worried about everyone, even Alison.

Meanwhile, Jack had more urgent things to spend his mental energy on. Carefully, he laid himself down between two of the cylinders, his shoulders and legs straddling them. It was, he discovered, a more or less comfortable position.

He didn't know the ship like Draycos did. But he *had* seen the rooms where the Valahgua had set up their precious Death weapons.

And Uncle Virgil had taught him all the best ways of getting into locked and guarded rooms. It was about time he put all those long years of criminal training to some use.

Lacing his fingers together behind his head, he closed his eyes and settled down to think.

CHAPTER 16

Back in the monitor room Jack had noticed that the two remaining Death weapons were in the same rooms on the starboard side of the ship as the two he and Draycos had already hit on the port side. One of those rooms had the same direct access to the tween gap as the last room they'd been in.

They would have to do it quickly, of course, before the Brummgas and Valahgua had time to figure out how the whole tween gap thing worked and come up with a way to block it.

Accordingly, as soon as Draycos returned with their supplies Jack laid out his plan. Draycos approved, and they headed out.

They reached the back-door entrance without incident. Draycos did his looking-over-the-wall trick, pinpointing the positions of all eight Brummgas who had taken up guard positions around the weapon.

With the previous attack still fairly recent, Jack figured the aliens would still not be completely up to speed. He was right. Draycos popped the door and Jack instantly opened fire with his tangler, nailing all eight aliens before they could do more than draw their weapons.

Still, they were more alert than he'd hoped. Even as the last one hit the floor the door across the room slid open and the backup group charged in.

Or at least, they tried to charge in. Jack had another clip in his tangler in time to nail the first two as they started through the doorway. They went unconscious as the shock capacitor knocked them cold, and sagged still more or less upright as the milky white tangler threads glued them to the sides of the doorway.

The rest of the Brummgas behind them howled in rage and frustration. A couple of the nearest lifted their guns over the heads of their unconscious comrades and blindly opened fire into the room.

Jack responded by shooting at the flailing arms with more tangler cartridges. That silenced the guns and added a couple more bodies to his makeshift roadblock.

He had drained that clip and was grabbing for a third when Draycos leaped back through the opening beside him. "Go," the K'da said, stretching his forelegs up toward the overhead bar.

Jack grabbed the panel's handles and shoved. As the panel slid shut, he caught a single glimpse of the pile of rubble that was the remains of the Death weapon.

Draycos had the bracing bar ready by the time the panel was back in place. Even so, they nearly didn't make it. A fraction of a second after Jack slid the bar into place there was a terrific thud that seemed to shake the whole bulkhead.

The impact jarred the bar partially loose. Jack and Draycos got to it at the same time, and with two hands and two paws tugging at it they managed to get it back in place before the next blow came. "Head aft," Draycos murmured, touching Jack's hand and sliding up his sleeve. *I want to take a different route back to the fire control room,* Draycos added as his contact reestablished their telepathic link. *There's another section of climbable mesh about twenty feet back.*

Jack nodded and headed down the narrow space. *That seemed*

to go well, he commented, wincing at the blows still slamming into the panel behind them. *They do seem a mite perturbed, though.*

As well they should, Draycos agreed. *Three Death weapons down. Only one to go.*

Jack grimaced. *Actually, it's probably more like two to go,* he said reluctantly. *Now that they're on to us, they're going to take a hard look at the one I gimmicked.*

Will they be able to fix it?

Theoretically, yes, Jack said. *Unless they're complete idiots, they'll certainly spot the first booby trap I set. The only question is whether they'll be happy with that, or whether they'll delve deeper and find the other one, too. I'm sorry—I should have tried to do more.*

You had limited time and opportunity, Draycos reminded him calmly. *If you'd taken too long, either the Brummgas with us or the watchers in the monitor room might have become suspicious. That would have ended the subtle approach right there.*

I suppose, Jack conceded. *I was still hoping I could do something more permanent to it.*

Things don't always work out as we hope, Draycos said. *That's the way with many endeavors, and warfare is no different. The warrior must always be ready to adapt to the unexpected.* The K'da paused, and Jack could almost see one of his open-jawed grins. *Wasn't that also true in your previous profession?*

Jack had to smile. *Believe it, buddy,* he agreed. *I can't even count how many times Uncle Virgil had to scramble like crazy to fix some plan that was about to go gunnybags on us.*

Then this is merely standard procedure for both of us, Draycos said. *Very well then. Two Death weapons to go. We'll leave yours for last, since there's a chance they won't find the damage—*

Hold it, Jack interrupted, frowning. Was that a light he was seeing in the distance ahead? *Close your eyes a second, will you?*

Obediently, Draycos shut his eyes, cutting off their green glow. It was a light, all right, Jack decided as he peered down the tween gap. Had the Brummgas found one of the other entrances?

A second later, he got his answer. With a thunderous roar that was even louder than usual in the confined space, someone ahead opened fire.

Draycos was off Jack's skin in an instant, grabbing the boy's arm and pulling him straight down. Jack landed on his chest on the meshwork floor, the impact knocking half the breath out of him. Another second, and he was slammed again as Draycos landed full length on top of him. "Draycos—!" he gasped with what air he had left in his lungs.

"Stay down!" the K'da shouted in his ear, the words barely audible over the gunfire. "Ricochets!"

Jack tensed. With the sound of the firing hammering his ears, he hadn't even heard the quieter impacts of the bullets themselves as they bounced their way between the walls of the tween gap.

A second gun joined the first, this one somewhere behind and above him. "Do we have a plan?" Jack called.

There was no answer, only a strange squirming of Draycos's body on top of his. The K'da's weight was still pressing him against the mesh, making breathing difficult.

A third gun opened up ahead and above him. Then a fourth added its roar to the din, and possibly a fifth. Jack pressed his cheek against the mesh, waiting helplessly for the bullet that he knew was bound to find him.

And then the mesh suddenly gave way beneath him, dumping him sideways toward the deep chasm below.

He yelped with surprise and a flash of panic. But even before the yelp made it out past his lips his fall was stopped short. There was another second of confusion and dizziness.

Then his brain cleared, and he understood. Draycos had cut the mesh floor beneath them on only three sides, and their combined weight had then bent it down like an opening trapdoor. Draycos, all four sets of claws gripping the mesh, was holding them sideways against the open flap. "We must get away from here," Draycos said in Jack's ear.

"I'm with you, buddy," Jack said. "How?"

In answer, Draycos stretched out his top two limbs a few inches, easing the pressure on Jack's body. Jack tensed again, but with the K'da's lower legs still hooked to the mesh flap he was in no danger of falling. "Roll over so that you're facing me," Draycos said.

It was tricky to maneuver in the cramped space and with the small amount of slack Draycos had given him. But the guns still thundering all around them made for good inspiration. Jack got himself turned around in Olympic-record time. "Now hold on tightly," Draycos said.

Jack wrapped his arms and legs around the other's torso. Draycos let go with his front paws, lunging forward and grabbing the underside of the mesh just in front of their hanging flap. He walked the paws forward, working his rear paws onto the mesh behind them.

And with that the K'da headed off, moving rapidly along the underside of the mesh.

With the long tween gap yawning under him, the booming gunfire rattling the metal above him, and the violent jostling as Draycos clawed his upside-down way beneath the mesh, all Jack could do was shut his eyes, wish he could shut his ears, and hold on for dear life. The bouncing went on and on. . . .

Abruptly, Draycos stopped. "Hold tighter," he ordered over the noise of the gunfire.

Jack nodded and got a fresh grip on the K'da's torso, pressing the side of his head against the other's scale-covered neck. Draycos let go of the mesh with his rear claws, and once again Jack's stomach churned with the brief sensation of falling. For another second the K'da continued to hang on to the mesh only with his front claws. Then Jack felt the rear paws find a grip, and a moment later he found himself again squeezed between Draycos and cold metal as the K'da climbed rapidly down another of the vertical mesh sections.

The gunfire above them was starting to slow down by the time they reached bottom. Bottom, in this case, was another mesh walkway. For a few seconds Draycos peered into the darkness, as if figuring out exactly where they were. Then, touching Jack's hand, he slid up his sleeve. *Straight ahead about fifty feet,* he said. *There should be another entrance panel on your right.*

Got it. Jack set off, his knees feeling a little wobbly.

The gunfire continued to slow down, and by the time they reached the panel it had stopped entirely. *Be careful as you open it,* Draycos warned. *They're undoubtedly listening now from above, hoping to hear what we might be doing.*

In that case, let's just hang here a minute, Jack suggested. *Sooner or later, they're bound to start making noise again.*

Draycos seemed to think about that, and Jack could sense his uneasiness with the situation. They were still very much exposed out here, and his warrior's instincts were probably screaming at him to get them under better cover. *Trust me,* Jack said.

Very well, Draycos said reluctantly. *But if I hear anyone approaching—*

He broke off as a soft metallic thud came from somewhere above and forward of their position. *Sounds like one of the mercenaries is coming in to look for our bullet-riddled bodies,* Jack said, getting a grip on the panel's handles. *That's our cue.*

He paused, his hands still on the handles, listening hard. Through the mesh he could now see the faint glow of a flashlight peeking through the mesh far above them. The footsteps started up, paused, then started up again, settling into a rhythm.

And with perfect timing, Jack popped the panel exactly as one of the footsteps sent its covering echo through the tween gap.

A minute later, they were through the doorway. Jack got a grip on the edge of the panel and pulled it back into place, again timing the event to coincide with the distant traveler's footsteps. *Okay,* he said, taking a deep breath. *I think we're in.*

I believe you're right, Draycos agreed. *Well done, Jack.*

Years of practice, Jack assured him. *With some of the crazy jobs Uncle Virgil had me pull, I had to raise running and hiding to a fine art.*

He looked around. The room they were in was long and narrow, with a ten-foot-tall, box-shaped cabinet on each of the fore and aft bulkheads. Control displays on each winked with colored status lights. Connecting the cabinets to the walls and ceiling were more stripe/spot-marked pipes. *Another fire control room?* he hazarded.

No, this is one of the ship's water-reclamation plants, Draycos said.

Really, Jack said, looking at the cabinets with new interest. *The crew drinks the stuff that comes out of these, do they?*

From these and nine other plants throughout the ship, Draycos said. *Why?*

Because there are two ways to keep a gun from going off, Jack said. *Wreck the gun, or stop the person from pulling the trigger.*

Are you suggesting we poison *them? The entire crew?*

We don't have to kill them, Jack said hastily. There had been an unpleasant tone in the K'da's mental voice just then. *I was think-ing we could find a way to knock them out. Or else make them so sick they can't function.*

Draycos was silent a moment. *We would need to sabotage all ten of the purifiers,* he pointed out. And *we would have to do all ten si-multaneously. Otherwise, once people started getting sick they'd realize something was wrong and guard the rest of the purifiers.*

True, Jack said. *We'd also have to find something that would affect humans, Brummgas, and Valahgua.*

And we'd need to deal with the emergency bottled water, as well, Draycos continued. *Those supplies are, unfortunately, scattered through-out the ship.*

Which means we'd have to hit them hard and fast, Jack said slowly, trying to think. Uncle Virgil had taught him a fair amount about incapacitating drugs and chemicals. Surely he could come up with something he could make up from stuff already aboard ship.

The big question was whether he could do it in time.

In time? Draycos asked.

We've got less than six days until we hit Point Three, remember? Jack said. *At that point, the Brummgas scream for help and Frost throws everything he's got at us.*

What if we destroy the radios? Draycos suggested. *That might at least buy us another few hours.*

Not worth the risks, Jack said. *Besides, even if we could take out all the actual radios, anyone with a comm clip will be able to punch a mes-sage across the kind of distance we're talking about.*

He grimaced. *Besides, whatever was going on with the* Essenay *just before we went on ECHO, there's a good chance Neverlin and Frost already know we're here. They'll be over as soon as we all come off ECHO.*

For a moment Draycos was silent. Jack tried to catch some of the K'da's thoughts, but they flashed by too subtly and too quickly. *Then we'll just have to make do with the time we have,* he said.

Right, Jack agreed. *Are there any other secret ways of getting around this ship besides the tween gap?*

There are the ventilation ducts, Draycos reminded him.

I meant for me, Jack said. *Unfortunately, my body doesn't compress nearly as well as yours and Taneem's do.* He shook his head. *I still can't believe she was able to get around the* Advocatus Diaboli *that way. What in the world did its designers think they were doing, making ducts that big?*

Actually, oversized ducts are a fairly standard large-ship design, according to the technical material I read in the Essenay's *encyclopedia,* Draycos said. *If there's a hull breach, you want to be able to deliver massive quantities of air to the affected area, thereby giving anyone trapped there a chance to escape or put on an emergency vac suit. A ship the size of the* Advocatus Diaboli *usually has plenty of air reserves available for such a purpose.*

He flicked his tail against Jack's leg. *I'm surprised Virgil Morgan never taught you about that.*

I'm not, Jack said sourly. *Uncle Virgil was strictly about practical stuff, and I outgrew ventilation ducts when I hit seven.*

Of course, Draycos said. *My apologies for bringing up an unpleasant subject.*

Don't worry about it, Jack assured him, shifting his thoughts firmly away from childhood memories. *Okay, we've got six days. Let's start by taking an inventory of what we've got to work with.*

CHAPTER 17

For Alison, the next six days went by smoothly and quietly. As near as she could tell, the time had gone equally smoothly for everyone else aboard the *Advocatus Diaboli*.

Neverlin and Frost met several times, discussing the final details of their plan. Sneaking through the vents, Taneem had managed to get close enough to eavesdrop on one of those talks.

But the two men had kept their voices too low for Alison to pick up more than a few words over Taneem's comm clip. Taneem had tried to repeat some of it to her later, but the conversation had been filled with technical terms that she didn't know and were therefore hard for her to remember.

It was frustrating, but there was nothing Alison could do about it. There were many unanswered questions about the details of Frost's plan, details that could prove critical in the days ahead.

As for Harper, he seemed to be spending most of his time in his stateroom, emerging only for meals or an occasional brief chat with Frost or one of the other Malison Ring mercenaries. Harper did walk around the ship at least once, but as far as Taneem could tell he never approached any of the vital control areas and never left the sight of one of the crew or passengers.

Like Neverlin, Harper seemed perfectly relaxed about the upcoming battle. But maybe that was just the man's personality.

Still, as the hours ticked down toward their arrival at Point Three, even Harper seemed to be picking up some of the tension beginning to pervade the rest of the ship.

Not only the ship but Alison herself. Very soon now she would learn if Jack and Draycos were really aboard the *Foxwolf*. And if they were, how much damage they had caused.

And at that point, she would have a decision to make.

She didn't want to confront Neverlin and Frost this soon. Not with the K'da/Shontine fleet still several days away.

But if and when Frost took over the job of finding and killing Jack and Draycos, she would have no choice.

The hours became minutes, the voices on the bridge softening as the tension and expectation grew. Taneem lay quietly in the duct, watching Neverlin and Frost and the Valahgua leader through the mesh and reporting as much of the situation as she could to Alison.

Which left Alison absolutely nothing to do except listen to Taneem's whispers, pace restlessly back and forth across the lifepod, and pray that Jack and Draycos had come up with some plan of their own.

And to pray even harder that they were both still alive.

The access crawl space beneath the *Foxwolf*'s main control complex, Jack reflected, was well named.

In his opinion, though, the creatures the ship's designers had expected to be crawling around in here were mice.

Okay, he said, rolling carefully onto his back and shining his light upward. Barely a foot directly above his head was a wide hole in the crawl space ceiling with an orderly tangle of wires and cables of various sizes coming out of it. In ones and twos the cables angled away from the hole, heading off in all directions toward the edges of the crawl space. To his right and left, he could see similar explosions of cables coming from other openings in the low ceiling. *Is this the right one?*

Draycos's head lifted slightly from his shoulder, peering at the markings by the hole. *Yes,* he said, sinking back down onto Jack's skin. *Do you need me to identify the wires for you?*

No, I got it, Jack assured him. A set of soft footsteps angled across Jack's ceiling to his left, reminding him—if he'd needed reminding—that the control complex directly above him was full of bad guys.

With a thick deck between them and him, they weren't likely to hear any noise he might make. Just the same, he was careful not to clink his flashlight as he set it down onto the deck beside his ear.

Reaching into his pockets, he removed his multitool and the cable-and-switch setup he'd put together. Studying the various stripe/spot patterns on the cables above him, he located the ones Draycos had described and set to work.

Jack had been highly trained in the art of bypassing security locks, alarms, and other complex electronics. This job, in comparison, was about as tricky as a walk in the park.

His first task was to connect three of the hyperspace control lines together, being careful not to trigger any flickers the computer might notice. Then he wired in one of the two high-voltage power lines that ran the console's display monitors, running that particular splice through the switch on his cable.

And he was done. *That's it,* he told Draycos. *I flip the switch, and the hyperdrive controls fry. That ought to hold their attention awhile.*

Let's hope it's long enough, Draycos said. Moving carefully in the cramped space, he slid out of Jack's sleeve. "I'll signal you when I'm in position," he murmured.

"Watch yourself," Jack warned.

The K'da flicked his tail in acknowledgment as he set off across the crawl space.

Jack watched him go, feeling a frustration that was edging toward despair. Every plan the boy had come up with over the past six days, every scheme he'd hoped to pull, had fallen apart in his hands.

His plan to drug the ship's water supply had come to nothing. There simply weren't enough of the proper chemicals aboard.

His backup plan, to fire a surge through the Death weapons' power lines, had merely ended up popping circuit breakers and getting them chased away again. The Valahgua had responded to that one by taking a bunch of their security cameras from other areas and installing them in the tween gap. By the time the Valahgua finished, all approaches to the two Death weapons were covered.

Draycos's plans hadn't fared much better. He'd tried using the ventilation ducts to approach the weapons, only to discover the Valahgua had tripled the guard. Many of the Brummgas were stationed outside in the corridors, and Draycos had concluded that a surprise attack from the duct would almost certainly succeed.

But with the tween gap now virtually closed to him and Jack, the ventilation system was their only means of traveling invisibly through the ship. With cameras still mounted in the weapons rooms, any attack from the ducts would give that secret away, leaving them nothing. Jack and Draycos had discussed the situation, and decided not to risk that until and unless they were desperate.

Now, with less than an hour before the *Foxwolf* reached Point Three, they were.

And so Draycos was going to go and try to take out the starboard Death, the one they knew was still operational.

Leaving the one Jack had tried to gimmick when they'd first come aboard. Which, by now, Jack knew, was probably also back to being operational.

He took a careful breath, trying to focus on the positive points. The Valahgua had had four Death weapons to use against the K'da and Shontine refugees. In a few minutes they would have only one. Surely that counted for something.

"Jack?" Draycos's voice came softly from Jack's comm clip. "I'm in the duct. Ten minutes and I should be there."

"Right," Jack said. "Just let me know when you're ready for me to turn their hyperdrive console into toast."

"I will." Draycos paused, and Jack could imagine his jaws cracking open in a grin. "Butter side down, of course."

Despite his gloom, Jack had to smile. "Butter side down," he confirmed.

"And then get out as quickly as you can," Draycos added, going serious again. "I'll meet you back in the recycling room."

"Sure," Jack murmured, his smile fading. *Toast, butter side down,* had been one of Uncle Virgil's favorite catchphrases.

Uncle Virgil. Virgil Morgan, professional thief, con man, and safecracker. Who had somehow ended up in possession of both Jack and the *Essenay* after Jack's parents were murdered eleven years ago.

How in the world had that happened?

Jack didn't know. It was possible he would never know. Uncle

Virge, the copy of his personality that Uncle Virgil had planted in the *Essenay's* computer, claimed he had no information about that part of Jack's life.

But Uncle Virge was in control of the *Essenay.* And despite Jack's instructions, the *Essenay* had apparently followed him to Point Two and rendezvoused with Neverlin's *Advocatus Diaboli.*

Neverlin, whose attempted frame-up of Jack for theft and murder had gotten him into this whole thing in the first place. Neverlin, who Jack had only recently discovered had been directly involved with the murder of Jack's parents.

Coincidence? Jack didn't know that, either.

He swallowed against a lump that had suddenly appeared in his throat. It was possible Uncle Virge had betrayed him. Maybe Alison had betrayed him, too. Certainly she wasn't someone he could completely trust.

But he had Draycos.

He could only hope that he could still say that fifteen minutes from now.

As part of their overall plan for the *Gatekeeper's* air ducts to double as back-door access routes, the ship's designers had made sure that the ventilation grilles would be difficult to see through from inside the rooms. Draycos was therefore able to move silently and invisibly toward his goal.

To his surprise, the invisibility part proved less important than he'd expected it to. At first there were plenty of Brummgas striding through corridors or lounging about the various rooms he passed. But as he approached the Number Four weapons bay, that number became less and less. The last three rooms he passed, in fact, were completely deserted.

Something was wrong.

He took the last stretch of duct at a careful crawl, his tongue flicking out as he went, trying to analyze the scents of Brummga and human and Valahgua drifting on the air around him.

And it was no doubt because he was taking such care that he spotted the small object sitting just inside the weapons bay's auxiliary control room grille.

He froze in place ten feet away, peering hard at the object. It looked like a tube or perhaps a section of thick cable, about six inches long and one inch in diameter. It was too wide to have gotten through the small holes in the grille, which meant someone must have opened the grille in order to put it there.

He flicked out his tongue again. This close to the grille, he should be able to pick out the specific scents coming from that room. There was one human in there, he decided, plus four or five Brummgas. No Valahgua.

He frowned, his tail arching with sudden suspicion. Only a handful of defenders for one of the precious remaining Death weapons?

Not a chance. Especially since his earlier checks had showed guard contingents three times that size. Could the rest of them be spread out in the corridor, where they would have a better field of fire?

Backing up, he slipped into the duct that paralleled the corridor outside the room. He flicked his tongue at the nearest grille, looking for the scent of nervous Brummgas.

But it wasn't there. The corridor was deserted, or nearly so.

Something was definitely wrong.

He returned to the room's duct again and took a cautious pair of steps toward the object lying inside the grille. From here he could see that it was vibrating slightly with the air flowing across it. Something light, then. Something light that had been rolled up into a cylindrical shape?

A piece of paper?

Carefully, he continued forward. It was a rolled-up piece of paper, all right, which had partially unrolled to its current diameter. Picking it up, he looked cautiously through the grille into the room beyond.

The room had changed since his quiet reconnaissance two nights ago. As he'd already surmised, the crowd of guards that had lined the bulkheads was gone. Instead, the walls were lined with a double bank of video monitors. It was hard to tell at his distance, but they seemed to be carrying the feeds from various security cameras. One group of monitors, he saw, showed images from the tween gap area.

As he'd also surmised, there were only five Brummgas in the room. Three of them were standing around the control end of the Death weapon, their backs to Draycos behind his grille. Two more were standing watchful guard by the door, with the grille at the edge of their peripheral vision.

Standing two paces behind the three at the controls, the stiffness of his back betraying his tension, was Wing Sergeant Langston.

Draycos eyed the group, his warrior's instincts tingling. Five Brummgas out of over three hundred, and a human whom they clearly didn't trust. Bait, if he'd ever seen it.

Which meant that this whole thing was a trap.

Taking one last look through the grille, Draycos picked up the rolled-up paper and retreated quietly along the duct.

He found a hidden spot away from any of the grilles, one where he had three different escape routes available to him. Crouching down, he unrolled the paper.

It was a note, as he'd expected, written in small but precise letters. Leaning close to give it all the light from his eyes that he could, he began to read.

Draycos:

I hope you get this message. I don't have much real information for you—they still don't completely trust me—but rumor is that the Valahgua are expecting you and Jack to try to hit the last two Death weapons before we reach Point Three.

They've now got cameras inside all the hull-gap access doors near both weapons bays to watch for your arrival. The ventilation system seems untouched so far—I don't think they realize you'll fit in there. I'm hoping that's the approach you'll use, since I can't get this note into any of the hull-gap doors without making a lot of noise.

Draycos nodded grimly to himself. Nothing really new, except that Langston had figured out the designers' system of back doors.

Unfortunately, as soon as he hit this particular Death weapon, the Valahgua would know about it, too. That would leave him only the equipment crawl spaces, which covered limited areas of the ship, and didn't reach the weapons bays at all.

They also fixed the Death weapon that you and Jack sabotaged. Not the two you shredded—they were furious about that, by the way—but the first one you hit, in the port-side weapons bay.

Again, nothing new there. The heavy guard on the other Death weapon alone had pretty well proved it had been fixed.

On the other hand, just because the Valahgua thought they'd fixed it didn't necessarily mean that they had. If they'd missed Jack's secondary sabotage, the weapon could still blow up in their faces when they tried to fire it. He could hope, anyway.

Speaking of that port-side weapon, rumor is that the Valahgua moved it sometime during ship's night. I don't know where.

Draycos frowned. They'd *moved* it? But it was already in as secure and inaccessible a place as the *Gatekeeper* had to offer.

And then, suddenly, he understood.

Langston and a handful of Brummgas, alone in a critical part of the ship. Bait for a trap, Draycos had already suspected.

Now he knew what the trap was.

"Jack, we're in trouble," he said quietly into the comm clip. "The Valahgua have moved the other Death weapon to cover this one.

"The minute I come into the open, they're going to kill me."

CHAPTER 18

For a few seconds Jack lay motionless in the crawl space, staring at the low ceiling above his head as he silently berated his carelessness. He'd gotten so used to dealing with Brummgas and their slow and unimaginative brains that he'd forgotten there were also humans and Valahgua in the mix.

Apparently, one of them had come up with something clever. "Jack?"

"Yes, I'm here," Jack said, kicking his brain into gear. "Start at the beginning."

He listened as Draycos read Langston's note and then gave his own observations and conclusions. "They're learning, anyway," Jack said when the K'da had finished. "Okay, let's think this through. First of all, I don't suppose you have any idea where they might have put the second Death, do you?"

"Jack, it could be literally anywhere aboard the ship," Draycos said heavily. "As I've told you, its beam can penetrate any number of decks and bulkheads."

"Right, but it'll also kill everyone in its path," Jack said. "I presume the Lordover won't want to sacrifice any more of his allies than he has to."

"Probably, but that's not much help," Draycos said. "He can easily move all the Brummgas and humans out of the line of fire."

"Except for those they *can't* move," Jack said. "What kinds of duty stations are there around the starboard weapons bay? Anything that absolutely *has* to be manned? Especially now, as we're about to come off ECHO?"

"There's nothing forward of the main control complex," Draycos said. "All the duty station functions in the bow can be handled from somewhere else. That leaves over a quarter of the ship as possibilities."

"Okay, then, how about power supplies?" Jack suggested. "You hinted earlier that the things had originally been set up in the weapons bays because they needed more power than your average crew mess or monitor station could deliver."

"True, and that *does* limit their choices somewhat," Draycos said, a cautious hope starting to filter into his voice. "But I'd need to either visit each room or else find a monitor station in order to find out which one they're using."

"Where's the nearest power monitor?" Jack asked, focusing on the ceiling over his head. "Better yet, can I tap into the one here in the control complex?"

"Theoretically, yes," Draycos said. "But you'd need a portable monitor, which we don't have. Other than that, the only centralized monitors would be in auxiliary control, just forward of the engine control complex."

Jack grimaced. The engine complex was way back in the aft section of the ship. "No good," he said. "It'd take you as long to get back there as it would to scope out all the possible rooms in the first place."

"Or at least nearly as long," Draycos conceded. "Perhaps we need to abandon the idea of attacking these weapons before we reach Point Three."

"No," Jack said firmly. "The minute we come off ECHO

we're going to have Frost breathing down our necks. If he doesn't catch us, he's sure going to pin us down. If we're going to take out this thing, we need to do it now."

"In that case, I'd best get started checking rooms," Draycos said. "If I find it quickly enough, I should at least be able to guarantee that that one's out of action."

"Assuming that isn't where they've shifted all the Brummgas that used to be guarding this other—" Jack broke off, his breath catching in his throat.

"Jack?"

"It's okay, buddy," Jack said, his brain suddenly racing. "I just had a sudden revelation. Did you actually see the Death weapon in the weapons bay?"

"Yes, of course."

"What direction was it pointing?"

There was a short pause. "It was pointing a hundred and ten degrees port side from the bow," the K'da said slowly. "Just aft of straight across. Odd. They've always been pointed forward, or a few degrees outward from forward."

"All aimed and primed and ready for their upcoming attack, in other words," Jack agreed. "Now, suddenly, they've got one pointed back inward toward the middle of their own ship."

"It's pointed at the other Death weapon," Draycos said, his voice suddenly charged with energy. "They're protecting *each other.*"

"Like a pair of chess knights in mutual guard positions," Jack said. "Now, knowing *that,* can you tell where the other one's been stashed?"

"Knowing that, there are only two possibilities," Draycos said slowly. "The forward machine shop, or the port-side power substation."

"Are both of them close enough?" Jack asked. "Back on Rho Scorvi, you said something about atmosphere limiting the Death's range."

"It's not the atmosphere itself but the density of life within it," Draycos corrected. "As the Death kills, some of its energy is absorbed by the life it's destroying. The atmosphere of a typical planet is full of microorganisms, spores, insects, and other life."

"And we were in a forest at the time," Jack said. "Probably one of your higher-density locations."

"Correct," Draycos said. "Also, the nearness of a planetary mass affects the Death in a way that the artificial gravity of a ship does not. As a result, on a planet the Death has a much smaller range."

"But none of that applies here."

"Correct," Draycos said. "Here the Death will have no problem cutting completely through the ship. However, in a choice between the machine shop and the substation, I would vote for the latter. It has more power available."

"Let's try that one first, then," Jack said. "How long will it take you to get there?"

"At least ten minutes," Draycos said. "The route isn't very straight."

Jack chewed at his lower lip. The idea that was taking shape in the back of his mind was straightforward but tricky.

It was also dangerous. And not just for him and Draycos.

"Shall I get started?" Draycos prompted.

"Better idea," Jack said. "See if Langston can give you a lift."

"You *are* joking, right?"

"Not at all," Jack said. "If you can get onto his skin without any of the Brummgas in there noticing, he can stroll down the corridor faster and easier than you can travel through the ducts."

"The ducts would be safer."

"Not necessarily." Jack hesitated. "Besides, we owe it to him to let him know what's coming."

There was another short silence. "Is there something coming that I don't know about?" Draycos asked.

"I think there is, yes," Jack hedged. "Let me think it through a little more. Meanwhile you go see if you think it's possible to get to Langston."

"Very well," Draycos said. "I'll speak to you again when I can." The comm clip went silent.

For another moment Jack lay where he was, gazing at the floor above him. Then, rolling over, he started crawling toward the next nearest group of wires and cables.

This was going to take more of a diversion than he'd originally thought.

The Brummgas hadn't moved from the positions where Draycos had left them a few minutes earlier. Langston, in contrast, had abandoned his place behind the Death weapon and was moving slowly around the room, gazing at each of the security camera monitors as he passed them.

His path, Draycos saw, would bring him directly beneath the ventilation grille. Keeping an eye on the Brummgas, Draycos got ready.

And as Langston passed beneath the grille, Draycos extended a claw and gave the edge of the grille three quiet scratches.

Langston paused, his head cocked. Draycos repeated the scratching. Langston half-turned to look at the Brummgas standing by the door, then turned back, leaning toward whatever equipment was directly beneath the grille as if he were studying it. "Hello?" he murmured, just loud enough for Draycos to hear over the quiet hum of the equipment.

"I'm here," Draycos murmured back, watching the guards closely. There was no reaction there that he could see. "I need to find the other Death weapon."

"I heard someone say they'd moved it to the conference room off the main control complex," Langston offered, pretending to make an adjustment.

"No, it's somewhere nearby," Draycos told him. "The Valahgua expect me to attack this weapon. When I do, they plan to use the other one to kill me."

Langston stiffened. "I see," he muttered. "I wondered why I'd been trusted with this job." He took a deep breath. "Okay. What do you need?"

"Jack has a plan," Draycos said, hoping it was true. "But I need to locate the weapon. I think I know where it is, but it'll be faster if you can carry me part of the way."

"Okay," Langston said. "You ready?"

"One moment." Pulling the comm clip off his ear, Draycos set it beside the grille. It would have been nice to be able to take it with him, but there was no way for a K'da to carry anything while in two-dimensional form. Another thought occurred to him, and he set the clip on mute so that Jack could still hear but not transmit. "Ready."

Langston turned toward the two Brummgas standing guard by the door. "Hey—Vimpru," he called. "How'd you like to hop over to the mess and get me a drink?"

All five Brummgas in the room turned to face him, identical expressions of disbelief and contempt on their faces. The two at the door looked at each other, then deliberately turned their faces away from him. The three at the Death's controls gazed at him a moment longer, then did likewise.

Smiling tightly, Langston lifted his hand and poked a finger through the grille. Draycos touched it and slid up the man's sleeve onto his arm.

Draycos felt a shiver run through Langston's skin as he settled himself across the other's back, legs, and arms. "Whoa," Langston murmured. "That's . . . interesting. Out of sight, now."

Turning on his heel, he headed for the door. "Fine—I'll get it myself," he said as he passed between the two guards. "Lieutenant Pickering won't be happy to hear you weren't being helpful."

Neither Brummga bothered to answer. Keying the door, Langston exited the room.

The corridor outside was very quiet. "I see they've moved everyone else out of the line of fire," Langston commented. "Which way?"

"To the right," Draycos said, flicking out his tongue. There was nothing nearby but Langston's own scent and that of distant Brummgas. "We're heading toward the forward power substation on the port side."

"Got it."

Langston started down the corridor, his footsteps sounding unnaturally loud in the quiet. Easing his head along the other's chest, Draycos peered out through his collar.

This wasn't one of the main cross-ship corridors that cut a nice straight path between starboard and port-side hulls. This was instead one of those that meandered all over the place, angling and teeing every thirty feet or so as it worked its way around the more oddly shaped rooms at the ship's bow.

"It's forward to that T-junction, left, right, and left again, correct?" Langston asked.

"Yes, but I can't let you go that far," Draycos told him. "You told the Brummgas you were going for a drink. Just take me to the nearest mess room and I'll be gone."

Langston continued on in silence another few steps. "I think I can do a little better than that," he said. "What's Jack's plan?"

"I don't know yet," Draycos admitted. "I'll need to get back in the ducts before I can find out."

"*He's* in the ducts, too?"

"No, but my comm clip is," Draycos said. "I can't carry anything in two-dimensional form."

"No problem." Langston dug something out of his side pocket and pressed it against the base of his throat. "Here."

Draycos lifted his head slightly and focused on it. "Your comm clip?" he asked, frowning.

"A spare, actually," Langston said. "You can reset it to your private frequency and pattern specs and call Jack without having to go back into the ducts."

"Excellent," Draycos said. "Thank you." Lifting his front paws from Langston's chest, he took the comm clip and started adjusting its settings.

He was still working at it when Langston took a sharp turn to the right, keyed open a door, and went inside a room.

A room with the well-remembered aroma of permanent disinfectant. "A *relief station*?" Draycos asked.

"Why not?" Langston countered. "Low ceilings, no cameras, and as much privacy as we're going to get. *And* we're only three rooms away from your power substation."

"You're also way too far from your station here," Draycos

warned. "There are two other relief stations closer to the starboard weapons bays."

"Both of which have been fitted with Brummga-sized equipment," Langston countered. "No, we token humans usually use one of the three that were left the way you and your Shontine friends originally had them. Perfectly normal behavior for me to be here. You ready with that yet?"

"Just finished." Draycos keyed on the comm clip. "Jack?"

"Here," Jack's voice came. "You find it?"

"Not yet," Draycos said. "But we're near the substation, and I can get into the ducts from here."

"Keep your voice down, will you?" Jack warned. "I can hear Brummgas in the background."

"That's coming from the comm clip I left by the weapons bay grille," Draycos assured him. "I'm using Sergeant Langston's spare comm clip."

"Oh," Jack said, sounding a bit taken aback. "Okay."

"Should I have hidden the other comm clip better?" Draycos asked. "It *is* muted, so they can't listen in."

"No, that's okay," Jack said. "Actually . . . yes, actually, that could turn out to be useful."

"I gather you have a plan?" Langston asked.

"Yes, I think so," Jack said. "How are you doing, Langston?"

"They don't trust me, but they're being good enough to give me plenty of rope with which to hang myself," Langston said.

"Sounds like Neverlin's style," Jack said. "How game are you to wrap some of that rope around your neck?"

"I'll do whatever's necessary," Langston said, his voice calm but deadly serious. "I'm a warrior." He looked sideways down at Draycos's face pressed against his shoulder. "Draycos understands."

"I think I'm starting to, too," Jack said. "Okay, here's the scheme."

Quickly, concisely, he laid it out for them. "Going to take some careful timing," Langston commented when he'd finished.

"Yes, but with three comm clips I think we can pull it off," Jack said. "*My* biggest question is for Draycos."

"Don't worry about me," Draycos told him, ignoring the creeping feeling shivering across his scales. No, he certainly didn't want to do this. Not this way.

But he could see no other way to do what had to be done. "As Sergeant Langston said, we're warriors. We do whatever is necessary."

"You also do what's right," Jack reminded him. "Is this going to conflict with that?"

"I do not kill without need," Draycos said. "Not even enemies. But this is a war of survival. I'll do whatever is necessary."

"Especially given what's at stake," Langston murmured.

"Yes," Draycos said. "Let's get on with it."

"Okay, then," Jack said. There was still some lingering doubt in the boy's voice, but he clearly knew better than to press the issue. "Get into the ducts and confirm the other Death is actually there. Langston, you get back to your station. Don't forget to pick up a drink on the way—that was your excuse for leaving, remember."

"Right," Langston said. "You need a hand, Draycos?"

"No, thank you." Draycos leaped out of Langston's collar, landing on one of the relief station's dividers. Balancing there, he got a claw under the corner of the ventilation grille and popped the hidden catch. "Ready."

"Good luck," Langston said, holding out his hand.

Reaching down, Draycos touched the outstretched hand

with his paw. "And to you," he said. Turning, he swung the grille open and crawled inside.

I'll do whatever is necessary, the words echoed through his mind as he started toward the power substation. *Whatever is necessary.*

CHAPTER 19

Two minutes later, as Jack finished setting up his additional sabotage, the word came through.

"It's here," Draycos's voice murmured from his comm clip. "Eight guards on duty, all Brummgas, with another bank of video displays showing the approaches and the other weapon's room."

"Any humans or Valahgua in sight?" Jack asked.

"Neither here nor in the corridor," Draycos confirmed. "And the weapon is definitely pointed at the other one."

Jack smiled grimly. He'd called it, all right. Langston's Death weapon was the bait, and this one was the hunter.

Only the Valahgua had been smart enough to hedge their bets in the other direction. If Draycos went for the more obvious bait, fine. But if he somehow sniffed out the location of this one, the result would be the same. The minute he appeared at either end of the shooting gallery, the other end would open fire.

No doubt the Valahgua had given clear and explicit instructions to the Brummgas manning the weapons. Though they'd possibly neglected to mention the fact that each group was in the other's sights.

But plans and instructions had a bad tendency to change in midstream. The Valahgua, clearly uninterested in risking their own precious skins, had pulled back to a cautious distance and left the front lines to the Brummgas.

That mistake was going to cost them.

"Okay," Jack said, working his way back to his original spot and the power line switch he'd wired into—now—three different consoles. "Touch-off in fifteen seconds, with diversion kicking in probably three minutes later. Listen for the signal, and don't go to sleep on me."

"Don't worry," Draycos said dryly. "And be careful."

"You, too."

Jack checked his pockets, making sure he had the two wire-wrapped bottles he'd managed to rig in the past few minutes. There was nothing but water in them, but the Valahgua leaning over their monitors wouldn't know that. Then, opening his flight suit collar to midchest level, he crossed his fingers and flipped his switch.

It was reasonably spectacular, as such things went. There was a multiple flash of muted sparks from the various sets of rigged wires, though most of the action was taking place up inside the consoles where he couldn't get much of a view. There was a soft hiss from one of the consoles, accompanied by the acrid stink of burned insulation and electronics.

And above him, dimly heard through the thick deck, the control complex erupted in chaos.

Thirty seconds later he was at the far end of the crawl space. With multiple footsteps now thudding back and forth over his head, he pushed open an access panel and climbed through into the midaft expansion conduit.

Two minutes after that, he had made it back into the starboard tween gap. "Here we go," he murmured toward his comm clip as he closed the panel behind him. "Look sharp."

Turning on his light, he headed forward at a dead run. Fifty yards ahead, Langston and his team of Brummgas were waiting expectantly around their Death weapon. Between Jack and them were the spy cameras the Valahgua had planted inside the tween gap one room over from them.

One room over from the waiting Death weapon. Distantly, Jack wondered whether anyone would be watching the camera monitors.

Draycos's count had just reached three minutes when the Brummgas in the room beneath him reacted. "There!" one grunted, pointing toward the bank of displays. "The boy!"

One of the others slammed a massive hand across the room's intercom switch. "Control; Mrishpaw," he called. "The boy is in the hull-gap near the starboard weapons bays."

There was no reply. Draycos peered through the grate as Jack's image hurried up to the camera. His foot loomed suddenly huge—

Abruptly, the image gave a wild twist and went black. The other monitor's image lasted perhaps half a second longer; then it, too, gyrated and went black.

"Control, the boy has destroyed the starboard cameras," Mrishpaw reported urgently. "Instructions?"

The intercom remained silent. But through the comm clip attached to his ear Draycos now heard a second call. "Control; Langston," Langston's voice came faintly from the comm clip hidden in the ventilation duct. "Morgan's in the hull-gap—starboard side near the weapons bays—and he's wrecked the cameras. Repeat: we've lost him."

Below Draycos, the two Brummgas at the Death's controls looked uncertainly at each other. Apparently, their instructions hadn't included this possibility. "Control; Mrishpaw," Mrishpaw tried again. "The boy is somewhere in the hull-gap, perhaps still near the starboard weapons bays. Instructions?"

"Control," a dark voice came over the speaker. "Was the K'da with him?"

Draycos felt a shiver of anger and disgust ripple through his scales. *That* was a voice and a tone he knew all too well.

Whatever damage Jack's sabotage had inflicted on the control complex, at least one of the Valahgua was still on top of the situation.

"I could not see him," Mrishpaw said, a note of relief in his voice. Finally, someone was there to tell him what to do.

"Instructions?" one of the Brummgas at the Death's controls called.

For a few seconds the speaker was silent. Draycos felt his claws sliding restlessly in and out of their sheaths as he watched the Brummgas fidgeting below him. If Jack's attack on the control complex had made the Valahgua too nervous, they might take the cautious way out and simply order the Death to be swept across the ship's bow.

If they did, Jack would die.

"Watch the monitors," the Valahgua ordered. "Let me know when the boy reappears."

Draycos breathed a silent sigh of relief. So the Lordover wasn't going to panic and blindly open fire.

But Draycos could also hear the suspicion in his voice. He knew there was some sort of plan going on here, and he was determined not to be taken in by it.

Unfortunately for him, he would be measuring the possibilities against what he knew about K'da battle tactics. Jack's con-man tactics might be something new.

"Control; Langston," Langston's voice came again in Draycos's ear. "Repeating: Morgan has passed by the starboard weapons bays and we've lost him. Do you have any orders?"

There was no answer. Either the Lordover was ignoring him or else Jack's sabotage had damaged the intercom to that area of the ship.

"I see him!" one of the Brummgas called, stabbing a finger at one of the other monitors. "There!"

"Lordover, the boy has reappeared," Mrishpaw said excitedly. "He is approaching the port-side weapons bay cameras."

"And he is carrying something," the first Brummga added, leaning close to the monitor. "Two bottles with something wrapped around their necks."

"They see you, Jack," Draycos murmured toward his comm clip. "Get ready."

"Control; Langston," Langston's voice came again, starting to sound agitated. "Morgan's coming up on the port-side weapons bays. Control, do you copy?"

Now, Draycos silently urged him. *Do it now.*

"Blast it," Langston snarled. "Intercom must be out. Vimpru— you and Galcra find a working intercom and let control know that Morgan's on the loose."

Draycos held his breath. If the two Brummgas obeyed Langston's order . . .

"We cannot leave," Vimpru said flatly. "Our orders are to stay and guard the weapon."

"Well, blast you, too," Langston snarled. "Fine—*I'll* go."

Draycos listened hard, and a moment later heard the sound of the door opening and closing. "He's clear," he murmured into his comm clip.

"Bottoms up," Jack murmured back.

Draycos peered through the grille at the monitors. The tiny figure that was Jack moved closer to the cameras, filling one of the two displays as he leaned over it.

And suddenly both displays went black.

"He has destroyed the port-side cameras as well," Mrishpaw said urgently into the intercom. "Instructions?"

"Hold position," the Valahguan voice said, and there was no mistaking the satisfaction there.

Because he'd figured it out. Leaning over the camera with his flight suit collar open, Jack had clearly demonstrated that Draycos wasn't riding his skin.

And if Jack was approaching the port-side weapons bay, where the second Death weapon had been located until a few hours ago, Draycos must therefore be preparing to attack the starboard weapon. A straightforward, coordinated two-prong attack, of the sort the Valahgua had seen a thousand times before.

Or else possibly Draycos was being subtle, with Jack merely a diversion to get their attention while Draycos launched a single-prong attack.

Fortunately, it didn't matter which of those conclusions the Valahgua jumped to. Jack's destruction of the starboard cameras as he passed was all the confirmation he needed that Draycos was lurking in the tween gap waiting for the moment to attack the bait.

And with the trap already set and primed, the Valahgua could afford the minor effort required to also eliminate the lesser of his two enemies. "Prepare to fire," the Valahgua ordered Mrishpaw. "As soon as the K'da has reached the weapon."

The voice went silent; and then, from the hidden comm clip,

the voice came again. "Readjust your aim to the boy's last position," he ordered Langston's crew. "Fire on my command."

"I obey," the response came. On the monitor below him, Draycos saw two of the Brummgas grab the front end of the other Death weapon and begin to swing it ponderously toward the port-side weapons bay.

And as its aim moved away from the room below him, Draycos pounced.

He shoved open the grille with his front paws and pushed off the duct's back wall with his hind paws, hurling himself out of the opening like a black-scaled missile. The Brummgas had just enough time to start to turn, their mouths dropping open.

And then Draycos was among them, slashing with his paws to stagger back the nearest alien, then slapping away the one behind him, clearing himself a path to the obscene killing machine mounted in the center of the room. From the intercom speaker he heard a Valahguan scream of fury, and through his comm clip he heard the Lordover howling at the Brummgas in the other room to stop what they were doing and turn the Death back toward the threat that had suddenly appeared behind them.

But it was already too late. Even as the Brummgas threw their weight against the weapon's muzzle, Draycos reached the center of his room. He ducked beneath the rear of the Death and came back up behind it.

And twisting back around to face the control panel, he keyed the firing button.

From its muzzle came a sickly yellow flash, and the all-too-familiar cone of violet light lanced out like the limb of some alien creature stretching out toward its prey. The violet light hit the bulkhead, and in his mind's eye Draycos could see it passing through the next room, and the next, and the next.

And on the monitor, the Brummgas still trying to wrestle the other Death weapon back into place collapsed to the deck.

The rest of the Brummgas in Draycos's room had recovered from their shock and were starting forward. But Draycos didn't have time to deal with them now. Giving the Death a quick but crippling double slash, he ducked under the charging Brummgas and made for the door. A flick of one paw at the control, a blind back-forth whipping of his tail to brush back pursuit, and as the door opened he slipped out.

He set off down the corridor at a dead run. All around him, the various room and corridor intercoms were alive with Valahguan and human voices shouting orders as they tried to get their troops to the scene.

But all the troops had been carefully moved out of the trap's line of fire, and it was an eternity too late to bring them back. Draycos took the corridor's turns at full speed, his paws climbing halfway up the walls as he did so.

Seconds later, he stood beside the fourth and final Death weapon.

Draycos had seen countless dead bodies during his people's war against the Valahgua. But there was something about bodies killed by the Death that especially sickened him. Keeping his eyes away from them, he slashed at the weapon itself, expending his fury and tension as he turned it into scrap metal.

"Draycos?" Jack's voice came in his ear.

Draycos took a careful breath. "I'm all right," he assured the other. "Get back to base. I'll meet you there."

"Make it quick," Jack warned. "I'm guessing they're not too happy with us just now."

Draycos looked down at the remains of the Death, scattered over the remains of the Brummgas the Death had killed.

The Brummgas *he* had killed with the Death.

Whatever is necessary . . .

"No," he agreed quietly. "I don't think they're happy with us at all."

CHAPTER 20

After only two months of being fully awake, as Alison sometimes referred to it, Taneem didn't consider herself very good at reading human expressions. But after these last few days aboard the *Advocatus Diaboli,* she *was* getting reasonably good at identifying anger.

And Neverlin was angry. Probably as angry as she'd ever seen a human being get.

"Unacceptable, Lieutenant," he ground out. He was standing behind his desk, glaring across the polished surface at the young man standing stiffly in front of him. "Completely unacceptable."

"I agree, sir," the other said, his voice as stiff as his body. "The conduct and performance of the Brummgas and Valahgua left a great deal to be desired."

"That's not what I meant." Neverlin glared at Frost, who was standing silently at the other side of Neverlin's desk, then shifted the glare to Harper, standing a little ways to Frost's right. "But as long as we're on the subject. Harper?"

"What do you want me to say?" Harper countered. Of all of those in the office, he seemed the calmest. "I already told you the Patri Chookoock had his doubts about some of his people. Obviously, he was right."

"I don't want you to *say* anything," Neverlin told him. "I want you to point the traitors out to me so that Colonel Frost can throw them out the airlock."

Neverlin looked back at the lieutenant. "And while he's thinking up names, I want to hear about our former StarForce Wing Sergeant Langston."

The lieutenant's eyes flicked to Frost. "There's not much to tell, sir," he said. His voice, if anything, had gone a little stiffer.

"Really?" Neverlin asked, looking at Frost again. "I understand he was off his post in the starboard weapons bay when Morgan and the K'da killed everyone else in there. Coincidence?"

"He'd left his post to try to contact the control complex," the lieutenant said. "He thought the one in the weapons bay had failed. He was on the intercom in fire control when the attack took place."

"Lucky for him," Neverlin said. "I also understand he walked right past Morgan when he first sneaked aboard without recognizing him. Was he looking for a working intercom then, too?"

"I've read that report," Frost spoke up before the lieutenant could answer. "It looks like he was simply preoccupied with other matters and never actually focused on Morgan."

"He didn't *focus* on him?"

"Morgan's KK-29 had already been cleared," Frost said. "There was no reason—"

"Cleared by *your* men."

"No reason for him to expect an enemy to pop out of the thing," Frost finished stubbornly. "*And* bear in mind a couple of dozen Brummgas passed him, too, and didn't think anything of it."

"Brummgas are incompetents," Neverlin growled. "I expect something more from Malison Ring mercenaries."

"We have Langston under confinement while we investigate his performance," Frost said. "If it turns out he's acted improperly, we'll deal with him."

"And if it turns out he's acting with Morgan?"

Frost's face darkened. "Then we'll *definitely* deal with him."

"Very commendable of you," Neverlin said acidly. "Considering it was you who brought him aboard in the first place."

"And it was Harper's friend the Patri Chookoock who brought the Brummgas aboard," Frost countered. "And *you* who brought the Valahgua aboard. If we're going to start passing out blame for this fiasco, I think there's more than enough to go around."

Neverlin's eyes flicked to the lieutenant, as if he suddenly realized their quarrel had an audience. "You're dismissed, Lieutenant," he growled. "Return to the *Foxwolf*. And *find Morgan and the K'da!*"

"Yes, sir." Turning to Frost, the lieutenant threw him a crisp salute. Then he turned and strode out of the office.

The door closed behind him, and for a moment there was silence. "Well, gentlemen," Neverlin said, sitting down at last in his desk chair. "Suggestions?"

"Obviously, the first thing we need to do is get the rotten apples out of there," Frost said. "Starting with Morgan and his friend."

"And how exactly do you intend to do that?" Harper asked. "Lieutenant Pickering's already tried the sensor route without getting anywhere. You really want to send your men into that hull-gap area to hunt for them?"

"I was thinking more of sending in some serious firepower,"

Frost countered. "If it didn't kill them it would at least keep them pinned down."

"I understand Pickering and the Brummgas tried that, too," Harper said. "The problem is that the K'da knows the ship far better than we do."

"So what do *you* suggest?" Neverlin asked him.

"Maybe we can draw them out some other way," Harper said. "I could try my Virgil Morgan impression, see if I can get Jack to show himself. At least maneuver him into a trap where we can grab him."

"Grab?" Neverlin asked, raising his eyebrows. "Not kill?"

"Grab," Harper said firmly. "If the K'da's not with him, we'll need a live hostage to draw him out." He smiled tightly. "Besides, the Patri Chookoock still wants to talk to Jack about his friend Alison Kayna."

"Does he, now," Neverlin said, his voice suddenly thoughtful. "Did I ever mention that I called the Patri a few days ago, after we went on ECHO?"

Harper shrugged. "You'd said you were going to."

"And I did," Neverlin said. "Would you like to know what he told me?"

It seemed to Taneem that a hint of a frown crossed Harper's face. "I assume he confirmed my story."

"Actually, I never talked to him," Neverlin said. "Somehow, the communications to the Chookoock family estate were always out."

Harper grunted. "That's Brummgan efficiency for you."

"Perhaps." Neverlin lifted a finger.

And suddenly there was a gun in Frost's hand.

Pointed squarely at Harper.

"Or perhaps it was someone else's efficiency," Neverlin went on quietly. "Someone with the resources of, say, Braxton Univer-sis. So Braxton sent you to track me down, did he?"

For a moment Harper studied Neverlin's face, as if he was trying to decide what to say. Then, he gave a small shrug of his shoulders. "Actually, my job was to locate Alison Kayna. He has a whole army of other people working on you."

"I'm flattered," Neverlin said. "What's Alison Kayna to him?"

"A corporate thief," Harper said. "She stole an especially im-portant trade secret. He wants it back."

"Of course he does," Neverlin said, in a tone that suggested that he didn't believe a word of it. "Well, we'll see. Colonel?"

Keeping his eyes and gun on Harper, Frost reached over to Neverlin's desk and touched a button on the intercom. "This is Frost," he said. "Close and drop ship."

"Wait a minute," Harper said, the first signs of concern or uncertainty crossing his face. "What are you doing?"

"If you're fronting for Braxton, he must have a way of track-ing you," Neverlin said. "That's why we just spent six days chas-ing our tails through hyperspace, actually. Now we say good-bye to your ship and head for the rendezvous point."

"This isn't it?" Harper asked. This time, there was no doubt about the concern in his face.

"You didn't really think I'd take you anywhere important on nothing but your word, did you?" Neverlin asked scornfully. "I hope Braxton's people bring enough supplies to have themselves a party. That's all they're going to get here."

"*Essenay* closed," a voice came from the intercom. "Confirm drop."

"Drop confirmed," Frost said.

Taneem didn't hear anything, but she felt the duct around her give a slight lurch. "*Essenay* away," the intercom said. "Drifting free and clear."

"Acknowledged," Frost said. He touched another intercom button. "All ships: you're cleared to proceed to rendezvous point. Repeat: all ships to rendezvous point. Go on ECHO when ready."

There were a dozen acknowledgments from a dozen different voices. "May I ask what you intend to do with me?" Harper asked as Frost shut down the intercom.

"That's entirely up to you," Neverlin said. "If you behave yourself, you might even live through all this."

Harper lifted his eyebrows. "Really."

"Really," Neverlin assured him. "You know a great deal about Braxton's security setup, knowledge that could come in handy when I'm ready to make my move against him."

"You really think I'll give any of that up?"

"I'm sure you will," Neverlin said casually. "With the proper persuasion, of course."

There was a beep from the intercom. "Mr. Neverlin, all ships except our fighter escort have gone on ECHO," the *Advocatus Diaboli*'s captain reported.

"Thank you, Captain," Neverlin said. "Signal the escort to follow, and take us out."

He clicked off the intercom. "And now it's time for you to go back into storage," he added, gesturing to Harper. "The guards outside will escort you to your stateroom."

"As you wish," Harper said, standing up. "You realize, of course, that this little maneuver has just given Morgan and Draycos more time to sabotage the *Foxwolf*."

"Hardly," Neverlin said. "It's only another two hours from here to the rendezvous point. I doubt even they can do much damage in that short a time."

"Not to mention that they've already done as much as they can," Frost said. He smiled. "Though not nearly as much as they *think* they have."

"But that's not your concern," Neverlin said. "Good-bye, Mr. Harper."

"Good-bye, Mr. Neverlin," Harper said. Inclining his head briefly to both Neverlin and Frost, he turned to the door and keyed it open. Peering through the grille, Taneem caught a glimpse of several armed humans waiting outside in the corridor.

The door closed behind him. "You think he'll behave?" Frost asked, putting away his gun.

"I doubt it," Neverlin said. "But he hasn't got the time or resources to make the kind of trouble he'd like to."

"You should let me kill him now."

"We'll wait," Neverlin said firmly. "An interrogation would be useful, and it might provide us an opportunity of seeing how the Valahgua handle such matters."

"As you wish." Frost made a face. "In the meantime, we still have Morgan and his K'da to worry about."

"Yes," Neverlin said, stroking his cheek. "A shame we didn't bring one of the other K'da/Shontine ships along. We could have transferred the *Foxwolf*'s personnel to it and then given our new ships some target practice."

"That would have been nice," Frost agreed. "But we *can* still have half of it. Once we're at the rendezvous, we could transfer everyone to the troop carrier and then open the *Foxwolf* to vacuum. That should do the trick."

"Eventually," Neverlin said, a bit doubtfully. "Remember that the K'da knows the ship. If there are vac suits or safe rooms anywhere aboard, he'll know where to find them."

"A temporary fix only," Frost assured him. "We've already

removed all the *Foxwolf*'s lifepods, and any other oxygen supply they find isn't likely to last more than a few hours."

"Will that give us time for the refitting?" Neverlin asked.

"If necessary, the Brummgas can start the job in vac suits," Frost said.

"Assuming we *want* the Brummgas handling that job."

"What, Harper's story about traitors in the ranks?" Frost scoffed.

"Someone did apparently try to get into my office," Neverlin reminded him. "Mrishpaw or someone else."

"Fine—my men can do it," Frost said, starting for the door. "I'll go clear the plan change with the Lordhighest."

"But don't tell him why," Neverlin said. "We don't want our guests thinking we're not all friendly trusting allies together."

"Right." With a tight smile, Frost left the room.

Taneem waited another minute, wondering if Neverlin would use the intercom to give any more orders. But he merely pulled out some papers and began to study them. Backing away from the grille, she found a place where it was safe to talk. "Alison?" she whispered.

"Yes, I heard," Alison said. "Get back here as quickly as you can. We need to get ready."

Taneem felt her muscles tense up. "We're going to battle to save Jack and Draycos?"

"We're going to save them," Alison said. "Hopefully, without a battle."

"How?"

"You'll see," Alison said. "Trust me." She paused. "Trust me," she said again, very softly.

CHAPTER 21

Two hours later, the *Advocatus Diaboli* came off ECHO in the midst of the rest of the fleet waiting at the rendezvous point.

And Alison was ready.

"We'll be leaving?" Taneem asked timidly from inside Alison's shirt.

"Yes," Alison said, sparing a moment from the lifepod's controls to glance down at the flat dragon head gazing up at her through her collar. Despite Alison's explanation, the K'da probably didn't really grasp what it was they were about to do.

Or else she knew full well what they were about to do and was wondering how they were going to live through it. "You'll leave before I will, though," Alison added. "In about a minute, you're going back into the ducts and getting as far away from this side of the ship as you can."

"Because when the lifepod leaves the ship, the ducts here will be closed off," Taneem said.

At least she'd gotten that part clear. "Because of the hole we melted in the duct, yes," Alison confirmed. "Popping the lifepod will open the duct to vacuum, and the system will react by isolating this area."

"But then how will you escape?"

"I'll already be out in the corridor," Alison said, feeling a flicker of impatience. They'd already been over this part of the plan twice. "There will still be air out there."

"But you'll also be isolated from the rest of the ship," Taneem said. "You'll be trapped here."

Alison grimaced. So Taneem *did* understand what they were going to do. "You have to trust me, Taneem," she said. "You just concentrate on getting yourself to safety."

"And then find you afterward?"

"Yes, but don't push your luck on that," Alison said. "You've got six hours—plenty of time for us to touch base again. You get yourself safe, and leave everything else to me."

She felt Taneem's tail flick against her leg. "I have been honored to be your friend, Alison," the K'da said quietly. "If we don't survive . . ."

"We'll survive, Taneem," Alison assured her.

Alison looked back at the lifepod's navigational display. The troop carrier was maneuvering close to the *Foxwolf* now, getting ready for Neverlin's planned transfer of the K'da/Shontine ship's crew and passengers. The *Advocatus Diaboli* itself was moving into the third point of the triangle, driven no doubt by Neverlin's usual desire to supervise everything.

Alison smiled to herself. Frost probably figured that removing the *Foxwolf*'s lifepods had eliminated the last obstacle to his plan for asphyxiating Jack and Draycos.

He was about to find out otherwise.

"Here we go," she said, lifting her hand to the hole in the duct.

With a surge of weight on her hand, Taneem slid off into the duct. "Hang on," Alison said, crossing to the packet she'd made of her comm clip and the equipment they'd borrowed from inside Harper's ventilation grille. Heading back to the duct, she maneuvered it through the hole. "Remember, as far across the ship as you can get," she reminded the K'da. "All the way on the far side would be best. And *don't* stop by any of the red-edged sections of duct—those are the emergency seals."

"Which could cut me in half," Taneem said. "Yes, I remember. Alison—"

"Be careful, and I'll see you soon," Alison cut her off. "Now scoot."

For a moment Alison could see a hint of gray scales in the gloom. Then, the scales stirred and were gone.

Alison returned to the lifepod's helm and sat down, giving her program one last check. All was ready. She counted out ninety seconds to let Taneem get some distance, then flipped up the protective cover on the drive control. "Incoming," she muttered, and threw the switch.

Instantly, the raucous clamoring of the separation alarm filled the lifepod. Getting up, she crossed to the door and slapped the release. It slid open, and she ducked out into the corridor.

The door slid closed. Three seconds later there was the multiple thud of explosive bolts as the lifepod blew free of the hull.

The decompression alarm hooted, and from all directions came the sound of multiple thuds as emergency seals slid into place across the various corridors around her. Over the alarm's bellowing Alison could hear the sudden hiss as her section was flooded with oxygen.

The hissing ended quickly as the damaged duct was sealed off and the sensors realized the corridor itself wasn't leaking air. Alison thought about sitting down, decided she'd rather meet Frost's men on her feet, and settled in to wait.

She didn't have to wait very long. Three minutes later, with another set of somewhat softer thuds, the emergency seals slid back into their slots.

And waiting behind them, their weapons drawn and ready, were a half-dozen men in Malison Ring uniforms. They spotted her, and at least three jaws dropped in expressions of stunned disbelief.

"Hello, Dumbarton," Alison said, nodding to the owner of one of those jaws. "Come on; come on. Frisk me or whatever you have to do, and then take me to Frost and Neverlin. They'll want to see me."

"Oh yes," Dumbarton said. His look of astonishment, she noted uneasily, was rapidly turning into one of malicious anticipation. "I'm sure they will."

She had thought they might take her to Neverlin's office for a more private chat. Instead, Dumbarton and his team escorted her to the *Advocatus Diaboli*'s bridge.

After frisking her for weapons, of course, rather more roughly than they really had to.

They reached the bridge to find Neverlin and Frost with their angry faces already in place. Alison expected Frost to get in the first word, and she wasn't disappointed. "Well, well," he said, his voice darkly sarcastic. "Why am I not surprised to see you?"

"Oh, come on, now—be honest," Alison chided him. "There's no way you aren't surprised to find me on your ship."

"Fine. I'm surprised." Frost nodded his head toward Neverlin. "Shall we just kill her now?"

"She certainly deserves it," Neverlin agreed. His voice, unlike Frost's, was utterly calm and cool.

Alison focused past Neverlin's shoulder on the main ship's

display. He was right, she had to admit. By his and Frost's standards, she probably *did* deserve to die.

The troop carrier was a mess. The deep dent her lifepod had made when it rammed into the ship's side was trailing tendrils of smoke and debris from a dozen different cracks in the hull. Through some of those cracks she could see a fiery glow, showing that some of the interior oxygen seals hadn't quite done their job.

"What I actually deserve is thanks," she said, looking back at Neverlin. "If I'd let you continue with this bonehead plan to kill Morgan's pet K'da, both of you would have ended up roasting over a slow fire."

"Really," Neverlin said. "And who, pray tell, was going to set up this roasting pit?"

"Don't tell us—let me guess," Frost said sarcastically. "You're working for the Patri Chookoock, right?"

"Hardly," Alison said, putting as much contempt into her voice as she could. "You know, you two are incredibly dense. Especially you, Colonel. You at least knew I'd been poking around one of the Malison Ring training centers."

"Is that what you call it?" Frost countered. "Poking around?"

"Also known as gathering evidence of misconduct by the base's commandant," Alison said. "But even without that, my name should have been enough for you. Alison? *Malison?*"

"Lock her up," Neverlin said, signaling to Dumbarton. "We'll decide what to do with her after—"

"You blithering fools," Alison cut him off, glaring back and forth between them. "You *still* don't understand, do you? The Malison Ring was *named* for me."

Neverlin looked sharply at her. "What in space are you talking about?"

"I'm talking about General Aram Davi," Alison said icily. "Founder and supreme commander of the Malison Ring. *And* father of one Alison Lorelei Kayna Davi."

She drew herself up. "Me."

For a long minute the entire bridge seemed to go silent. Alison looked around the room, her eyes pausing an extra fraction of a second on each of the men wearing Malison Ring uniforms. "You can prove this, of course?" Frost asked at last.

In answer, Alison dug into the sleeve of her shirt and pulled out a long white strip not much thicker than a cat's whisker. "Micro-etched, with an internal codex core for confirmation," she said, holding it out toward Frost.

Frost glanced at Neverlin, then stepped forward and took it from her. "Is that a codex-four?"

"It has a four, a five, *and* a six," Alison said. "Feel free to run it through the whole checklist."

"Trust me, we will," Neverlin said as Frost stepped back. "Of course, if you're telling the truth, it's all the more reason for us to make sure you disappear quietly."

"It might, if Dad was mad at you," Alison said. "Actually, he's more intrigued than angry."

"Meaning?"

"Meaning all sorts of interesting things." Alison looked significantly around the bridge. "But I think we might want a little more privacy before we discuss them."

"My office," Neverlin said. He started to point toward the door Alison had come in by, then dropped his arm. "But you already know where it is, don't you?"

"Of course," Alison said. "And maybe we can also get something to eat. Seventeen days on lifepod rations gets pretty tiresome."

"I'll have something brought in," Neverlin said. There was still a fair amount of sarcasm in his tone, she noted.

But she also noted that the sarcasm was now edged with a little caution. As well it might be. "Good," Alison said, gesturing him forward. "After you."

"Let's start with the obvious," Neverlin said when he, Frost, and Alison were seated together in his office. "How did you get aboard this ship?"

"Inside the K'da safe, of course," Alison said. "Another one you really should have figured out, given that you know I know how to open them."

"So you're working with Jack Morgan?" Neverlin asked, a hint of threat beneath his voice.

"He was a useful ally as long as our goals weren't bumping heads," Alison said. "He *and* that highly interesting poet-warrior friend of his."

"Who's already played havoc with our attack plan," Frost said accusingly.

"Don't look at me," Alison countered. "*You* were the ones who let him come in. *And* the ones who didn't have anything but a bunch of incompetent Brummgas standing in his way."

"You sound like another of our uninvited guests," Neverlin said.

"Who, Harper?" Alison snorted. "The man has chutzpah; I'll give him that."

"Wait a minute," Frost growled. "How do you know about Harper?"

"How do you think?" Getting up from her chair, Alison squatted down and retrieved the needle microphone from under the desk. "You really should sweep your personal areas for bugs more often," she said, setting the needle onto the desktop in front of Neverlin.

"So it was *you* who decoyed my men away from their posts," Frost said. "And then framed Mrishpaw for it."

Alison shrugged. "What can I say, except that Brummgas pretty much invite that sort of thing."

"I gather General Davi doesn't think much of Brummgas?" Neverlin asked.

"Do *you*?" Alison countered. "*I* certainly don't. Especially not after this last fiasco."

"The general doesn't think much of most non-humans, actually," Frost said.

"And for good reason," Alison said. "Draycos, though, is one alien he's *very* interested in."

"What does he want to do, recruit him?" Frost asked.

"In a manner of speaking, yes," Alison said. "The K'da ability to attach themselves to humans has all sorts of interesting possibilities. But without a subject to study, the bioweapons labs aren't going to be able to coax out that secret."

"So you came to plead for the refugee fleet?" Neverlin asked.

"Hardly," Alison assured him. "All Dad wants from that part of the operation is a fair cut."

"A fair *cut*?" Frost demanded. "What kind of cut does he think he deserves?"

"The kind of cut due a new partner," Alison said calmly. "Especially a new partner who can free you from the burden of ever again having to rely on the Patri Chookoock and his brain-dead muscleheads. From now on, if and when you need manpower, the Malison Ring will provide it."

"If the general is feeling so accommodating, why didn't he simply direct the Driftline commandant to give us the extra ships we wanted?" Frost asked, his tone still suspicious. "It would have been considerably easier on Sergeant Chapman and his team."

"He would have if he'd known where you were planning your raid," Alison explained patiently. "This isn't exactly something you put on the Malison Ring newslist."

"That's his excuse," Neverlin spoke up. "What's *yours*?"

"What's my what?"

"Your excuse," Neverlin said. "You sit around quietly in a lifepod for seventeen days, and then your first word of greeting is to wreck our troop carrier?"

"I thought you or Colonel Frost might put up a fight over whether or not we try to keep Draycos alive," Alison said. "This way, the point is moot. You don't have enough spare room among the rest of your ships to accommodate that many Brummgas while you open the *Foxwolf* to space." She shrugged. "Besides, the carrier is probably more use to you wrecked than it is whole."

"How do you figure that?" Neverlin asked.

"I presume the plan is for you and the *Foxwolf* to go running to the refugee fleet as soon as it arrives, claiming the big bad wolf is behind you and pleading for protection. Am I close?"

"Go on," Neverlin said.

"So now you've got a ship with genuine damage that you can show them," Alison said. "It'll also make a good place to stash Morgan and the K'da while we deal with the rest of the fleet."

"Assuming we can coax them out of hiding," Neverlin said. "Or did you have a plan for that, too?"

"Of course I do," Alison said scornfully. "Jack and I are buddies, remember? All you have to do is have the *Foxwolf* put you on their intercom system and announce you've captured me. I moan a few pitiful words about being alone and scared and tortured, and he'll fall all over himself trying to rescue me."

"Oh, please," Frost said with a snort. "Even if Morgan's stupid enough to fall for that, I hardly think the K'da will."

"Of course he won't," Alison said. "But that doesn't matter. Draycos is noble to the point of practically being a cartoon figure. He'll figure that he'll be able to rescue me no matter what the odds or the situation."

"Not a chance," Frost said flatly. "He's a soldier in a war. He's not going to give up a strong, defensible position just because the enemy asks him to."

"Then he gives it up because he doesn't have any other choice," Alison said. "Because you'll also threaten to pull the Brummgas and Valahgua off and open the *Foxwolf* to vacuum." She shrugged. "After all, *he* doesn't know I wrecked the troop carrier."

Frost looked at Neverlin. "What do you think?"

"Actually, it might just work," Neverlin said thoughtfully, his eyes steady on Alison. "It may also give us a chance to kill a second bird with the one stone."

"I hope you meant that figuratively," Alison warned. "Dad wants them alive and unharmed."

"Purely a figure of speech," Neverlin assured her with a genteel smile.

There was a beep from his intercom, and he leaned forward to touch the switch. "Yes?"

"Dumbarton, sir," Dumbarton's voice came. "Ms. Davi's ID checks out."

Alison felt a quiet flicker of relief. *Ms. Davi,* he'd called her. *And* he'd said it with the proper tone of respect. So they were indeed convinced.

And everyone in the Malison Ring knew General Aram Davi's reputation for ruthlessness. If Neverlin and Frost decided they wanted her dead, they'd now have to work over, around, or through the rest of the Malison Ring soldiers aboard to make her that way.

But if any of those thoughts were running through Neverlin's mind, they didn't show in his face. "Thank you, Sergeant," he said, and switched off the intercom.

"Well?" Alison prompted.

"We'll try it," Neverlin said. "If Morgan and the K'da take the bait, I want a proper reception ready for them. Colonel?"

"I'll make the arrangements," Frost said, starting for the door.

"One other thing first," Neverlin said, motioning for Frost to stop. "One other question."

"Yes?" Alison asked.

"What exactly did you steal from Braxton Universis?"

"Who says I stole anything?" Alison asked evenly.

Neverlin didn't reply, but merely continued to stare at her. Alison stared back a few seconds, then shrugged. "Fine," she said. "It was one of those high-tech ship tracers you used to follow the *Essenay* to Rho Scorvi. Dad had heard rumors, and decided he wanted one for himself."

She smiled tightly. "If we'd known you'd already made off with one of them, I wouldn't have bothered."

"They're very useful devices, aren't they?" Neverlin agreed. "At least now we know why Harper was so interested in tracking you down."

"And why I was so interested in getting away," Alison said.

"Yes," Neverlin murmured. "I gather, then, that it was *you* who were on Rho Scorvi with Jack Morgan." His face suddenly darkened. "*You* who were shooting at Colonel Frost's men."

"Colonel Frost's men were shooting at me first," Alison countered stiffly. "Besides, at that point they were technically deserters." Deliberately, she turned to Frost. "As were you, Colonel. I had a perfect right to execute any of you if the opportunity arose."

"I'm so glad we're on the same side now," Frost murmured.

"If I were you, I wouldn't be too flippant," Alison warned. "You may have heard that the commandant of the training center I was at was arrested right after I had that run at his computers. As far as Dad's concerned, you're still very much on probation."

"I'll keep that in mind," Frost said.

"Good," Alison said. "Then get busy and set up that reception we discussed."

She looked at Neverlin. "And while he attends to that," she added, "maybe we can finally get that decent meal."

CHAPTER 22

Jack had just unwrapped a ration bar when he heard a crackling sound through the deck above the crawl space where he and Draycos had taken up temporary residence. "Attention, Jack Morgan," a familiar voice called, the tone muffled by the deck. "This is Arthur Neverlin."

He's not actually there, Draycos said into Jack's mind. *He's speaking through the ship's intercom.*

Jack nodded. He'd already figured that one out.

"Jack, I know you can hear me," Neverlin continued. "I have something here that I believe belongs to you."

There was a short pause. "Jack?" a new voice called.

It was Alison.

Jack felt his heart seize up. *Oh no.*

"I'm sorry, Jack," Alison said. Even through the deck Jack could hear a slight quavering in her voice. "They—I couldn't— *aah!*"

Involuntarily, Jack twitched. The pain in her voice right then—

"Don't worry, Jack," Neverlin said. "She's not seriously hurt. Yet. But that could change."

Steady, Jack, Draycos cautioned. *He's trying to draw us into the open.*

Jack grimaced. He knew that. But knowing it didn't help his tight muscles in the slightest.

And if Alison was being tortured, what had happened to Taneem? Surely this time Neverlin and Frost couldn't possibly have missed finding the K'da riding on her skin.

"Believe it or not, though, you're in a more serious position than she is," Neverlin went on. "You see, now that the fleet has reassembled, all my ships are available to me. Including the troop carrier, with plenty of passenger space aboard. I presume you understand the full ramifications of that."

Do we? Jack asked.

Unfortunately, we do, Draycos answered grimly. *He can now take all the crew and passengers off this ship, put them in the carrier, and open our ship to vacuum.*

Terrific, Jack replied, glancing around the crawl space. *I don't suppose you know where some vac suits are stashed?*

Even if there are any still aboard, it would be a futile gesture, Draycos said. *Vac suit oxygen supplies are limited to a few hours at the most, while Neverlin can leave the Brummgas in the carrier almost until the K'da/Shontine fleet is due to arrive.*

Which is, what, another ten days?

Unless they're ahead of schedule, Draycos said. *Call it somewhere between four and ten days. We can't possibly hold out here that long.*

Aren't there any spare oxygen tanks?

Only a limited supply, Draycos said. *And most of them are in five centralized locations. Neverlin could easily destroy them before the crew was evacuated.*

"So it's up to you," Neverlin went on. "I'd actually prefer to have you alive, and if you come out now and surrender peacefully I give you my word you won't be harmed. But bear in mind that this is a limited-time offer." With another crackle, the intercom went silent.

Okay, Jack said, trying to think. *If we can't hold out, what are our other options? Assuming we can find a vac suit, can we sneak outside and float our way to one of the other ships? Or could we even take over the* Foxwolf *itself and fly it somewhere?*

I doubt either plan would work, Draycos said reluctantly. *The other ships will surely be too far away for us to make a quick transfer, and of course there's no practical way to hide either our departure or our crossing. As for taking command of this ship, Neverlin will surely be prepared for us to try that.*

Jack swallowed. Suddenly, the crawl space seemed a lot tighter than it had before. *So what are we going to do?*

For a moment Draycos was silent, his background thoughts rushing past Jack's mind like the rapids of a mountain stream. *We surrender,* the K'da said at last. *If all he wanted was our deaths, he could simply have removed all the Brummgas and suffocated us as he threatened without giving us a warning.*

So if he doesn't want us dead, what does *he want?*

I don't know, Draycos admitted. *But if we stay here, we'll surely die. Alive, even in Neverlin's hands, there's always hope.*

Jack took a deep breath, eleven years' worth of Uncle Virgil's warnings and counsel flowing through his mind. *Run away. Protect yourself. Don't stick your neck out for anyone. Run away.*

Run away. . . .

But he couldn't run away. Not this time.

Okay, he said with a sigh. *Let's go.*

Even with Neverlin's promise, Jack half-expected them to be gunned down as soon as they emerged from the tween gap.

Certainly there were enough armed Brummgas waiting to have made quick work of them.

But apparently for once Neverlin had been telling the truth. "Okay, I'm here," Jack said, trying to sound as if stepping into a circle of guns was something he did every day.

"So we see," a tall human said as he pushed his way through the wall of glowering Brummgas. "Lieutenant Pickering, captain of the *Foxwolf*." His eyes flicked up and down Jack's form. "I trust your friend is with you?"

"I'm here," Draycos confirmed, lifting the top of his head from Jack's shoulder.

Pickering didn't take a step backward, but Jack had the feeling that he very much wanted to. "Yes, I see." He lifted a finger and beckoned.

And to Jack's surprise, Langston stepped into view. "Hello, Jack," the other said darkly. "Nice to actually *see* you this time."

"Hey, it's not *my* fault you can't walk and read at the same time," Jack countered, picking up instantly on the cue. Langston must have played Frost the same scenario he'd pretended to play for Jack, that he'd been too busy studying his notepad to focus on the pilot who came out of that KK-29 patrol ship. "Come on; let's get this over with."

Langston jerked a thumb over his shoulder. "This way."

They walked in silence to the docking bay. Brummgas lined the whole route, most of them fidgeting with their guns. Langston stepped to the side of the open hatchway and gestured Jack to go in.

Jack did so, and found himself in the KK-29 he'd borrowed from Chiggers back on Bentre. "I would have thought they'd have moved it by now," he commented.

"They did," Langston said, coming in and closing the hatch.

"Frost had it brought back for the occasion. Come on—you might as well sit up front."

They headed forward to the cockpit. The ship was all powered up, Jack saw as he sat down in the copilot's seat. So were the weapons boards, he noted with interest. "A functional ship with functional weapons," he pointed out as Langston took the pilot's seat. "You'd think they *wanted* us to make a run for it."

"It does look that way, doesn't it?" Langston agreed. He checked his displays and hit the release control, and the patrol ship floated free. "Maybe they do. Maybe all this is just more of Frost's fine-weave rope."

"Could be," Jack conceded. "He's probably hoping we'll try something and he'll have an excuse to blast us to dust."

"I don't think so," Langston said as he eased in the drive, moving them away from the *Foxwolf*. "See those Djinn-90s over there?"

Jack peered out the canopy where the other was pointing. In the distance he could see three of the heavy fighters, drifting silently along. "Look like they're minding their own business, don't they?"

"That's the point—they *are* minding their own business," Langston said. "So is everyone else. If we made a break for it now, we'd be on ECHO before anyone could stop us."

Jack frowned, searching the sky. He didn't know nearly as much as Langston did about military ships and tactics, but he was willing to trust the other's judgment. "So what's the scam?" he asked. "They want some practice with the Death?"

"What Death?" Langston countered. "The only one left is on the *Advocatus Diaboli,* and it's way out of position to hit us back here."

"Then maybe we're booby-trapped," Jack suggested.

Langston shook his head. "I already ran a check on the air system and did a quick visual," he said. "There's nothing aboard they could use to gas us. And they sure aren't going to blow up one of their ships just to take us out. They need all of them they've got."

Jack chewed at the inside of his cheek. "Draycos?" he asked. "What do you think?"

"I agree with Sergeant Langston," the K'da said from his shoulder. "The entire setup is strange."

"So what do we do?"

"We continue on to the *Advocatus Diaboli,*" Draycos said.

"Because of Alison, I suppose?" Langston said.

"In part," Draycos said.

"Yeah," Langston muttered. "I don't know, Draycos. Something about her seems fishy to me."

"Join the club," Jack said dryly. "But you know how stubborn K'da poet-warriors can get when they're being noble."

"I suppose." Langston looked sideways at Jack, a crooked smile on his lips. "Lucky for me."

"Jack?" a whispered voice came from Jack's comm clip.

Jack jerked in surprise. Had Alison gotten free?

"Who's that?" Langston asked, frowning at him.

And then Jack's brain caught up with him. "It's Taneem," he said. "Taneem? Are you all right?"

"For now, yes," Taneem said. Even in a whisper Jack could hear the misery in her voice. "Jack, she lied to us. She lied to all of us."

"Calm down, Taneem," Draycos said, gently but firmly. "Tell us what she lied about."

"Everything," Taneem said. "She's not a thief. She's General Aram Davi's daughter. I heard her say so."

Jack frowned. Why did that name sound familiar?

"The Malison Ring's *commander*?" Langston demanded, sounding stunned.

And then it clicked. "Oh, boy," Jack muttered.

"No wonder she had his voice pattern on the *Essenay*'s computer," Taneem continued. "No wonder she had such wonderful burglary equipment."

"Okay, calm down," Jack said. "Given Frost's shenanigans with Malison Ring men and equipment, having Davi's daughter in the game may not be such a bad thing."

"You don't understand," Taneem said. "She's gone over to them. She and her father both. She's not in danger—she just pretended to be to get you and Draycos out of hiding."

Jack felt his stomach tighten. "Then Neverlin wasn't going to pull the Brummgas off the *Foxwolf* and try to kill us?"

"He couldn't," Taneem said. "Alison wrecked the troop carrier."

"I'll be swiggled," Langston said, peering at one of his displays. "She's right. There's a great big air-leaking dent in its side."

"Okay," Jack said. He was rather surprised at how calm his voice sounded. "We're definitely butter side down now. What do you think, Draycos? *Now* do we make a run for it?"

For a few seconds there was nothing but the rapid flow of Draycos's thoughts against his mind. "No," the K'da said. "For one thing, Sergeant Langston's observations and conclusions haven't changed. If Neverlin truly hopes we'll try to escape, we must definitely not do so."

"So we just walk into this other trap instead?"

"If it *is*, in fact, a trap," Draycos said. "Taneem, where are you right now?"

"In one of the ducts near Neverlin's office," Taneem said. "Not close enough for him to hear us."

"How much of the conversation did you hear where Alison revealed her true identity?"

"All of it, I think," Taneem said. "They didn't believe her at first, but she had something hidden in her sleeve that proved it."

"I'm sure she did," Draycos said. "Question: did she ever mention *you*?"

There was a short pause. "No, she didn't," Taneem said. "She said her father wanted you alive so they could learn the secret of how you can go onto people's skin."

"But she never mentioned you?" Draycos persisted.

"No, not that I heard."

"So what does that prove?" Langston asked, frowning.

"It proves she's still playing games," Jack told him, some of the weight lifting off his lungs. "And not just with us."

"What do you mean?" Taneem asked. "Is she *not* General Davi's daughter, then?"

"I don't know who she is," Jack said. "Not that I ever did, come to think of it. But if she'd really betrayed us, she should have betrayed you, too."

"She *did* tell Neverlin you'd been a useful ally while your goals weren't bumping heads," Taneem said. "Maybe they still aren't."

"Maybe," Jack said. "Draycos?"

"I'm willing to trust her a while longer," Draycos said.

"That's good enough for me," Jack said. It was almost the truth, too. "Meanwhile, Taneem, you stay hidden. Listen in as much as you can, but stay hidden."

"What about my six-hour limit?" Taneem asked. "Over half of that has already passed."

And Alison was probably going to be cooped up with Neverlin and Frost for the rest of it, Jack suspected. "That's okay—you and Draycos can take turns on me," he said. "Just track us down after they lock us up."

"All right," Taneem said. "Be careful. I hope you're right about Alison."

"We will, and we hope so, too," Jack said. "We'll talk to you later."

The transmission clicked off. "That assumes they'll put you some place where she can get to you," Langston warned.

"*And* that we're not under constant surveillance," Jack said grimly. "I know. But I don't know what else to do."

"Maybe I can find an excuse to go aboard later," Langston suggested. "Do you still have that spare comm clip I lent Draycos?"

"Right here," Jack said, digging it out of his pocket and handing it to the other. "It's still set on our frequency."

"Good," Langston said, slipping it into his own pocket. "If I can get back in time, I'll give her a call and arrange a rendezvous."

"But don't take any unnecessary risks," Draycos warned. "At the moment we want you alive and with as much freedom of movement as possible."

"He's right," Jack seconded. "Don't worry about Taneem. Between Alison and me, we should be able to cover her."

"Okay," Langston said. "You two watch yourselves. Whatever Neverlin's got up his sleeve, I'm guessing you're not going to like it."

CHAPTER 23

Another cluster of guns was waiting when Jack and Langston emerged from the patrol ship into the *Advocatus Diaboli*. This time, though, the guns were being held by humans instead of Brummgas.

"Hello, Jack," Frost greeted him gravely. He was, Jack noted, standing between and slightly behind two of the other Malison Ring mercenaries. Apparently, he didn't trust Draycos quite enough to be at the front of the line. "You've been a busy boy."

Jack shrugged. "Idle hands are the devil's workshop, Uncle Virgil always said."

"And he would know," Frost said. "Where *is* your elusive uncle, by the way?"

For a moment Jack was tempted to tell him the truth. Frost's reaction to the news that the man he'd been chasing for the past six months had in fact died nearly a year and a half ago might be amusing.

But it was never a good idea to give away information for free. "I'm sure he's out there somewhere," Jack said instead. "Lurking, you know. Uncle Virgil's very good at lurking."

"Apparently so," Frost said. "Fine. Turn around and get back into the patrol ship. You too, Langston."

"First let me see Alison," Jack said. "I want to see that she's all right."

"She's fine," Frost said. "She's waiting for us at the troop carrier."

Jack frowned. "The troop carrier?"

"Your new temporary home." Frost waved Jack back toward the patrol ship. "If you please?"

Draycos?

Do as he says, Draycos said. But there was a dark grimness to his tone.

A grimness Jack himself was also feeling. Because if he and Alison were both aboard the carrier—and if they both *stayed* aboard the carrier—Taneem was going to be in serious trouble.

"Unless you'd rather go out right now in a blaze of glory," Frost suggested as Jack hesitated.

Jack grimaced. "Sorry," he said, backing toward the hatchway. "Got caught up in the scenery."

A few minutes later, Jack, Langston, Frost, and half a dozen of the mercenaries were again moving through space, this time making for the troop carrier. "You're probably wondering what happened to it," Frost commented as they approached the flashing lights of a docking station.

"A little," Jack said, gazing out at the ship's crushed side. Up close, it didn't look as bad as it had earlier on the KK-29's display. "Someone run a red light?"

"In a manner of speaking," Frost said. "There's a vac suit in the rack behind you. Put it on, and rig it for long term."

Jack glanced back at the rack. "No thanks," he said. "I'm fine."

"Put it on or die right here."

Jack shivered. Frost hadn't even raised his voice, but there was something in his tone that told him the man wasn't in the mood for flippant remarks.

Silently, Jack got up and put on the suit. Rigging for long term meant hooking up the food and bathroom facilities, which he did. "Now what?" he asked, leaving the helmet attached to his belt.

There was a gentle bump as Langston docked them with the carrier. "We go inside," Frost said, standing up. "Follow me. Langston, you stay here."

The airlock was larger than those Jack was familiar with. Probably designed to handle a dozen vac-suited soldiers at a time, he decided. Frost led them through the lock, out another door into a supply and maintenance room, then through a heavily armored door into a long, high-ceilinged chamber.

Midway along the chamber's long inner bulkhead, leading farther into the ship, was another airlock-style door. Nearby was an equipment cart containing a selection of tools, including a small welding torch. Across from the airlock, on the hull side of the chamber, there was a long hatchway that was nearly as large as the room itself. "What's this, a docking bay?" Jack asked.

"Yes, for one of the two scout ships," Frost confirmed. "They're usually not well armored, so they're kept inside where the carrier's main hull can protect them. Bucket on, then over against the wall by the tool cart."

I think I'm going to hate this, Jack warned Draycos as he slipped his helmet over his head and snugged it into place.

Which part?

The tool cart part, Jack told him. *I take it you hadn't noticed the welding gear.*

Draycos flicked his tail against Jack's leg. *No, I hadn't,* he said. *You're right. I think we may soon both hate this.*

Jack crossed to the inner bulkhead as ordered. At Frost's direction, two of the mercenaries wrapped short lengths of cable around the wrists of Jack's suit and locked them in place. They then held the other ends of the cables against the bay's inner bulkhead while a third man quick-welded them to the metal. Jack's ankles were next, followed by a larger loop around his waist.

"There," Frost said, running a critical eye over the work. "That should hold you awhile."

"You promised I could see Alison," Jack reminded him.

"And so you will," Frost said. Right on cue, down the bulkhead came the hiss of the airlock door opening.

Jack craned his neck to look as five vac-suited figures strode into the bay. Three of them carried heavy rifles, which they lowered to point at Jack as soon as they had a clear line of fire. The other two were unarmed.

But even with the partial concealment of their helmets Jack had no trouble identifying them.

One was Neverlin. The other was Alison.

"Hello, Jack," Neverlin's voice came through the speaker in Jack's helmet. He sounded almost cheerful, or at least as cheerful as the man probably ever got.

"And good-bye, Jack," Frost added. He gestured to his own group of mercenaries, who holstered their weapons and followed Frost into the airlock.

The door hissed closed behind them. A moment later, as he pressed his back against the bulkhead, Jack felt the rhythm of the pumps as they started pulling the air out of the bay.

"So nice of you to join us," Neverlin said. He gestured to Alison. "As you can see, she's safe and sound."

"You okay, Alison?" Jack asked.

"Yes, I'm fine," Alison assured him, her voice subdued and quavering.

It was, Jack thought, the very image of a scared, helpless little girl. *Quite the little actress, isn't she?* he commented sourly. *I just hope it is an act.*

Remember Taneem, Draycos reminded him.

Right. "Nice little box, this," Jack commented, looking back at Neverlin. "I was just wondering a few days ago how you would go about keeping a K'da poet-warrior neutralized."

"Now you know," Neverlin said. "Actually, to be fair, it was Ms. Kayna's idea."

Play dumb, Draycos warned.

Relax—I'm on it. "What was her idea?" Jack asked, frowning.

"Putting you in here," Neverlin said. "Now that we've evacuated the air, the K'da can't use his claws or teeth without opening your suit to vacuum, thereby killing you both. Very clever."

"You're too kind," Alison said. She straightened up.

And suddenly the helpless little girl was gone. "But then, I *have* spent the last couple of months thinking about it."

"What are you talking about?" Jack asked, letting his puzzlement move toward disbelief on its way to outrage.

"Sorry, Jack," Alison said. "I'm sure your uncle Virgil warned you against trusting people. Now you know why."

"Allow me to present Ms. Alison Davi," Neverlin said, gesturing to her. "Daughter of the Malison Ring's supreme commander."

Jack looked at Alison, tightening the muscles in his throat and cheeks. Most of the dramatic acting was wasted, he knew, with his helmet's faceplate obscuring a lot of Neverlin's view. But some of it would be visible, and he had to play this exactly right.

"Of course," he said. "I knew something was wrong with her. I should have guessed it was because she's a killer's daughter."

Alison started to take a step toward him, broke off the movement. "That's rich, coming from the son of thieves," she bit out.

"Uncle Virgil is a thief," Jack said stiffly. "My real parents were Judge-Paladins."

"Right. Like I said." Deliberately, Alison turned to face Neverlin. "So what's the plan, now that you're down to one Death weapon?" she asked. "Take the *Advocatus Diaboli* in with the *Foxwolf* and do what you can with the one you have aboard?"

"Certainly we'll be going in together," Neverlin said, a nasty sort of slyness creeping into his voice. "But whoever said we were down to *one* weapon?"

Alison glanced at Jack, a frown creasing her forehead. "I thought the K'da shredded all the others."

"He shredded all those aboard the *Foxwolf,* yes," Neverlin confirmed. "Unfortunately for him, I'd already taken two of them out and loaded them aboard a pair of our Djinn-90s prior to Sergeant Chapman's raid on the Malison Ring depot at Drift-line."

"Sounds a little risky," Alison said.

"Sounds very much necessary," Neverlin corrected. "Your doing, as it happens."

"Mine?" Alison asked, frowning a bit harder.

"Thanks to that trouble you stirred up with your father's people last month on Brum-a-dum," Neverlin explained. "With the entire Malison Ring now presumably on alert, I thought Chapman might have trouble picking up the Rhino-10s we wanted. I thought giving him two of the Death weapons might be useful in case they needed to shoot their way out."

"I see," Alison said, her voice just a little too casual. "And did they?"

"As it happens, they did," he said, his voice a bit odd. "But not from any Malison Ring ships. At least, nothing carrying a Malison Ring insignia."

"Just like your ships," Jack put in. "Maybe it was another renegade like Frost."

"Maybe," Neverlin said. "But whoever they were, they were foolish enough to challenge Chapman as he and his new ships headed for deep space. The last thing they ever did."

Jack winced. Who had they been? he wondered. Local law enforcement? Pirates? "Better be careful," he warned. "You don't want to run down the clock on your new toys. Be embarrassing to have them burn out just when things with the K'da and Shontine start getting interesting."

"I appreciate your concern," Neverlin said, smiling through his faceplate. "But our friends have assured us we'll have plenty of time to complete our mission."

"Good of them," Jack said. "You really think they'll still be your friends once the K'da and Shontine are dead?"

"At any rate, we'll be leaving you now," Neverlin said, ignoring the question. "I have a pair of Death weapons to transfer back aboard the *Foxwolf,* and—"

"Because once the K'da and Shontine are dead, what's to stop them?" Jack cut in, raising his voice. "What's to keep them from turning on you and the Malison Ring and the Patri Chookoock—?"

Neverlin stepped up to Jack, glowering behind his faceplate, and with a flick of his finger cut off Jack's radio. *Good-bye, Jack,* he mouthed in the sudden silence.

Gesturing to Alison, he crossed to the airlock. Alison gave Jack a single unreadable glance and then followed. They stepped inside, and Jack felt the bulkhead behind him vibrate as the pumps once again started shifting air around. *I think you annoyed our host,* Draycos said dryly.

All part of the grand plan, buddy, Jack assured him. *He wouldn't have been so quick to cut off my ranting if there weren't other people who could hear it. That tells us there's still someone aboard.*

The damage didn't seem all that great, Draycos agreed. *It's probably still flyable.*

And if there are people aboard, then all the other amenities of life should be, too. Pulling on his wrist straps, Jack pressed his back firmly against the bulkhead. *Take a peek and see what you can see.*

Draycos slid around on his skin, and Jack felt the K'da lean his fourth-dimensional way over the wall behind them. He held the pose for a few seconds, then came fully back onto Jack's skin. *Neverlin and Alison are removing their suits,* he reported. *There are also two Brummgas there—Neverlin appears to be giving them some instructions.*

Hopefully having to do with changing our oxygen tank every couple of hours, Jack said. *What sort of room is it?*

It appears to be a preparation room, Draycos said. *There are two racks of vac suits, plus oxygen tanks, maneuvering units, and tool cabinets like the one they used to attach your suit to the wall.*

Perfect, Jack said.

How exactly is it perfect? Draycos asked.

There's air over there, and it looks like the whole crew is Brummgas, Jack explained. *Knowing Neverlin, he would have given his orders to humans if there were any aboard.*

He smiled tightly. *And what none of them know is that you can fall over that wall any time you want to.*

Yes, Draycos agreed thoughtfully. *So Alison is indeed still on our side.*

Never doubted it for a minute, Jack said. *The only question now is when exactly we want to make our move.*

Not soon, I'm afraid, Draycos said. *We don't know how many crew are aboard, or the deck plan, or what sort of flight and combat capabilities the ship has.*

And we're not likely to get any of that, either, Jack said with a grimace. *Unless you go on a little search on your own. But there's no way you'd be able to get back in here without them knowing something had happened.*

Then I'm afraid our best strategy will be to wait until the operation has begun, Draycos said. *That may mean some of my people will die, but we'll need the chaos and distraction to take over the ship.*

And if it turns out the blasted thing can't fight, we won't be able to do anyone any good, Jack said heavily. *But I suppose you're right. I just hope we'll know when—*

Shh! Draycos cut him off. *Do you feel that?*

Jack frowned. There was an odd vibration rumbling through the deck beneath his feet. He cocked his head, trying to listen.

And suddenly, he got it. *It's a dual-stage ECHO system coming up to speed,* he told Draycos. *That's the kind that's used in some larger military ships.*

I see, Draycos said, suddenly thoughtful. *So that's why Neverlin didn't seem worried about us escaping on the flight from the* Gatekeeper *to the* Advocatus Diaboli.

Because we weren't actually at the rendezvous point, Jack said, nodding as he understood. *Guy's full of tricks, isn't he?*

Circles within circles, wheels within wheels, Draycos agreed. *Still, it's often the case that a clever man outsmarts himself.*

Let's hope Neverlin's one of those, Jack agreed. *So what do we do until your people arrive?*

We do what surveillance we can, Draycos said. *Your back to the wall, please. I'd like to spend some time studying the preparation room behind us.*

CHAPTER 24

The latest trip had been made, this one much shorter than the previous ones. Though there were two men on duty on the bridge, most of the rest of the *Advocatus Diaboli*'s crew and passengers seemed to have retired to their staterooms for ship's night.

But not Neverlin, Frost, or Alison. The three of them were still in Neverlin's office. The two men seemed to still have a lot of questions for Alison concerning her father, General Davi, and his work.

Watching them through the ventilation grille, Taneem wondered what it would be like to die.

She didn't know. But she would soon find out. The end of her time limit was rapidly approaching, when she needed to go two-dimensional on a host's body or disappear into death.

But she had no host. Jack had been taken off somewhere and hadn't returned. Langston had been refused permission to come aboard the *Advocatus Diaboli* to pick up some specialized tools.

And Alison was with Neverlin and Frost, with no sign that their conversation would be ending any time soon.

Silently, Taneem backed away from the grille and set off through the *Advocatus Diaboli*'s maze of air ducts. She didn't really have any place to go, but she couldn't bear to stay by Neverlin's office any longer.

She didn't want to die within sight of her host, the human girl she'd grown to know and love over the two short months they'd been together.

The ducts were vibrant with an ever-shifting mix of aromas. The smell of human and Valahguan bodies combined with a blend of cooking and engine lubricant and a dozen other scents. She sniffed at the air as she worked her way through the ducts, wondering if it all smelled richer now than it had earlier. Draycos had told her of legends that said K'da senses grew sharper as death approached. But she couldn't tell if that was happening or not.

And then, suddenly, one particular aroma seemed to leap out at her from the mixture. A very individual, very familiar human scent.

Harper.

She frowned, looking around her. Sure enough, her aimless wanderings had brought her to the part of the ship where Harper had been locked up. With nowhere else to go, she headed for the duct that would take her by his stateroom. Reaching the junction, she turned the corner.

And stopped short. Five paces ahead was the opening that led into Harper's room.

Only the grille was no longer fastened the way it was supposed to be. It was instead hanging at an angle, held in place by a single corner bolt.

Cautiously, Taneem moved forward. Had be been putting more items into the duct and been caught? But he was still in the room—the scent whispering past her snout and tongue showed that much. She reached the duct and eased an eye around the corner.

Harper was there, all right. He was lying on his side in his bed, the blanket pulled up to his shoulders, his right arm half tucked beneath his pillow.

His *bare* right arm . . .

It was insane, Taneem knew. Completely insane. Even if Harper managed to sleep through it, he would spot her as soon as he opened his eyes.

But if she waited here, she was dead.

She had nothing at all to lose.

Keeping her eyes on Harper, she eased around the edge of the hanging grille and dropped into the room. There was no reaction. Padding over to the bed, she gingerly touched his forearm and slid up onto his skin.

It was like the first sip of cold water from a mountain-fed stream after hours of wandering through the forest with nothing but warm and stagnant tree stump water to drink. Taneem closed her eyes, feeling the tension and fear and hopelessness draining out of her as peace and strength flowed in to take its place.

Yes, this would work. An hour on Harper's skin and she could go back for another six hours in the ducts. Surely before those hours were up Neverlin and Frost would tire of asking their questions and send Alison off to her own room to sleep.

She would just have to make sure she was gone before Harper woke up. Easy enough to do. Readjusting herself on the man's skin, she settled down to wait.

Ten minutes later, she was fast asleep.

She awoke with a start, her heart thudding with the awful feeling that something was wrong.

It was dark, for one thing. Darker than it had been when she'd come into Harper's room.

And then, to her relief, she understood. While she'd been asleep Harper had merely pulled the blankets all the way up over his shoulders. Carefully, stealthily, she shifted around on his skin, trying to find a place where she could see the clock by the side of the bed.

"Good morning," Harper said softly.

Taneem froze. Had he been talking to *her*? Or was there someone else in the room?

She flicked her tongue out a bit. Aside from her and Harper, the room was empty.

"Come on; I know you're awake," Harper went on in the same quiet voice. "Cat got your tongue?" With a sweep of his arm, he flung back the blankets.

And to her horror, Taneem found herself looking up at his fully awake face.

She reacted instantly, hurling herself backward off his skin and landing in a crouch on the deck past the end of the bed. She glanced up at the grille, preparing to leap into the opening and escape.

Only the grille was no longer hanging by a single bolt. It was back in its proper place, secured at all four corners.

"You must really have been tired," Harper commented. He'd made no move to follow her, but was still lying in bed propped up on one elbow. "You didn't even wake up when I put the grille back."

With an effort, Taneem found her voice. "What do you want?" she asked. She had hoped to sound as strong and commanding as Draycos, but the words came out sounding merely weak and scared.

"I want to help you," Harper said. "Why do you think I left the back door open for you in the first place?"

Taneem flicked another glance at the grille. "Was it a back door? Or was it a trap?"

"You've been here for over five hours," Harper pointed out. "If I wanted to turn you over to Neverlin, I could have done so long before now."

It all seemed reasonable, Taneem had to admit. But there was still something odd about it. "Why do you care what happens to me at all?"

"Lots of reasons," Harper said. "You ever hear the expression 'the enemy of my enemy is my friend'?"

"No."

"Basically, it means that if Neverlin is fighting against both of us, we have some common ground to join forces against him," Harper explained.

"And against Alison, too?" Taneem asked.

"You still trust Alison?" Harper countered.

"She didn't betray me to Neverlin," Taneem said. "I don't know who she is anymore, but I know she's still my friend."

"Good enough," Harper said, nodding. "And by that same logic, I'm your friend, too."

Taneem flicked her tongue out, wishing again that she knew how to read human emotions from the changes in their scents. "But you lied to Neverlin," she said. "How do I know you're not lying now?"

"I don't know how to answer that, Taneem," Harper said, his voice low and earnest. "I can't prove anything I'm telling you. All you have is the fact I didn't turn you over to Neverlin and Frost."

"That's not very much," Taneem said. "You could just be

protecting me so that you can take me back to Braxton Universis with you and learn how to turn my abilities into a weapon. Just like General Davi wants to do."

"That's not what I want," Harper assured her. "But even if I did, you'd still do better to stay with me. Mr. Braxton is a much better person to deal with than General Davi."

Taneem flicked her tail in frustration. "I don't know what to do," she whispered. "I don't understand any of this."

"I know," Harper said sympathetically. "It's a crazy business, keeping up with us humans. All you can do is hold on to the fact that Alison's still your friend, and that I'm your friend, and trust us to protect you as best we can."

Taneem looked back at the grille. "Maybe I should go and see if Alison's all right."

"I wouldn't," Harper said. "In fact, I'd stay away from her completely for the next few days. Neverlin's going to be keeping her close from now until the refugee fleet arrives. We don't want him or any of the others spotting you."

"Whereas no one's going to look at you?"

Harper smiled. "Exactly," he said. "Sometimes it pays to be a prisoner."

He pointed toward the small bathroom. "But you should probably go hide in the bathroom for a bit," he said. "They'll be delivering my breakfast soon, and we don't want the delivery boy to see you."

"Very well," Taneem said, padding toward the door. Suddenly, she realized how long it had been since her last meal. "Is there any chance I might be able to take a little of your food?"

"Every chance in the galaxy," Harper assured her. "From now on, what's mine is yours."

He smiled again. "And while we eat," he added, "perhaps

you'll tell me more about yourself. And about Jack, and Alison, and Draycos."

The next three days went by slowly for Taneem. Slowly, but in some ways far too fast.

She spent a fair amount of her time roaming the *Advocatus Diaboli*'s ventilation ducts, keeping an eye on Alison and watching Neverlin and Frost at their various activities.

For much of that time, watching the latter two meant crouching by the bridge air duct. Taneem couldn't tell what exactly was happening with the attack force, but they seemed to be moving their various ships in strange ways.

Harper, when she brought back the news of these events, concluded they were doing something he called maneuvers. Those were practice sessions, he told her, to make sure all the ships' crews knew what they were supposed to do when the refugee fleet arrived.

He was eager to learn the details of the maneuvers, and Taneem tried her best. But many of the words Neverlin and Frost used were ones she didn't know and because of that were difficult to memorize. She could only remember bits and pieces, not nearly enough for Harper to put together into a clear picture.

She could tell he was frustrated by her fumbled words and half-remembered phrases. But he never complained. Nor did he criticize Taneem for her shortcomings.

Taneem was grateful for that. She was grateful to him for many other things, too. She still missed Alison, missed her terribly, in fact. But though Harper was a different sort of friend, at the end of those three days Taneem knew that he really *was* a friend. Like Jack and Draycos, she was slowly coming to realize, friends came in different forms.

Oddly, though, in many ways Harper reminded Taneem more of Alison than he did of either Jack or Draycos. She wasn't sure why.

She was still pondering that puzzle when their friendship came to its end.

CHAPTER 25

Taneem knew something important was happening the minute she eased her head around the edge of the grille and peered down into the *Advocatus Diaboli*'s bridge. Not only were Neverlin and Frost present, but so were Alison and the chief Valahgua, the one they called the Lordhighest.

And all of them had the same sense of tension and alertness about them.

Had the refugee fleet arrived?

Taneem listened closely, trying hard to sort through all the strange terms and phrases. Harper had taught her some of them, so it was a little less confusing than it had been in the beginning. But there were so many of them, and all this was still so very new to her.

Once, she saw Alison glance directly up at the grille she was hiding behind. Taneem tensed, but the girl looked away again without any reaction or comment.

And then, Taneem heard the word Harper had told her specifically to listen for. "Hammerfall One, deploy," Frost ordered toward the radio microphone. "Hammerfall Two, prepare to deploy on my command. Hammerfall Three, continue to hold position."

Deploy. Taneem flicked her tail. Harper had made it clear what she was to do when she heard that word. Letting her eyes linger for a moment on Alison, Taneem backed away from the grille and headed back for Harper's stateroom prison.

He was lying facedown on the floor in his underwear when she arrived, doing an exercise he had told her was called push-ups. "Harper?" she called softly from the grille.

"Yeah," he grunted, hopping back to his feet and stepping to the grille. Lately they'd been leaving the grille in place, lest one of the Malison Ring mercenaries catch it open.

But only the top two screws were fastened, and those only loosely. Harper pulled up the bottom of the grille, angling it up far enough to get a hand in. Taneem touched the hand and slid onto his skin.

And then right back off onto the deck. "They said the word," she reported. "Frost said, 'Hammerfall One, deploy.' Then he said for Hammerfall Two to get ready to deploy when he told them to, and that Hammerfall Three was to hold position."

"I see," Harper said, sitting down on the edge of the bed. His manner had gone suddenly quiet and dark. "Did you take the long way around and go by Neverlin's office like I asked you to?"

"Yes," Taneem confirmed. "There were three men standing guard outside the door."

"Were they bunched up?" he asked. "Standing in a close group, I mean?"

"Not really," Taneem said. "There were two right by the door and one a few steps away from them."

Harper hissed between his teeth. "Frost shows his ability to learn," he murmured.

"I don't understand," Taneem said, swishing her tail back and forth as she gazed into his face. There was something about this new Harper that frightened her.

"Either he doesn't completely trust Alison or he isn't convinced that I'm as far out of circulation as he'd like," Harper explained. "Either way, he doesn't want anyone skulking around and using his InterWorld transmitter without permission. The two access points are the bridge, where he's got lots of people to watch for trouble, and his office, where he doesn't. Only now he does."

"You want to call someone?" Taneem asked, grabbing onto the part of that she understood.

"I *need* to call someone, yes," Harper said grimly. "Unfortunately . . . well, there's always another way, isn't there?"

"Do you want me to help you?" Taneem asked hesitantly. "I can fight, a little."

He smiled. "I have no doubt you can," he said. "But even with your help, there are too many of them."

"I also have the special needles you put into the duct when you first came aboard," Taneem reminded him. "Alison gave them to me to hide."

"That would work if I didn't have to cross half the ship to get there," Harper said. "From here, though, I'd never make it that far without someone spotting me."

"Then maybe I could do it for you," Taneem offered. "I could get to the office through the ducts. If you could teach me how to work the controls, maybe I could make the call for you."

For a moment Harper gazed into space, his expression tight and thoughtful. But then he shook his head. "No good," he said. "It's too complicated for me to explain, and any fumbling would tip off the people on the bridge that someone was in there. Then they'd shut down the system, maybe even dismantle it."

He forced another smile. "Besides, you could hardly get in and out alone without leaving a trail. A lot of sliced ductwork, if nothing else."

And once Neverlin knew about her, Taneem knew, he and Frost would hunt her down and kill her. "I don't care," she said, trying hard to be brave. "If it's that important, I'm willing to risk my life."

"I know you are," Harper said gently. Reaching over, he stroked the top of her head, scratching his fingertips briefly against the scales behind her ears. "But I *do* care, and I'm not willing to risk you. Not just yet."

"Then when?"

"I don't know," he said. "But the longer you stay hidden— the longer they don't know about you—the better the chance that you can help Alison later on. Perhaps for something even more important than this."

Standing up, he held out his hand to her. "You'd better get back to the bridge and see what they're up to," he said, his tone suddenly brisk and businesslike.

"What about you?" Taneem asked, ignoring the hand.

"I'm going to do what has to be done," he said. "I've enjoyed our time together, Taneem. I wish it could have been longer. But in life you take what you can get."

"Are you going to attack those men by yourself?" Taneem persisted.

"And thank you especially for trusting me," he added. "Come on, now—up and at 'em. We've got work to do."

Reluctantly, Taneem touched his hand and slid up onto his skin. He stepped back to the grille and slipped his hand into the duct, and Taneem slid off again into the narrow space. "Thank you for protecting me," Taneem said.

"My pleasure," Harper said quietly. "*And* my honor." He wiggled his fingertips at her. "Now scoot." Pulling his hand out, he closed the grille.

For another minute Taneem stayed where she was, watching as he sat back down on the bed and began scratching at the inside of his upper right thigh. Exactly the same way, she remembered, that he'd scratched at his forearms just before he pulled away those pieces of pretend skin.

And sure enough, as she watched he pulled away an identical flap from his leg.

She waited until he'd pulled a similar flap from his other leg. Then, as he gathered his clothing and began to get dressed, she finally moved away down the duct, her heart heavy.

Something bad was about to happen. Something very bad.

And somewhere deep inside her, Taneem knew she'd never see him again.

"Jack?"

Jack jerked awake, blinking his eyes violently. In that first confused moment he tried to bring his hands up to rub his eyes and wondered why he couldn't.

Then his brain cleared a bit, and he remembered. He was in a vac suit, hung up on a bulkhead like a slab of fresh meat, locked inside a half-wrecked troop carrier with a bunch of Brummgas. Had been all that, in fact, for the past three days.

"Jack, can you hear me?"

He tensed, this time coming fully awake. It wasn't Draycos's voice speaking directly to his mind, as he'd first thought.

It was Langston's voice, coming from the comm clip on his collar.

"Langston?" he croaked back, his mouth dry from his sleep. For a second he had a flash of fear, wondering if Langston's voice was even now being transmitted straight to Neverlin via the radio in Jack's suit.

But no. Neverlin had shut off his radio, and none of the Brummgas who'd been changing his oxygen tanks over the past three days had bothered to turn it back on.

"Yes," Langston confirmed. "I just wanted to take a moment to thank you and Draycos for everything you did for me on Semaline."

"No big deal," Jack said, frowning. Why was Langston doing this? More important, why was he doing it *now*?

"It most certainly was," Langston said. "Draycos nearly got himself killed in the process. So did you, for that matter. Anyway, I wasn't sure I'd ever thanked you properly. So this is it."

"You're welcome," Jack said. At the edges of his mind he could feel Draycos listening silently but alertly. "What's going on out there?"

"Our group's about to be deployed," Langston said. "That means that Neverlin's false starts are over, which means we're finally at the real rendezvous point."

Something cold closed around Jack's heart. "And?" he asked carefully.

"Someone has to stop these people," Langston said, his voice hard and determined. "But we're going to need help. I'm going to try to call that help."

"What are you talking about?" Jack asked. "Langston?"

"He's talking about sending a message," a new voice put in quietly. "In the only way any of us can."

Jack blinked. Was that—? "*Harper?*" he demanded.

"But you're too late, Langston," Harper went on, a touch of

grim humor coloring his voice. "You hear me? You be a good boy, and play it cool, and stay in formation. I've got this one."

"Now, what are the *two* of you talking about?" Jack demanded. "Come on—someone talk to me."

"I appreciate the offer, Harper," Langston said. "But this isn't your fight."

"It's very much my fight," Harper said softly. "Besides, I've already burned all my bridges behind me. I can't be of any more use in this war. But there's a chance you can be."

"But—"

"No buts, soldier," Harper said firmly. "You're still a Star-Force officer. Consider this an order."

There was a faint hissing sound as one of the two men exhaled at the comm clip. "Understood, sir," Langston said, his voice stiff and formal and unhappy. "Good luck, sir."

There was a double click as both comm clips shut off. "What the blaze was *that* all about?" Jack snarled, fear and uncertainty and helplessness rising in his throat and threatening to choke him. "Draycos? What was that all about?"

I don't know, the K'da's voice came grimly in his mind. *But nothing good. I'm afraid, Jack, that the battle has begun.*

"Hammerfall groups have reached their positions," Frost reported, half-turning to face Neverlin and Alison. "Backstop ready to deploy."

"I trust you approve of our tactical landscape?" Neverlin asked Alison.

He was half-joking, Alison knew. But only half. He and Frost and the Valahgua had clearly worked out all this in advance, probably months ago.

But the opinion of General Davi's daughter was apparently still worth something. Even if only for amusement value. "Looks reasonable enough," she said. "Your three main forces—the Hammerfalls—are set in a wide triangle formation behind you, perfect for herding you toward the refugee fleet. They're also positioned far enough back that they won't overtake you before you get there. That's the tricky part, really—making it look like they're trying to get to you when they really aren't."

"True," Neverlin said. "On the other hand, the K'da and Shontine aren't going to know how fast Djinn-90s, KK-29s, and Rhino-10s can fly."

"Point," Alison conceded. "At the same time, you don't want them so far back that they'll overtake you too slowly. That might give the K'da and Shontine too much time to stop and think while you're barreling toward them."

"Which is the reason for the five Djinn-90s of the Backstop group," Neverlin said, clearly pleased that he and Frost had anticipated that question and had an answer ready for it. "As our supposed rear guard, they can move up toward us if we need the Hammerfall groups to speed up, or else fall back if we need them to slow down."

"Clever," Alison said. She'd already figured that out, actually, but it wouldn't hurt to stroke Neverlin's ego a little. "You can't risk any direct radio communication with the Hammerfall ships—the K'da would definitely find that suspicious if they spotted it. This way all the Hammerfall Leaders have to do is monitor the Backstop group's position relative to the *Advocatus Diaboli* and they'll know what you want them to do."

"Exactly," Neverlin said. "The Lordhighest doesn't think the fleet would pick up a tight beam pointed at such angles, but it's better to be safe than—"

"Sir!" the *Advocatus Diaboli*'s captain spoke up sharply. "We've got lifepod separation. Number two, port-side bow."

"What?" Neverlin demanded, crossing over to stand behind him. "Who in—?"

"Never mind *who*," Frost cut him off. "Where's he going?"

"He's curving around," the captain reported, peering at his displays. "Looks like he's trying to—correction: he's curving around again. Picking up speed."

"Evasive!" Frost barked. "Backstop group—emergency close and engage!"

"What's going on?" Neverlin demanded. "Frost?"

"He's going to ram," Frost snarled. "I said *evasive*, frunge you."

"Trying, sir," the helmsman shot back. "We're not as maneuverable as he is."

"Backstop?" Frost snapped.

"Backstop Leader," a tight voice came back. "We're out of position, Colonel. No way to get to him in time without hitting you."

Frost glared at the displays, muttering under his breath. Then, abruptly, he turned on the Lordhighest. "The Death," he ordered. "Get him with the Death. Now!"

"You do not order us in that tone—"

"To blazes with my tone!" Frost snapped. "Just *kill him*."

For a moment the Valahgua gazed at him. Then, he muttered a pair of guttural-sounding words toward his shoulder. There was a slight flicker of the bridge lights—

"Got him," the captain announced. "Helm: hard about."

"Too late," Neverlin said, pointing at the display. "He's going to hit."

The captain must have seen that, too. "Collision!" he shouted. "All hands!"

Lunging to the nearest console, Alison grabbed the handgrip and braced herself.

A fraction of a second later, the lifepod hit.

It wasn't a big impact, not nearly as big or violent as Alison had expected. The *Advocatus Diaboli* shuddered like a dog giving a final shake as it shed the last bit of water after a dip in a cold lake. But the bridge didn't fill with the screaming of the hull-breach alarm, or even the slightly less strident hooting of the decompression warning.

She took a careful breath, feeling slightly ridiculous. Given the urgency of Frost's warning, she'd expected something a lot more dramatic.

Neverlin apparently had, too. "Is that it?" he asked, sounding flustered and more than a little annoyed.

"No, that is *not* it," Frost bit out. "Captain, get someone to the InterWorld transmitter and shut it down."

"Shut it *down*?" Neverlin put in. "But it's not on."

"You worthless fool," Frost snarled at him. "What do you think an emergency beacon *is*?"

Neverlin stiffened. "Oh no."

"Exactly." Snarling a curse, Frost left the bridge at a dead run.

"What has happened?" the Valahgua demanded. "Neverlin, explain."

"Later," Neverlin said, starting to follow Frost.

"Not later," the Valahgua insisted. "Now."

With a visible effort, Neverlin slowed to a stop. "This ship is equipped with an emergency distress beacon," he ground out. "That beacon is connected to our InterWorld transmitter. In an emergency—such as a lifepod ramming our hull—it sends out a signal that anyone within range can pick up."

He glared at Alison. "*And* can trace."

"Don't look at *me*," Alison warned. "Whatever happened, it wasn't my—"

She broke off as a brief staccato of shots sounded in the distance. What in the *world*? "Whatever happened, it wasn't my doing," she went on, fighting to keep her voice calm and even. The daughter of Aram Davi shouldn't be startled by a little random gunfire, after all. "I suggest you or Colonel Frost start by taking a head count and finding out who's missing."

"No need," Neverlin said bitterly. "It was Harper. It had to be him."

Alison felt her stomach tighten. Harper. Of course. "All by himself?" she asked pointedly. "An interesting trick."

"Braxton's full of interesting tricks," Neverlin said. But there was a glint in his eye as his gaze drifted around the bridge.

Across the bridge, the door opened and Frost reappeared. "The transmitter's been shut off," he said. "If we're lucky, we got it fast enough that no one was able to get a solid fix on it."

"That was my *transmitter* you were shooting at?" Neverlin demanded. "Blast it all, Colonel—"

"Would you rather have Harper's friends drop in on us while we're in the middle of looting the refugee ships?" Frost asked. "If someone followed Harper to Point Two they're only four days away."

Neverlin's lips pressed together into a thin line. "Captain, get your men busy making repairs to the InterWorld transmitter," he growled.

"Yes, sir," the captain said.

Neverlin looked at Alison. "And once it's back together, have them disconnect the emergency beacon system," he added.

"Do not fear the friends of our enemies," the Valahgua said.

"If any come, they will die as surely as will the K'da and Shontine."

"Let's just hope your K'da and Shontine are on time," Frost put in darkly. "If they're late, we could end up being caught between two different groups of enemies. That's generally considered a bad idea."

"Do not lecture me on military truths," the Valahgua said stiffly. "And do not concern yourself with such matters. If our enemies arrive together, they will die together."

"I'm sure they will," Neverlin said before Frost could answer. "Meanwhile, we have our final few ships to deploy."

"Not yet," the Valahgua said. "You have tracked the lifepod that carried the traitor?"

"I don't know," Neverlin said. "Captain?"

"Yes, sir, we have its trajectory," the captain said, peering at his displays.

"You will retrieve it," the Valahgua said. "Send your ships now."

"Lordhighest, all we have available right now are the five Djinn-90s of the Backstop group," Frost reminded him. "Everyone else is over a thousand miles behind us at the three Hammerfall start points."

"If you're worried about the refugee fleet spotting it, we can simply destroy it," Neverlin offered.

"You will retrieve it intact," the Valahgua said. "We have never before used the Death on a human. I wish to study exactly how its effect has been."

Neverlin looked at Frost, and Alison could sense a sudden uneasiness in both men. "There's no need to make a full investigation," Neverlin said, his voice studiously casual. "You told me you and your colleagues would be leaving as soon as the K'da and Shontine were destroyed."

"There is science to be done, Neverlin," the Valahgua said. "The science *will* be done. Retrieve the lifepod and the body."

Neverlin's lip twitched, but he nodded to Frost. "Go ahead, Colonel," he said, again working at sounding casual. "I'm sure your pilots can figure out some way to grab the lifepod."

For a half-dozen heartbeats Frost continued to glower at the Valahgua. Then, with clear reluctance, he gestured to the captain. "Feed Backstop Leader the lifepod's trajectory and order him to retrieve it," he said shortly. He looked back at Neverlin. "Anything else?"

"No, that will be all." Neverlin turned to Alison. "Would you care to sit in on the autopsy?"

"No, thank you," Alison said. "If you don't mind, I'd like to go back to my stateroom for a while and get some rest."

"Good idea," Neverlin said, his eyes suddenly thoughtful as he gazed at her. "Yes. A very good idea."

As always, Alison gave her stateroom a quick sweep with her sensor as soon as she was inside. As usual, she found they'd planted another bug while she'd been out. Dealing with it, she lay down on the bed.

And let her heartache wash over her.

It was all going wrong. All of it. Spectacularly and devastatingly wrong. Taneem was probably dead, drifting off into that strange fourth-dimensional world, all because Alison hadn't been able to break free from Neverlin and Frost in time. Jack and Draycos didn't seem to have made any move to take over the troop carrier, like she'd expected them to. Maybe Neverlin had changed his mind and they were dead, too.

And Harper *was* dead. Killed quickly, quietly, and efficiently by the Valahgua and their monstrous Death weapon.

It was all coming apart.

And it was all her fault.

What in space had ever made her think she could pull off something like this, anyway?

She didn't know how long she lay there, staring at the ceiling and condemning herself and her failures. All she knew was that she was suddenly startled out of a light doze by a soft scratching at the ventilation grille.

She bounded off the bed onto her feet, staggering a little as the blood level in her brain dropped briefly before her heart got up to speed again. "Taneem?" she called softly, afraid to hope.

But for once, hope hadn't abandoned her. "Yes," the K'da's familiar voice came back. "May I come in?"

"Of course, of course," Alison said, grabbing the desk chair and pulling it over to the grille. "I don't suppose you still have the screwdrivers we borrowed from Harper?"

"Yes, I've had everything waiting right here," Taneem said. A thin piece of plastic slid into view through one of the openings in the duct. "Here."

Alison took it and set feverishly to work. It was the flat-head screwdriver, not exactly suited to the crosshead bolts the grille was fastened with.

But it was good enough, and Alison was inspired, and within two minutes she had the grille open far enough for her to wedge her hand up into the duct.

Two seconds after that, Taneem was once again nestled against her skin.

"Thank God," Alison murmured as she refastened the grille. "Thank God. I was hoping you'd found a safe haven."

"I couldn't get to you," Taneem murmured back. "You were with Neverlin and Frost the whole time."

"I know," Alison said, climbing off the chair and putting it back in its place by the desk. Going back to the bed, she lay down again.

But this time, it was relief that washed through her instead of heartache. "I tried every trick I could think of to get away, but they weren't buying any of them," she went on. "I couldn't even go the bathroom alone for those first few hours. I don't think they completely trusted me back then. Probably still don't," she added, remembering the look on Neverlin's face as she'd left the bridge just now. "All I could do was hope you could find a sleeping crewman or someone else you could borrow long enough to get by." She was babbling like an idiot, she knew. But strangely enough she didn't care. "I tried to point you forward toward the crew section a couple of times—did you notice?"

"I did better than that," Taneem interrupted her gently. "Harper let me stay with him." She paused, and Alison winced with the sudden sadness she could sense in her friend. "He's dead, isn't he?"

"Yes, he is," Alison said, fresh tears misting across her eyes. "He died trying to save Draycos's people."

"Did he succeed?"

Alison swallowed hard. "Not by himself," she said. "Maybe not even with all the rest of us to help."

She wiped at her eyes with her sleeve. "But it's not over yet," she added firmly. An hour ago, all her hope had been gone. But now some of it was back. Maybe enough of it. "Not by a long shot."

There was a soft knock on the door. "Hide," she whispered urgently to Taneem as she stood up. She waited until the K'da had settled herself out of sight beneath her clothing, then keyed the door open.

It was Neverlin. To Alison's mild surprise, he was alone. "Ms. Davi," he greeted her courteously. "May I come in?"

"As you wish," Alison said, stepping back out of the doorway, her heart thudding suddenly in her chest. Could he have recognized her, as Frost had back on Brum-a-dum? "Please; sit down."

"Thank you." Stepping to the desk, he swiveled the chair around and lowered himself into it. "I trust you had a good rest," he continued as Alison perched herself on the corner of the bed facing him.

"I'm feeling much better, thank you," Alison said, telling the complete truth for once.

"Good." Neverlin paused. "Tell me, how soon do you think your father could get a full military force out here?"

"Not nearly soon enough," Alison said. "The refugee fleet could be here, what, as early as tomorrow?"

"Theoretically, yes," Neverlin said. "Though personally I'm not expecting them for another four to six days. But I wasn't thinking about a force for the attack itself."

"Then for what?"

"For the work afterward." Neverlin gave her a small smile, his eyes glinting unpleasantly. "For the looting."

"For the looting?" Alison asked pointedly. "Or for protecting us from any friends Harper might have on the way?"

"You mean his friends in Braxton Universis Security?" Neverlin snorted. "Actually, I rather hope they do show up. The more of them our Valahguan friends take care of here, the fewer I'll have to deal with later when I take over the company. The Valahgua have finished their examination of Harper's body, by the way."

Alison forced herself not to look away from him. "Any surprises?" she asked.

"Not really," Neverlin said. "The Death apparently kills humans as efficiently as it does everyone else."

"An interesting weapon," Alison said.

"Which I hope never gets a foothold in the Orion Arm," Neverlin said, his voice going odd. "That's one of the reasons I was hoping your father could get a force out here, in fact."

Alison frowned at him. "Are you asking my father to help you kill the *Valahgua*?"

"Perhaps the Valahgua," Neverlin said, shrugging slightly. "Or perhaps others. I presume you noticed Colonel Frost's confrontation with the Lordhighest just before you left the bridge. He nearly came to blows with him."

"I'm not sure I'd call it coming to blows, exactly," Alison hedged. "I've seen you and Frost lock horns as solidly as they were doing."

"Exactly my point," Neverlin said. "The colonel has been growing more and more erratic lately. That's not a good thing for a delicate alliance like ours."

"So you're thinking it might be a good time to clean house?" Alison suggested.

"Something like that." Neverlin paused, considering. "Perhaps both the house *and* the barn."

Alison stared at him. "Are you suggesting getting rid of Frost *and* the Brummgas?"

"You said your father wanted a fair cut," Neverlin pointed out. "This would certainly leave a larger share for him."

"It would indeed," Alison said, forcing her voice to remain calm. Neverlin was even more cold-blooded than she'd thought.

"How would you explain the loss of his troops to the Patri Chookoock?"

"This is war," Neverlin reminded her. "People die all the time in wars."

"True," Alison said. "Well, it certainly wouldn't cost anything to ask Dad what he thought about all this. How long until the InterWorld transmitter is up and running again?"

"Another hour at the most," Neverlin said. "We've now removed all the bullets Frost fired into it." He grimaced. "As I said, he's getting more and more erratic."

"I wish you luck trying to take his guns away from him," Alison said dryly. "Fine. As soon as the transmitter is working again—"

Beside her bed, the intercom gave a ping. "Mr. Neverlin?" the *Advocatus Diaboli*'s captain's voice came. "Bridge to Mr. Neverlin."

Alison reached over and keyed the switch. "Yes, Captain?" Neverlin called.

"We've got five ships coming off ECHO directly ahead," the captain said.

"Range?" Neverlin demanded, scrambling to his feet.

"About five thousand miles," the captain said. "Correction—there are now twenty ships. No; fifty. A hundred twenty. Good God—it's over three hundred. And they're still coming."

Neverlin looked at Alison, his eyes dark. "The K'da and Shontine," he said. "They're here."

CHAPTER 26

Frost and the Lordhighest were already on the bridge when Neverlin and Alison arrived. Frost gave the newcomers a quick and slightly curious look before returning his attention to the main status board. "What's happening?" Neverlin asked as he stepped to Frost's side.

"Nothing yet," Frost told him. "The fleet is still dribbling in off ECHO, though it finally looks like they're almost finished. Over nine hundred ships so far, including between fifty and sixty major warships in vanguard position."

"We will destroy them all," the Valahgua rumbled.

"I'm sure you will," Neverlin said briefly. "Are we moving yet?"

"Yes, sir," Frost confirmed, pointing at the display. "The *Fox-wolf*'s taken point, with us riding her aft starboard flank and Backstop forming up in rear-guard position behind us."

"What about the troop carrier?" Neverlin asked. "Never mind—I see it."

"I've got it limping along after us," Frost said. "A noble and valiant ally who's been wounded but is still trying gamely to stay with us. The Lordhighest says the K'da and Shontine are suckers for that sort of thing."

A brief smattering of alien speech came over the bridge

speaker. "That's the fleet again," Frost said. "They've already called once, while you were on your way here."

"Are we going to answer?" Neverlin asked, looking at the Valahgua.

"Not we," the alien said. "The Lordover of the *Foxwolf* will reply for us."

The alien words came over the speaker again. This time, they were answered, by what sounded to Alison like the same language and a very similar voice. "The *Foxwolf*'s Lordover?" she asked.

"Yes, speaking through a voice changer," the Lordhighest said. "He welcomes the fleet after their long journey and tells them he also brings a new ally."

There was another rapid-fire exchange, followed by another. "What are they saying now?" Neverlin muttered.

"The Lordover speaks of the force that attacked and nearly annihilated us," the Lordhighest said, a macabre amusement in his voice. "He warns that we may not have completely escaped them."

"Very well." Neverlin took a deep breath. "Colonel? Do it."

Frost nodded and gestured to the captain. "Order Backstop Leader to pull forward two hundred yards," he said.

"Will that be enough?" Neverlin asked. "Two hundred yards won't look like much from the Hammerfalls' distance."

"It's more than enough," Frost assured him. "Especially with the troop carrier now falling back from us. A simple ranging pulse between us, the carrier, and the Backstop ships will give them everything they need."

"Hammerfall groups on the move," the captain reported.

Another burst of alien speech came from the speaker, this time with a sense of urgency to it. "The *Foxwolf*'s Lordover has pretended to notice the pursuit," the Lordhighest translated. "He is calling on our friends in the refugee fleet for protection."

"Sir, the *Foxwolf* is increasing speed," the helmsman said.

"Match him," Frost ordered, his eyes flicking between the forward and aft tactical displays. "Signal Backstop to maintain current distance from us. We don't want the Hammerfalls closing too fast."

"Troop carrier is falling farther behind," the captain said.

"Signal them to maintain their current speed," Frost said. He turned a tight smile on Neverlin and Alison. "Our valiant ally, unable to keep up."

"Six of the refugee warships are moving forward," the captain said. "Angling outward toward the Hammerfall groups. Other warships are moving to fill the gaps."

"They want to help, but they're still not sure about us," Frost said.

"The *Foxwolf's* Lordover will convince them," the Lord-highest said, a repulsive anticipation bubbling beneath his voice. "Victory is ours, Neverlin."

"Let's not count our profits too soon," Neverlin warned. "Even with the Death on our side, there's still a battle to be fought before—"

He broke off as a small but brilliant flash appeared on the aft display. "What was that?" Alison asked, pointing to it.

"Some kind of explosion aboard the troop carrier," Frost said, frowning as he leaned closer to the display.

There was another flash, then another, then two more in rapid succession. "What in the name of—?" Neverlin demanded.

Abruptly, something seemed to fade into view beside the troop carrier. Something small and quick, firing its missiles into the carrier's small weapons pods and bridge.

And Alison caught her breath. "Chameleon hull-wrap," she murmured.

Frost swore viciously. "It's the *Essenay*," he snarled. "It's the damn frunging *Essenay*."

It had been over three hours since that last communication with Langston and Harper, and Jack had heard nothing else from anyone.

He'd tried to ask for details from the next Brummga who came to change his oxygen tank, hoping to find out what all that had been about. But his vac suit radio was still shut off, and he doubted the big alien had even noticed the prisoner's lips moving.

And then, even as he and Draycos were trying to decide whether it was finally time for Draycos to go on the offensive, the troop carrier gave a lurch and began to move.

Any ideas? Draycos asked.

None whatsoever, buddy, Jack answered grimly, pressing his helmet against the bulkhead behind him and trying to decipher the hums and crinkles he could hear through the metal. *It sounds like we're under way, but at only half speed. Maybe less.*

More maneuvers?

Could be, Jack conceded. *You getting anything?*

There was a brief sense of movement as Draycos leaned off his back and peered over the bulkhead. *The preparation room is still deserted,* Draycos reported.

For a few minutes they listened together in silence. The carrier had turned slightly to port side, Jack decided, and was now heading straight forward. If this was some kind of maneuver, it was a pretty simpleminded one.

And then, the faint engine and maneuvering-jet sounds were abruptly drowned out by a much louder thud. It was followed by another, then another, then by a quick one-two pair.

Those are missile impacts, Draycos said suddenly. *Someone is shooting at us.*

Are we shooting back? Jack asked, straining his ears. To him, all the pounding just sounded like someone taking a large hammer to the carrier's hull.

Yes, Draycos said. *But too little and too late. It sounds like the attacker has finished with the defenses and has moved on to the bridge—*

"Jack?" Uncle Virge's voice came from Jack's comm clip. "Jack lad? Can you hear me?"

It took Jack a second to find his voice. "Uncle Virge? Where are you? What are you doing?"

"At the moment, beating the stuffing out of the troop carrier you're on," Uncle Virge said with clear satisfaction. "You're still in the starboard scout ship bay, right?"

"Fine time to ask, but yes," Jack said. "How did you know?"

"Langston told me," Uncle Virge said. "He has your comm clip's frequency and pattern—did you know that?"

"Yes, I gave them to him," Jack said. "How did you get in so close without being spotted?"

"I just drifted in nice and slow with the hull-wrap going," Uncle Virge said. "Turns out it works even better in space than it does on the ground, provided you don't lean on the drive. There we go—all finished."

The impacts, Jack realized suddenly, had stopped. So had the sound of the carrier's drive. "Great," he said. "Now all we need to do is figure out how to get me out of here."

"Leave that to me," Draycos said. "Uncle Virge, bring the *Essenay* to the starboard scout ship hatch and wait."

You sure you know what you're doing? Jack asked.

Very sure, Draycos said. *Back to the bulkhead, please. I'm getting off.*

"Destroy them!" Neverlin snarled. "You hear me, Frost? I want Morgan and that blasted kid killed."

Alison felt Taneem stir nervously on her skin. Those were her friends out there. . . . "No," Alison spoke up firmly. "Dad wants the K'da alive."

"To hell with the K'da," Neverlin said, throwing her a quick glare. "Frost?"

"We can't reach them," Frost ground out between clenched teeth. "They're out of range."

"Don't be ridiculous," Neverlin snapped. "Turn a couple of Backstop's Djinn-90s around and deal with them."

"We can't move the Backstop ships," Frost said. "They're the ones the Hammerfalls are watching, remember? You want them to end up falling back, then surging forward, then falling back, then surging forward again?"

"If you think I'm going to let them get away now—"

"Enough," the Valahgua cut him off. "The K'da and his boy cannot harm us. Merely jam all communications so he cannot speak to the fleet."

Neverlin took a deep breath, his eyes burning as he glared at the alien. "Full-spectrum radio bubble, Captain," he ordered. "Lock out everything except ours."

"First signal the Backstop ships to go wide and institute bubbles of their own," Frost added. "And have them spread outward to the sides as far as they can and still keep their bubbles overlapping ours. If we're going to make a blank spot, we might as well make it a good, wide one."

"Yes, sir," the captain said. He tapped a key and started giving orders.

As he did so, Alison felt a movement on her skin. She looked down as Taneem's head slid up her shoulder and neck just far enough to see through the opening in her collar. "Hey," Alison whispered, tapping urgently on her shoulder. If Frost or Neverlin should happen to glance over here, the whole game would be up.

The captain finished relaying the orders and keyed another pair of switches. "Bubble activated," he reported.

Alison tapped again on her shoulder. This time, to her relief, Taneem slid back down out of sight.

"Fine," Neverlin said, still glowering at the Lordhighest. "Continue the operation."

With a shove from his hind paws, Draycos leaped off Jack's shoulders, through the vac suit and bulkhead, and into the preparation room next door.

The question of how to take over the troop carrier had occupied most of Draycos's thoughts for the past three days. Without knowing the ship's layout or crew complement, he'd known from the beginning that such an undertaking would have only a small chance for success.

Now, to his relief, all those thoughts and concerns had become irrelevant.

Bounding across the room, he reached the rack of oxygen tanks fastened to the sidewall. There were exactly twenty-eight of them, he noted in passing as he began slashing through the metal with his claws.

Within a minute the rack was wobbling violently back and forth as the compressed air spewed out into the room. Crossing to the airlock that led into the hangar bay, Draycos keyed open the inner door. Waiting until the extra air pressure in the room began to hurt his ears, he slashed through the airlock's inner door.

His eardrums fluttered at the sudden change in pressure as the air in the preparation room began to flow into the vacuum of the hangar bay. Draycos waited, crouched against the wind, hoping the oxygen from the bottles he'd opened would be enough to fill the bay.

It was. A few seconds later, as the pressure between the two areas evened out and the wind slowed to a stop, he keyed open the inner door.

Jack was watching anxiously as Draycos stepped into the bay. The boy's worried look changed to one of relief as Draycos hurried over to him. "I was hoping all that wind was your doing," Jack's voice came faintly through the helmet.

"All part of the plan," Draycos assured him. Five more slashes of his claws, and Jack was no longer anchored to the bulkhead.

"It's always nice when these plans work," Jack agreed as he popped off his helmet. "Come aboard and let's get out of here."

Draycos touched the boy's neck and slithered onto his skin. Jack hurried toward the main hatch controls, putting his helmet back on as he jogged across the bay. He reached the controls, double-checked his helmet seal, and flipped up the opening switch's safety cover. "Get ready, Uncle Virge," he called. "Here we come."

"Ready, Jack lad."

Getting a grip on the handhold, Jack threw the switch.

The hatch slid open, creating an instant hurricane as the air Draycos had just poured into the bay went pouring right back out again. Jack held on gamely until the wind had stopped, then looked out.

Draycos slid up his neck and looked out, too. The *Essenay* was right outside the hatch, pacing the carrier no more than fifty yards away, its hatch wide open. *I guess we jump?* Jack asked.

Yes, but not too fast, Draycos said. *Remember that the only thing available to slow us down is the airlock's back wall.*

Got it, Jack said dryly. Taking a deep breath, he bent his knees, leaned halfway out of the hatchway, and shoved off.

"The *Essenay* is still pacing the carrier," the captain reported. "No indications yet that the prisoner has escaped."

"That won't last long," Neverlin growled, pounding his fist rhythmically on the edge of the captain's chair back. "All Morgan has to do is blow the hatch, suit up, and unweld the kid from the bulkhead."

"And then get to the edge of the jamming bubble in time to warn the refugees," Frost said. "Maybe we *should* detach one of the Djinn-90s from Backstop and have it deal with them."

"If the Hammerfall Leaders are confused by one ship out of five being diverted, they have no business being the leaders of anything," Neverlin agreed. "Do it."

"Just a minute," Alison spoke up, leaning toward the display. "Are we sure Virgil Morgan is actually aboard that ship?"

"If it's not Morgan, who is it?" Frost retorted.

"Maybe no one," Alison said. This was one of Jack's deepest secrets, she knew, and she felt a little funny about revealing it without his permission.

But she needed to buy him some time, and making his situation look more hopeless than it really was might do the trick. "I keep thinking about the fact that in all the time I flew with him Jack never once called or met up with his uncle."

"Then who's flying the *Essenay*?" Frost persisted.

"I don't know," Alison said. "But didn't Jack say his parents had been Judge-Paladins?"

"I'll be cursed," Frost breathed, his anger and impatience suddenly gone. "I'll be double cursed. That's his *parents' old ship.* Morgan must have stolen it the same time he hooked up with the kid."

Neverlin barked a short laugh. "Well, well. A Judge-Paladin ship, eh? No wonder we haven't been able to find Virgil Morgan all these months."

"Explain," the Valahgua demanded.

"We couldn't find him because he isn't aboard that ship," Neverlin said. "Not anymore. He's dead or just gone—it doesn't really matter which."

He pointed to the display. "What matters is that that ship is being run by a very sophisticated computer."

He smiled maliciously. "And a computer can't suit up and cut Jack free."

"Which means Jack is still out of the picture," Frost said. "He'll stay chained to the bulkhead until all this is over and we go back and get him."

"Assuming he lives that long," Neverlin said. "If his ship has managed to kill all the Brummgas, he and the K'da will die as soon as their current air tank runs out."

Neverlin looked at Alison. "In which case we'll try to keep one of the civilian refugee ships intact for your father," he added.

"I'd appreciate that," Alison said, breathing a quiet sigh of relief. Finally, something she'd done had worked.

"There—see," the Lordhighest put in. "They have increased speed. The warships are coming to our aid. They will now be the first to die."

"Patience, Lordhighest," Neverlin said calmly. With Jack and Draycos off the threat list, his plan was back on track again. "We're going to allow those six ships to go past us unharmed. Perhaps we'll let the next batch through, too, assuming the Lordover on the *Foxwolf* is able to persuade them to send a second group. We want as many enemy ships out of position before we show what we have waiting."

Alison gazed at the displays, estimating times and distances. If every ship kept to its same course and speed, she realized with a sinking feeling, Neverlin's plan was going to work beautifully. Those six K'da/Shontine warships would be completely out of the fight by the time the *Foxwolf* and *Advocatus Diaboli* opened up with their Death weapons. If the K'da and Shontine detached another group of warships as well, Neverlin could probably take out a good percentage of the remaining defenders before they even realized what they were facing.

And then, as she watched, another group of ten K'da/Shontine warships moved away from the refugee fleet. Forming up into a loose combat array, they started forward.

And Alison came to a decision.

"I'll be back in a minute," she said, heading for the bridge door.

No one bothered to answer. With their attention on their incoming prey, possibly no one even heard her. Leaving the bridge, she headed aft.

Back on Brum-a-dum she had promised Taneem she would

help protect Draycos's people. Up to now, everything she'd done toward that goal had been relatively safe and easy and ineffective. But all of that was about to change.

All of it.

CHAPTER 27

The trip across the fifty-yard gap seemed to Jack to take forever. But then, all at once, the *Essenay*'s open hatchway loomed in front of him.

And then he was through the opening and flying across the airlock way faster than he'd realized he was going. He threw out his arms and braced himself.

He hit the far wall, thankfully not as hard as he'd expected. His arms took the impact with ease, and even as he bounced back again he felt the flow of air against his vac suit as Uncle Virge closed the hatch behind him and started filling the airlock.

"Are you all right, Jack lad?" the computer's voice came as Jack unfastened his helmet. He'd barely gotten it off before Draycos leaped out of his collar and took off toward the cockpit. "Langston said Harper got killed ramming the *Advocatus Diaboli*—"

"Later," Jack interrupted. Stripping off the vac suit, he headed after Draycos.

He was halfway to the cockpit before Uncle Virge's last comment suddenly registered.

Harper had been *killed*?

But there was no time to think about that now. He and Draycos had a fleet to save.

Jack reached the cockpit to find Draycos standing behind the pilot's seat, his forepaws resting on the back of the chair, his long neck moving back and forth as he scanned the *Essenay*'s displays. "How's it look?" Jack asked, slipping past him and sitting down.

"The fleet's still far out of the Death's range," Draycos said. "But several of the warships have left position and are moving forward. They seem to be angling toward three areas to the rear of the *Advocatus Diaboli*."

"Great," Jack grunted, glancing over the *Essenay*'s systems as he strapped in. The only ships he could see ahead of them were the *Advocatus Diaboli*, the *Foxwolf*, and five of Frost's Djinn-90s. The latter, to Jack's mild surprise, had spread themselves wide to all sides instead of flying in a group between him and two bigger ships. "Uncle Virge, do you have a tag on the rest of Neverlin's fleet?"

"They're about a thousand miles behind us," Uncle Virge said. "In three different groups, like Draycos said. All three groups are moving up fast."

"Pretending they're chasing the poor defenseless *Foxwolf* and *Advocatus Diaboli*," Jack said, nodding grimly. "Uncle Virgil and I ran this scam I don't know how many times."

"How do we defeat it?" Draycos asked.

"All it takes is a toot on the whistle," Jack said, keying the long-range transmitter. "K'da/Shontine fleet, this is the *Essenay*," he said. "Please respond."

There was no answer. "K'da/Shontine refugee fleet, this is Jack Morgan aboard the *Essenay*," Jack tried again. "I have someone here who needs to speak to you." He gestured Draycos toward the microphone. "Draycos?"

Draycos let loose with a torrent of alien speech. Jack listened in fascination at the flow of the words, regretting the fact that he wouldn't be able to understand and therefore fully appreciate the astonishment that would undoubtedly be part of the fleet's response.

But there was no response, astonished or otherwise. "Uncle Virge?" he asked.

"Radio's working perfectly, Jack lad," Uncle Virge assured him. "Neverlin must be jamming or bubbling the signal."

"Of course he is," Jack said, disgusted with himself for not having realized that sooner. "That's why those five Djinn-90s are flying wide—they're adding their own jamming to the mix."

"What method of jamming is he using?" Draycos asked.

"Either a blank bubble or a jamming static field," Uncle Virge said. "I can't tell which from this distance. A bubble absorbs or scatters all radio signals passing through it, while a static field simply broadcasts noise on all frequencies so as to drown out everything else."

"It's probably a bubble," Jack said. "It's classier and a lot more subtle. It's also easier to keep your own communications open with a bubble than it is with static."

"If the *Advocatus Diaboli* is able to signal through the bubble, does that mean we can do the same if we use its frequency and pattern?" Draycos asked.

"In theory, yes," Jack said. "In practice, we'll never find the pattern in time."

"Then what do we do?"

Jack gazed out the canopy at the drive glows ahead in the distance. "We get past the bubble," he said, getting a grip on the control yoke and firing up the main drive. "And since those Djinn-90s were kind enough to pull way out to the sides out of the way, it looks like our best bet will be to go straight up the middle."

"Up the *middle?*" Uncle Virge echoed. "Jack, you don't mean—?"

"I sure do," Jack confirmed as he ran the drive to full power. "We're taking this crate right up the *Advocatus Diaboli's* tailpipe."

The *Advocatus Diaboli's* living areas were deserted as Alison made her way aft from the bridge.

Not surprising, really. All of the crew were at their emergency stations, and all the Malison Ring mercenaries still on board were guarding the bridge, the Death, and other vital areas.

One of those areas was Neverlin's office, she saw as she rounded the final corner and came within sight of the office door. There were three men on duty: two flanking the door, the third holding station down the corridor halfway between the office and Alison.

There was no way she could take out all three of them, positioned as they were, at once, not even with Taneem to help. Alison would have to play it another way.

"I need to get into Mr. Neverlin's office," she announced as she strode forward.

The nearest of the guards stirred, as if preparing to move into her path. Alison gave him a brief, lofty look, and he seemed to think better of it. "It's a thumbprint lock, Ms. Davi," he said instead.

"I know," Alison said. "He's already programmed me in."

The other's lip twitched. "Colonel Frost left orders that no one was to be allowed near the office."

"Colonel Frost isn't in charge of Mr. Neverlin's office," Alison countered as she strode past him. "You can check with Mr. Neverlin if you want."

She got two more steps before the sergeant at the door

worked through his own hesitation and nodded to the man now behind Alison. "Give him a call, Halberd," he said.

Alison glanced back over her shoulder as the mercenary tapped his comm clip. "Halberd for Mr. Neverlin," he called.

Alison kept going, forcing herself to maintain a calm, even pace. Neverlin hadn't been wearing a comm clip, which meant Halberd's call would have to go through one of the *Advocatus Diaboli's* crew, all of whom were rather busy right now. With luck, that would give her the time she needed.

She reached the door and stepped between the two guards. "A minute, please, Ms. Davi," the sergeant said, holding his hand out to block her as she lifted her right thumb toward the waist-high reader.

"Fine," Alison said with an annoyed sigh. Turning around, she leaned her back against the door.

And as she did, she pressed her left thumb against the base of her left forefinger and slid her implanted lockpick out from beneath the fingernail. Keeping the hand behind her back, she eased the pick into the programming notch beneath the reader.

Private ship locks, which were usually only accessible by trusted friends and employees, were seldom very well defended. This one was no exception. Within a few seconds she felt the gentle snick that signaled that the lockpick had done its electronic magic. The lock was open to receive new data.

She looked down the corridor. Halberd was still talking quietly on his comm clip, but his forehead was starting to crease into a frown. Sliding the lockpick back beneath her nail, Alison reached her left hand a little higher behind her back and pressed her thumb to the reader.

Behind her, the door slid open. "Hey!" Halberd shouted, pointing toward her.

The other two turned to look. Their eyes widened as Alison took a long step backward into the office and slapped the lock control.

One of the guards lunged sideways, making a last-second grab for her. But the door was faster, sliding into his arms and batting them aside and back out into the corridor.

"That was close," Taneem murmured as Alison circled Neverlin's desk and headed for the door to the communications nook. The K'da lifted her head from Alison's shoulder, then bounded out through her collar. "What do you want me to do?"

"Right now, just stay out of the way," Alison said. She opened the door to the nook and sat down at the console. Keying for long-range radio, she hit the switch. "Attention, K'da/Shontine refugee fleet," she said into the microphone. "Attention. You're in danger. The ships coming toward you are not, repeat *not,* friends or allies. They're enemies attempting to get behind your defenses—"

"Identify yourself," a voice demanded in heavily accented English.

Not a human voice, Alison decided, or Valahguan or Brummgan, or even K'da. Shontine? "My name is Alison Kayna," she said. "I'm a friend of Draycos, poet-warrior of the K'da, who arrived six months ago aboard the *Havenseeker.*"

"Let me speak with Draycos."

"He's not here with me," Alison said. "He's in another ship, whose communications have been cut off."

"Which other ship? Can you prove you are friend of Draycos?"

"He has golden scales, each with a red edge—"

"Not description," the other cut her off. "Can you prove you are friend of Draycos?"

Alison felt her stomach tighten. It had never occurred to her that the refugee fleet might not believe her story. From the way Draycos had talked, she'd assumed they would be coming in alert and suspicious and not trusting anybody or anything.

But of course, the Lordover on the *Foxwolf* had gotten to them first. In fact, he was probably talking to the fleet right now, feeding them his version of who and what Alison was. "No, I can't prove it," she gritted. "But you have to—"

And then, to her surprise, Taneem leaned over her shoulder, her gray-scaled snout pointed toward the microphone. " 'The sky was fair,' " she said. " 'The evil's lair

> " 'Was scattered on the hill's black side.
> " 'The warriors grim, in light so dim
> " 'Were gathered like the ocean's tide.
> " 'For evil they would not abide.
> " 'Though death await, if death their fate,
> " 'From this their faces would not hide,
> " 'For evil they would not abide.' "

She seemed to shake herself. "The start of *Troodae's Saga*," she identified it. "Translated into English by the poet-warrior Draycos."

"Well?" Alison prompted.

There was no answer. "Refugee fleet?" she called again, looking over at the status display.

One look was all she needed. "Neverlin's cut us off," she said, standing up and crossing back into the main office.

There she came to an abrupt stop. There were voices coming from the corridor. Lots of them. None of them sounding friendly.

"What do we do?" Taneem asked nervously from behind her.

"We surrender." Alison eyed Taneem. "Or rather, *I* surrender. Come on."

Alison retreated again into the communications nook. "No time for subtlety," she said, pointing up at the room's ventilation duct. "Shear off the bottom two bolts, then get aboard."

Taneem leaped up, slicing the heads off the bolts with two quick swipes of her claws. She landed on the deck and bounced up again, touching the back of Alison's neck and melting onto her skin.

Alison reached up to the grille and managed to force her fingers under the now-loosened bottom. "Go," she ordered.

A moment later the K'da was safely in the duct. "Stay there until the cavalry arrives," Alison said. "Good luck."

"Wait," Taneem called softly. "What about you? And what cavalry?"

"I'll be all right," Alison said, hoping fervently that that was true. "And by cavalry I mean Jack and Draycos."

"They're aboard?"

"Not yet," Alison said. "But they will be."

"How do you know?"

"Because they know we're here," Alison said. "And I know Draycos." She paused. "And I know Jack, too. Now scoot."

Taking a deep breath, she stepped back through the door into the office.

The Malison Ring soldiers were just charging in, guns ready in their hands. "Easy," Alison called, holding her hands up, palms outward, as the weapons swiveled in her direction.

From outside in the corridor, Neverlin pushed his way between two of the soldiers. His face was carved from stone, his eyes blazing with barely controlled fury. "So here we are," he said, his voice deathly quiet.

"Here we are," Alison agreed, rather surprised at how calm she sounded. "It's still not too late to call this whole thing off."

His lip twitched in a sardonic half smile. "Don't be ridiculous, child. You think your pathetic little effort has made any difference?"

"The fleet's been alerted," Alison pointed out. "You're not going to be able to split up the defenders now the way you hoped."

"I never thought that trick would work in the first place," Neverlin said casually. "Frankly, I was surprised they fell for it at all. No, my dear Alison whoever-you-really-are, that was simply our most optimistic Plan A. Plan B has already been implemented."

Alison gazed into his eyes. If the man was lying or bluffing, she couldn't see it. "You're still way outnumbered," she said.

He barked a short laugh. "You still don't understand, do you? We were monitoring your call. We heard everything you managed to get out before we cut you off."

Alison felt her pulse pounding in her ears. What had he heard that she'd missed? "And?" she asked carefully.

Neverlin smiled, the smile stopping halfway to his eyes. "You were so busy trying to convince them to listen to your poem," he said softly, "that you never got around to mentioning the Valahgua. Or the Death."

Alison felt her chest tighten. He was right. Mother of God, he was right.

"And so the defenders will regroup to cautiously intercept us and escort us into a protected place away from the main fleet while they try to figure out which of us is telling the truth,"

Neverlin went on. "And when we have them all neatly bunched up, we'll kill them. All of them."

He held out a hand to her. "Come," he said. "You'll have a much better view of the slaughter from the bridge."

"Thanks," Alison said through dry lips. "I'll pass."

"The Lordhighest insists," Neverlin said, his hand still stretched toward her. "I've promised the Valahgua they could have you to deal with as they see fit after this is all over."

He raised his eyebrows slightly. "I trust General Davi won't mind his daughter being tortured to death?"

"Would it matter if he did?" Alison asked.

"Not really," Neverlin said. "But then, General Davi has never even heard of you, has he? Come. The K'da and Shontine are waiting."

CHAPTER 28

"Something's happening," Uncle Virge called over the roar of the *Essenay*'s drive. "The K'da/Shontine warships seem to be changing formation."

"Let me see," Draycos said, raising his head from Jack's collar for a better look at the displays.

The computer was right. The K'da/Shontine defenders were definitely reconfiguring.

"Maybe Alison got through to them," Jack suggested. "If the *Advocatus Diaboli*'s radio is set up to transmit through the bubble, she might have gotten to it and clued them in."

Draycos didn't answer, his eyes on the *Essenay*'s display. The defenders finished their maneuvering. . . .

"No," he told Jack. "She didn't get through. At least, not enough."

"What do you mean?" Uncle Virge asked.

"That's an intercept-and-capture formation," Draycos said, flicking his tongue toward the display. "Not the pattern they would use if they knew they were facing the Death."

"Great," Jack muttered. "You sure? I mean—no offense."

"None taken," Draycos assured him. The boy's question had no implied insult to it, he knew. "A Deathguard formation cannot be mistaken for anything else."

"I didn't think so," Jack said.

Draycos lowered his head back flat onto Jack's shoulder, feeling the dark stream of his host's thoughts. No, there hadn't been any insult in Jack's question.

Because there hadn't even been a real question there. Jack's words had been little more than sound designed to fill an empty space that would otherwise have held a terrible truth, and a dark conclusion.

A conclusion Draycos himself had already come to.

"More movement," Uncle Virge said. "This time it's those three crowds of Neverlin's ships angled out behind us. They've put on a burst of speed."

"How soon before they catch up with the *Advocatus Diaboli?*" Jack asked.

"At current speeds, roughly the same time the *Advocatus Diaboli* and *Foxwolf* reach the defenders."

Jack exhaled in a long hiss. "So the scam part is officially over," he said. "They've switched to your basic full frontal assault."

"So it would seem," Draycos agreed.

"Blast it all, why don't they just run?" Uncle Virge asked tensely. "I mean the K'da and Shontine. Why don't they just turn the fleet around and run?"

"They can't," Draycos said. "Our hyperdrives need time to cool down and reset before they can be used again. They won't be able to escape into hyperspace for at least eight hours."

"By which time they'll all be dead," Jack murmured.

Draycos studied Jack's face out of the corner of his eye. The boy had seen the truth, all right, and had come to the same decision Draycos had. The only decision possible for a K'da warrior. "As things stand now, yes," he confirmed.

"So what do we do?" Uncle Virge asked.

Jack took a deep breath. *Draycos?*

I understand, Draycos said. *But you don't have to do this. You could eject in the* Essenay's *lifepod. Someone might arrive to rescue you before the air ran out.*

Someone besides Neverlin's goons? Jack countered. *Thanks, buddy, but I'd rather go out with you than with them.*

"So what do we do?" Uncle Virge asked again. "Draycos?"

"We can't get through the bubble fast enough to alert the refugees," Jack told him. "Not forward, and not sideways. At least, not before Neverlin calls in one of those outriding Djinn-90s to blow us to bits. So we're going to do something else."

"Such as?"

Draycos felt Jack brace himself. "We're going to attack the *Advocatus Diaboli* and try to knock out its Death weapon."

"We're *what*?" Uncle Virge demanded. "Jack lad, in case you hadn't checked the weapons board lately, we're out of missiles. I used them all getting you off that troop carrier."

"I *did* notice, thanks," Jack said. "I also know our meteor-defense lasers and particle beam probably won't even scratch Neverlin's paint."

"So how do you intend to attack?"

"The only way we can," Jack said quietly. "We're going to ram him."

"Oh no," Uncle Virge said, his voice horrified. "No, no, *no*. Jack lad, you can't—Draycos, please. Talk him out of it."

"It has to be done, Uncle Virge," Draycos said gently. "I've already offered Jack the option of ejecting before then."

"And I've already refused it," Jack said.

"It won't work," Uncle Virge insisted. "Langston said Harper rammed, too, remember? Neverlin won't risk that happening again, especially not with a ship this size. He'll use the Death on you, just as he did on Harper."

"Which will accomplish the same thing," Jack said. His voice and thoughts, Draycos noted, had gone strangely calm. The same calm he'd seen many times in fellow warriors preparing to face death. "If Neverlin uses the Death on us, the K'da and Shontine will see it and know what they're up against. Either way, we win."

"You'll also *die*."

Jack looked down at Draycos. "It's sometimes a warrior's duty to die for his people," he said. *Isn't it, Draycos?*

It is, Draycos assured him, feeling a stirring of emotion he hadn't felt in a long, long time. *I knew from the first, Jack, that you were more than you seemed. Far more than your uncle Virgil had allowed you to become. I'm so very gratified to see that I was right.*

I'm kind of surprised myself, Jack replied dryly, giving Draycos a somewhat forced smile. *Let's do it.*

Draycos lifted his head again to look out the *Essenay*'s canopy at the drive glows of the *Advocatus Diaboli* and *Gatekeeper* in the near distance.

And beyond them, at the last hope of his people. *Yes,* he confirmed. *Let's.*

This time, they made sure to handcuff Alison's wrists behind her.

The bridge hadn't changed much since she'd last been there, she noted as she was led through the door, a burly Malison Ring mercenary on either side keeping a cautious grip on her upper arms. Even with the handcuffs, Neverlin had finally learned not to take chances with her.

"There you are," Frost greeted her, as calmly as if she'd just been out getting the mail. "I understand we've been a busy girl. Again."

"Not as busy as I would have liked," Alison admitted, studying his face. He seemed way too calm for someone who'd been taken in by her con as thoroughly as he and Neverlin had.

But then, Frost could afford to be calm. Certainly calmer than Neverlin. With the collapse of her Alison Davi soap bubble, Frost's own position in this group was suddenly back to normal again. "Well, we'll be making up for that soon," he said. "Let me see; what's been happening since you left? The Lordhighest informs me the K'da/Shontine warships are now poised to intercept and detain us, still with no idea that we have the Death waiting for them. The rest of our attack force has abandoned the original game and is speeding to join us in a straight-up battlefront configuration."

He gave her an evil smile. "And your friend Jack Morgan has just put on a burst of speed, apparently in hopes of getting past us and out of the bubble in time to warn his K'da friends."

Alison looked over at the tactical, her mouth going dry. Frost was right—the *Essenay* was charging straight up the *Advocatus Diaboli*'s drive trail. "He can't possibly make it in time," she said. "You can just ignore them."

"It does look that way, doesn't it?" Frost agreed. "But I think it's a little late to start taking unnecessary chances. Especially now." His eyes flicked over Alison's shoulder to Neverlin. "Especially with this particular boy and K'da."

"The story I spun you before wasn't completely bogus," Alison persisted. "A live K'da would bring an astronomical price at any bioweapons lab."

"And I thank you for suggesting it," Neverlin said, coming up beside her. "But there will be plenty of safer specimens for us to choose from later." He waved toward the display. "Right now, I'm rather looking forward to watching Jack and his K'da die."

Alison swallowed hard. "You'll be using the Death on him, I suppose?"

"I think he's counting on that, actually," Neverlin said. "Our use of the Death would finally alert the refugee fleet to the surprise we have aboard." He smiled at Alison. "But only if they see us use it."

Alison frowned, looking again at the tactical display. What was Neverlin up to now?

And this time she saw it. "You're letting the *Foxwolf* pull ahead," she said. "You're going to lure the *Essenay* in close, where the *Foxwolf*'s bulk will block the refugees' view when you fire the Death."

"Very good," Neverlin said approvingly. "You really *could* have been General Davi's daughter, couldn't you?" He smiled. "Of course, there are a few details you don't know."

"It won't work," Alison said, trying one last time. "It *can't* work. There's no way you can use the Death against enough of them before they realize what's going on."

"We'll see," Neverlin said calmly. "In the meantime, we have Jack and his K'da to deal with."

At the sensor station, one of the displays began beeping urgently. "Sir, we have incoming spacecraft," the captain snapped, swiveling in his seat and keying some switches. "Thirty of them, approximately eight hundred miles aft. All craft accelerating in our direction."

"Identify," Frost ordered, moving up behind him.

"ID coming up now," the other said. "Sixteen are Malison Ring Shrike fast-attack fighters. Thirteen register as Braxton Universis Security cruisers. The thirtieth—"

He swiveled around to face Neverlin, his eyes wide. "It's the *Angelside*," he breathed.

Alison felt her breath catch in her throat. The *Angelside*? Cornelius Braxton's personal yacht was *here*?

This was not good. Not good at all.

"Interesting," Frost said, his voice glacially calm. "Signal Hammerfall One that we have some fresh targets. He's to split Outriders Two and Three from his group and send them back to deal with the intruders."

"Belay that order," Neverlin said. His voice, too, was calm, but there was a simmering hatred beneath it that froze Alison's blood. "Hammerfall One will continue its mission to support the *Foxwolf*'s attack. Backstop will turn back to intercept the intruders."

"Sir, five Djinn-90s can't take on two wings of Shrikes," Frost said urgently.

"Don't worry, Colonel; they'll have all the help they need," Neverlin assured him. "As soon as we've dealt with the *Essenay*, we'll be circling back to join them."

He half-turned, and it seemed to Alison that he was looking straight at her. "I'm going to deal with Mr. Braxton personally. Captain, what's the *Essenay*'s status?"

"Coming up fast, sir," the captain said. "Another thirty seconds and he'll be alongside us."

"And the *Foxwolf*?"

"In position and ready," Frost assured him. "The enemy ships won't see a thing."

Neverlin nodded. "Good. Lordhighest, contact your operators." He looked again at Alison. "Tell them to prepare to fire."

The *Essenay* was nearly to the *Advocatus Diaboli*'s stern now. "Steady on," Jack said aloud. They were empty words, he knew, said for no better reason than to fill the empty space around him. In less than a minute the *Essenay* would be alongside Neverlin's ship.

And with a push of an alien's hand on a button, Jack and Draycos would die.

There is no shame in being afraid, Draycos's thoughts came through the pounding of Jack's heart.

I know, Jack said. But he couldn't help but feel some shame anyway. Some shame, some fear, and a lot of regret.

He didn't want to die. But then, he didn't suppose anyone ever really *wanted* to die.

Careful, Jack, Draycos warned. *The* Gatekeeper *has positioned itself directly in front of us. Its drive glow may mask the refugees' view of the* Advocatus Diaboli *as it fires.*

Already spotted that, Jack assured him. In his own ham-handed way, he thought with dark amusement, Neverlin was still trying to outthink him and Draycos. *You just watch and—*

He broke off the thought. No, Draycos wouldn't watch and learn. Very soon now, neither he nor Draycos would ever learn anything again. *Here we go,* Jack said instead. Twisting the control yoke completely around, he sent the *Essenay* spiraling into a half circle around the *Advocatus Diaboli,* coming out on the far side of the ship and well clear of the *Foxwolf*'s blockage.

And it was time. *It's been an honor to know you, Draycos,* he told the K'da, reaching down to stroke the K'da's head as it lay flat against his right shoulder. Strangely enough, the words didn't sound corny to him, as he'd been afraid they would.

And an honor to know you, as well, Jack, Draycos replied. *Good-bye, my friend.*

Good-bye. Taking a deep breath, Jack threw full emergency power to the *Essenay*'s drive, sending the ship jumping forward and outward along the *Advocatus Diaboli*'s side.

He had just enough time to see the burst of debris and dust and compressed air that exploded from the *Foxwolf*'s side, swirling blackly directly in his path and completely blocking the view of the distant K'da/Shontine defenders.

And then, the violet cone of the Death cut across space in front of him, slicing across his view of both the *Foxwolf* and the masking cloud of debris.

He twisted the control yoke again, trying to pull the *Essenay* out of the beam's path.

But it was too late. Before he could do more than gasp, the violet cone swept back toward him, passed unhindered though the canopy—

And cut through him like a tingling knife.

CHAPTER 29

The voices were still murmuring around Alison, murmuring like a mountain brook in the distance. There were words there, too, she knew.

But with her head bowed, her eyes closed, and her heart aching, she hardly heard any of it.

Jack and Draycos were dead.

Vaguely, distantly, she heard someone calling her name. Blinking the tears out of her eyes, she looked up. "What?" she asked.

"I was just telling you not to take it so hard," Neverlin said. "After all, you'll be joining them soon enough."

Alison took a deep breath. This was no time to fall apart. "As will you and Frost and the Valahgua," she said. "I know Cornelius Braxton, and you're not going to find him an easy nut to crack."

Neverlin shook his head. "You still don't get it, do you, Alison? Even having seen it demonstrated right in front of you, you still don't get it. The Death is literally the ultimate weapon. It doesn't matter how many people Braxton brought with him. He's dead, and so is everyone with him."

"Sir, the *Essenay's* gone into a half-powered drift," the captain reported.

"Very good, Captain," Neverlin said. "Swing us around and bring us up behind Backstop. No rush—give them time to re-form into their attack cluster."

"Yes, sir."

"It's a shame we couldn't be on the same side, Alison," Neverlin went on, his voice lowered. "You're obviously a girl of many talents."

Alison flicked her tongue across her upper lip. There was only one chance left for her now. "What if I told you I was ready to join up with you?" she asked.

Neverlin smiled. "You really think I'd believe you?"

"I could pay for my life," Alison offered. "I still have a few secrets. Things I know that would be very valuable to you."

"What sort of secrets?"

"The sort that would be very valuable to you," Alison repeated. "Or to anyone else who knew them."

For a moment Neverlin eyed her closely. Then, he looked at the two Malison Ring mercenaries still holding on to her upper arms. "Three paces back and wait," he ordered them.

One of the soldiers glanced at the other. "Sir, Colonel Frost said—"

"Three paces back," Neverlin repeated.

"Yes, sir." Letting go of Alison's arms, the two men stepped back as ordered.

"Now," Neverlin said, his eyes back on Alison. "Go on."

"Your side of the bargain first," Alison said. "I want in on the deal with you and Frost. I especially want in on anything the weapons labs turn up out of all this."

Neverlin smiled thinly. "You have a particular interest in weapons?"

"My father does, yes," Alison said. "And of course, I want to not be turned over to the Valahgua."

"That might be difficult," Neverlin warned. "You've cost them a great deal of time and trouble."

"You're helping them get what they want," Alison countered. "I think they can afford to concede a point or two."

"Sir?" the captain called. "The *Essenay*'s on the move again."

"It's just the ship's computer flailing around," Neverlin called back. "Ignore it."

"Yes, sir."

"Well?" Alison asked.

"All right, I'll play," Neverlin said, inclining his head to her. "If these supposed secrets are actually worthwhile, you have a deal."

Alison took a deep breath. Taneem would understand, she told herself. Surely Taneem would understand. "Okay," she said. "Here it is. . . ."

Before Jack could do more than gasp, the violet cone swept back toward him, passed unhindered through the canopy, and cut through him like a tingling knife.

Nothing happened.

Carefully, Jack opened his eyes, only then realizing that he'd even shut them. *Draycos?* he asked warily.

I'm here, Draycos said, just as warily. *What happened?*

You tell me, buddy, Jack countered, looking down at his chest. Draycos's gold-scaled head was visible through the open collar, one green eye looking up at him. *I thought the Death killed everything it hit.*

It does, Draycos said, sounding as puzzled as Jack felt. *It always does.*

Well, it didn't this time, Jack said. *Not unless incredibly grubby flight suits are allowed into the afterlife.*

Could they have missed? Draycos suggested doubtfully. *That tingle felt rather like a near miss.*

That was no miss, near or otherwise, Jack said firmly. *I saw it go through me. I felt it go through me.*

Then I have no idea, Draycos conceded.

"Jack?" Uncle Virge asked tentatively. "Are you all right, lad?"

"Apparently so, Uncle Virge," Jack assured him. He blinked once, shook his head to clear it, and for the first time since the Death had passed through him he focused on the view through the *Essenay*'s canopy.

Not surprisingly, he'd let go of the yoke when the Death hit. As a result, the *Essenay* was more or less in drift mode, its nose angling off its original course, its engines backed off to half speed. The drive glows of the *Foxwolf* and *Advocatus Diaboli* were already a good distance ahead, still heading for the refugee fleet.

And then, as he watched, the *Advocatus Diaboli* detached itself from the larger ship and started an almost leisurely curve to the side. "Neverlin's pulling away," he announced.

Weight came onto his shoulder as Draycos raised his head for a look. "What do you think?" Jack asked. "Mechanical trouble?"

"I'm not reading anything obvious," Uncle Virge said. "But those five Djinn-90s that used to be riding wide cover have also turned around. Maybe they're all heading back to deal with the Malison Ring and Braxton Universis ships coming up behind us."

"The *what*?" Jack demanded, looking at the aft display and

keying for a tactical overlay. There were new drive glows back there, all right, coming up fast behind them.

He looked back at the *Advocatus Diaboli*. It was halfway through its curve, still looking like it wasn't in any particular hurry to take the Death to the incoming ships.

He probably isn't *in a hurry,* Draycos pointed out. *He'll want to make sure the Djinn-90s are in position to give him cover before he gets within range of the attackers' weapons.*

That sounds like Neverlin, Jack thought back. On the other hand, the *Advocatus Diaboli*'s leisurely turn, coupled with the *Essenay*'s own drifting course . . .

"Okay," he said aloud. "Here's what we do. Uncle Virge, plot me an intercept course with the *Advocatus Diaboli*—minimum time, maximum surprise, and I want to end up running parallel along its flank."

"Jack lad, this is insane," Uncle Virge protested. "As soon as Neverlin sees you moving, he'll fire the Death at us again. You and Draycos were lucky once. You can't count on being lucky again."

"It wasn't luck," Jack insisted. "I don't know what it was, but it wasn't luck."

"But how will this gain us anything?"

"I'm going to try for a crash-dock," Jack said. "Hopefully, before they can figure out what we're doing and get the hatchway blocked. If we can get inside and stop the jamming, we can finally warn everyone about the Death weapons."

"*If* you survive," Uncle Virge said stiffly. "You may be somehow immune to the Death, but I doubt that'll carry over to old-fashioned gunfire."

"Probably not," Jack agreed. "If we don't make it, *you'll* have to warn them. Draycos?"

"I'm with you, Jack," the K'da said.

As if Jack had had any doubts on that score. "Okay, Uncle Virge, ball's in your court."

The computer speaker gave a long, pained sigh. "Course plotted and ready, Jack lad. But even minimum-time approach will take you a few minutes to get there."

"Good enough." Jack got a grip on the control yoke, glancing over the course details as Uncle Virge scrolled them across the navigational display. "Okay, Neverlin. Here we come, ready or not."

". . . so Frost knows about everything you had in that big walk-in safe," Alison concluded. "I know he found out about the KK-29 patrol ships from the information in your office safe. I'm sure the papers in the big one were even more interesting."

The wary anticipation in Neverlin's eyes darkened into anger. "That's it?" he demanded. "*That's* your big impressive secret?"

"Not all of it, no," Alison stalled. Out of the corner of her eye she could see Frost and the *Advocatus Diaboli*'s captain conferring behind the helmsman. Still too close to the communications section of the board. "I also know Braxton has been monitoring Jack Morgan's movements, including his little side trips to Rho Scorvi and Semaline. How could he have done that without someone in Frost's group feeding him information?"

"With Braxton's resources?" Neverlin said with a snort. "He could have found Morgan in any of a dozen ways."

"I'm just saying there are things going on under the radar," Alison said. Across the bridge, Frost and the captain moved a few feet over to study the sensor station's tactical displays.

And it was time.

Alison braced herself for action. She was probably about to die, she knew. Chances were she would die without even accomplishing her goal.

But she had to try. She could only hope Taneem would understand why she'd done it.

"This is nonsense," Neverlin declared. "And you're wasting my time." Lifting his eyes, he beckoned her guards forward again.

And as he did, Alison ducked down, rammed her shoulder into his chest as hard as she could, and charged toward the communications board.

But she'd only gone two steps before a hand grabbed her forearm from behind. She tried to twist away, but the grip was solid, bringing her desperate rush to a sudden halt. The hand yanked at her, spinning her around again.

"You little fool," Neverlin said, his free hand pressed against his chest where her shoulder had rammed him. "Did you think I wasn't expecting something like that?"

He let go as her two Malison Ring guards caught up and locked their own massive hands around her upper arms. "What happened?" Frost demanded, hurrying up to them.

"She tried to get to the jamming control," Neverlin told him. "Probably figured that the *Essenay*'s computer would spot that the bubble was down and send out a warning."

Frost glowered at Alison. "With your permission, sir, I think we've had enough of Alison Kayna for one day."

"Agreed," Neverlin said. "Take her to her stateroom—"

With a horrible screech of shredded metal, the ventilation duct across the bridge disintegrated.

And a black-scaled fury hurled herself into the room.

The bridge exploded in pandemonium. Neverlin shouted

something incomprehensible, practically falling over as he backed hurriedly away. The hands gripping Alison's arms were suddenly gone as the soldiers went for their guns. Frost had the presence of mind to grab Alison's shirt collar with his left hand as he went for his own gun with his right.

But Taneem hadn't come for vengeance or war. That single leap landed her on the deck beside the communications board.

And with three slashes of her claws she disintegrated the section that controlled the radio bubble.

"You got it!" Alison called to her, twisting around in Frost's grip and kicking hard into the side of his knee. He spun halfway around, grunting in pain as his shot buried itself in the bridge ceiling instead of Taneem. "Now get out of here!" Alison shouted as she bounced her shoulders sideways off her two Malison Ring guards, trying to wreck their aims, too. "Go somewhere safe and hide. *Go!*"

Taneem's silver eyes flicked once to her. Then, to Alison's relief, the K'da bounded back up through the shredded grille and disappeared down the duct.

"Hold your fire," Frost snapped as the mercenaries finally got their guns lined up again. His own weapon, Alison noted uneasily, was pointed at her. "No point. It's gone."

The Valahgua stepped toward Frost, his tentacles writhing like twin snakes caught in an electric fence. "How a K'da here aboard?" he demanded. "How a K'da here *aboard*?"

"I don't know," Frost said, his eyes steady on Alison over the barrel of his gun. "But I can guess."

"Alert the crew and soldiers," Neverlin ordered, his breath coming quick and shallow. "If they see it, they're to shoot to kill."

Across the room, an alarm warbled. "Proximity warning," the helmsman called tensely. "It's the *Essenay,* coming in fast."

"Evasive," Frost ordered. "Morgan must have left a last-ditch ramming order on the computer before he died. Keep us away from the ship. And get that jamming bubble back up."

"Too late," the captain said. "The *Essenay's* transmitting."

He hit a switch. Alison held her breath. . . .

"Attention, K'da and Shontine," a familiar voice boomed. "Attention, Braxton Universis ships."

And Alison felt her heart surge, the ashes of defeat blazing again with sudden fire.

It was Jack.

"Attention, Braxton Universis ships," Jack called, watching the *Advocatus Diaboli*. The bigger ship had finally noticed the *Essenay* bearing down on it and was trying to veer away. Turning the control yoke, he swung back toward them. "The ships heading your way are carrying your enemies. For you Braxton people, that includes Arthur Neverlin and Colonel Maximus Frost of the Malison Ring. For you K'da and Shontine, it also includes a group of Valahgua.

"Most important, for all of you, the ships are carrying three Death weapons."

"Identify yourself," a voice demanded, his English carrying an accent Jack didn't recognize.

Draycos lifted his snout from Jack's shoulder and poured out some more of his alien speech. The voice answered back in the same language, and for a few seconds they conversed in short sentences.

Midway through the discussion the violet beam of the Death again swept through the *Essenay's* cockpit. Again, Jack felt nothing but an unpleasant tingle.

The conversation ended. *They're convinced,* Draycos said, going flat onto Jack's skin again.

Good, Jack answered. *Let's just hope we can convince Braxton's people, too.* "Braxton Universis ships—"

"Hello, Jack," a voice cut him off. "Where are you?"

Jack stared at the bridge speaker. "Mr. *Braxton?*"

"Yes indeed," Braxton confirmed. "Where are you?"

"I'm in the *Essenay,*" Jack said, his mind flashing back to what Harper had said about Alison's thefts from his company. Braxton must want her *really* badly to have come all this way personally to get her. "Currently working my way toward the *Advocatus Diaboli.*"

"You mean you're in the ship that was just hit with the Death?" Braxton asked.

Jack blinked. "You know about the Death?"

"I know everything," Braxton said. "But if the Death hit you, why are you still alive? Doesn't it work against humans?"

"Oh, it works just fine against humans," Jack said grimly. "And as you saw, Neverlin's got one of them aboard the *Advocatus Diaboli*. You and your people need to back away before he gets it into range."

"Understood," Braxton said. "But you haven't answered my question."

"I don't know why we're alive," Jack said. "Somehow, a human/K'da combination seems to be immune." He grimaced, belatedly remembering that Braxton didn't know what a K'da was. "A K'da is a sort of—"

"That doesn't make sense," Braxton interrupted. "The Death has no trouble killing K'da/Shontine combinations."

Jack blinked. *How in blazes does he know all this?*

I don't know, Draycos said. *But I have had a sudden thought. With your permission . . . ?*

Go for it, buddy.

Draycos lifted his head off Jack's shoulder. "Mr. Braxton, this is Draycos," he said.

"The K'da who saved my life on the *Star of Wonder*," Braxton said. "I hadn't had a chance yet to thank you for that."

He does *know a lot, doesn't he?* Draycos thought toward Jack. "You're welcome," he said aloud. "There is an analogy I've used regarding the Death. If you wished to destroy the core of a planet, a normal weapon would have to first blast through the crust and mantle to reach it. The Death instead seeks out that core directly, without needing to expend energy on the destruction of its victim's flesh and blood and bone."

"All right," Braxton said. "And?"

"Perhaps a K'da/human combination acts like a double planet," Draycos said. "As the Death seeks out the center of that combination—"

"It seeks out the center of mass," Braxton said, a sudden interest in his voice. "And the center of mass of a double planet is halfway between them. *In empty space.*"

"Exactly," Draycos said. "Again, I don't know how accurate the analogy is. But the fact remains that a human/K'da combination appears to be safe from the Death."

"Interesting," Braxton said softly. "Very interesting indeed."

"Turn it off," Neverlin said quietly.

Like a man awakening from a strange dream, the captain stirred and touched the radio control. The voices cut off.

A deathly silence settled onto the bridge. Alison looked around the room: at Neverlin, at Frost, at the other Malison Ring soldiers. All looked stunned, or worried, or quietly but helplessly furious.

And finally, she turned to the Valahgua. "So that's the secret," she said. "That's the reason you came all the way across the galaxy to the Orion Arm just to kill the K'da. You knew, maybe from the beginning. You knew the K'da originally came from Earth."

"They came from *Earth*?" Frost echoed.

"That is only a theory," the Valahgua rumbled. "It has not been proven."

"Oh, it has now," Alison told him. "That's why Draycos has been picking up new abilities over the past six months. With Jack as his host, he's found a part of himself he hadn't even realized was missing."

More and more of those on the bridge, she noticed, were starting to transfer their attention from the silenced radio speaker to the Valahgua.

And some of those stunned expressions were starting to give way to anger. The Valahgua had kept a vital secret from them, and all of them knew how disastrous that could be in the middle of a battle.

"You didn't dare take the risk that the K'da would find us and figure this out for themselves," Alison continued. "So you came to Neverlin and dangled big rewards in his face and got him to—"

"Enough," Neverlin said.

Alison stopped, a sudden chill running up her back. There was nothing of the growing sense of outrage or betrayal in Neverlin's own voice or expression. There was nothing there but a dark and deadly determination. "This is all very interesting," he said quietly. "But it changes nothing. There's only one human/K'da combination in the galaxy, and it won't be around much longer."

He looked at Frost. "Meanwhile, we still have the Death, and we have solid Valahguan tactics with which to use it against both the invaders and Braxton."

"And those other Malison Ring ships, too?" Frost asked, an odd edge to his voice.

"Did General Davi develop immortality for his men when I wasn't looking?" Neverlin retorted. "Of course those other Malison Ring ships, too."

"I was thinking of the possible future consequences," Frost persisted. "Those Shrikes wouldn't be here if General Davi didn't already know what was going on."

"But he *doesn't* know what's going on," Neverlin reminded him smoothly. "He has only Braxton's version of events, a version that won't survive beyond the next few hours. Don't worry, Colonel. *Our* story is the only one that will ever leave this place."

He turned back to the Valahgua. "The mission is still on, Lordhighest. Order your people to continue as planned."

"They will continue until death," the Valahgua promised. "What of Morgan and the K'da?"

"As I said, they won't be around much longer," Neverlin assured him. "Since Morgan was kind enough to warn Braxton about the Death, I notice his ships have scattered out of their attack clusters. While they're trying to figure out how to regroup to face us, we'll have the Backstop force come back and deal with the *Essenay*. Colonel?"

Frost pursed his lips but nodded. "Yes, sir," he said. "I'll give the order."

CHAPTER 30

"Oh, for crying out loud," Jack growled as, for the third time, the *Advocatus Diaboli* veered sharply away just as the *Essenay* was getting close. "Hold *still,* will you?"

"So that you can dock and get aboard?" Uncle Virge said. "Not likely."

Do you want me to try? Draycos offered. *I know some maneuvers Neverlin won't be expecting.*

Thanks, but I'd rather have you riding my skin in case they try the Death on us again, Jack said. *Don't worry—he can't outrun us forever.*

"Movement," Uncle Virge said. "Those five Djinn-90s ahead of us are looping back."

Jack looked at the display. The fighters were curving around, all right, heading back toward the *Advocatus Diaboli* and *Essenay.*

And meanwhile, the *Advocatus Diaboli* had just straightened out again. Straightened out very invitingly, in fact.

Draycos spotted it, too. *He's trying to lure you onto a path that will give the Djinn-90s a clear shot,* the K'da warned.

Just means I have to finish this before they get in range, Jack said.

But that was easier said than done. The *Advocatus Diaboli* kept backing away as Jack tried to get the *Essenay* close enough for a crash-dock. He kept half an eye on the bigger ship, the other half on the ranging data for the Djinn-90s scrolling across the navigational screen.

It was going to be close.

"Wait a minute," Uncle Virge said, sounding puzzled. "Something's wrong. Three of the Braxton ships have started in toward us again. On full power, too."

"Which three?" Jack asked.

"The big yacht and two of the Security ships," Uncle Virge said. "They're moving into attack formation."

Braxton's trying to draw away the Djinn-90s? Draycos suggested.

Jack hissed between his teeth. Yes, that was exactly what Braxton was trying to do.

The problem was, by the time they got into attack range of the Malison Ring fighters, they would themselves be within range of the Death. "Get me a signal to them," he told Uncle Virge. "Mr. Braxton? Yo—Mr. Braxton?"

"I'm here, Jack," Braxton's voice came. "Hang on—we're coming."

"Well, don't," Jack said tartly. "Didn't you hear what I said about the Death?"

To his amazement, Braxton actually chuckled. "Perfectly," the older man assured him. "It just so happens I have a little surprise for Mr. Neverlin. Suban, would you like to say hello to Jack?"

Jack frowned. What in the world—?

And then a strangely deep, strangely alien voice came over the speaker. "Hello, Jack," it said. "It is good to hear your voice again."

Again? "Who is this?" Jack asked.

"I am now called Suban," the other said. "But you knew me as Snip."

Jack frowned even harder. *Snip?* It sounded familiar. . . .

He caught his breath. "*Snip?*" he said. "You mean . . . *Special Needs Phooka?*"

"You used to rub my ears and jaw to calm my fears," Suban confirmed. "I am pleased you remember me."

Jack shook his head wordlessly. He'd left Snip and the rest of his fellow Phookas back on Rho Scorvi with the Erassvas who served as their hosts. "How did you get—I mean—?"

"We rescued them, of course," Braxton came back on. "A lost colony of K'da would have been far too tempting a target for Neverlin if he'd found out about them. We took them off Rho Scorvi, woke them up, and brought them along as a good-faith gesture of friendship to the K'da and Shontine."

He chuckled again. "Ironic, isn't it? All along I assumed we were the ones protecting them. Now, it seems, they're going to be the ones protecting *us*."

"And you all have them?" Jack asked, just to make sure.

"Everyone aboard these three ships," Braxton confirmed. "That's why we're the ones moving in."

"But how did you even know about them?" Jack asked.

"Later," Braxton said briskly. "Right now, I see that Mr. Neverlin has noticed our intentions."

Jack looked at the display. Three of the five Djinn-90s that had been on course for the *Essenay* had turned around again, heading back to intercept the incoming Braxton Universis ships. "Leaving us only two to handle," Jack muttered. "I guess that's better than nothing."

"It's a lot better than nothing, Jack lad," Uncle Virge said, a dark slyness in his voice. "One of those two ships is Langston's."

He'd barely finished the comment when the rearmost of the two approaching Djinn-90s blew the other one out of the sky.

"You're clear, Jack," Langston's voice came over the radio. "What else do you need?"

"Nothing," Jack said. The *Advocatus Diaboli,* its use as bait suddenly gone, twisted violently away again.

Only this time the maneuver was too late. "Just get yourself clear," Jack added as he turned the *Essenay* to follow. "Go hook up with the rest of Braxton's group and wait to help with the cleanup."

"What about you?"

The *Advocatus Diaboli* loomed directly ahead. Clenching his teeth, Jack turned the control yoke hard to the left.

With a horrendous grinding of metal the two ships slammed together. For a long second the *Essenay* slid forward along the bigger ship's side, still grinding metal.

And then, with a lurch that threw Jack hard against his straps, the *Essenay* came to an abrupt halt. "Hatches linked," Uncle Virge announced. "Or at least, close enough."

"Jack?" Langston called. "What are you doing?"

"We're going to destroy the Death," Jack told him. "I don't suppose you happen to know where they've got it mounted?"

"I saw them kill Harper with it, remember?" Langston said grimly. "It's in the forward bulk storage room: upper deck, all the way at the bow."

"Got it," Jack said. "Thanks."

"Good luck," Langston said. "I'll see you later."

Jack grimaced. "Let's hope so."

The *Advocatus Diaboli* shuddered with the impact, the distant scream of tortured metal echoing through the empty corridors all the way to the bridge. Alison winced, her ears throbbing with the screeching.

And then she was nearly knocked off her feet as the *Essenay* caught the larger ship's docking collar.

"He's here," Frost spat. "Sergeant, get a squad to the starboard docking station."

"No," the Valahgua ordered. "We go instead to the bow. Everyone goes."

"You want to give Morgan the run of the ship?" Frost demanded.

"He may have all that he wishes," the Valahgua said coldly. "When we stand beside the Death, we will release it from its mount and sweep it through everywhere else."

"And then what?" Frost asked. "He and the K'da are immune, remember?"

"Only if they're together," Neverlin said. "I think we can arrange something that'll get them apart. Get everyone to the Death weapon chamber."

"I hope you know what you're doing," Frost warned. "Both of you."

"We do," Neverlin said. "Now get moving."

He gestured to the guards holding Alison's arms. "And bring her, too. If the Death isn't enough bait for Morgan and the K'da, maybe she will be."

The *Advocatus Diaboli*'s airlock had been slightly warped by the impact. But it was functional enough. Slipping inside, Jack pressed his back against the inner door. *What kind of reception committee have they got waiting?* he asked Draycos.

The K'da peered over the door. *I see nothing,* he reported, sounding both surprised and more than a little suspicious. *They may have set up an ambush in one of the cross-corridors.*

Let's find out. Hefting his tangler, Jack keyed the door.

It slid open with another screech of tortured metal. He ducked out into the corridor for a quick look, then ducked back into cover again.

No one shot at him. *I don't smell anyone nearby,* Draycos said, his tongue flicking up from Jack's shoulder. *Shall I go investigate?*

Better not, Jack said. *An ambush we can hopefully spot before we get in range. They don't have to be nearly that obvious to turn the Death around and shoot it at us.*

Then let us deal with it, Draycos said firmly.

They set off down the corridor, Jack holding his tangler ready, Draycos's tongue rhythmically darting out and tasting the air.

But for all the signs of life they found, the ship might have been deserted. *Where is everyone?* Jack asked as they passed the ship's midpoint.

In the bow, Draycos said. *You were right—they're planning to use the Death against us.*

Good luck to them, Jack said. *How do they think they're going to get you to come off me?*

By also attacking us with normal weapons, Draycos said. *Frost knows I'll have to leave you if I'm going to defend you against his men.*

Jack chewed the inside of his cheek. Unfortunately, that made a lot of sense. *So we need to get you to the Death before he can get his guns lined up?*

Or get me past the guns before we attack the Death, Draycos said.

Jack grimaced. *Sounds like your classic chicken-and-egg problem.*

Pardon?

Never mind—tell you later, Jack said. *I guess we're playing this one by ear.*

They continued forward through the still-deserted ship. *Maybe we can get to the Death room from underneath,* Jack suggested as they walked. *Or maybe we can just cut off the power.*

We can try, Draycos said doubtfully. *But I suspect Frost has blocked any threats that obvious.*

Frost had. They reached the middeck bow to discover that all the forward compartments had been sealed. *And no one's getting in there any time soon, either,* Jack said, pointing to a red light on the door's release switch. *They've opened that whole section to vacuum.*

Including all the power connections to the Death room?

And including the section's backup generator, Jack confirmed. *I guess it's a frontal assault or nothing.*

Then let us not keep them waiting, Draycos said.

Fine with me, Jack said, feeling his heart start to race again. *But we've got one more stop to make first. If they've moved the Death into a bulk storage room, it stands to reason they must have moved all the bulk storage itself out. Let's find out where they put it.*

"Hurry up with that thing," Frost growled as the two Valahgua worked at disassembling the swivels of the Death weapon's mount. "Come on; come on."

"It is not easy to work in these confines," the Lordhighest countered stiffly.

He had a point, Alison had to agree. The storage room followed the shape of the ship's bow, reasonably wide at the aft end by the door but narrowing considerably toward the bow where the Death weapon had been mounted.

And with Neverlin, Alison, Frost, the three Valahgua, and six crewmen crammed in that narrower area, the Valahgua didn't have a lot of extra room to work with.

"Relax, Colonel," Neverlin said calmly from Alison's side. "We have time." He nudged Alison's shoulder, nodding back toward the door. "I trust you approve of our tactical landscape?"

Alison looked toward the room's door, her stomach tightening. The ship's twelve resident Malison Ring mercenaries were facing the door, five of them kneeling, another five standing behind them, the last two another pace back from the double firing line as backup. "It's beautiful," she said. "Draycos will cut through it like winter wheat."

"I hope he tries," Neverlin said. "I understand K'da evaporate into thin air when they die. I'd like to see that."

Alison's eyes flicked up to the ventilation grille just above the door. She hadn't seen Taneem since the K'da had wrecked the jamming equipment and Alison had ordered her to go hide.

She hoped Taneem had obeyed. She hoped even more that the K'da had found a hiding place somewhere forward and in the lower deck where Neverlin's planned sweep of the *Death* might miss her.

Jack found the displaced storage items on the third door he tried, two doors aft of the *Death* room. Everything he'd hoped for was there.

Three minutes later, he was ready.

Okay, he said, running a critical eye over his masterpiece: a rolling cart with three oxygen tanks strapped to it, twenty feet back from the *Death* room and lined up squarely on its door. *We're good to go. You ready?*

Yes. Draycos hesitated. *Jack . . . if this doesn't work . . .*

It's okay, symby, Jack said, a lump coming to his throat. *We already said our good-byes, remember?*

Yes, Draycos said. The moment had passed, and he was all business again. *Do you want me to take another look over the door?*

No time, Jack said. *They looked like they might have the Death free any second now. Besides, where could anyone possibly have moved in there?*

Point, Draycos agreed. *Then let's do it.*

He leaped out of Jack's collar and landed on the deck beside the cart. Jack moved up to the door, his usual full-size tangler in his right hand, Harper's tiny palm-grip tangler hidden in his left. Holding the butt of his tangler an inch away from the door release, he looked back at Draycos and nodded.

With a triple slash of his claws, Draycos sliced the ends off all three oxygen tanks.

The cart surged forward, picking up speed as the escaping gas drove it forward like a small, rolling rocket. Draycos loped along beside it, picking up his pace as the cart sped up, nudging it back on track whenever it started to drift off-target. Jack watched it come, holding out his left hand toward Draycos as he judged his timing.

A second before the cart reached the door, Draycos leaped up and forward, catching the back of Jack's hand and melting onto his arm. A half second later, with the cart still picking up speed, Jack tapped the butt of his tangler into the release.

The door opened, and Jack leaned around the edge. "Catch!" he called, tossing his tangler in a high arc into the room. Several of the mercenaries instinctively looked upward toward the flying weapon, before suddenly spotting the cart roaring through the door toward them.

The soldiers directly in front of it scrambled to get out of its way. As they did so, Jack lifted his left hand and fired both shots of Harper's tangler.

The cartridges hit the side of one of the oxygen tanks and burst open, their milky white threads snagging the nearest of the kneeling mercenaries and anchoring him solidly to the careening cart. The sudden drag sent the cart pivoting sharply to the side, changing its course and bouncing it into and across more of the mercenaries.

And as it careened through their neat double line, Draycos leaped out of Jack's sleeve.

He landed in front of the nearest mercenary just as the other got clear of the cart and started to bring his gun back around toward his attacker. The K'da got there first, slapping his paw against the man's gun hand and deflecting it to the side.

But instead of leaping to the next soldier in line, the K'da simply vanished up the first man's sleeve.

Someone gasped a curse. But before anyone could move, Draycos was back, bounding out of the back of the man's collar toward the soldier behind him. Again his outstretched paws caught the man's hand and he slid out of sight up his sleeve, his tail managing to slap across the head of the next man in line before he vanished.

"Now!" Neverlin bellowed over the chaos. "Shoot them!"

Draycos leaped out of the mercenary's collar, headed for a man a couple of steps farther back on the right-hand side of the group. Beyond him, a pair of Valahgua heaved the long Death weapon cylinder off its mount and swiveled it around toward Jack.

And as it started its turn, the end erupted with the familiar sickly yellow flash and the violet light of the Death. Cutting through the soldiers to Jack's left, it swept ponderously toward him.

There was nowhere to go. Nowhere to hide. Instinctively,

Jack leaped forward into the room, diving for the deck. His last glimpse before the struggling soldiers blocked his view was that of Alison breaking free from Neverlin's grip and throwing her body at the side of the weapon in a desperate attempt to slow it down.

But it was a futile gesture, and Jack knew it. Even with her interference, he had no more than a second before the beam would sweep over him. Alison could do no more; Draycos was already an eternity too far away. Jack hit the deck chest-first, the impact knocking half the wind out of him, and prepared himself to die.

And then, the rest of the air was knocked out of him as something hard and heavy slammed into his shoulders and the back of his neck. The sudden weight vanished as suddenly as it had appeared—

The violet beam swept over him, and he felt the by now familiar tingle. The tingle, and nothing else. He heard the hum of the weapon change pitch slightly as it halted its swing and came back toward him to try again.

And then, the hum was drowned out by the thunder of a pair of gunshots.

The hum vanished, and the room fell abruptly silent. Cautiously, Jack raised his head.

The mercenaries who had been standing in front of him were lying crumpled on the deck. All dead. The Death weapon itself was lying on the deck, too, as were the two Valahgua who had been holding it. A third Valahgua was still standing, something that looked like a weapon in his hand and pointed down at Alison, who was sprawled frozen on the deck looking up at him.

To Jack's right, Draycos was crouched on the deck, poised to spring. His green eyes glittered as he stared unblinkingly at the

Valahgua. Pressed against the curved bulkhead, as far back as they could get, were Neverlin and six white-clad crewmen.

And standing between Draycos and the Valahgua, no more than a step back out of their line of sight, was Frost. His gun was in his hand.

Pointed at the Valahgua.

"Lower the weapon," Frost told the alien. "You hear me?"

"They must die," the Valahgua insisted, his voice sounding utterly alien. "They must all die."

"There's no point," Frost said. "It's over. It's all over. Surrender, and you can still live."

The Valahgua snarled something in his own language. "Do not mock me!"

"He isn't mocking you," Draycos said. His voice was low and bitter and deadly. "If you surrender, you will be allowed to return with a message."

"What message, K'da?" the Valahgua spat.

"That the power of the Valahgua is broken," Draycos said. "That if you ever come again to this region of space, you will be destroyed." His tail flicked. "But you will only live to carry that message if you lower your weapon."

"Better take him up on the offer," Jack advised, standing up and taking a couple of steps toward the standoff. A risky move, he knew, but giving the Valahgua one more target to choose from might give Draycos the opening he needed. "You don't want your people always wondering what happened out here, do you?"

The Valahgua flashed Jack an unreadable look. "Come on," Jack cajoled. "You don't want to die, do you?"

The Valahgua looked down at Alison. "Don't do it," Jack warned.

And with a scream that seemed to shake Jack's teeth, Taneem

leaped out of his collar. The Valahgua twisted his arm up and around, trying to bring his weapon to bear on this sudden new threat.

He never made it. Before the gun was even halfway to its target, Draycos leaped across the open gap and buried his claws in the Valahgua's throat.

The gun went off, sizzling a blast of blue-white energy into the ceiling, then dropped to the deck.

"*Now*," Draycos said, "it is over."

Jack took a deep breath. "I guess they'll never know what happened now, will they?" he said.

"Perhaps not," Draycos said, turning to face Frost.

Frost, whose gun was still pointed at the dead Valahgua. Only now, Jack realized suddenly, it was pointed at Draycos.

Neverlin spotted it, too. "Do it," he muttered urgently, taking a step forward.

Without even looking at him, Frost swiveled his gun away from Draycos and pointed it at Neverlin. "As he said, sir. It's over." He looked at Jack. "Give Braxton a call," he said. "Tell him I want to make a deal with him. And *only* with him."

"Sure, no problem," Jack said. Picking his way through the sprawled Malison Ring bodies, he stopped in front of Frost and held out his hand. The other hesitated, then turned the gun around and handed it to Jack. "The keys to Alison's cuffs would be nice, too," Jack suggested as Alison got awkwardly back to her feet.

Frost shook his head. "I don't have them. Not sure who does."

"Allow me," Draycos said. Inserting one claw into the handcuff chain, he sliced through it.

"Thanks," Alison said, wincing as she brought her hands back around again. "That's hard on the shoulders," she commented. "You all right?"

"I'm fine," Jack assured her.

"Yes, I can see that," Alison said dryly. "I was talking to Taneem."

"I'm also fine," Taneem said. Somewhat hesitantly, she moved forward. "I know you told me to hide, but I couldn't leave you alone. I hope I did all right."

"You did more than all right, Taneem," Alison assured her, reaching over to stroke her head. "I'm sure Jack and Draycos agree."

"And then some," Jack agreed. "Thanks for saving my life."

"You did the same for me on Rho Scorvi," Taneem said simply. "I'm glad I was able to repay you."

Jack cleared his throat. "Speaking of payments and paybacks, we'd better get Braxton on the radio." He eyed Alison. "Did you know he came all the way out here personally to find you?"

Alison shrugged. "I thought he might."

"I hope he hangs you," Neverlin said bitterly. "Whoever you really stole that tracer for, I hope he well and truly hangs you."

"He *does* seem to want you pretty badly," Jack warned.

"Yes, I suppose he does," Alison agreed. She smiled at Neverlin. "But then, grandfathers are like that."

CHAPTER 31

"That's it," Alison announced, dropping one last folded shirt into the carry bag laid out on her bunk in the *Essenay*'s second cabin. "You know, I'm really going to miss this place."

"Not that you ever spent much time in here," Jack pointed out.

"Oh, I don't mean the room," she said, looking around the cabin. "Not even the ship, really."

"The company, then?" Draycos asked from the corner where he and Taneem had stretched out on the deck to watch Alison's packing.

"Yes," Alison said. She gave Jack a wry look. "Strange though that may sound."

"That's okay—it's been a day for strangeness," Jack assured her. Oddly enough, he thought, he was going to miss her, too. "You're really Mr. Braxton's granddaughter?"

She nodded. "On my mother's side," she said. "My dad, on the other hand, is an Internos Intelligence agent."

"Must have made for an interesting childhood," Jack said. "So you're an Internos agent. And I thought the Whinyard's Edge recruited them young."

A shadow seemed to pass across Alison's face. "I'm a special case," she said quietly. "Do you remember, after you got back from Semaline, when you asked if I knew what it felt like to have people die because of me?"

"Yes," Jack said, wincing at the memory of that day. He'd been full of anger and pain and guilt, and had lashed out completely unfairly at her.

"I was nine at the time," Alison went on, her eyes staring into infinity. "My best friend's brother told me in secret that he was going to run away from home and join a mercenary group."

"How old was he?" Draycos asked.

"He'd just turned twelve," Alison said. "Two years too young to legally join. But he was tall for his age, and he really wanted to go." She closed her eyes briefly. "Three months later, he was dead. Killed in combat."

"I'm sorry," Jack said quietly. "But it was *his* decision, not yours. What happened wasn't your fault."

"Yes, it was," Alison said. Her voice was calm, but Jack could hear old pain still lurking beneath it. "I could have told someone. I *should* have told someone. But I thought the whole thing was terribly grown-up and too glamorous for words."

Jack nodded as he suddenly understood. "So *that's* what you were doing in the Whinyard's Edge. You were looking for evidence of underage recruitment."

She gave him a wry half smile. "You *are* pretty good at this, aren't you? Yes, that was my mission in life. I'd already infiltrated Weber's Hellions and the Malison Ring and pulled data on them. This time, it was the Whinyard's Edge's turn."

"The whole thing your dad's idea, I suppose?"

"Actually, Dad was dead-set against it," she said, her smile vanishing into memory again. "As were Mom, Grandfather, Grandmother, and pretty much everyone else. But I had righteousness on my side. And guilt."

"And you wore them down."

"More or less," Alison said. "Dad finally agreed, on the condition that I go through a full five years of training first. He probably figured I'd get tired of it and drop out."

"Only you didn't," Jack said.

"Like I said, righteousness and guilt." She cocked her head. "And then I met you, and a whole lot of really interesting questions came tumbling out into the light. After we escaped from Sunright I contacted Dad. We put two and two together, and figured out that you were the same Jack who'd saved Grandfather's life on the *Star of Wonder*. After a little discussion, we agreed I should change missions and concentrate on you for a while."

She snapped her fingers. "Which reminds me, I've got the footlocker you left at the Whinyard's Edge camp."

"With my leather jacket inside?" Jack asked. "Great! I thought that was gone forever."

"No, Dad's got it, all safe and sound," Alison assured him. "We'll pick it up after we get out of here. Anyway, we lost you for a bit while you were on Brum-a-dum, then picked up your trail again after you freed all those Chookoock slaves. I followed you to Bigelow, where you promptly got yourself captured trying to sneak into the Malison Ring HQ there."

"Which Draycos and I could have gotten out of on our own," Jack said, his face warming at the memory. "So that was why I spotted Harper hanging around your ship. He was your excuse to talk me into giving you a ride?"

"Yes." Alison lowered her eyes. "He was also . . . bodyguards aren't supposed to be your friends, you know. But he was anyway."

"Sometimes it's a bodyguard's duty to die for those he protects," Draycos said. "Just as it is a warrior's."

"I know," Alison said. "And we'd probably all be dead if he hadn't sacrificed himself to set off the *Advocatus Diaboli*'s emergency beacon that way. But it still hurts."

"He wouldn't want you to hold on to the pain, Alison," Draycos said gently. "But you may always honor him in your memory. As I will."

"As we all will," Jack promised, searching for a way to get Alison off this subject. "So that whole thing about meeting friends on Rho Scorvi was just a bucket of soap bubbles?"

Alison's eyes and mind seemed to come back. "Basically," she said. "Though someone would have come eventually to check if I hadn't surfaced. Grandfather's scientists had analyzed the scratch mark Draycos made on the bottom of his rejuvenation cylinder, and they'd somehow deduced that it was a Phooka claw mark. So I maneuvered you into going there, just to see how you'd react."

She smiled at Taneem. "Little did I know. Anyway, once we got off-planet again, I called my contact on your InterWorld transmitter. I told him about the Phookas and had Dad go in with a team and spirit them away. I didn't want Neverlin killing them or, worse, using them to scam the refugee fleet when it arrived."

Jack looked over at the computer module. Uncle Virge was being awfully quiet about all this. "How did you bribe Uncle Virge into not telling me about the call?"

"No bribery needed," Alison said. "I'd already figured the *Essenay* was either a diplomatic or governmental ship, and their computers always come with a privacy lock-out. I just said the magic words, and Uncle Virge basically went to sleep."

Jack nodded. "Is that also how Harper got you on Bentre, Uncle Virge?"

"Yes," Uncle Virge said, a strangely thoughtful tone to his

voice. "He shut me off, got out of his cuffs, unwired the sopor mist canisters you'd hooked up, flew us to the Braxton Universis office on Keeleywine, and dropped Chiggers off with the security people there. Then he woke me up again, explained the situation, and gave me a take-it-or-leave-it offer to help out."

"And so the two of you came to Point Two to masquerade as Uncle Virgil and infiltrate Neverlin's group," Jack said, shaking his head. There was nothing like suddenly getting an entirely new angle on a situation you'd thought you understood.

"And to bring me some emergency equipment," Alison said. "He was also there on Brum-a-dum, by the way, the night I locked myself in Neverlin's safe."

"I remember," Jack said, an odd memory suddenly kicking in. "When Frost and Neverlin came charging into the hangar, you said *both of us* weren't supposed to rescue you."

"Right," Alison said. "I'd given him a comm clip with your frequency and pattern so he could keep track of what we were up to." She grimaced. "Of course, if I'd realized that Frost and Neverlin were still on Brum-a-dum, I'd have called in a full Braxton Security force to grab them as they left the Chookoock estate. We could have ended the whole plot right there."

"That wouldn't have ended it," Draycos said. "The Valahgua and their Death weapons were still free. Even without Neverlin and Frost, they would have found a way to attack the refugee fleet."

"I suppose," Alison said reluctantly. "Anyway, you know the rest."

"All except your story about being General Davi's daughter," Taneem spoke up. "How did you create that fiction?"

"It's no trick for Intelligence people to create false IDs," Jack explained. "Her dad probably also gave her all those voiceprints

Uncle Virge told me she had stashed away in case she needed them."

"Jack's right," Alison said. "But in this case, we also had General Davi himself ready to back up my story if Neverlin decided to check up on me. After I called his forces in on the Patri Chookoock last month, Dad had to tell him the whole story to keep him from launching a full investigation and maybe knocking over my personal applecart in the process."

"I'll bet he was thrilled," Jack murmured.

"He was several miles north of furious," Alison agreed. "Not at us, but at what Frost had done with his men and equipment. He agreed on the spot to cooperate with us."

"Hence the Malison Ring contingent your grandfather brought in with him," Jack said dryly. "Probably the main reason Frost switched sides there at the end. He knew he'd lost, and figured he'd better surrender to your grandfather before Davi got to him."

"Something like that." Alison shook her head. "I just wish we could have persuaded the Patri Chookoock to cooperate, too. But he wouldn't. All Dad could do at that point was block his communications so that he couldn't bring the hammer down on Harper."

"Though Neverlin still guessed the truth," Taneem said.

Alison sighed. "Yes."

"So why didn't you just tell me from the start who you were?" Jack asked. "It would have made things a lot easier."

Alison shrugged uncomfortably. "In the beginning, because we weren't sure whether we could trust you," she said. "You *or* Draycos."

"Oh, that's nice," Jack growled.

"No, she's right, Jack," Draycos said. "She had only my side of the story, after all. There was no way for her to know we weren't a group of invaders planning a conquest of the Orion Arm."

"At least not until I got to know him," Alison agreed. "By then—" She grimaced. "You'd gotten it into your head that Grandfather might have been involved with your parents' death. At that point, I didn't dare tell you the truth."

"You don't still think that, do you, Jack?" Taneem asked.

"Not really," Jack assured her. "Besides, if Alison can accept the whole K'da race based on Draycos's character, I suppose I can accept Mr. Braxton based on hers."

"Which makes him a good man?" Taneem suggested.

"It certainly makes him a conniving man," Jack said blandly. "Also smart-mouthed, underhanded—"

"Hey!" Alison protested.

"—but probably not a murderer," Jack finished. He turned innocent eyes on Alison. "You say something?"

"Listen, buddy-boy," she said, leveling a finger at him, "if you want to talk about *conniving*—"

"Please," Taneem interrupted anxiously. "Please don't fight."

"They're not fighting," Draycos soothed her. "This is a rather silly game humans sometimes like to play together."

"You'll get used to it," Alison assured her, sending Jack's innocent look right back at him.

Jack felt his stomach tighten. "Yeah," he muttered.

"What, you don't think she will?" Alison asked, frowning.

"I don't think she'll have a chance," Jack told her. "As soon as—"

He broke off at the sound of a footstep down the corridor. "Hello?" he called.

"It's just me," Braxton's voice came back. "Where are you?"

"Second cabin," Alison called back. "Down the corridor aft."

There were more footsteps, and Braxton appeared in the cabin doorway. "There you are," he said, crossing over to the bunk and sitting down. "You ready, Alison?"

"Almost," Alison said. "Is the battle over?"

"Actually, the battle never got started," Braxton said, looking thoughtfully around the room. "We were able to get through to the Brummgas on the *Foxwolf*—" He looked at Draycos. "Excuse me: the *Gatekeeper*," he corrected himself. "They decided there was no sense in throwing their lives away and mutinied against the Valahgua."

"Lucky for them," Alison said.

"Not for all of them," Braxton said soberly. "The Valahgua turned the Death weapons around and killed over a hundred before they were finally overwhelmed."

The room went quiet. Jack glanced at Draycos, seeing his own revulsion and regret in the K'da's expression. Even big, dumb lummoxes like the Brummgas didn't deserve to die that way. "Rotten losers, aren't they?" he murmured.

"Yes," Draycos said, his voice dark. "They are."

"Well, they'd better get used to it," Alison said. "Now that you're back where you belong, they're done for."

"Yes," Braxton agreed. He finished his survey of the room and turned to Jack. "Speaking of being back where they belong, Jack, you and I need to discuss your future."

"What future?" Jack said sourly. "Now that everyone knows Uncle Virgil's dead, some Internos bureaucrat's bound to take the *Essenay* away from me. Then they'll put me in school, or with some strangers—"

He broke off. "Sorry," he apologized. "I suppose I should just be happy I'm still alive."

"Yes, you should," Braxton said. "But I think we can do a little better than your rather unappetizing scenario."

He gestured to Draycos. "You see, as it happens, Braxton Universis still owns Iota Klestis."

Jack eyed him suspiciously. "And?"

"Oh, don't worry," Braxton hastened to assure him. "The K'da and Shontine are welcome to it, for as long as they want to stay. But instead of giving it to them outright, I thought I'd give them a permanent lease at a dollar a year."

"Why is that better than selling it to them?" Jack asked.

"Or just giving it to them?" Alison added pointedly.

"A mere dollar a year fee *is* giving it to us," Draycos told her.

"May I speak?" Braxton asked. "Thank you. There are two reasons to lease instead of sell. One: those Internos bureaucrats Jack just mentioned also have their own ideas as to what should be done with refugees and displaced persons. If I still own Iota Klestis, I can let anyone move in there that I want."

"Giving the K'da and Shontine time to negotiate their way through the paperwork?" Alison suggested.

"Exactly," Braxton said. "And two: since I own the world, I can hire anyone I want to be ambassador to the residents."

"Ambassador?" Draycos asked.

"Technically, he'll be a corporate liaison," Braxton said. "But the duties will be effectively the same. Naturally, I'll need someone who knows and understands the K'da."

He looked at Jack. "Ideally, one who is also already known and trusted by them."

Jack frowned . . . and then, suddenly, he understood. "You can't be serious," he said.

"I certainly can," Braxton said. "My planet, remember?" He looked around the room again. "And of course, an ambassador needs his own personal diplomatic ship." He smiled. "It needs a little hull work around the hatchway, but I think it'll do."

"But I'm just a kid," Jack protested.

"But you have the gifts of insight and compassion and justice," Draycos said. "Speaking on behalf of the K'da and Shontine, we would be honored to have you among us."

"Then it's settled," Braxton said, standing up. "Once the fleet's ready to move, we'll escort them to Iota Klestis. I've already alerted the nearest Universis depots, and they're putting together an initial supply run to help with the transition."

"Thank you," Draycos said.

"My pleasure," Braxton replied, inclining his head. "I'm very much looking forward to working with you and your people."

He crossed back to the door. "As soon as you're all ready, come on over to the *Advocatus Diaboli*. I've decided to stay aboard for the trip to Iota Klestis." His face tightened a little. "And to make sure that Death weapon is well and truly destroyed."

"I would be happy to assist in that," Draycos offered grimly.

"I was hoping you would," Braxton said. "See you all soon."

He left, his footsteps retreating again down the corridor. "Well," Alison said. "What do you think of that?"

"I don't know yet," Jack said. "This is all coming way too fast."

"You've got time," Alison said quietly. "The point is that you're finally safe. You're safe, and you're among friends. Just like Draycos and his people are."

"You're safe, Jack lad?"

Jack frowned at the computer module. It had been Uncle Virge's voice . . . but there'd been something odd about it. "Yes, I think maybe I really am," he said. "Who'd ever have guessed, huh?"

"The people responsible for your parents' murder are dead?"

"Dead or in custody," Jack said. "Why?"

"Just a minute."

There was a long pause. "What's going on?" Alison asked.

Jack shook his head. "I don't know."

There was a click from the speaker. "Hello, Jack lad," Uncle Virge said.

Jack tensed. Because it *wasn't* Uncle Virge, the personality Jack's uncle had programmed into the *Essenay*'s computer. This voice was subtly but definitely different.

It was Uncle Virgil himself.

"I apologize for speaking to you through this recording," Uncle Virgil went on. "I presume from the fact that you *are* listening to it means I'm dead or in jail or otherwise unavailable to give all this to you in person.

"But I wanted you to know how it was you ended up living with me aboard your parents' ship."

Silently, Draycos got to his feet and crossed the room to stand at Jack's side.

"It *was* their ship, if you haven't already figured that out. A beautiful Judge-Paladin ship, loaded to the intakes with all the finest equipment money can buy.

"Unfortunately, not all of us have that kind of money. So seeing as I was a thief by profession, I set out to steal it."

Jack glanced at Alison. She was staring at the speaker, an intense look on her face.

"Not that I specifically targeted your parents' ship. That was just . . . I don't know. Luck? Fate? I can never tell about these things. I just needed one of the ships to put down at some out-of-the-way place where the alarm would take a while to get out. The Hreenwoth Canyon on Semaline was the perfect spot."

Jack looked down at Draycos. All that time they'd spent in that canyon, all that danger, and he'd never even known its real name.

"I knew the Golvins had requested a Judge-Paladin to come mediate their dispute with Triost Mining, so I got there first and arranged to have myself arrested. Nothing serious, just some minor theft that would give me an excuse to hang around the valley. Once your parents arrived and settled down to business, I slipped out of custody and got over to their ship.

"I had just popped my way through the lock when the Lesser Assembly Hall blew up."

Jack closed his eyes. The image of that explosion . . .

"I didn't have time to think," Uncle Virgil went on. "My first instinct was to get out, and to get out fast. I got to the cockpit, froze out the computer that was trying to block me, and took off."

"Must have been fewer guy wires linking the pillars back then," Draycos murmured. "Otherwise, the *Essenay* could never have landed in the canyon."

"I figured that whoever had had the chutzpah to kill a pair of Judge-Paladins would have been smart enough to have some air backup ready. But he'd missed out on that one. I got into space and on ECHO before the planetary space control even realized anything was wrong.

"It was only then that I found out I had a passenger. You.

"It was quite a shock, as I'm sure you can imagine. You were in your bunk, sleeping like a—well, I suppose like a three-year-old, a remote sitting beside you."

"A remote?" Draycos asked.

"It's an electromechanical robot linked to the ship's computer," Jack said. "Huh. I'd forgotten all about that."

"Not entirely," Draycos said. "Do you remember when we stumbled into that Wistawki bonding ceremony on the Vagran Colony?"

Jack nodded. That had been right after he and Draycos had met, while Jack was still trying to get out from under the theft charge Neverlin had framed him with. "I called you my electro-mechanical assistant."

"The remote had stopped when I froze out the computer," Uncle Virgil continued. "I got rid of it right away. Hate the things. Then you woke up, and—well, again, there wasn't time to think. I got you something to eat and spun you a story about your parents asking me to watch you for a while. I figured I'd drop you off with the authorities on the next planet.

"Only before we got to the next planet I finally *did* have time to think. I didn't know why whoever it was had killed your parents, but it occurred to me that if it was personal rather than business, he might not want their son to live, either. So I decided to hang on to you until I had a better handle on what was going on.

"But that was going to take some time, and meanwhile you were starting to ask questions. So . . . well, you know the rest. I told you I was your uncle Virgil and that your parents had been killed in a mine accident. And I sort of . . . adopted you."

"And turned me into a thief," Jack murmured.

"I know you're probably not happy with some of the things I did," Uncle Virgil said, an odd note of pleading in his voice. "Changing your name and . . . well, teaching you something of my profession. But you have to remember that I didn't know who or what we were up against. I had to keep your real identity hidden from everyone, including you. At the same time, I needed to give you the tools you'd need if I didn't solve the puzzle and you had to track down the murderers yourself.

"But you're safe now. Somehow, you're safe. Otherwise the computer wouldn't have been able to find and unlock this recording. You don't need me anymore. And for that I'm glad. I really am.

"So I guess this is good-bye, Jack lad. I know you'll probably hate me for what I did to you. I wish I could have done better, but it's too late for that now. Just please try to believe that I did the best I knew how."

The voice stopped. Jack took a deep breath, let it out in a slow sigh. "So," he said, just to fill up the silence.

"*Do* you hate him?" Taneem asked quietly.

Jack looked at her. "No," he said, and was rather surprised to discover that he meant it. "He made mistakes. We all do. But he kept me alive for eleven years." He considered. "And I guess he really *did* give me the tools I needed to bring Neverlin down."

He looked back at the computer module. "Thanks, Uncle Virge."

There was no answer. "Uncle Virge?" Jack called again.

"Good afternoon," a courteous feminine voice said. "How may I assist you?"

Jack swallowed. "Never mind," he said.

"I'm sorry, Jack," Alison said gently.

Jack blinked back sudden tears. "Don't be," he said. "Uncle Virgil died a long time ago." He looked at Draycos. "And he was right. I don't need him anymore."

He took another deep breath. "So what are we hanging around here for, anyway?" he said, forcing some cheerfulness into his voice. "Let's get over to the *Advocatus Diaboli* and wreck a Death weapon. And after that, we can introduce Taneem to her people."

"Will you stay with me awhile, Alison?" Taneem asked, almost shyly.

"As long as you need me," Alison promised. "I'm looking forward to meeting your people, too." She picked up the carry bag and looked at Jack. "You ready?"

"Go ahead," Jack told her. "I'll be along in a minute."

Alison glanced at Draycos, then nodded. "Okay," she said. "But make it snappy." With Taneem padding along behind her, she left the room.

"Are you all right?" Draycos asked gently.

"I don't know," Jack said. Suddenly, to his surprise and embarrassment, more tears were flowing from his eyes. "I just feel sort of . . . I don't know. Sort of lost."

"That's to be expected," Draycos said. "For the past six months you've been on the run, living with fear and danger and a burden no one your age should ever have to carry. Along the way, you've grown a great deal as a person, as well as learned things about yourself and your history you thought you'd never know."

He reached up a paw and rested it gently on Jack's arm. "You've never had a chance to truly grieve for your parents. Now, finally, you have that chance."

"I guess," Jack said, swiping a hand across his eyes. "But it hasn't just been the last six months. With Uncle Virgil, and then after he died . . ." He shook his head. "That was my life, Draycos. It was all I ever knew. Now, suddenly, everything's changed."

"Yes, it has," Draycos said. "It's called being at peace. Being at rest. It's something you haven't experienced since you were three years old." He lashed his tail gently. "To tell you the truth, it's something I've never truly experienced, either."

Jack looked down at the K'da, a wave of tangled thoughts and emotions swirling through him. There was grief for his parents, certainly, along with the scary sense that his life had changed forever. There was also a little shame that he was even carrying on like this when Draycos and his people had suffered so much more than he had.

But on top of all the rest of it— "We did it," he murmured, the fact suddenly and truly sinking in. "We saved your people. We actually *did* it."

"We did, didn't we?" Draycos said, his jaws cracking open in a K'da smile. "You and I, and Alison and Taneem."

"And Langston, and Mr. Braxton," Jack added. He felt his stomach tighten. "And Harper."

"All of us together," Draycos agreed quietly. "We're safe, Jack. *You're* safe."

Safe. The word flowed through Jack's mind like a gentle summer breeze. *Safe.*

"Hey, in there?" Alison's voice drifted back down the corridor. "You two get lost?"

Quickly, Jack wiped the last of the tears from his eyes with his sleeve. "Keep your socks on," he called back. "We're coming."

"Then do it," Alison said as she and Taneem stuck their heads around the doorway into the room. "Grandfather's waiting, and you *don't* want him mad at you."

"Oh, right," Jack said dryly. "What's he going to do, take away the dessert cart?"

"Worse," Alison said solemnly. "He might limit you to a single day at Great Galaxy Romp next time he takes us there. And no roller coasters at all."

"Actually, no roller coasters would be fine with me," Jack assured her. He gave Draycos a lopsided grin. "I'm at peace now, you know."

"Not for long," Alison warned. "You're an ambassador to a

whole race of people. Two whole races, actually. Your future's about to get really complicated again."

"Complicated, but good," Draycos said. "For all of us."

"Absolutely," Alison agreed, reaching down to stroke Taneem's neck.

"You really think so?" Jack asked.

"Oh yes." Alison smiled. "Bet on it."

Timothy Zahn is the author of more than thirty original science fiction novels, including the very popular *Cobra* and *Blackcollar* series. His first novel of the *Dragonback* series, *Dragon and Thief*, was named "A Best Book for Young Adults" by the American Library Association. Jack Morgan's adventures continued in *Dragon and Soldier, Dragon and Slave, Dragon and Herdsman,* and *Dragon and Judge*. Zahn's recent novels include *Night Train to Rigel, The Green and the Gray, Manta's Gift, Angelmass,* and *Blackcollar: The Judas Solution*. He has had many short works published in the major SF magazines, including "Cascade Point," which won the Hugo Award for best novella in 1984. He is also the author of many bestselling *Star Wars* novels, including the all-time bestselling *Star Wars* spin-off novel, *Heir to the Empire,* as well as *The Hand of Thrawn* duology and, more recently, *Outbound Flight* and his latest, *Allegiance*. He currently resides in Oregon.